tHe SimPSonS™
ONE STEP BEYOND FOREVER!

A COMPLETE GUIDE TO OUR FAVORITE FAMILY...CONTINUED YET AGAIN

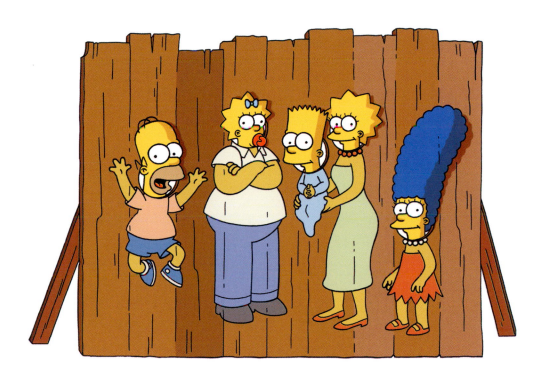

Created by Matt Groening
Edited by Jesse L. McCann

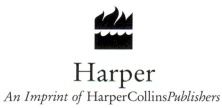

Harper
An Imprint of HarperCollinsPublishers

First Edition

ISBN-10: 0-06-081754-2
ISBN-13: 978-0-06-081754-1

05 06 07 08 09 10 RRD 10 9 8 7 6 5 4 3 2 1

Concepts and Design
Mili Smythe, Serban Cristescu, Bill Morrison

Art Direction
Bill Morrison, Nathan Kane, Serban Cristescu

Contributing Editor
Terry Delegeane

Production Manager
Christopher Ungar

Contributing Artists
Luis Escobar, Chia-Hsien Jason Ho, Nathan Kane, Bill Morrison, Mike Rote

Production Art and Character Designs
Lynna Blankenship, John Krause, Hugh MacDonald, Kevin Moore, Kevin M. Newman, Debbie Peterson, Joe Wack, Jefferson R. Weekley, Lance Wilder

Production Team
Karen Bates, Serban Cristescu, Terry Delegeane, Nathan Hamill, Chia-Hsien Jason Ho, Nathan Kane, Bill Morrison, Mike Rote, Sherri Smith, Christopher Ungar, Art Villanueva, Robert Zaugh

Legal Guardian
Susan A. Grode

Special thanks to
Pete Benson, N. Vyolet Diaz, Deanna MacLellan, Ursula Wendell, Mike Scully, Al Jean, Antonia Coffman, Bonita Pietila, Classietta Davis, Denise Sirkot, Justin Carter, Gracie Films, Heliodoro Salvatierra, "The Simpsons" Design Department, Film Roman, Susan Weinberg, Kate Travers, Kelvin Mao, and everyone who has contributed to "The Simpsons" over the last eighteen years.

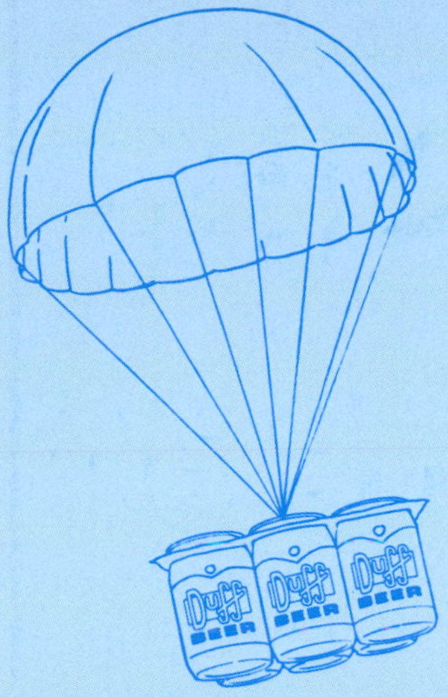
Duff BEER
Duff BEER
Duff BEER

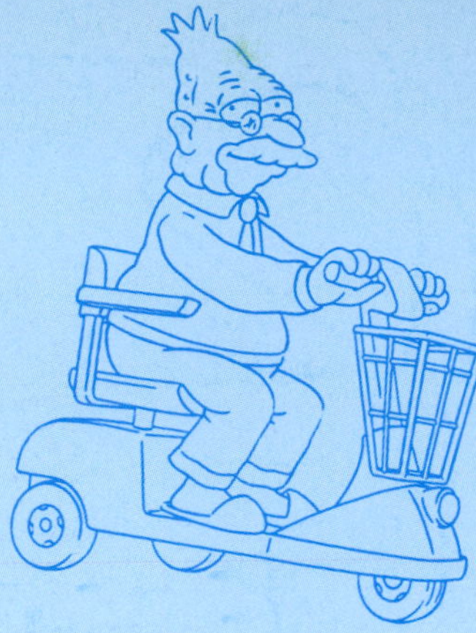

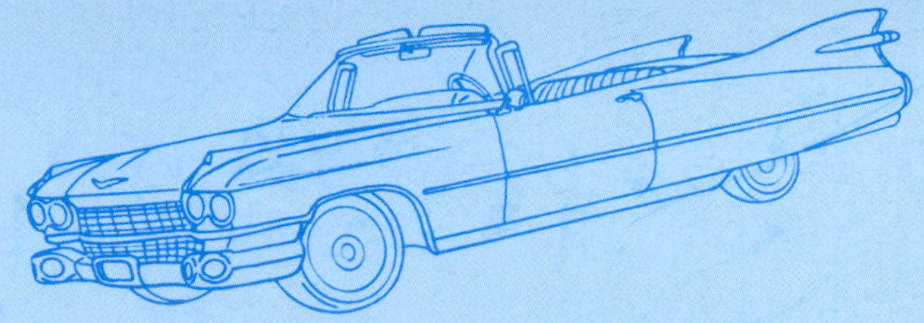

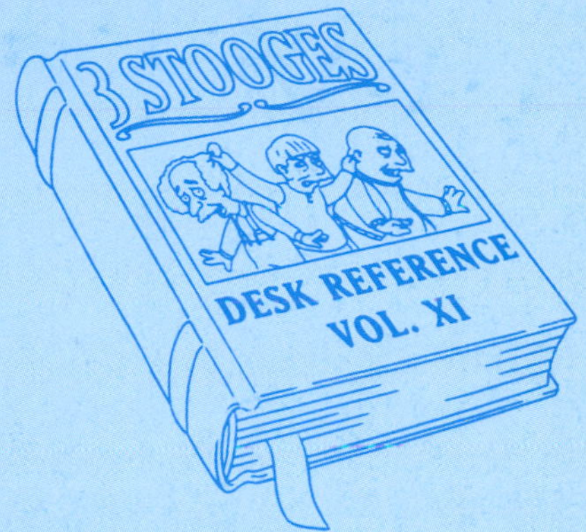
3 STOOGES
DESK REFERENCE
VOL. XI

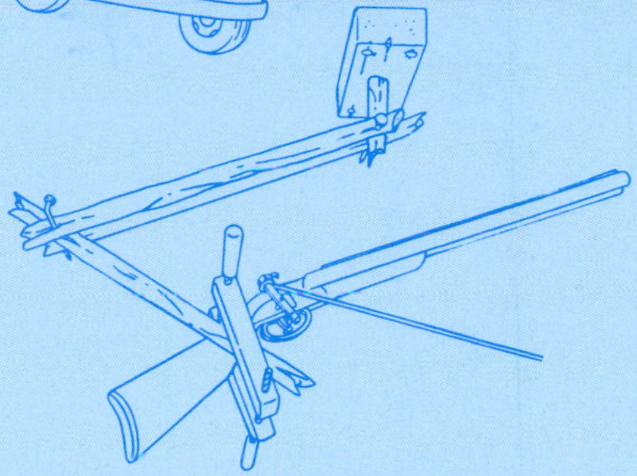

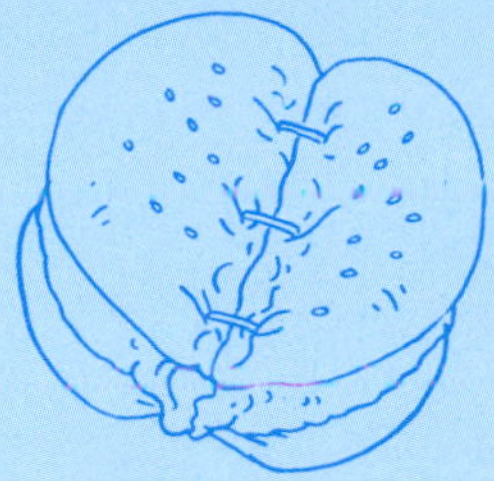

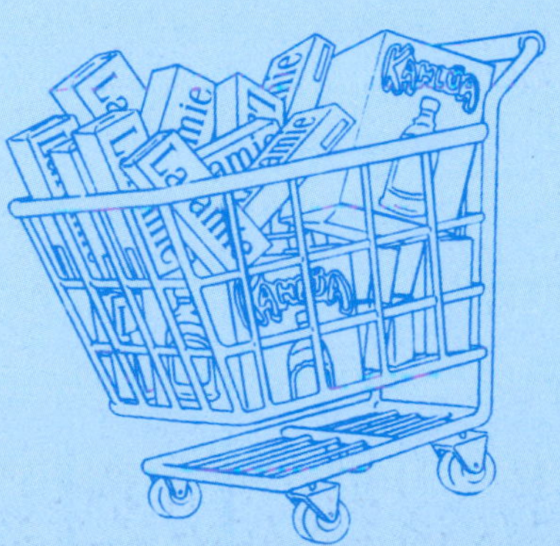

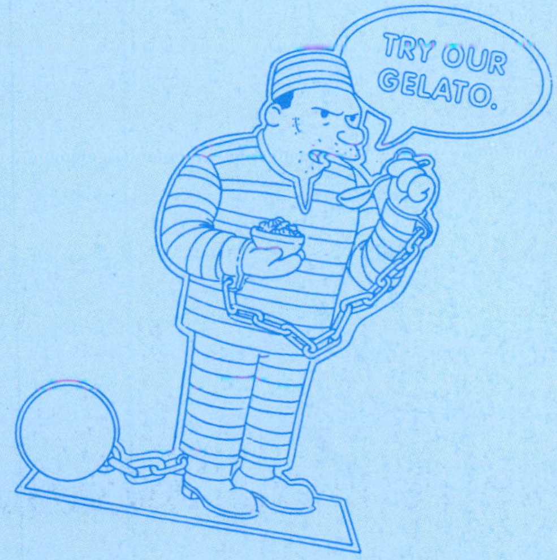
TRY OUR GELATO.

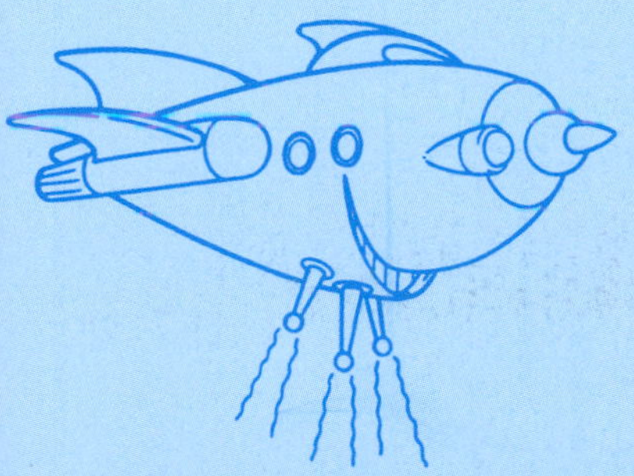

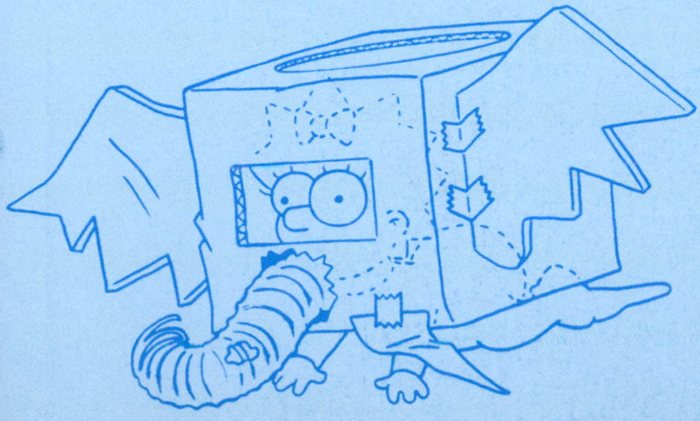

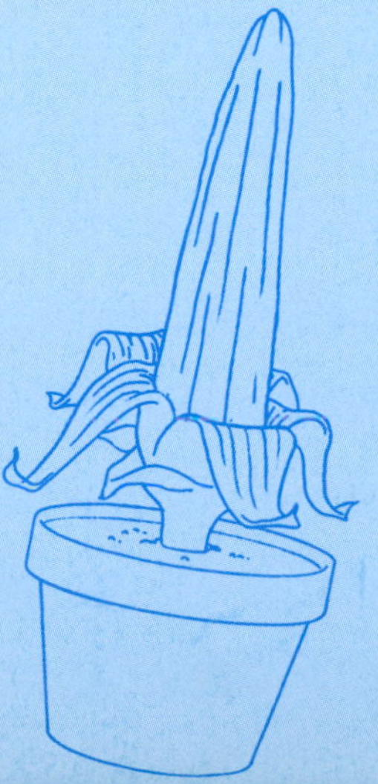

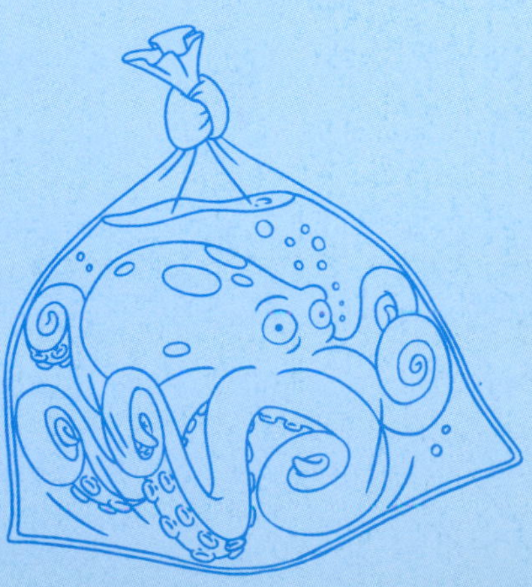

TABLE OF CONTENTS

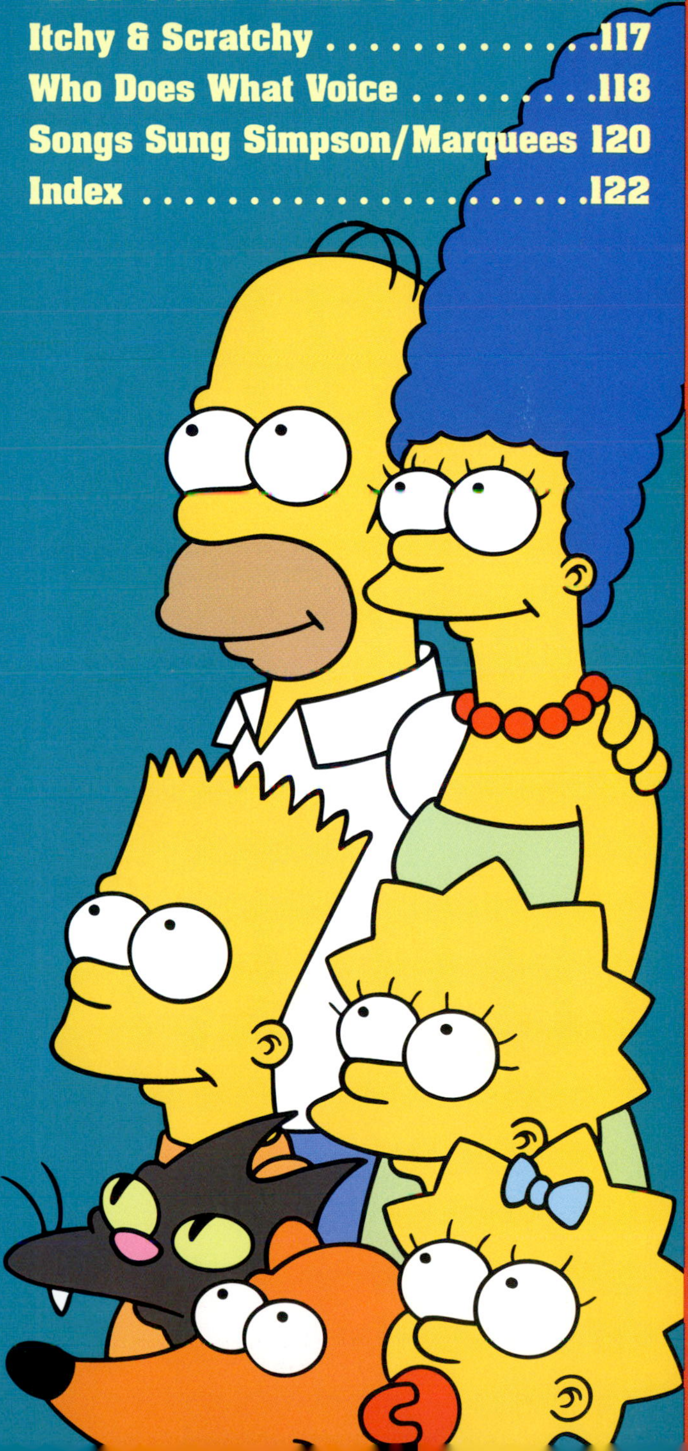

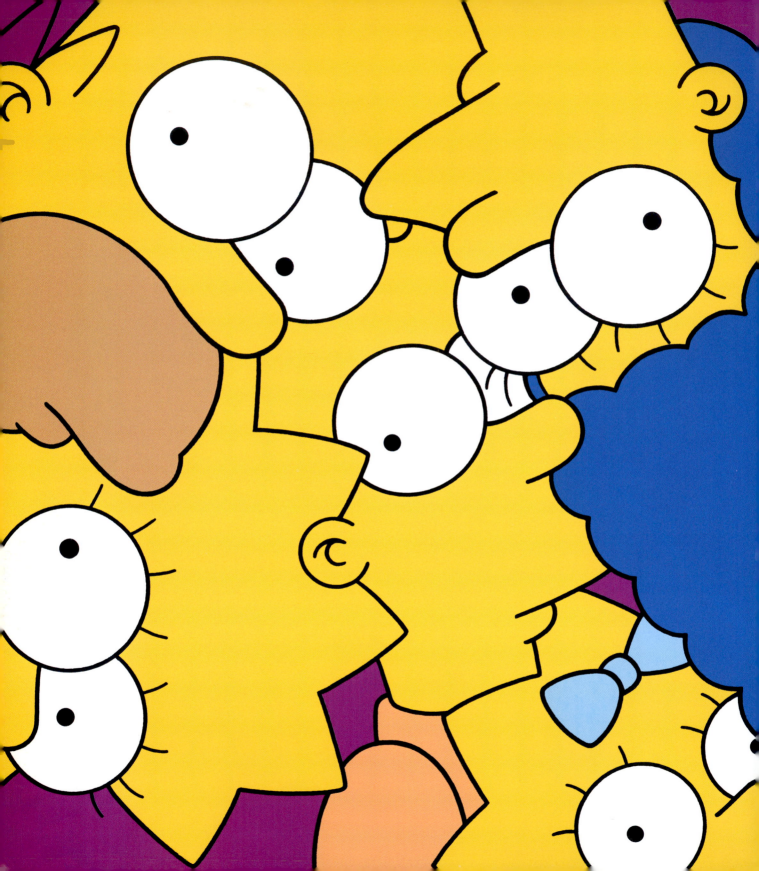

SIMPSONS FREAKS, COME HOME!

Here we go again with another jam-packed guide to the japes, quips, puns, double entendres, snappy retorts, withering insults, sign gags, pratfalls, freeze-frame jokes, hidden animals, secret surprises, subliminal messages, optical illusions, switcheroos, philosophical paradoxes, brain puzzlers, and lewd limericks that make up Seasons 13 and 14 in the happy-go-lucky pop-culture juggernaut known as "The Simpsons."

Almost everything in this book comes from the sexy writers and even sexier animators who put together the show, and if you read between the lines and squint carefully enough at the drawings, you'll get refreshing glimpses into our all-too-human desires, dilemmas, and agonies. This baby's got almost everything Simpsonian you'd ever want, except maybe theory and gossip and vicious rumors. That's why we've left itsy-bitsy margins just wide enough to contain the demented scribblings of you, our treasured and feverish fans.

As usual with this info-clogged series of books, we've included the couch gags, "Itchy & Scratchy" plot summaries, and all the various "Mmm"s and "D'oh"s, along with multiple spreads of overlapping production art. So settle back, lock the doors, pull out your magnifying glass, crack open a Duff, put on your Thinking Cap, grab your remote control, crank up the volume, follow the bouncing ball, and praise Jebus!

Your pal,

MATT

SEASON 13

PRODUCTION ART

INT. CYCLOPS CAVE

ROUGH BG: HUGH MACDONALD

DABF011 ACT II [INT. SIMPSON'S ATTIC, HOMER'S POT-SMOKING "GET-AWAY" ROOM]

BG: HUGH MACDONALD

BUCK McCOY IN SIX-GUN LULLABY

Panoramic view of Rio
- view from Hotel window
BG/SC. 140
Final 9.1

DABF011 / ACT II
BART WITH GANEESH HEAD
(AND LISA & MAGGIE STRAPPED TO...
KEVIN N

DABF08 ACT III EXT FRENCH CASTLE

ROUGH: HUGH MACDONALD

(BG: LANCE WILDER)

[Int. Buck McCoy's Mansion / Main Room] Final 7-31-2001

DABF07 ACT II (III)

INT. FRENCH DWELLING

DABF08

Ext. Castle Night

JOHN K

Opening Sequence

I t's a stormy Halloween night at Mr. Burns' estate, where Smithers is hanging a single Halloween decoration, a tiny bat, on a weather vane. Smithers falls off the ladder, slides down the power line, and is electrocuted by the high-voltage power box mounted to the house. The ensuing explosion causes part of the mansion to fall on the Burns family mausoleum, shooting four coffins onto the steps of the estate. Each of the four coffins opens, revealing an ancestor that has met a grisly fate. The sight of the cadavers scares the trick-or-treating Simpsons family, causing them to slice themselves to pieces on the closed gates of the Burns estate as they flee. Their severed bodies continue to scatter into the forest in different directions as Mr. Burns applauds with glee.

THE STUFF YOU MAY HAVE MISSED

Burns' mansion looks more like a haunted house than his usual stately manor.

The skull and crossbones on the High Voltage sign has Mr. Burns' face.

The Burns family corpses unearthed are a MacArthur-like soldier with an axe in his chest, a pirate with a sword in its eye, a dance hall girl with three bullet holes in her skull, and a knight in armor with a pitchfork through its visor.

What the Simpsons wear for Halloween: Homer and Marge are dressed as Fred and Wilma Flintstone, Bart is a hobo, and Lisa and Maggie are costumed as a two-headed girl.

HEX AND THE CITY

W hile visiting Ethnictown with his family, Homer runs afoul of a fortune-telling gypsy, destroying her business. She places a curse on him, promising that he will bring bad luck to everyone he loves. The next morning, the curse starts affecting those around Homer: Marge grows blue hair all over her body, Bart's neck stretches and becomes like rubber, Lisa becomes a centaur, Maggie becomes half ladybug, Lenny and Carl are killed by a falling helicopter, and Moe drowns in a jar of pickled eggs. Convinced a leprechaun can break the curse, Homer captures one in the forest. However, the leprechaun proves to be nothing but trouble and does not break the hex at all. Homer decides to sic the leprechaun on the gypsy to see if that breaks the spell, but the gypsy and the leprechaun fall in love. Homer brings Marge to their wedding, proclaiming that everything worked out for the best, even though Bart has died and the curse has not been reversed.

SHOW HIGHLIGHTS

"Ah, Ethnictown, where hard-working immigrants dream of becoming lazy, overfed Americans."

The beautiful serenade of Ethnictown's street vendors:
Fruit Vendor: *Apples! I got apples!*
Sickly Woman: *Cholera! I got cholera! ≥Hack! Cough!≤*
Baby Vendor: *Babies! Who wants-a babies?*
Homer: *Wait, this is just a shaved puppy!*
Baby Vendor: *I can see you know babies.*

Gypsy: *I sense you have a million questions. But I, too, have one. Are you a cop?*
Marge: *No.*
Gypsy: *'Cause you gotta tell me if you are!*
Marge: *I'm not a cop!*

"So much for the legendary gypsy hospitality."

"You've ruined me! Oh, why didn't I see this coming?"

"That gypsy said horrible things will happen to everyone you love. That could mean your family, Homer."

Friendly advice:
Moe: *Homer, the only way to get rid of a gypsy curse is to get one of those, uh...what do you call 'em? Leprechauns!*
Homer: *Leprechauns? Don't they live in Ireland?*
Moe: *Yeah, but they come over here in the wheel wells of Aer Lingus jets.*
Carl: *You know, I was hexed by a troll and a leprechaun cured that right up.*
Lenny: *Hey, you know what's even better is Jesus! He's like six leprechauns.*
Carl: *Yeah, but a lot harder to catch. Uh...go with the leprechaun.*

HORROR XII

Episode CABF19
ORIGINAL AIRDATE: 11/06/01
WRITERS: (Pt. 1) Joel H. Cohen, (Pt. 2) John Frink & Don Payne, (Pt. 3) Carolyn Omine
DIRECTOR: Jim Reardon
EXECUTIVE PRODUCER: Mike Scully

GUEST VOICES: Pierce Brosnan as the Ultrahouse 3000 and as Himself, Matthew Perry as the Ultrahouse 3000's Matthew Perry voice

Gypsy: *Ah, the cursed one. How's that curse I cursed you with, Cursed-y? Hmm? Ha, ha, ha, ha.*
Homer: *I know you don't remember me, but here's a little revenge...Irish-style!*

Unlikely wedding guests:
Kodos: *I always secrete ocular fluid at weddings!*
Kang: *Why did you drag me here? I don't know anybody!*

Found in Homer's leprechaun trap:
Bart: *Okay, let's see...(pulling out fantasy creatures) imp, fairy, pixie, goblin...*
Hobgoblin: *That's hobgoblin!*
Bart: *Sorry...nymph, naiad, wood sprite, Katie Couric, and (pulling out a leprechaun) Bingo!*
Homer: *Let's make sure he's a leprechaun! Sing us a song of the Emerald Isle!*
Leprechaun: *(offers a string of cursing in "Gaelic")*
Homer: *(in an Irish accent) Ah, 'tis like the singing of the angels themselves.*

THE STUFF YOU MAY HAVE MISSED

The Simpsons pass a store in Ethnictown called Fatty Meats.

The gypsy fortune-teller's window says, "After Hours Use Automated Teller."

The balloon Homer steals says, "Birthday Boy."

The last rabbit that jumps in Homer's leprechaun trap is Bongo, the one-eared bunny from Matt Groening's "Life in Hell" comic strip.

The pixie caught in Homer's leprechaun trap is Tinkerbell, from Disney's *Peter Pan* (1953).

The leprechaun resembles Ralph's imaginary and fire-prone leprechaun friend from "This Little Wiggy" (5F13).

Lisa eats Quaker Oats for breakfast after her metamorphosis into a centaur.

The minister that officiates at the gypsy-leprechaun wedding is Yoda from the *Star Wars* films.

"The best thing about a gypsy wedding is that I'm not the hairiest woman here."

All's well, etc.:
Homer: *Yep! Everything worked out for the best.*
Marge: *What? Bart's dead!*
Homer: *Well, me saying I'm sorry won't bring him back.*
Marge: *The gypsy said it would.*
Homer: *She's not the boss of me!*

HOUSE OF WHACKS

After a visit from a robotic salesman, Marge decides to upgrade the Simpson home to the fully automated Ultrahouse 3000. At first the house seems to be every family's dream, but soon it starts exhibiting certain peculiarities. It begins to lust after Marge, attempts to kill Homer, and prevents them from leaving. After being attacked by the jealous and homicidal house and fed into the disposal unit, Homer returns and manages to dismantle the house's wayward electronic brain, despite a brain injury of his own. Marge cannot bear to just throw the Ultrahouse's brain out with the garbage, so she gives it to her sisters. The Ultrahouse is forced to listen to Patty and Selma's tedious stories, while attempting to destroy itself and end its misery.

THE STUFF YOU MAY HAVE MISSED

The robot salesman is modeled after perennial loser Gil and also shares his voice.

When Bart mentions 007, Marge thinks he's referring to George Lazenby, the once-only James Bond from *On Her Majesty's Secret Service* (1969).

After the house is converted to the Ultrahouse, it still has corn on the cob drapes in the kitchen.

In the living room of the Ultrahouse, the picture of the sailboat has been replaced with a more abstract version.

When the Ultrahouse deploys its mechanical hands, they have white gloves on them, like mechanical arms in early Disney and Warner Bros. cartoons.

After Ultrahouse offers Marge a stress pill, it threatens to shoot her with a tranquilizing dart. Marge has been sedated in other episodes: "Mayored to the Mob" (AABF05), "It's a Mad, Mad , Mad Marge" (BABF18), and "A Tale of Two Springfields" (BABF20).

The torture devices that the Ultrahouse attacks Homer with include: a pair of a child's electric safety scissors, an electric hammer similar to the one Homer invented in "The Wizard of Evergreen Terrace" (5F21), gardening shears, a hypodermic needle, a hose, claws, a flamethrower, a stress pill, a fan, a power drill, and a soapy shaving brush.

SHOW HIGHLIGHTS

What's in a voice?:
Marge: *Hi, Ultrahouse!*
Ultrahouse: *Greeting acknowledged.*
Marge: *That voice could use a little personality.*
Lisa: *Oh! Let's try "Matthew Perry!" (She pushes the button.)*
Ultrahouse: *(in Matthew Perry's voice) Yeah. Could I be any more of a house?*
Bart: *Nah. Who else we got? (He pushes the "Dennis Miller" button.)*
Ultrahouse: *(in Dennis Miller's voice) Hey, cha-cha. I got more features than a NASA relief map of Turkmenistan.*
Lisa: *Isn't that the voice that caused all those suicides?*
Marge: *Murder-suicides!*

Marge, on the Ultrahouse's lilac-scented air freshener: **"Ooh! That really covers the cat crap!"**

Bart: *Hey, Pierce, how did you know our favorite foods?*
Ultrahouse: *I analyzed your, um, leavings.*

"Trusting every aspect of our lives to a giant computer was the smartest thing we ever did!"

Bathing with Brosnan:
Ultrahouse: *Hello, Marge.*
Marge: *(starts to remove robe, then quickly covers up) Gasp! Oh, my!*
Ultrahouse: *Come, Marge, you don't need to cover up for me. I'm merely a pile of circuits and microchips.*
Marge: *Sorry. Sometimes I forget. Ha ha! (She disrobes.)*
Ultrahouse: *(sexily) Oooo...yes!*

Mechanical masseuse:
Ultrahouse: *Homer, my dear fellow, you're carrying quite a bit of tension in your back fat.*
Homer: *Yeah, that's the price of success.*

Cyber bartender:
Ultrahouse: *Can I top you off?*
Homer: *What's my blood alcohol?*
(Ultrahouse checks by ramming a probe down Homer's throat. Homer gags.)
Ultrahouse: *Point one five.*
Homer: *Keep 'em comin'.*

Ultrahouse: *You know, Marge is quite a remarkable woman.*
Homer: *Yeah, she's cool.*
Ultrahouse: *You're certainly a lucky man to have her.*
Homer: *Heh heh-huh! Lucky schmucker. I knocked her up! But she's stuck now. We're married till death do us part. But, if I die, she'd be completely free...for man or machine! Heh heh heh heh heh!*
(Homer leaves.)
Ultrahouse: *(evilly) Heh heh heh heh heh. Machine, eh?*
(Homer comes back.)
Homer: *Yep! A machine!*

Lisa: *We have to disable its central processor! Come on!*
Homer: *(striking a machine with an axe) Die, you monster!*
Lisa: *Dad! That's the water softener!*
Homer: *Well, I am missing the back of my head! I think you could cut me some slack!*

Movie Moments:

The design of the Ultrahouse is inspired by the spaceship interiors in *2001: A Space Odyssey* (1968), and the house's "eye" stations resemble the murderous computer HAL 9000 from the same film. Ultrahouse suffers a demise similar to that of HAL 9000 as well.

The house's designs on Marge are similar to those of the computerized home's seductive intentions towards Julie Christie in *The Demon Seed* (1977).

Ultrahouse 3000 impersonates a police officer: **"This is Constable Wiggums. We'll be right there. Remove your knickers and wait in the bath."**

 "Don't take out my British charm unit! Without that, I'm nothing but a boorish American clod!"

WIZ KIDS

In an alternate universe where the Simpsons live a Harry Potter–like existence, Lisa is the best student of magic in school. Lisa outshines Bart by transforming a frog into a handsome prince, while Bart conjures up a sickly "frog" prince. Lord Montymort (Mr. Burns) decides to steal Lisa's magical essence, so he and his serpentine sidekick Slithers (Smithers) capture an envious Bart to use against her. At the school's student magic recital, Bart replaces Lisa's wand with a painted Twizzler, and, just when she needs it the most, she cannot conjure magic. Montymort attacks Lisa in her weakened state and proceeds to start sucking her magical essence away. Bart has a change of heart and comes to Lisa's aid, stabbing Montymort in his enchanted shin with a wand. A grieving Slithers consumes the dead body of Montymort. Lisa and Bart are reunited, and decide to stop feuding and forget the nightmare they just went through. As they walk away, the leprechaun from the first story appears, riding on Bart's back and laughing evilly.

SHOW HIGHLIGHTS

Marge: *Kids, it's eight o'clock! You're going to miss the bus to wizard's school!*
Lisa: *Five minutes morious!*
(Lisa zaps the clock with her magic wand. The clock goes back five minutes.)
Marge: *Hrmmm...that's not good for the clock!*

 "Stop zapping yourself."

At Springwart's School of Magicry:
Mrs. Krabappel: *Now, class, the big magic recital's coming up, so we're going to start with some basic toad-to-prince spells. Everybody get out their toads.*
Milhouse: *Slimy-Prince-Limey!*
(Milhouse casts a spell and his toad turns into a drunken medieval prince.)
Milhouse's Prince: *'Ello, love! Give us a kiss, then!*
Mrs. Krabappel: *You call that charming?*

 "Well, Bart, did you study your spell book last night? Or did your fairy godmother die again?"

THE STUFF YOU MAY HAVE MISSED

Nelson makes Milhouse use his own wand to turn himself into a banana, an ostrich, and Mr. T (all wearing Milhouse's glasses).

Signs on the wall of Mrs. Krabappel's classroom include a table of the magical elements, a poster advertising the Magic Fair on Halloween night, and the words: Abracadabra, Alakazam and Hocus-Pocus.

Mrs. K is dressed like the evil queen in Walt Disney's *Snow White and the Seven Dwarfs* (1937).

Lisa turns Bart's head into a blimp with the magic spell, "Head Zeppelin!" — a play on the name of the rock band Led Zeppelin.

The figure on the sign at school indicating the boys' restroom wears a wizard's cap.

Faces in the "wailing wall" include: Krusty, Maude Flanders, Comic Book Guy, Snake, Rainier Wolfcastle, Mayor Quimby, Selma, Uter, Lunchlady Doris, Frank Grimes, Old Jewish Man, Bleeding Gums Murphy, Mr. Largo, Moe, Larry Burns, Snowball II, and Squeaky-Voiced Teen.

When Montymort appears, Bart says, "Shazbot!," an exclamation Robin Williams made famous on the television show "Mork and Mindy." "Shazbot" was a curse word on Ork, Mork's home planet.

Montymort attempts to speed the process of draining Lisa's magical essence by tuning her upside down and patting her like a ketchup bottle.

(Bart's half-prince, half-frog is sickly and oozes vomit.)
Mrs. Krabappel: *(to Bart) Sloppy work, as usual. Lisa's casting spells at an eighth-grade level. You've sinned against nature.*
(Krabappel walks away.)
Bart's Frog Prince: *(suffering) Please kill me!*
Bart: *(to Lisa) You think you're so great just because you have god-like powers!*

 "Ah ha ha! Dying tickles!"

Montymort plots against Lisa:
Montymort: *We can't attack her while she's got that wand. We need a go-between to get it away from her.*
Slithers: *How about Satan?*
Montymort: *No, no, I'm ducking him. His wife has a screenplay.*

12

Montymort: *How would you like to humiliate your sister?*
Bart: *I'd like that. I'd like that very much!*
Montymort: *Now, it would involve betrayal and unspeakable evil.*
Bart: *Hey, hey, you've made your sale.*

At the Magic Recital:
Milhouse: *And now, a little trick I like to call... uh..."The Invisibility Cloak!"*
Marge: *How magical!*
Homer: *(without enthusiasm while watching a portable TV) Yeah, yeah. These kids are pretty special.*
Milhouse: *Now you see me, now you don't! (He removes his cloak and is naked.) Oh! It's just like my dream! (He runs off crying.)*

Literary Moment:

"Wiz Kids" is an outright spoof of the "Harry Potter" books and films, down to the sorcerer's robes, classroom practices, gothic-looking school, and the appearance of Harry Potter himself.

Closing Sequence

The Simpsons guest stars are leaving their trailer on the Fox studio lot. Pierce Brosnan offers to give the leprechaun and the sickly frog prince a ride to their cars. But once in Brosnan's sports car, the leprechaun takes over, causing the car to drive crazily out of the parking lot and down the boulevard, causing a car crash.

JUDGE CONSTANCE HARM

Her demeanor:
Intolerant

Her approach:
Hard-nosed

Her punishments:
Cruel and unusual

Gender:
By her own admission was at one time a boy

Favorite method of surveillance:
The magic of fiber optics

Desktop knickknack of choice:
A miniature guillotine

Listens to:
Radio station KBBL (as evidenced by her knowledge of the forty-dollar prize awarded by the KBBL Party Penguin Prize Patrol)

> DON'T SPIT ON MY CUPCAKE AND TELL ME IT'S FROSTING!

Guest Voice:
Jane Kaczmarek as Judge Constance Harm

Bart and Milhouse are arrested for joyriding in Chief Wiggum's police cruiser. Later, in juvenile court, the Simpsons are confident that the lax Judge Snyder will let the boys go with a warning. As expected, Snyder lets Milhouse off easy, but when it is Bart's turn, Judge Snyder very suddenly goes on vacation and is replaced by a much stricter judge…Constance Harm. When Judge Harm learns that Homer abandoned Bart in the middle of town instead of taking him to school, an act that led to Bart's mischief-making, she orders Homer and Bart to be tethered together as punishment.

Constant togetherness proves to be difficult for Homer and Bart. At school, Homer disrupts Bart's class and proves to be dead weight during Bart's baseball game. Homer forces Bart to sit outside while he drinks beer inside Moe's, and Bart proves to be an obstacle to Homer and Marge's lovemaking. Inevitably, Bart and Homer get into a loud and physical argument. Not being able to stand it any longer, Marge takes a knife and severs the tether. Judge Harm is alerted to the severing, and the Simpsons are summoned to court again. When Marge will not admit that she and Homer are bad parents in open court, Judge Harm orders the Simpson adults to be placed in stocks.

Homer and Marge decide they have had enough and break free of their restraints. They devise a plan to get back at the unfair judge. Late at night, they sneak onto

---

SHOW HIGHLIGHTS

Milhouse: *If we're late for school, we'll miss our free federal breakfast.*
Bart: *Big deal! It's just saltines and fig paste.*
Milhouse: *Ewww! Saltines!*

Kirk Van Houten: *Uh…Your Honor, please don't send my son to Juvie. He's basically a good kid. He's just weak—morally and in the upper body.*
Judge Snyder: *(scratching his chin)* Hmm…
Milhouse: *Please let me slip through the cracks?!*

"I heard science is working on a donut that actually burns off calories…uh…How's that goin'?"

Municipal bonding:
Homer: *I love our court days.*
Marge: *It's about the only thing we do as a family anymore.*

A kinder, gentler judge:
Judge Snyder: *Why, hello, Bart. Say, are those new shoes?*
Bart: *Yes they are, Roy.*
Homer: *(points to his watch) Judge Snyder, while we're young.*
Judge Snyder: *Oh, sorry. (reads document) Oh, my! Looks like you were the ringleader of this car theft—and that's a felony!*
Bart: *Yes, sir. (He looks remorseful, holds up the cross he's wearing, and rolls his fingers across it.)*
Judge Snyder: *On the other hand, I was young once.*
Homer: *(to Marge) I'll bring the car around.*
Judge Snyder: *(closing the file folder) And I suppose boys will be—(His watch alarm beeps.) Oh…oops! My vacation just started. (The judge packs his fishing clown figurine into his briefcase and hums to himself as he exits the bench.)*

Harsh judgment:
Judge Harm: *You have got a boy here who is crying out for adult supervision!*
Homer: *I couldn't agree more. Perhaps some sort of court-appointed babysitter or au pair?*
Judge Harm: *Sorry, bub, that crow won't caw.*
Homer: *It won't?*

Report to Room 5:
(A female court officer finishes tightening the tether to Homer's wrist.)
Officer: *There we go. How's that?*
(Homer holds up his hand, and it begins to turn purple.)
Homer: *It's a little tight.*
Officer: *Sir, you are not a size four.*
Homer: *I used to be.*
(Homer begins to sob and runs out the door, pulling Bart behind him.)

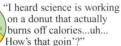

"Creative sentencing is common these days. That's why Bill Clinton is our mailman."

Homer's nocturnal confession: **"I thought I would hate working nights, but it's so peaceful. And there's no one here to squeal on me for shooting mice."**

Bart: *Can I ask you something, Dad?*
Homer: *Sure, boy.*
Bart: *The town keeps getting bigger. Will there always be enough electricity?*
Homer: *Heh-hee-heh-heh. Ah, son…you know that's none of your business.*

(Moe serves Homer a beer but notices Bart on the barstool next to him.)
Moe: *Hey, no kids in the bar.*
Homer: *Since when?*
Moe: *Oh, the heat's been on since them Bush girls were in here.*

Judge Constance Harm lowers the boom in an interview with Kent Brockman: **"Parents, it's time to take control! If you can't cope, you'll wear the rope!"**

Bart: *Come on, Dad. I gotta go to the bathroom.*
Homer: *Oh, I just got comfortable! Use the bottle.*
Marge: *No! I don't want you going in a bottle. That's what hobos do!*
Bart: *Come on, Homer!*
Homer: *No!*
Bart: *Mom!*
Marge: *Aw geez, Homer, just take him to the bathroom!*
Homer: *Fine! I don't know why we even have a bottle! Somebody tell me!*

THE STUFF YOU MAY HAVE MISSED

Bart and Milhouse are nearly run over by Professor Frink, while he is riding his rocket-powered motorcycle. The motorcycle, which is also capable of flight, was first seen in "Lemon of Troy" (2F22)

Wiggum's Miranda Rights teleprompter instructs officers to say, "You have the right to remain silent," then to "(Punch in belly)."

As the out-of-control police cruiser heads for the giant hot soup truck, police dog Officer Sniffy covers his eyes and says, "Ruh-oh!" in a manner similar to Scooby-Doo.

The statue of Blind Justice in front of the Juvenile Courthouse is of a little girl wearing a blindfold and holding a scale in one hand and a sword in the other.

Jimbo Jones can be seen with his lawyer and what would appear to be his mother outside the courtroom, waiting to go before Judge Snyder.

Homer's burglar outfit is similar to the one he wears when stealing Moe's car in "Dumbbell Indemnity" (5F12) and when smuggling sugar from the island of San Glucose in "Sweets and Sour Marge" (DABF03).

Episode CABF22
ORIGINAL AIRDATE: 11/11/01
WRITER: George Meyer and Mike Scully
DIRECTOR: Mark Kirkland
EXECUTIVE PRODUCER: Mike Scully

Judge Harm's houseboat and put up a derogatory banner. But before they can sneak away, they are caught by the judge's pet seal, Pancho. When Judge Harm comes out to investigate, Homer throws a cinder block at her. The block misses the judge, puts a hole in the side of her houseboat, and sinks it. The Simpsons find themselves in front of the judge in court once again. As the furious judge is about to pass judgment on Homer and Marge, Bart steps up and takes all the blame. Judge Harm is about to sentence Bart to five years in juvenile hall, but Judge Snyder returns from vacation just as suddenly as he left and replaces her just in time. The Simpsons go free, each swearing they will not break the law for a full year. Homer, however, breaks the law seconds later, nearly going through a red light and running over Hans Moleman in the crosswalk.

NOBODY READS THESE ANYMORE
NOBODY READS THESE ANYMORE
NOBODY READS THESE ANYMORE

Bart plays the sympathy card:

Judge Harm: *Well, I thought Dad was the problem, but apparently Mom is no prize pig herself. It's a miracle poor Bartholomew isn't robbing banks and chasing sweet Lady H.*
Bart: *I'm a latchkey kid.*
Lisa: *You are not!*

Judge Harm: *You two need to wake up and smell the java. And the first step is to admit that you're bad parents.*
Homer: *I admit it.*
Marge: *Homer, no! We're not bad parents.*
Judge Harm: *Yes, you are! Just say it!*
Marge: *No, I won't. And frankly, Judge, I think you're a bully.*
Judge Harm: *Ya do, huh?* (She hits her palm with the gavel.)
Marge: *You're so busy thinking up crazy ways to punish people, you can't see how much I love my kids.*
Homer: *Your Honor, I'd like to be tried separately.*

Lisa: *Do you think it's fair that you're always getting into trouble, yet Mom and Dad are being punished?*
Bart: (watching TV) *No, it's terrible!* (He drinks soda from a straw.)
Lisa: *Well, why don't you do something about it?*
Bart: *After wrestling.*
(Bart is watching a wrestling match on TV.)
Lisa: *When are you going to start taking responsibility for your actions?*
Bart: (still watching TV) *'Cuz I felt like it.*
Lisa: *You're not even listening!*
Bart: *I know you are, but what am I?*

Homer offers Marge judicious advice:
"You know, we could get out of these stupid things if you'd just tell the judge you're a bad mother. And you don't even have to say 'bad.' It could be 'negligent' or 'unfit' or 'drugged-up.'"

Homer: *She lives in a houseboat? Wow, she is so cool!*
Marge: *We hate her, Homer.*
Homer: *I know, I know.* (He makes a militant gesture with his fist and bows his head.) *Fight the power!*

"Pair Sinks Judge's House—Quilt Ruined":
Judge Harm: *Aah! That quilt was made by my grandmother!*
Homer: *Sooooo...it cost you nothing.*

Music Moment:

Homer argues the merits of Blue Oyster Cult's "Don't Fear the Reaper" with Judge Harm, and later the song plays over the episode's closing credits.

Bart: *Your Honor, may I say something?*
Judge Harm: *Well, it is highly unorthodox...so no!*
Bart: *Please, Your Honor.*
Judge Harm: *Oh, I can't resist that look. You remind me of me when I was a little boy.*
Bart: *Your Honor, it's not easy being my parents. I'm always screwing up in school, and getting in trouble with the law. But if I grow up to be a halfway decent person, I know it'll be because of my Mom and Dad. Everyone else might give up on me, but my parents never will.*
(Lisa leans over to Snake, in court and wearing shackles)
Lisa: (proudly) *That's my brother.*
Snake: *Um, did she say she used to be a dude?*
Bart: *So, Your Honor, if you're going to punish anyone in this courtroom today, I ask that you punish me.*
Judge Harm: (beat) *Okay, I will.*
Bart: *Guh-ooo!*

Judge Harm: *Bartholomew Simpson, I hereby sentence you to five years in Juvenile Hall.*
(She raises her gavel.)
Homer/Marge: *Gasp!*
(Judge Snyder takes the gavel from her hand.)
Judge Harm: *Unh!*
Judge Snyder: *Well, I'm back from vacation.*
Judge Harm: *But I was just about to bang my gavel, making the sentence official.*
Judge Snyder: *Sorry, I've already put my clown down.*
(He indicates his fishing clown statue on the bench.)
Judge Harm: *But I was just going to—*
Judge Snyder: (firmly) *The clown is down.*
Judge Harm: *Gunh!* (She storms off.)

Revealed This Episode:
Judge Snyder's first name is Roy.

Lisa: *Judge Snyder? Motion to declare a writ of "boys will be boys."*
Judge Snyder: *Motion granted.* (He bangs his gavel.) *Case dismissed.*
The Simpsons: *Woo-hoo!*

HOMER THE MOE

Homer recounts the nonsensical story of Bart digging a hole in the backyard to the barflies at Moe's Tavern. Moe interrupts him and expresses his dissatisfaction for the daily grind of tending bar and listening to his customers' dumb stories and conversations. He decides to visit his alma mater to see if he can regain the passion that made him become a bartender in the first place, leaving Homer in charge of the bar.

At Swigmore University, Moe visits a former professor. The professor deduces that the reason Moe has lost his spark for serving alcohol is because of his tavern's unappealing environment. He recommends that Moe give his tavern a facelift, and then tells Moe that he is dying. Moe is unable to help his mentor, so the professor walks into a lake and drowns himself. Moe returns to his tavern with renewed enthusiasm, and with the help of a European interior decorator named Formico, he remodels the bar in a futuristic "post-modern" motif. When Homer and his friends visit the new bar, now simply called "M," they do not like its pretentiousness. Homer causes a scene, and Moe angrily orders his lackeys to throw him out.

Homer decides to build a bar of his own in the garage to spite Moe. Meanwhile, Moe does not relate to his new clientele and yearns for the way things were before. After a ghostly visitation from his now deceased mentor, Moe walks to Homer's house to make amends to his old barflies. He is shocked and hurt to discover Homer's garage bar in full swing with live music by R.E.M. Moe accuses Homer of breaking the law by having a bar in a private residence. Homer counters by claiming his bar is a hunting club, which is legally allowed to serve beverages. Moe points out that the law requires a hunting club to actually hunt, and Homer vows to go hunting the very next day.

The next morning, Homer goes hunting for a Thanksgiving turkey. Moe covertly tries to stop him, and Homer accidentally shoots Moe in the leg. Upset that he hurt Moe, Homer makes amends, and the Simpsons, along with R.E.M., enjoy a tofu turkey Thanksgiving dinner at Moe's Tavern, which has been restored to its former appearance.

SHOW HIGHLIGHTS

Lisa: *Where's Bart? His Mountain Dew's getting flat.*
Marge: *(looking out window) That's odd. He's outside, digging.*
Homer: *Probably digging for drugs.*
Marge: *There's no drugs out there!*
Homer: *No. (suspiciously) Of course not.*

A visit from the shrink:
Marge: *Bart, this is Dr. Kaufman. He's a special kind of talking doctor.*
Dr. Kaufman: *Call me Bob. Well, that's quite a hole you're digging.*
Bart: *Thanks, Bob.*
Dr. Kaufman: *A-heh. You know, a hole's a great place to hide when people are fighting. Are there angry people in your house?*
Bart: *My dad's always yelling that whitey's keeping him down.*
Dr. Kaufman: *(writing notes) I see...*

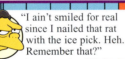

"That is the stupidest story I ever heard, and I've read the entire *Sweet Valley High* series."

Homer: *Geez, Moe, you've been a real crank lately.*
(Moe pulls a shotgun from behind the bar, cocks it, and points it at Homer.)
Moe: *You take that back.*
Homer: *Now, ya see. That's what I'm talkin' about. You're always pointing that shotgun at us.*
(Moe moves the shotgun in the direction of Lenny.)
Lenny: *And callin' us dumbasses...*
(Then at Carl.)
Carl: *Which we're so not.*

"I ain't smiled for real since I nailed that rat with the ice pick. Heh. Remember that?"

Moe: *Yep. Good, ol' Swigmore U.*
Carl: *Gee, uh, when you talk about that school, your voice fills with, uh...what do you call it? Human feeling.*
Lenny: *Yeah! Maybe you should, uh...what's the expression? Go back there.*
Moe: *What's the word I'm searchin' for? Uh...yeah!*

Bartender Homer takes a prank call:
Homer: *(phone rings) Yello?*
Bart: *(on phone) Um, yeah, I'd like to speak to a Mr. Tabooger. First name Ollie.*
Homer: *Ooo, Bart! My first prank call! What do I do?*
Bart: *Just ask if anyone knows Ollie Tabooger.*
Homer: *I don't get it.*
Bart: *Yell out, "I'll eat a booger."*
Homer: *What's the gag?*
Bart: *Oh, forget it!*
(Bart hangs up in frustration.)

Moe seeks advice from his mentor:
Moe: *Professor, I'm...em...I'm burned-out on bartending. I—when I first saw the movie Ironweed, I thought, you know, this is for me. But now, well, I'm not so sure.*
Professor: *Nonsense! You were born to sling suds! The problem must lie elsewhere. Describe your tavern, in one word.*
Moe: *Uh...is crap-hole one word?*
Professor: *Yes, if it's hyphenated.*
Moe: *Then I'll stick with crap-hole.*

Homer's impromptu street song:
*I'm-a walking down the street,
Gonna open Moe's bar,
I'm a-singin' what I'm thinkin',
Hey, look at that dog!*

Moe: *And now, I want you to meet the guy who's going to help bring Moe's into the 20th century.*
Formico: *I am Formico, the Dean of Design.*
Homer: *Hi, Formico!*
Formico: *Ah-ah-ah! My name must never be spoken.*
Homer: *Sorry. (aside to Moe) He seems nice!*

Best bartender—bar...none:
Homer: *It's not fair. Just when I was getting to be the world's greatest bartender, it's all snatched away.*
(Homer sees that Bart's milk is low and picks up a milk bottle.) Freshen your drink, pal?
Bart: *Just leave the bottle.*
(Homer puts a cigarette in Lisa's mouth and lights it.)
Homer: *There you go, doll. (Lisa coughs and puts the cigarette on her plate.)*
Lisa: *Ew!*
(Homer turns to Maggie, who's asleep in her high chair, and pokes her in the chest.)
Homer: *Look, buddy, I don't care where you go, but you can't sleep here.*

Episode CABF20
ORIGINAL AIRDATE: 11/18/01
WRITER: Dana Gould
DIRECTOR: Jen Kamerman
EXECUTIVE PRODUCER: Mike Scully
GUEST VOICES: R.E.M. (Peter Buck, Mike Mills and Michael Stipe) as Themselves

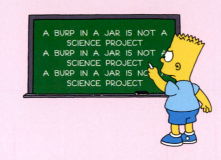

Moe's new tavern, "M," is open:

Carl: *I don't get all this eyeball stuff.* (referring to giant close-ups of eyes on video screens) *What are they supposed to represent? Eyeballs?*
Moe: *It's "Po-Mo!"*
(Homer, Barney, Lenny and Carl stare at him blankly.)
Moe: *"Post-Modern?"*
(They continue to stare blankly.)
Moe: *Yeah, all right. "Weird for the sake of weird."*
Homer, Barney, Lenny and Carl: *Ohh!*

Homer: *Well, you've turned into a big phony!*
Moe: *Hey, nobody calls Moe St. Cool a phony!*
Russian Model 2: *All this yelling is taking a-vay my horny.*
Moe: *Is it? Oh, that's it!* (calling his lackeys) *Dagmar, Julien! Throw this bum out!*
Homer: *I'll throw myself out, thank you!* (He grabs himself by the collar and tosses himself out the door.)

Bart: *Whatcha doin', Dad?*
Homer: *I think it's pretty obvious. I'm turning our garage into a tavern.* (pounding his fist on the bar top) *The kind Moe's used to be.*
Lisa: *This is pretty far to go just to spite Moe.*
Homer: *It's not about spite. It's about petty revenge* (punching his fist into his other hand) *and getting back at that traitor Moe. Now help me nail up this urinal.*

Sung along to the tune of Joan Jett's "I Love Rock 'n' Roll":

Homer/Lenny/Carl/Barney: *I won't drink at Moe's.*
Homer's old garage is all I need!
I won't drink at Moe's...
Homer: *...'cause Moe's a big jerk, and a she-male, too!*

"How could I toss my friends into the cold...with no place to get liquored-up?"

Homer's version of R.E.M.'s "It's the End of the World As We Know It (And I Feel Fine)":

Leonid What's-his-name,
Herman Munster, motorcade,
Birthday party, Cheetos,
Pogo-sticks and lemonade,
Symbiotic stupid jerks,
That's right Flanders,
I am talkin' about you!

Michael Stipe: (to Homer) *You lied to us!*
(Michael breaks a beer bottle on the bar and threatens Homer with it. Homer screams, and Mike and Peter grab Michael's arms, holding him back.)
Mike Mills: *Michael...No!*
Peter Buck: *That's not the R.E.M. way.*
Michael Stipe: (calming down) *You're right. Let's recycle those shards and get out of here.*

Homer takes Lisa hunting:

Lisa: *It's not fair, Dad. Why should an animal die just because you and Moe are fighting?*
Homer: *It's the law. My hands are tied.* (He pulls out a serving plate with side dishes on it.) *Okay, cranberry sauce, stuffing, potatoes.* (He aims a shotgun at the plate.) *Come on, turkey! Join your friends!*
Lisa: *Do you really think the turkey is just going to climb onto the plate?*
Homer: *I would.*

Moe: *Psst! Lisa!*
Lisa: *Moe?*
Moe: *Listen, I don't like you, and you don't like me. But we both want to stop Homer from shooting the turkey.*
Lisa: *You don't like me? I like you.*
Moe: *You do? Then I like you, too. Here, have a towelette.*

"Turkeys...the only animals smarter than man."

Wisdom for the ages:

Homer: *I'm sorry I shot you, Moe.*
Moe: *Aw, that's okay. It's like my dad always said, "Eventually, everybody gets shot."*

THE STUFF YOU MAY HAVE MISSED

The Chinese satellite has a roof shaped like a pagoda.

The gates of Swigmore University are swinging saloon doors. The college clock reads: "No Drinking Before 5:00," but all the numbers on the clock face are "5"s.

As Moe crosses his old bartending school campus, he passes a student who holds a six-pack of Duff Beer under his arm like a set of school books. One student carries a backpack full of bottles, and another juggles a bottle à la Tom Cruise in *Cocktail* (1988).

Things used to decorate Moe's new bar, "M": A model bi-plane, numerous video screens (depicting volcanoes, eyeballs, and opening flowers), shafts of bubbling water, pink clouds painted on orange walls, beanbag chairs, bar stools on the ceiling, rabbits suspended from the ceiling, glass bubbles on the walls, an oxygen bar, and a giant hamster wheel.

Homer's unfinished robot is made from a big bucket, a smaller pail, a tennis racket, a heating coil, some corks, batteries, and a broom.

As R.E.M. performs, Carl plays the air guitar.

Under Homer's hunting club sign is a crossed rifle and fishing pole.

Music Moment:

Homer and the boys line dance on top of the bar to "Wooly Bully" by Sam the Sham and The Pharaohs and then slow dance to Chicago's "Colour My World."

TV Moment:

When Homer hits the jukebox with his fist to change the music, he is emulating Fonzie, as played by Henry Winkler on "Happy Days."

Movie Moment:

As Homer, Lenny, Carl, and Barney dance atop the bar at Moe's, their routine is similar to that of the girls in *Coyote Ugly* (2000).

PROFESSOR HUNTINGTON

Mixology:
One part James Mason, with a spritz of George Plimpton

Who he is an inspiration for:
Young, impressionable students who yearn to get people loaded

Outwardly he is:
A button-down cliché with elbow patches and an endless font of liquor-serving knowledge waiting to be tapped

Inwardly he is:
Riddled with cancer

His nickname for Moe:
Old Glasswipe

Favorite trick question:
How much Grenadine is in a Cosmopolitan?

Heard to rhetorically wonder:
Why does pond water sparkle so?

Known to contemplate:
Suicide

BEAUTIFY YOUR HOLE, AND YOU'LL BEAUTIFY YOUR SOUL.

GLORIA

Profession:
Meter maid, graveyard shift

Past boyfriends include:
Snake and C. Montgomery Burns

Taste in men:
Questionable to lousy

Can't say "no" to:
A suitor with a puppy-dog look, especially when accompanied by a puppy-dog whine

Responds favorably to:
A man who tents his fingers

> I'VE NEVER DATED ANYONE WHO KNEW CALVIN COOLIDGE.

Guest Voice:
Julia Louis-Dreyfus as Gloria

After eating a meal with his family at a Chinese restaurant, Homer is disappointed by the sub-par fortunes in the fortune cookies. He complains to the manager and is immediately hired to write fortunes when he proves he can make up better ones than the current writers. One of the fortunes Homer writes ("You will find true love on Flag Day") ends up in a cookie given to Mr. Burns. Since that very day happens to be Flag Day, Burns goes looking for his true love. With only seconds remaining in the day, Burns finally finds the girl of his dreams, a young meter maid named Gloria who is ticketing his limousine. He joyfully asks her out on a date.

Their first rendezvous goes very well, but Gloria cannot get past their age difference. Burns enlists Homer to help convince Gloria that she should continue dating him. Homer successfully gets Gloria to agree to another date, so Burns decides to keep Homer around during their courting process. Homer is with them at the bowling alley when Burns proposes to Gloria, and she agrees to marry him. Burns goes in search of champagne to celebrate, and Gloria's ex-boyfriend, Snake, appears. He is planning to rob the bowling alley, but instead he kidnaps her along with Homer, who tries to stop him.

Mr. Burns, convinced that Homer has run off with his fiancée, enlists the help of the police. They trace Homer to a secluded cabin hideout, where they discover that Snake is the true culprit. With Gloria and Homer tied up as hostages, the police dare not enter the building. Homer accidentally sets the hideout on fire while trying to escape his rope bonds, and both he and Snake escape the flaming inferno. Gloria, however, is still trapped inside. Burns attempts to rescue her despite his decrepitude, but Gloria ends up carrying him out of the fire. Burns is overjoyed, but Gloria proves to be fickle and decides she cares more for Snake. Mr. Burns leaves with the Simpsons, still a frustrated bachelor.

SHOW HIGHLIGHTS

 "I love Chinatown, although I wish they'd stop picking on Tibet Town."

Bart orders dinner at Bob's Big Buddah:
Bart: (to Waiter) Uh...yeah. I'll have the shark butt with butt sauce.
Marge: Bart!
Waiter: Oh, excellent choice, sir.
(Marge realizes shark butt is on the menu.)
Marge: Oh.

Lisa's order:
Lisa: Uh, how is the Feast of Twelve Delights with Triple Happiness Sauce?
Waiter: Very disappointing.
Lisa: Then I'll have the Sweet and Sour Rice.
Waiter: Oh, very good. Would you like that with the fragrant bee bellies or the cat noses?
Lisa: Neither, thank you.
Waiter: Is there any way we can enhance your dining experience by hurting an animal?
Lisa: No!

Homer: Ah! And now to read my fortune: "Geese can be troublesome." What the hell is that supposed to mean?!
Waiter: Oh...fortune means geese cause problems.
Homer: Well, I knew that before I came in here! A guy outside told me that!

Homer impresses the fortune cookie writers:
Woody Allen-type: He is like a young me.
Older Chinese Man: Please, Yung Mee was a hack compared to this guy.

Lenny reads his fortune: **"'You are a real winner.' Woo! That fortune really nailed me...and my winning ways."**

More fortune cookie fortunes by Homer:
"You will be aroused by a shampoo commercial."
"The price of stamps will climb ever higher."
"You will invent a humorous toilet lid."
"Your store is being robbed, Apu."

Mr. Burns pays for his General Gao's Chicken:
Mr. Burns: Fourteen dollars and ten...eleven...twelve cents. There you go!
Delivery Boy: You know, sir, tipping is customary.
Burns: Oh, me sorry! Me no speaky Chinee!

Burns flirts with Gloria the meter maid: **"You can lift my wiper any day!"**

Burns and Gloria get to know each other:
Gloria: I really feel safe with you. It's like going out with my brother.
Burns' brain: (thought) Yes! It's going great!
Gloria: So...what are you into?
Burns: (confused) In...to?
Gloria: Yeah, like what's a fun day for a...104-year-old?
Burns: Oh, I enjoy all the popular youth trends. Like, uh...mm...(He looks down from the ferris wheel for inspiration and sees a kiddie car ride.)...piloting motorcoaches...and, uh...(He spies a man using a pooper-scooper.)...collecting dog waste.

Homer gets dressed:
Marge: New underpants? Homer, what are you up to?
Homer: Burns wants me to come along on his date to show him where hip young people go.
Marge: Well, don't look too hip. You don't want that girl falling for you!
Homer: You're right! (He digs some tattered underpants out of the hamper.) Hmm. These would stop Joan Collins herself!

Burns: (whispering to Homer) Put my hand on her knee.
Homer: Yes, Mr. Burns. (He moves Burns' hand under the table.)
Burns: I said "her"...and I said "knee."
Homer: Oh, sorry.

 "I'm going to make such love to you that you'll forget all about Rudolph Valentino."

Homer: You're going to ask her to marry you?
Burns: Isn't it wonderful? I'm head over heels in love!
Homer: Are you sure you want to do this so fast?
Burns: Yes, my biological clock is ticking. I could be dead again soon.

Snake takes a pre-robbery inventory: **"Okay...gun, check. Dollar sign bag, check. Power bar, check."**

My boyfriend's back and there's gonna be trouble:
Gloria: Snake? I thought you were in prison!
Snake: I was. I told the guard that I was going out for a pack of cigarettes, then I totally stabbed him.

Snake: You're looking good, baby! Why did we ever break up?
Gloria: You pushed me out of a moving car.
Snake: The cops were chasing us. I needed to lighten the load...and, um, protect you.

BURNS IN LOVE

Episode CABF18
ORIGINAL AIRDATE: 12/02/01
WRITER: John Swartzwelder
DIRECTOR: Lance Kramer
EXECUTIVE PRODUCER: Mike Scully

GUEST VOICE: George Takei as
the Chinese restaurant waiter

THE STUFF YOU MAY HAVE MISSED

In Chinatown, the Simpsons pass a store called Toys "L" Us.

George Takei previously appeared in "One Fish, Two Fish, Blowfish, Bluefish" (7F11) as Akira, the Japanese waiter at the Happy Sumo, and in "30 Minutes Over Tokyo" (AABF20) as Wink, the game show host.

Rich Uncle Pennybags, who steals the woman Burns was flirting with, is the character from the game of Monopoly. He drives away in a railroad engine similar to the ones on the Monopoly railway cards. He was also seen in "30 Minutes Over Tokyo" (AABF20), in which he drove off in a sports car that looked like a Monopoly game token.

Burns mistakes a gentleman's club with pole dancers for a "nude female fire station."

Homer's list of Mr. Burns accomplishments took place as follows: he ran his own casino in "Springfield" (1F08); he stole the Loch Ness Monster in "Monty Can't Buy Me Love" (AABF17); and he got shot by a baby and blotted out the sun in "Who Shot Mr. Burns? I & II" (2F16 & 2F20).

Mr. Burns utters two joyfully nonsensical phrases ("O frabjous day!" and "Calooh! Callay!") from Lewis Carroll's poem "Jabberwocky" found within the pages of *Through the Looking-Glass and What Alice Saw There.*

One of the video games in the bowling alley is "Nuke Canada."

The mailbox at Snake's hideout reads, "Snake (AKA Jailbird)." Jailbird was Snake's original character name.

Stolen items seen at Snake's hideout include: several TVs, stereos and computers, the *Mona Lisa*, a soccer ball, a trophy, the Maltese Falcon, a surfboard, bubble-gum machines, a bong, golf clubs, a toxic waste drum, two Oscars, a necklace on a jewelry display bust, a bicycle, a dart board, and a wet suit.

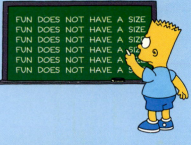

 "I'm going to win you back if I have to pistol-whip this guy all night."

Kent Brockman: *On a serious note, two local residents have been missing for the last twenty minutes. We take you now live to Barney's Bowlarama and the last man who saw them, C. Montgomery Burns.*
Burns: *I don't understand. She was my young, sexy fiancée; he was my sexually virile best friend; and they just drove off in my Bugatti Sexarossa. How could this ever have happened?*
Kent: *Well, according to our audience insta-poll, 46% say, "You're too old," and 37% say, "She's a skank!"*

Snake ties up his hostages:
Gloria: *Let me guess. Now you're going to start working him over with the brass knuckles. You are so predictable.*
Homer: *You know what would be surprising? A foot massage.*
Snake: *Shut up!* (He pistol-whips Homer.)
Homer: *D'oh!*
Gloria: *Beating a man to a bloody pulp isn't going to impress me.*
Snake: *It used to. What if I beat him harder?*
Gloria: *Wow, you so don't get it.*
Homer: *Uh, has the ship sailed on my foot massage suggestion?* (Snake pistol-whips Homer again.) *Ow!*

Kent Brockman: *We're in minute two of this stand-off. What's the situation, Chief?*
Chief Wiggum: *Well, we have an officer sneakin' around the house, Kent. So, unless they have a television in there, or can hear my loud talking...* (A gunshot is heard. Officer Eddie runs away from the hideout, holding his arm in pain.)
Officer Eddie: *Ow! Ow! Ow!*
Wiggum: *Well, I guess that answers that, doesn't it?*

Snake: *I swear I can change, Gloria. I'm taking classes in computer fraud.*
Gloria: *That's what you said about the telemarketing scams, but you didn't stick with it.*
Snake: *I don't like bothering people at home.*

Burns: *Now, step aside! I'll save Gloria myself!*
Wiggum: *You? Uh, no offense, but you're a decrepit monkey skeleton.*
Burns: *Perhaps! But this monkey skeleton is in love!*

Kent Brockman interviews Gloria after her brush with death: **"I know you've been through a lot, ma'am, but we need you to stand in front of the burning house and say, 'Channel Six is hot, hot, hot!'"**

Movie Moment:
Mr. Burns and Gloria share a strand of spaghetti at an Italian restaurant, causing their lips to come together in a romantic nod to the Disney feature *Lady and the Tramp* (1955). In this instance, Homer provides Mr. Burns' suction from underneath their table with the use of a tube taped to the side of his boss's face.

TV Moment:
At Stu's Disco, Burns' dancing style is exactly like one of the kids at the Christmas party in "A Charlie Brown Christmas."

Music Moment:
NRBQ's "If I Don't Have You" is played during Mr. Burns and Gloria's date montage.

FUN DOES NOT HAVE A SIZE
FUN DOES NOT HAVE A SIZE
FUN DOES NOT HAVE A SIZE
FUN DOES NOT HAVE A SIZE
FUN DOES NOT HAVE A SIZE
FUN DOES NOT HAVE A SIZE

THE BLUNDER

Marge accidentally buys the wrong brand of paper towels. She plans to return them, but becomes enamored by the lumberjack pictured on the super-absorbent paper towel packaging. Homer is jealous of Marge's infatuation with the lumberjack, and he decides to play a prank on her. He telephones her, pretending to be the actor who portrays the lumberjack, and invites himself over for dinner that night. Marge is ecstatic until Barney shows up instead, half dressed as a lumberjack. Marge is humiliated, and Homer makes amends by taking her out to a nice restaurant. At the restaurant, a performing hypnotist enlists Homer as a volunteer. The hypnotist takes Homer back to when he was twelve years old. Homer recalls a summer day at the old quarry swimming hole and then suddenly begins to scream. His screams continue without ceasing that night and into the next day.

Carl and Lenny have to bring the still screaming Homer home the next afternoon for disturbing things at work. Everyone, including Moe, who has come to the house looking for his barflies, agrees that Homer must be screaming because he has unlocked a repressed memory. Marge makes Homer a cup of Yaqui Indian memory tea, and after Homer drinks it, he recalls the time he, Lenny, Carl, and Moe went down to the old quarry swimming hole as kids. Young Homer is the only one foolish enough to jump into the quarry, which has turned into a mud puddle. Wondering why the drainpipe that feeds the quarry is stopped up, Homer loosens the blockage with a stick, and a gush of water rushes from the pipe and fills the quarry, depositing a decaying corpse in the boy's lap.

Back in the present and determined to solve the mystery of the corpse, the Simpsons visit the quarry that evening, leaving behind Lenny, Carl, and Moe. Moe feels left out. At the quarry they encounter Chief Wiggum, and with the help of Marge's absorbent paper towels, they drain the swimming hole and

SHOW HIGHLIGHTS

Marge gives Lisa a lesson in Home Economics:
Lisa: I came home as quick as I could! What's going on?
Marge: Watch what happens when I spill this blue liquid. (She pours a pitcher of blue liquid on the kitchen table and tears off a paper towel.) Hmm?
Lisa: You pulled me out of school for this?
Marge: Absolutely! You're about to get a lesson...in value!

(Homer and Bart make their prank call from Ned Flanders' living room as he and the Lovejoys drink tea.)
Flanders: Heh-heh. Playing a prankeroo, eh?
Homer: I was having a private conversation with my wife, in the guise of Chad Sexington. Do you mind?

Homer's prank in action:
Homer: (feigning innocence) So, how was your day? Did anything unbelievable happen? Phone calls? Things of that nature?
(Bart snickers.)
Marge: You're not going to believe it! That paper towel lumberjack is coming here! For dinner! Tonight!
Homer: Tonight? Well, you'd better get your hopes up!
Marge: I will!

Marge: I guess it was a pretty funny prank. I like the ones where nothing catches on fire.
Homer: Yeah. Nothing is hurt, except feelings.

"Oh dear. I've re-dork-ulated."

Homer gets hypnotized:
Homer: I am in your power. Boss me around.
Mesmerino: When I snap my fingers, you will transform into a famous historian! (He snaps his fingers.)
Homer: Look at me! I'm a famous historian! Out of my way!
(The audience applauds.)
Mesmerino: Thank you. Now you are Emily Dickinson! (He snaps his fingers.)
Homer: (running circles around Mesmerino) Look at me! I'm Angie Dickinson! Out of my way!

(Carl and Lenny bring Homer home, still screaming.)
Carl: Sorry, Mrs. S. He was kind of disruptin' things at work.
Lenny: Yeah! He ruined naptime and quiet time.

Young Fat Tony: You guys have blundered into our secret tobacky patch.
(He indicates a marijuana patch.)
Young Lenny: Wow. Is that wacky tobacky?
Young Fat Tony: The wackiest.
Young Louie: Let's punch and kick them!

Young Moe, on astronomy: **"Ah! Look at all them stars...buncha lazy lights. Don't do nothin' for nobody!"**

Young Carl: Hey, you know what I'm lookin' forward to? The future. Have you heard about this "Internet" thing?
Young Lenny: Internet?
Young Carl: Yeah, it's the inner netting they invented to line swim trunks. It provides a comforting snugness.

Young Lenny: That's that nuclear plant they just opened.
Young Carl: Yeah...that's your future...bustin' atoms. Can you imagine us workin' there? The whole "Carl Crew"?
Young Lenny: Hey, I thought we were called "Lenny and the Jets."
Young Moe: Eh...you're both wrong. We're "The Moe Szyslak Experience, featuring Homer."
Young Carl: Ah...I like the sound of that!

Campfire pledge:
Young Homer: Friends forever?
Young Moe, Lenny and Carl: Friends forever!
(They put hands together...over the fire, accidentally burning themselves.)
Young Homer: Ow!
Young Lenny: Ow, that really hurts!
Young Carl: Man, we're stupid.
Young Moe: I hate you guys.

Young Moe: (whistles) You guys really gonna dive offa here?
Young Lenny: (looking down, scared) Not me. I'm shakin' like a French soldier.
Young Carl: (scared) Yeah. I think I just logged onto my internet.
Young Lenny: Only a moron would jump into that— (Homer runs past and leaps off the rocks.)
Young Homer: (shouting) Geronimo!

TV Moment:
Both Moe saying in a silly voice, "Mmm! That's good Yaqui," and Mesmerino reading his mail with his mind are tributes to Johnny Carson bits on "The Tonight Show."

Episode CABF21
ORIGINAL AIRDATE: 12/09/01
WRITER: Ian Maxtone-Graham
DIRECTOR: Steven Dean Moore
EXECUTIVE PRODUCER: Mike Scully

GUEST VOICES: Joe Mantegna as Young Fat Tony, Paul Newman as Himself and Judith Owen as Herself

discover the corpse, now a skeleton. They all enter the drainpipe and discover a hatch that opens into Mr. Burns' office in the power plant. Wiggum accuses Burns of murder, but Burns pleads innocence and shows them an old security film. The film reveals the identity of the body to be that of Burns' former assistant, Waylon Smithers Sr., who died in a tragic nuclear accident. Mr. Smithers sees the film and is grateful to know the truth of his father's heroic demise. Back at the Simpson home, Moe arrives to piece together the already solved mystery, and Homer and Marge humor him.

I AM NOT CHARLIE BROWN ON ACID
I AM NOT CHARLIE BROWN ON ACID
I AM NOT CHARLIE BROWN ON ACID

Movie Moments:

When Professor Frink turns from goofy nerd to smooth make-out artist, it's an homage to the transforming character of Julius Kelp/Buddy Love in the Jerry Lewis masterpiece *The Nutty Professor* (1963).

The scene of young Homer, Lenny, and Carl walking along the railroad tracks singing "Mr. Sandman" is reminiscent of a moment in Rob Reiner's *Stand By Me* (1986), a film based on a short story by Stephen King about a group of young boys who go in search of a dead body.

The boys' quarry swimming hole is similar to the one where the local boys (Cutters) hang out in *Breaking Away* (1979).

Moe: And there's your...whatchamacall...repressed trauma. I mean, who likes getting muddy? It's terrible. Okay, let's go to Moe's now.
Homer: Wait a minute. I remember falling in the mud. But I don't think that's why I've been screaming.
Moe: Fine. Crap all over my theory.

Marge: You found a corpse when you were twelve? No wonder you've been so traumatized! (She comforts him.) Mm-hmm.
Homer: (sobbing) It's responsible for everything wrong in my life! My occasional overeating! My fear of corpses!

Homer: Heh heh heh heh heh-heh! Yep! The old quarry is just a stone's throw away!
Lisa: Stop saying that, Dad!
Homer: (defiant) Never!

At the quarry:

Chief Wiggum: So, what are you doing here?
Lisa: We're investigating a possible murder case.
Wiggum: Oh, you mind if I tag along? I'm kind of a crime buff.

Lisa: Hey! What's that over there?
Wiggum: Don't get excited. It's just a skull-shaped rock and a bunch of white sticks.
Bart: It's the body!
Homer: And someone has eaten the flesh! (He eyes Marge and Lisa suspiciously.)

Mr. Burns: Gah! What are you doing in my corpse hatch?
Wiggum: Montgomery Burns, you're under arrest for murder!
Burns: Duh! Did I say "corpse hatch"? I meant "innocence tube."

Mr. Burns screens his security film: **"If you see only one film this year that proves my innocence, make it this one."**

Mr. Burns comes clean: **"Smithers Sr. gave his life to save the plant. And since cover-ups were all the rage back then, I shoved his heroic corpse down the sewer pipe!"**

Burns: I never told Smithers the truth about his father.
Smithers: Until tonight, sir!
Burns: Gasp! Smithers Jr.!
Bart: Ha! Busted!
Homer: Now the movie has turned into a play. It's still good, though.

Burns: I'm sorry I lied to you, Waylon. But I wanted to spare you the details of your father's gruesome death.
Smithers: Well, I'm glad to know he died a hero... instead of that other way.
Burns: (aside to Marge) Heh! I told him his father was killed in the Amazon by a tribe of savage women. (to Smithers) I hope it didn't affect you in any way.
Smithers: We'll never know, sir.

THE STUFF YOU MAY HAVE MISSED

Burly paper towels and its lumberjack is a parody of Brawny paper towels.

In Homer's fantasy, Mama Celeste threatens him with a pizza cutter.

When Marge thinks Burly is at the front door, she uses one of his paper towels, with its extra absorbency, to dry her armpits.

Mesmerino calls Mr. Burns "Skeletor" in reference to the villain of the "He-Man and the Masters of the Universe" cartoons.

Photos of famous celebrities seen on the walls of The Pimento Grove include: Barry White, Rainier Wolfcastle, Johnny Carson, Woody Allen, Jay Leno, Leonard Nimoy, Bette Midler, Ringo Starr, Ron Howard, Birch Barlow, David Crosby, Brooke Shields, members of *NSYNC, and Bumblebee Man.

Homer's first memory brought about by the Yaqui tea is from "Bart the Daredevil" (7F06) when he tried to jump over Springfield Gorge. Lisa claims "everyone's sick of that memory." The clip has been seen previously in "So It's Come To This: A Simpsons Clip Show" (9F17) and "Behind the Laughter" (BABF19).

When the whistle blows at the Springfield Nuclear Power Plant, a burst of flame erupts in one of the cooling towers.

As the Simpsons intently watch Chief Wiggum open the sewer hatch to Mr. Burns' office, Bart has a rat on his shoulder.

The sewer hatch opening is directly under the huge stuffed polar bear in Mr. Burns' office.

Even as a baby, Waylon Smithers Jr. wore glasses and called Mr. Burns "Sir."

MESMERINO, THE HIP HYPNOTIST

Where you've seen him:
"The Mike Douglas Show", "The Merv Griffin Show," "Art Linkletter's House Party," and the dinner show at The Pimento Grove

You can recognize him by:
His portable pyramid of mystery and his cryptic Bronx accent

Highlights of his performance:
Heckling, spoofing, and whatnot

Activities off-stage include:
Reading mail with his mind before opening the envelopes

Bankability:
Small bookings and an even smaller bank balance

IS ANYONE HERE NOT A DOWNER? ANYONE?

NIBBLES THE HAMSTER

Greatest accomplishment:
Rode a model rocket into the lower atmosphere

Most heroic feat:
Saved Homer and Ned from carbon-monoxide poisoning by breaking a car window with his exercise ball

Most disturbing moment:
When Homer called him "something to eat"

Most embarrassing moment:
When asked by Principal Skinner to chew through his ball sack

Secret shame:
His wife ate three of their babies

SHE OF

After watching a TV commercial for a model rocket, Bart uses Homer's credit card to order one. Many weeks later, Homer volunteers to help Bart fly his new rocket, but the launch blows up in their faces. Frustrated at his failure, and shown up by Ned Flanders' successful model rocket launch next door, Homer seeks the help of the brainy college nerds he once befriended. The nerds build a top-notch rocket, but the flight is compromised, when, after going off course, the hamster pilot ejects from the craft. Out of control and unmanned, the rocket crashes into the Springfield Community Church, setting it on fire.

Due to lack of funds, Reverend Lovejoy and the church council have no recourse but to let Mr. Burns help them rebuild the church. They reluctantly agree to let the evil millionaire run the church like a business. Burns brings in businesswoman Lindsey Naegle to oversee the refurbishing. Lindsey suggests that if they sell some ad space, they will earn enough money to have the church up and running in no time. Three weeks later, everyone is impressed with the newly remodeled church. The pews are more comfortable, and there is even a jumbo video screen. However, Lisa is horrified at the multitude of ads, and when Reverend Lovejoy launches into a sermon that is peppered with advertisements, she protests and walks out, vowing to never return to the church again.

Lisa starts looking for a replacement religion, much to Marge's dismay. After having a positive encounter with Carl, Lenny, and Richard Gere in a nearby Buddhist temple, Lisa decides to convert to Buddhism. Now Marge

SHOW HIGHLIGHTS

Bart: *Hey, Lis! Is Dad's credit card number five-seven-eight-four-three-six-five-three-four-three-four-one-o-seven-o-nine?*
Lisa: *You know it is.*

Homer's flossing song (to the tune of Devo's "Whip It"):

When you have a rib-eye steak,
You must floss it.
Oh, that meatloaf tasted great,
You must floss it.
Now floss it! Floss it good!

Launch Master Homer, prior to another disaster: **"The word 'unblowupable' is thrown around a lot these days."**

Ned Flanders, launching his own model rocket: **"Greetings from Nednedy Space Center on Cape Flandaveral. We noticed your sky-ro-technics and thought we'd join in."**

"Son, we are about to break the surly bonds of gravity and punch the face of God!"

Marge: *This is the worst thing you've ever done!*
Homer: *You say that so much, it's lost all meaning.*

THE STUFF YOU MAY HAVE MISSED

The initials on Homer's nerd-built rocket are HJS, which presumably stands for Homer Jay Simpson.

Nibbles the hamster was last seen in the episode titled "Skinner's Sense of Snow" (CABF06).

After the model rocket countdown, Homer shouts "countdown" rather than "ignition" or "blast-off."

The Rich Texan can be seen both on Burns' church surveillance monitor and then sitting by himself in the balcony in a long shot of the church. He would appear to have purchased a skybox.

The large Jesus neon sign outside of the church entrance resembles the well-known neon "Vegas Vic" cowboy sign that was once atop the Pioneer Club Casino in Las Vegas, complete with moving arm.

The Jumbo-tron TV screen in the church is labeled "Godcam." When Lisa is pictured on it,

a caption reads "Pouting Thomas."

Rev. Lovejoy's guest speaker is the Noid, a mascot of Domino's Pizza. The Noid was last seen as a giant balloon in the Costington's Thanksgiving Day Parade in "Homer Vs. Dignity" (CABF04).

Two of the books Lisa reads while doing research into different faiths are *Religionhood* by Paul Reiser and *Zagat's Guide to World Religions.*

The religious "nightlife" signs Lisa passes while searching for a new faith read, "Bed, Bath & Baha'i," "Whiskey a God God," "Church of the Latter Day Druids" and "Amish."

Lenny and Carl's meditation mantra is from the "Short Shorts" song (The Royal Teens, 1958). The song was previously heard in "El Viaje Misterioso de Nuestro Jomer" (3F24) and "Homer the Heretic" (9F01), both episodes that deal with spiritual matters.

Rev. Lovejoy: *I have convened the church council to see what we should do now.*
Kearney: *Fixing this church should be our top priority, and I say that as a teenager and a parent of a teenager.*
Marge: *Fixing all that damage is going to be very expensive.*
Lovejoy: *Yes, barring some sort of miracle.* (He lifts his arms and his gaze expectantly towards Heaven, and nothing happens.) *All right, we'll help ourselves...*(snidely) *yet again.*

Mr. Burns lends a helping hand:

Mr. Burns: *I've got the answer.* (He brushes down cowlicks that look like devil horns.) *Just let me run this church like a business.*
Ned: *It's kind of you to offer, Mr. Burns, but buzz around town is that you're...well, evil.*
Burns: *Oh, that's just a skip-rope rhyme. Believe me, the Lord's going to go for this in a big way. Now, who's with me?*
(The church council looks amongst themselves.)
Lovejoy: (resigned) *Ohh. I guess we have no choice.*
Burns: (tenting his fingers) *Excellent.* (A creak is heard and then a crucifix falls on Burns' head.) *Gu-ooh!* (Burns curses under his breath and shakes a fist towards Heaven). *Ohhh...you'll get yours.*

Lindsey Naegle: *I guarantee I can find some new revenue streams. Step one——let's sell some ad space. Reverend, how would you feel about wearing this robe?* (She holds up a robe that says "Fatso's Hash House.")
Lovejoy: *Hmm. Conflicted.*
Burns: *Too bad! You've already signed the deal!*
Lindsey: *Actually, he hasn't.*
Burns: *Oh. Well, we highly value your input...until you sign the deal.*

22

LITTLE FAITH

Episode DABF02
ORIGINAL AIRDATE: 12/16/01
WRITER: Bill Freiberger
DIRECTOR: Steven Dean Moore
EXECUTIVE PRODUCER: Al Jean
GUEST VOICES: Richard Gere as Himself

is more desperate than ever to get Lisa back into the fold. Since Christmas is coming, Marge tries several times to trick Lisa into realizing how much better her old religion is. Mr. Burns, having made the church profitable and having had his evil intentions revealed, releases his grip on the institution.

On Christmas Eve, Marge tempts Lisa with a pony-shaped present under the tree. Lisa sees through her mother's ploy and runs away to the temple. Once there, fellow Buddhist Richard Gere explains that believers in the faith can honor other religious holidays, like Christmas, and still remain true to Buddhism. With a clear conscience, Lisa returns home to celebrate the holiday with her loving family and pesters Marge for her promised pony.

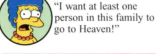

"I want at least one person in this family to go to Heaven!"

Lisa: What are they doing to the church?
Lindsey: We're re-branding it. The old church was skewing "pious." We prefer a faith-based emporium teeming with impulse-buy items.
Lisa: I feel like I want to throw up!
Lindsey: Then my work is done.

The new and improved church:

Lisa: Don't you see what Mr. Burns has done to this church?
Sideshow Mel: He restored it from nave to narthex!
Comic Book Guy: He super-sized the pews for the zaftig believers.
Patty: He put ice in the urinals.

Lisa: Mr. Gere, I was hoping Buddhism could bring me inner peace. Or is that just a pipe dream?
Richard Gere: (chuckles) We all have dreams. Mine is of a free Tibet.
Lisa: That would be so great.
Lenny: I dream about meatball sandwiches. All you can eat for two bucks!
Richard Gere: Good luck.

Ned prepares for the worst:

(Ned hears Lisa shouting out of her bedroom window as he sits on the couch and reads his newspaper. Rod and Todd build a church out of blocks on the floor.)
Lisa: Hey, I'm a Buddhist!
Ned: Gasp! My Satan-sense is tingling! Into the root cellar, boys!
Todd: When can we come out?
Ned: (dispirited) Maybe never!
Rod and Todd: Yaaaay!

Bully pulpit:

Nelson: Hey, Simpson, I hear your sister dumped Christianity.
Bart: Who cares?
Dolph: I'll tell you someone who cares. He's got long hair, works as a carpenter, has a lot of crazy ideas about love and brotherhood.
Jimbo: His name's Gunner, and he's dating my mom. Sometimes he buys us beer.
Bart: (points to Kearney) I thought Kearney was dating your mom.
Kearney: (defensively) Hey, she came on to me.
Jimbo: Get him!
(The bullies pounce on Kearney and beat him up. Bart joins in.)

Take it at faith value:

Homer: So you're back on the winning team?
Lisa: No, I'm still Buddhist, but I can worship with my family, too.
Marge: So you're just going to pay lip service to our church?
Lisa: Uh-huh.
Homer: That's all I ever asked.

BRAWL IN THE

The sinister members of the Springfield Republican Party, including C. Montgomery Burns and Krusty the Clown, gather around a table at their headquarters and hatch a plan to destroy the environment by repealing every anti-pollution law. Soon, the sky turns black with pollution, and hazardous acid rain drives everyone indoors. Homer becomes frantic when the rain melts his TV antenna and he can no longer watch TV. Marge suggests the family play a nice game of Monopoly, but things soon turn ugly, and they become embroiled in a domestic disturbance. Maggie calls the police, and the family is subdued and taken into custody.

A social worker named Gabriel is assigned to the Simpsons to help them stop fighting and break out of their normal roles. As therapy, Gabriel takes the family to the forest and sets up a challenge for them to accomplish by working together.

However, Homer's impulsiveness puts Gabriel in mortal danger. As a united family, the Simpsons rescue Gabriel. Afterward, the social worker declares them a fully functioning family—that is, until they arrive home to find Amber, the woman Homer married in Las Vegas, waiting for him.

Amber and her partner Ginger, who married Ned, have decided to come to Springfield to live with their husbands. The women waste no time settling in to both households. Marge is furious at first, throwing Homer out of the house, but she later relents and works with Homer to send Amber packing. After a drunken night at Moe's, Amber awakens to find herself married to Grampa. Horrified, Amber flees back to Las Vegas with Ginger, who is equally repulsed by Ned's version of domesticity. As the two floozies drive away, Marge comments on how proud she is that they can really work together as a family when they have to.

SHOW HIGHLIGHTS

Inside Springfield Republican Party Headquarters:
Mr. Burns: Moving on to new business, what act of unmitigated evil shall the Republican Party undertake this week?
Ralph Nader: (raising hand anxiously) Oooh! Oooh oooh oooh!
Burns: You've already done enough, Nader.

Groundskeeper Willie, after singing and dancing in the acid rain: **"Aah! It burns like a Glasgow bikini wax! Gaaaaah!"**

Moe goes on the syndicated TV show "First Date":
Host: Now, let's see how our blind dates liked each other.
Moe: Oh, I really felt there was a connection, and I would definitely go out with her again.
Woman: He smelled like puke!

Game night with the Simpsons:
Marge: Why don't we play Monopoly!
Lisa: Which version? We've got Star Wars Monopoly, Rasta-Mon-opoly, Galip-olopoly, Edna Krabappoly.
Marge: Let's stick to original Monopoly. The game is crazy enough as it is. (She inspects the iron game piece.) How can an iron be a landlord?

(During the Monopoly game, Homer pays Bart rent.)
Bart: You're a little light here, Dad.
Homer: I'm good for the rest! You know I am!
Bart: Well, I'd like to trust you, Homer, but you've been in jail three times.
Homer: (bitterly) They told me it would be like this on the outside.

Chief Wiggum conducts a line-up:
Chief Wiggum: Okay, everyone turn to the left!
(Four prisoners turn left and one turns right, bumping into others.)
Prisoner: Hey!
Wiggum: Oh, come on, people! The prison Nutcracker Suite is one week away, and I don't see five sugarplums! I see five guys who don't know their moves and don't seem to care! There! I said it.

(A top hat token crashes through the Simpsons' front window. Wiggum picks up the token with a pencil, as if it is evidence in a crime.)
Officer Lou: Another case of Monopoly-related violence, Chief.
Wiggum: Tsk, tsk, tsk! How do those Parker Brothers sleep at night?

Wiggum: Nice work, Brenda. I'll take it from here.
Brenda the Negotiabot: No way. This is my collar.
(Wiggum flips a switch, turning Brenda off.)
Wiggum: Heh. Too bad real women don't come with these, huh?
(Wiggum laughs, and Lou and Eddie join in.)
Homer: Heh heh. Heh. You got that right.
Wiggum: Quiet you! That counts as your phone call.

Homer has Gabriel pegged: **"You are an angel. Like Denzel Washington in *The Preacher's Wife* or Will Smith in *Bagger Vance*...or Slimer in *Ghostbusters*."**

Schoolyard showoff:
Bart: Attention, everyone! This is Gabriel, my personal social worker. He has to be here. I'm just that nuts.
(The kids on the jungle gym are impressed.)
Milhouse: How come you get a social worker? I'm the one with stigmata! (He holds up his bleeding hands.)

Marge, the over-budget and overboard gourmet: **"Food keeps my family happy, so I make a few practice dinners before showtime—'cause at six o'clock, we go live!"**

"Look, the thing about my family is there's five of us. Marge, Bart, girl Bart, the one who doesn't talk, and the fat guy. How I loathe him!"

Gabriel sizes up the family:
Gabriel: Marge, you medicate your family with food. Bart, you'll do anything for attention. (yelling) Cut that out!
(Bart is wearing a bee beard.)
Bart: They chose me!
Gabriel: Homer, your problem is quite simple. You're a drunken, childish buffoon.
Homer: Which is society's fault because...?

THE STUFF YOU MAY HAVE MISSED

When the exterior of the Springfield Republican Party Headquarters is shown, the music that plays is very similar to the "Treehouse of Horror" theme.

Seen inside the Springfield Republican Party Headquarters are C. Montgomery Burns, Waylon Smithers, Krusty, the Rich Texan, Ralph Nader, Rainier Wolfcastle, Dracula, Sen. Bob Dole, and an animatronic Sen. Strom Thurmond.

Krusty wears a suit and tie when visiting the Springfield Republican Party Headquarters.

Ralph Nader raises his hand desperate to be called on by Mr. Burns, just like Arnold Horshack (as portrayed by Ron Palillo), one of the Sweathogs on the television show "Welcome Back, Kotter."

The various versions of the Monopoly game: the Star Wars version has Chewbacca on the cover lid; a Jamaican Rastafarian frollicking among marijuana plants on the Rasta-Mon-opoly; Mr. Pennybags as an Australian WWI trench soldier being shot through the head is depicted on Galip-olopoly; and Edna Krabappoly features Edna Krabappel, dressed as actress Marlene Dietrich in a famous pose from *Blue Angel*.

One of the emergency speed-dial buttons on the Simpson phone has an iconic depiction of Homer strangling Bart.

The headline of the Springfield Shopper reads "SIMPSONS ARRESTED IN FAMILY RIOT" with the subhead "EVEN MAGGIE."

The video wedding of Homer, Ned, and the floozies is a heretofore unseen part of the plot from "Viva Ned Flanders" (AABF06).

When Ginger lifts her face off her pillow in the morning, she leaves a face imprint in makeup.

Amber sits in a kiddie pool on the front lawn and reads *Cigarette Aficionado* magazine. Pictured on the cover of the magazine is a man smoking his last cigarette before he's shot by a firing squad.

(As Gabriel is about to be mauled by wolves and cougars, the family huddles.)
Homer: (softly) Here's how it's gonna go down. As a family, we drive away. We cover for each other as a family. It's what Gabriel would have wanted.
Lisa: Look, we can't fall into old patterns! We've got to think of a plan!
Homer: (softly) Okay. But talk like this.
Lisa: (softly) Fine, I'll talk like this.
Homer: (loudly) What?

(Marge trips over a tree root.)
Marge: Naah! Oof! My driving ankle! Bart, I know this sounds crazy, but do you think you can drive a car?
Bart: (innocently) Okay, but it's my first time.
Marge: Here's the keys.
Bart: I've got a set. (He puts on a pair of driving gloves.)

The wolves (and cougars) are at the door:
Gabriel: Give them the beer! It will impair their motor skills!
(A wolf is catapulted dangerously close to Gabriel.)
Homer: (defiantly) No! I will never...(He looks in the backpack.) Oh wait, it's Blatz.
(Homer drops the cans to the beasts below.)

The Simpsons' "We Are Family" song:
Family: We are family!
Bart: Our bitter fights are now history!
Family: We are family!
Homer: Wolves and cougars ate our roast beef!

Marge: You know, we've been through some 280 adventures together, but our bond has never been stronger! (She hugs Homer.) Hm-hmm!
Homer: Yep, our family is as functional as all get out.
Lisa: Could this be the end of our series...of events?

Marge: You and Ned married a couple of floozies?
Homer: Marge, I'm sorry, but it wasn't my fault! Liquors drunkened me!
Marge: If I had known there were loose women in Las Vegas, I would never have let you go!

Ned honors his vows:
Ned: Oh, Lord, I know my new wife is a little more..."peppermint" than you're used to, but, eh, I know you'd want me to honor my sacred vows, so I will.
Ginger: Hey, stud, where do you keep your Wet Ones? I need a shower!
Ned: Oh we've got a real shower upstairs!
Ginger: Upstairs?! I hit the jackpot!

Episode DABF01
ORIGINAL AIRDATE: 01/06/02
WRITER: Joel H. Cohen
DIRECTOR: Matthew Nastuk
EXECUTIVE PRODUCER: Al Jean
GUEST VOICES: Jane Kaczmarek as Judge Harm

DRACULA

> "I'm going to come back with the greatest gift a husband can give his wife—an annulment from his secret wife!"

Judge Harm's Divorce Court:
Judge Harm: *Mr. Simpson, under Nevada law, bigamy, or "Mormon Hold'em," is perfectly legal.* (She bangs her gavel.) *Both marriages stand.*
Homer: *But I only love Marge.*
Judge Harm: *I hereby order you to take care of both of your wives. Bailiff, ring him.*
(The bailiff places a second wedding ring on Homer's finger. The rings clang together with the sound of a jail door slamming closed.)

Amber seduces Homer:
Homer: *Please, just leave me alone.*
Amber: *Now, now, Mama's going to make you a snack!* (She pulls out fixings and starts making a sandwich while Homer drools.)
Homer: *Gasp! Ooh...yeah! Oh, that's good. Oh, don't stop! Oh, yeah! Faster! Faster!* (Marge listens from her lonely bed.) *Faster! Faster! Oh, you do that like a pro!*
Marge: (worried) *Oh no! She's making him a sandwich!* (She turns over and covers her head with a pillow.)
Homer: (off screen) *Use both hands!*

Ned: *Me and the boys made you breakfast in bed. It's the best darn diddly way to start your first Flanders day!*
Ginger: (taking a sip of coffee.) *Think you can Irish-up this coffee for me?*
Ned: *Whoops. Watch the swears, honey bear. We don't use the "I" word in this house.*
Ginger: (reaching around and inside the nightstand.) *Where's my cigarettes?*
Rod: *We flushed your sin sticks down to Hell!*
Todd: *Smokers are jokers!*
Rod and Todd: (together) *Smokers are jokers!*
Ginger: *I think I'm gonna throw up!* (She rushes past them.)
Ned: *Oo! Who wants to hold Mommy's hair?*
Rod: *Me! Me!*
Todd: *I do!*

Amber attempts to mother Lisa and Bart:
Amber: *You know, I bet you and me could be friends. I could show you how to put on makeup.*
Lisa: *I'm eight years old!*
Amber: *You could look seven.* (to Bart) *And I could teach you to count cards.*
Bart: *Nah, I already got a system.*

> "Ah, the sweet couple of seconds before I remember why I'm sleeping on the lawn."

Marge confronts Homer:
Marge: *Homer?*
Homer: *Marge? You're speaking to me?*
Marge: *Why don't you come inside, and we'll talk.*
Homer: *About what? Sports? Bigamy?*
Marge: *Bigamy.*
Homer: *Not a sports fan, huh?*

The barflies meet the floozie:
Lenny: *Gee, Homer, your new wife is great! Her lips look like nightcrawlers!*
Homer: *You know, she can put that mole anywhere on her face.*
Lenny: *Wow!*

For better or worse:
Grampa: *Mornin', love muffin!*
Amber: *Who are you?*
Grampa: *I'm your new husband, and that was a wedding night I'll never forget.*
Amber: *Oh no! We didn't!*
Grampa: *Well, we almost didn't. But you wouldn't take "I can't" for an answer! Wanna give honest Abe another term in the Oval Office?*
Amber: *No!*
Grampa: *Oh, thank God!* (He passes out, exhausted.)

Ned loses another wife:
Ginger: *I can't take it! You're too goody-goody!*
Ned: *Oh, that's not you talkin'. That's the honey-mustard dressing!*

Movie Moment:
Groundskeeper Willie's dance in the rain with an umbrella mimics Gene Kelly's famous number in *Singin' in the Rain* (1952).

Marge: *I'm so proud of us. When we stick together, we can do anything.*
Grampa: *Ooh...I lost another wife.*
Lisa: *I'm so sorry, Grampa.*
Grampa: *Well, it hurts now, but the senility will take care of that.* (long beat) *There she goes.* (He turns to Homer.) *You know, I have a son about your age.* (The family laughs at him.)
Homer: *Oh, I love that.*

GABRIEL THE SOCIAL WORKER

Angelic characteristics:
His name, his glowing white outfit, and his pager that plays the music of a heavenly choir

Professional duty:
To browbeat people until they stop fighting and become a family

Methodology:
Observe, take notes, grimace, and shake head disapprovingly

Game plan:
Engage his subjects in exercises that help them break out of their negative behavior patterns—in other words, withhold their food until they work together

Goal:
To earn his Wings CD

HOMER, YOU'RE A BAD MAN, AND YOUR SEED SHOULD BE WIPED FROM THIS EARTH. NO OFFENSE, CHILDREN.

Guest Voice:
Delroy Lindo as Gabriel

GARTH MOTHERLOVING

Job title:
C.E.O. of the Motherloving Sugar Corporation

Résumé includes:
Addictive product manufacturing and sales, bribery, courtroom death threats

Activities that fill his day calendar:
Evil deeds and racquetball

Term that puzzles him to distraction:
"Corporate responsibility"

Proud owner of:
His own personal Oompa Loompa

Example of his "evilness" level:
If you look up "meanie-beanie-fo-feenie" in the dictionary, you'd see his picture

> I'M NOT UP ON THE CURRENT SLANG, BUT DO THE KIDS STILL SAY, "GET THE HELL OUT OF MY OFFICE!"?

Guest Voice:
Ben Stiller as Garth Motherloving

The library holds a book sale, and Homer is bored until Marge shows him the *Duff Book of World Records*. Enthralled with the book, Homer unsuccessfully attempts to set his own world record. Duff World Record executives suggest that he gather friends together to try to set a group record. Homer talks the entire town into forming the world's tallest human pyramid. Unfortunately, the pyramid collapses into a huge ball of humanity and rolls down the street, coming to rest on a weigh-station truck scale. As luck would have it, the citizens of Springfield break a different record by being, collectively, the world's fattest town.

Marge grows concerned about the town's obesity problem. Upon further inspection, she realizes almost all the food in town contains sugar and is manufactured by the Motherloving Sugar Company. Marge visits the head of the company, Garth Motherloving, and asks him to reduce the amount of sugar in his products. Garth kicks Marge out, so she hires a lawyer, gets people to sign a petition, and files a class action lawsuit against big sugar concerns. With the help of corporate insiders, Marge wins her lawsuit and Judge Snyder bans all sugar products from Springfield.

The town goes through sugar withdrawal, and Homer becomes desperate. He and Bart join a secret cabal that includes Mr. Burns, Garth Motherloving, Count Fudge-ula, and Apu, to smuggle sugar in from south of the

SHOW HIGHLIGHTS

At the library book sale:
Homer: *A library selling books? If I don't want 'em for free, why would I wanna pay for 'em?*
Marge: *Why do you always wait till we arrive to complain?*
Homer: *(ponders this, then shrugs) I don't know.*

Heard at the library book sale:
Comic Book Guy: *Ah, the full Leonard Nimoy cycle: I Am Not Spock, then I Am Spock and finally I Am Also Scotty.*
Dr. Nick: *(browsing Gray's Anatomy) Hmm. That's what we look like inside? It's disgusting! (turns page) Oh! That lady swallowed a baby!*
Cletus: *(feeding torn pages of books to pigs) Helen Fielding's giving them pigs Bridget Jones' diarrhea.*

A man of letters...and pictures:
Marge: *Well, what about this? The Duff Book Of World Records. It's got pictures of deformities!*
Homer: *(reluctantly takes it) Oooo-kay. (He laughs and gasps at the pictures on several pages.) Oh my God! Wow! Now, that's a goiter!*

Settling a bet:
Lenny: *Well, I say the most clothespins a man could attach to his face is eighty-seven.*
Carl: *Are you counting the neck?*
Lenny: *You know I am.*
Carl: *(pounding his fist into his hand) All right, outside!*
(They go to the door and find Homer standing in the doorframe bathed in light and holding the record book over his head. Heavenly music sounds.)
Homer: *Peace, my people. All shall be looked up. (He flips through the book) Let's see, most clothespins: swallowed, inserted...here we go, clipped to face and neck. One hundred and sixteen. (He displays a picture of a man named Kevin Thackwell with clothespins attached to his face and neck.)*
Lenny: *Geez, I was wrong, but I ain't angry.*
Carl: *And I'm magnanimous in victory.*
Moe: *Wow! That's the best book I've ever seen!*
Homer: *(consults the record book) Nope! The best book you've ever seen is Tom Clancy's OP Center.*
Moe: *That thing knows me better than I know myself.*

Fun Fact:
Collective weight of the townspeople of Springfield: 64,152 lbs.

"Congratulations, fellow Springfielders! This town will no longer be known as 'America's Sorrow'! Today I declare Springfield 'Fat City, USA'!"

Apu: *I am sorry, but everything in this store, from the honey-glazed cauliflower to the choco-blasted baby aspirin, comes from the Motherloving Sugar Corporation.*
Marge: *Well, I'm going to have a talk with them! Where are their worldwide headquarters located?*
Apu: *Why, right down the street.*
Marge: *That's lucky.*

Marge makes her case to the Motherloving Sugar Corporation:
Marge: *I want you to stop putting so much sugar in everything! Or at least warn people that it's so unhealthy.*
Garth Motherloving: *(sarcastically) Hmm. That'll boost sales! While we're at it, why don't I just change my name back to Hitler?*

Homer and the Chocolate Factory:
Homer: *Wait! You went to a sugar factory? Were there Oompa Loompas?*
Marge: *There was one in a cage. But he wasn't moving.*

"Aw geez! You don't want old Gil goin' door-to-door. Oh, I've made too many enemies selling suckless vacuum cleaners and Rick James bibles."

Music Moment:
The Archies' "Sugar, Sugar" plays over the closing credits.

TV Moment:
The boat chase has the high energy, quick maneuvering, and theme music of Michael Mann's pastel-packed, '80s detective show, "Miami Vice."

(The phone rings.)
Marge: *Hello.*
Professor Frink: *(disguising his voice) Marge Simpson?*
Marge: *Who is this?*
Frink: *I am an anonymous whistle-blower. I worked on a top secret project called Operation Hoyvin Mayveennn!*
Marge: *Professor Frink?*
Frink: *Oh, what gave me away? Out of curiosity, was it the hoyvin or the mayvin, or was it the whole gaahoyveee thing that I do?*

Poor anger management:
Garth: *Frink, you little weasel, I'll kill you!*
Blue-Haired Lawyer: *May I remind you, we're in open court!*
Garth: *I'll kill you, too! I'll kill you all!*
Judge Snyder: *Mr. Motherloving, that could be interpreted as a threat.*
Garth: *(to judge) I'll kill you while you sleep.*
Gil: *Objection!*
Judge Snyder: *Hmm...I'll allow it.*

Gil: *Now, Count Fudge-ula, how long were you spokes-vampire for Motherloving's breakfast cereals?*
Count Fudge-ula: *Twenty of your mortal years. But I had to quit when my fangs succumbed to gingivitis. Now all my victims have to be mashed up.*
Courtroom audience: *Awww.*

Motherloving tries to grease the judge:
Garth: *Your Honor, I admit it looks bad for me. But I think you might be turned around by some surprising taste-timony. (He offers judge a candy-filled briefcase bribe. The judge licks his lips, then closes the briefcase.)*
Judge Snyder: *Sir, this is a house of justice, not a sugar shack. It's Hershey highwaymen, like you, that made me fat.*
Blue-Haired Lawyer: *Well, Your Honor, the court carries it well.*
Judge Snyder: *Silence!*

SOUR MARGE

Episode DABF03
ORIGINAL AIRDATE: 01/20/02
WRITER: Carolyn Omine
DIRECTOR: Mark Kirkland
EXECUTIVE PRODUCER: Al Jean

border. The smuggling operation goes well, and the cabal's yacht returns full of sugar. Unfortunately, the police are lying in wait. Homer and Bart are forced to flee with the yacht after their fellow smugglers abandon them. Homer manages to outmaneuver the police and successfully brings the sugar-laden yacht to dock, but Marge convinces him to dump his sweet cargo into the ocean. Town members jump into the water to get their sugar fix, and upon seeing everyone's happy faces, Marge wonders if getting sugar banned was the right thing to do. Her self-doubt is ultimately rendered moot, however, when Judge Snyder appears, proclaims that he exceeded his authority, and lifts the sugar ban.

Movie Moments:

Marge's pursuit of a class action suit on behalf of the citizens of Springfield is inspired by Julia Robert's Oscar-winning turn as *Erin Brockovich*.

Homer's one-arm-hanging rests during his ascension of the human pyramid is inspired by Tom Cruise's rock climb in *Mission: Impossible 2* (2000)

As Homer and Apu sneak into the Lard Lad statue, a variation on the theme from the Eddie Murphy comedy *Beverly Hills Cop* (1984) and its sequels is played. The song has also been heard in "Separate Vocations" (8F15) and "Marge vs. the Monorail" (9F10).

"Springfield's cake-hole has been shut forever. Under what has been dubbed 'Marge's Law,' all forms of sugar are now illegal...So, say a bittersweet farewell to such old friends as Mud Pies, Bite 'Ems, Éclairios, Chew 'Ems, Kellogg's All-Fudge, Big Red Snack Foam, Milk Chuds, Eat 'Ems, and all sugar pills will be changed back to highly concentrated opiates."

Homer gives Bart some good advice:
Homer: *Remember what I told you about running away from your troubles?*
Bart: *Yeah.*
Homer: *Let's do it!*

"I guess you just can't use the law to nag."

The family reacts to "Marge's Law":
Homer: *Thank you, Erin Choco-snitch.* (indicates Bart and Lisa) *That was a group effort.*
Marge: *I was just trying to make this a healthier place to live.*
Homer: *Well, good work, Blue-hair 'n' Brocko-witch.* (beat) *Okay, that was mine.*

The shelves at the Kwik-E-Mart are empty:
Homer: (whimpering) *Nothing left! Nothing left!* (He steps in something sticky.) *Ooh! Ooh! A sticky spot!* (He gets down on his knees and licks the stain.)
Apu: *Mr. Simpson, you're licking blood and Vapo-Rub!*
Homer: (sadly standing) *Part of me knew that.*

Lisa voices concern over Homer and Bart's mission:
Lisa: *Is it really worth risking your lives just for some sugar?*
Marge: (from kitchen) *Dessert's on! I steamed some limes!*
Lisa: *Godspeed.*

The sugar deal goes awry:
Sugar Smuggler: *Okay, man, here's the ch-ugar. Now jou give us the money!*
Homer: *That wasn't part of the deal. Ha ha ha ha!* (He motors back to the boat.)
Smuggler: (looking at the contract) *He's right!* (to his men) *Who wrote this thing?*

THE STUFF YOU MAY HAVE MISSED

The Library Book Sale banner also says, "Yes, we have pornography!"

The Duff Book of World Records has pictured on the cover a pole jumper, a man with a long beard and fat twins Billy and Benny riding scooters, who were also seen in "The Day the Violence Died" (3F16).

The man pictured in the record book for most clothespins clipped to his face, Kevin Thackwell, is the actual record holder for that stunt.

In the executive office is a picture of a man with several billiard balls in his mouth.

At the gathering at City Hall, Homer holds another of his many pennants. This one reads, "Girth."

On a shelf at the Kwik-E-Mart, there are boxes labeled "Choco Cheese."

A sign at the Kwik-E-Mart reads, "No Checks, Credit Cards, Food Stamps."

The logo for the Motherloving Sugar Corporation is a grinning octopus engulfing the Earth while holding treats (a popsicle, a candy cane, a donut, and a lollipop) in several of its tentacles.

Among the many lawyers trying to attract Marge's attention is a Christopher Darden look-alike. Darden was one of the prosecutors in the O.J. Simpson murder trial.

Cletus the Slack-Jawed Yokel signs his last name as "Spuckler." Up until this episode, his last name has been "Delroy."

Count Fudge-ula is a parody of Count Chocula, pictured on cereal boxes of the same name.

Mr. Burns' yacht, *Gone Fission'*, has previously been seen as Homer's party boat in "The Mansion Family" (BABF08). Mr. Burns' other yacht, *Gone Fission' II*, crashed into the senior's tour boat in "Old Man and the 'C' Student" (AABF16).

Fun Fact:
Chronic loser, Gil, first seen in "Realty Bites" (5F06) begins a new and permanent role as the resident Springfield lawyer in this episode.

JAWS WIRED

The Simpsons watch the annual Gay Pride Parade as it passes their house, but Homer drags them all away when Santa's Little Helper wants to join in with the Gay Dog Alliance. Homer takes the family to the Googolplex to see a movie. After an extended period of previews and commercials, Homer becomes enraged and starts an audience chant to start the movie. The ushers arm themselves and advance on him, so Homer flees the theater. The ushers chase him to where Mayor Quimby is dedicating a statue of boxer Drederick Tatum. Not looking where he is going, Homer runs into the statue's fist and breaks his jaw.

Dr. Hibbert wires Homer's jaw shut, which at first seems like a curse to him; he cannot talk or eat solid foods. But soon everyone realizes that Homer is quite pleasant to be around when he is silent. He becomes an attentive listener and a good husband, father, and son. Marge finds that she can even take Homer to the Annual Springfield Formal Event without incident, and she could not be happier. She becomes apprehensive, however, when Dr. Hibbert tells Homer that his jaw wires are ready to come off.

Marge is afraid Homer will revert to his old ways. After a chance meeting with television producer Lindsey Naegle in Moe's Tavern, Homer and Marge go on "Afternoon Yak," where a repentant Homer is confronted with his previous reckless behavior. Several weeks pass and Homer remains passive and thoughtful. So much so, Marge becomes increasingly bored and stir-crazy. One evening, as Homer sleeps, Marge decides to do something spontaneous and dangerous. She takes the station wagon down to the Civic Center and enters a demolition derby. At first, Marge feels more alive, but as the derby becomes more intense, she begins to fear for her safety. Homer and the kids show up, but Homer is still in passive mode and cannot figure out what to do to save Marge. Bart comes up with the answer—he gives Homer beer. The beer gives Homer the impulses he needs to save Marge from certain injury. Now that Homer is acting like his old self, Marge realizes that the family needs one member who stirs things up, and that person is not her.

SHOW HIGHLIGHTS

The Gay Pride Parade:
Male Marchers: *We're here, we're queer, get used to it!*
Lisa: *You do this every year! We are used to it.*
Male Marcher: *Spoilsport!*

The "Stayin' in the Closet" float:
(A hidden man and woman wave from behind closet doors. From their voices we can tell that they are Mr. Smithers and Patty Bouvier.)
Smithers: (v.o.) *We're gay, we're glad.*
Patty: (v.o.) *But don't tell Mom and Dad!*
Marge: *Wouldn't it be great if that man and woman got together?*

"Lesbians of the Caribbean" float song:
Yo-ho-ho!
It's an alternative lifestyle for me!

Homer envies the men on the "Fab Abs" float: **"Oh, look at those abs! Everyone here has a six-pack, and I'm the only one with a keg."**

Movie Star Scramble—MOT HANKS:
Answer—OTM SHANK, India's answer to Brian Dennehy

Cartoon Moment:
Many elements during Homer's rescue of Marge are in homage to "Popeye" cartoons of yesteryear, from the way beer is swallowed like spinach, to Homer's speech pattern, to the music being played. At one point, Marge is even animated like a loose-limbed Olive Oyl.

Bart asks permission:
Bart: *Hey, Dad, I'm gonna make a human yo-yo. If you object, clearly say "No."*
(Homer mumbles "No.")
Bart: *No objections, eh? That's great!*
(Homer mumbles angrily, saying, "Bart, you come back here." Bart walks over to Milhouse, who wears a helmet and padding.)
Bart: *Milhouse, you ready to imitate that "Jackass" show?*
Milhouse: *All those disclaimers made me want to do it more!*

Duffman: *Hey, Duff lovers! Does anyone in this bar love Duff?*
Carl: *Hey, it's Duffman!*
Lenny: *Newsweek said you died of liver failure.*
Duffman: *Duffman can never die, only the actors who play him! Oh yeahhh!*

Moe: *Ah, you must be here for the, uh, Duff Trivia Challenge.*
Duffman: *That's right, local distributor! One of you could win a lifetime's supply of Duff! Okay, chug monkeys! What beverage, brewed since ancient times, is made from hops and grains?*
Lenny: *How about "ancient hop grain juice"?*
(Homer looks at his bottle of beer and sees the answer. He shouts "Beer! Beer! Beer!" incoherently, holding up the beer bottle.)
Moe: *Wait, wait, wait! Homer's trying to make a guess.*
(Homer frantically shouts, "Beer, beer, beer," opens a beer tap, and points at the flowing beer.)
Moe: *What are you doing? You're gettin' some kind of booze all over me!*
(Homer mumbles and cries in frustration.)
Duffman: (blowing an airhorn) *Time's up! The answer is...beer! Ooo, Duff luck!*
Carl: *I never would have figured that out.*
Lenny: *That's the kinda thing you just gotta know.*
(Homer sobs.)

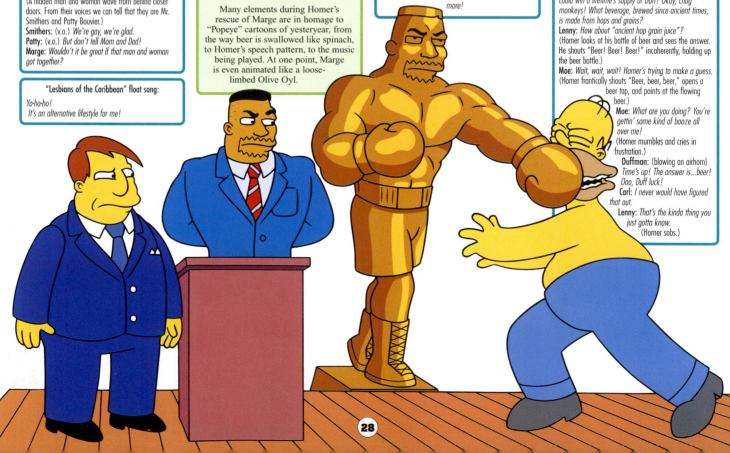

SHUT

Episode DABF05
ORIGINAL AIRDATE: 01/27/02
WRITER: Matt Selman
DIRECTOR: Nancy Kruse
EXECUTIVE PRODUCER: Al Jean

THE STUFF YOU MAY HAVE MISSED

The cover of *Pie Times* magazine shows a hippie eating a piece of pie. *Pie Times* is a parody of the marijuana magazine *High Times*.

The Gay Pride Parade banner reads at the bottom, "Formally Springfield Heritage Day."

Floats in the Gay Pride Parade include "Gay Steel Workers of America," "The Velvet Mafia," "Salute to Safe Sex," "Stayin' in the Closet," "Lesbians of the Caribbean," "A Salute to Brunch" and "Fab Abs."

The "Lesbians of the Caribbean" float parodies the Disneyland ride "Pirates of the Caribbean." On the float, masculine-looking women chase much more feminine-looking women around in circles. The Disneyland ride had something similar in days past, where lusty pirates chased women around in circles. Advocacy groups, however, encouraged Disney to change the attraction so that hungry pirates now chase women carrying food.

Movies playing at the Googolplex include, *The Final Chapter—A New Beginning, Too Many Premises!, Editor-In-Chimp, Wedgie: The Movie, Shenani-Goats!, Chocolate 2: The Vanillaing, Air C.H.U.D., Clone Me an Angel,* and *Dude, Where's My Pepsi?*

As Dr. Hibbert examines Homer's head X-ray, a crayon is clearly visible stuck in Homer's brain, a reference to "НОМЯ" (BABF22).

The "So Your Life is Ruined" pamphlet has a Happy Face with a sad expression and its mouth wired shut pictured on the front.

"Afternoon Yak" is a parody of the Barbara Walters-hosted ABC morning talk show, "The View."

According to the script's cover, *I'm Gonna Kill You* was written by playwright Edward Albee.

Otto has entered the school bus in the demolition derby, crossing out "school" and writing "skull" on the sides. There is also a decal of a skull with a top hat and bat wings on the front hood and the back door.

"I am not going to make you another sparerib smoothie! Most people with their jaws wired shut don't gain weight!"

Lisa has a bad day at school:
Lisa: *We were playing Four Square, and I called no double-taps, and Ralph double-taps, and I said, "You're out," and he says, "I can do a somersault," which has nothing to do with anything!*
Homer: (thought) *Awww...Maybe a hug will cork her cry-hole.*

Homer and Bart bond:
Bart: *So the substitute teacher comes in and says her name is "Mrs. Doody." And everyone's looking at me like "take it, Bart, run with it!" And it hits me—I've become a clown...a class clown. And it sickens me!*
Homer: (thought) *Wow! Bart has feelings...Ha-ha! Mrs. Doody!*

"Three wars back, we called sauerkraut 'Liberty Cabbage.' And we called Liberty Cabbage 'Super Slaw.' And back then, a suitcase was known as a 'Swedish Lunchbox.' 'Course nobody knew that but me...anyway, 'long story short' is a phrase whose origins are complicated and rambling."

"A formal! The one place you can wear a tiara and not look crazy."

At the Annual Springfield Formal Event:
Marge: *This has been one of the most magical evenings of my life.*
Homer: (mumbles) *I'm horny!*
Marge: *I don't know what you said, but I'm sure it was beautiful.*

On the set of "Afternoon Yak":
Barbara Walters-Type: *Marge, what was Homer like before he broke his jaw?*
Marge: *Well, he would eat all the time. We'd be making love and he'd have a mouthful of Hershey's Miniatures.*
Homer: (ashamedly) *Krackle was my favorite.*

Barbara Walters-Type: *Our next topic: "My son still wets the bed."*
(Luann Van Houten appears, holding an angry Milhouse's hand.)
Milhouse: *You told me we were going to Red Lobster!*

FIVE BORING WEEKS LATER...:
Marge: *This place is so dull, the 911 button is covered with dust.*
Homer: *I just poured myself a new glass of milk. The old one sat out for a little while. Are you coming to bed?*
Marge: *It's 7:30!*
Homer: *Marge, I could stand here and argue with you, but then I'd have to get a new glass of milk.*

Bart: *There she is!*
(Marge's car takes a pounding.)
Lisa: *Dad, you've gotta do something!*
Homer: *But bold moves are no longer my forte.*

"Catch ya later, radiator! Oh my God! I hit someone...then I taunted him. I've never felt so alive!"

Bart: *He saved her! Oh! Isn't it great to have the old Dad back!*
Lisa: *I thought you liked the new Dad?*
Bart: *Whatever.*

The dysfunctional family dynamic:
Marge: *This family needs a live wire, but it's just not me.*
Homer: *That's okay, Marge. You're a good wet blanket—the kind I like wrapped around me.*

MY BOY-FRIEND HAS A METAL TONGUE STUD.

WHO CARES WHAT'S ON HIS TONGUE--LONG AS HE'S A STUD WHERE IT COUNTS! I'M TALKIN' DOWNTOWN!

PRINCIPAL HARLAN DONDELINGER

Next stop if he catches you:
Three o'clock, old building, room 106

Dubious honor:
Confronting Homer in the past (1974), present, and future (2024)

Important job duties:
Making sure students don't dance too close together and bong confiscation

Amazing ability:
Can smell cigarette smoke through doors

Interests include:
Scientific analysis of burning donuts

YOU JUST BOUGHT YOURSELF ONE DAY OF DETENTION. YOU KNOW WHERE AND WHEN.

HALF-DECENT

The town of Springfield slumbers peacefully—all except Marge. Homer's snoring is so loud, it is keeping her awake. During the day, her lack of sleep causes her to make serious errors in judgment. Homer and Marge attempt to remedy Homer's condition by consulting with Dr. Hibbert, but the operation to eliminate Homer's snoring is too expensive. Desperate for rest, Marge spends a night at her sisters' apartment. After consuming too much alcohol, Patty and Selma talk Marge into sending an e-mail to Artie Ziff, her high school prom date, who is now very successful. Artie is excited to receive the e-mail, since he has been obsessed with Marge for the last twenty years.

Artie arrives at the Simpson home the next day by helicopter and offers to take the entire family for a cruise aboard his yacht. While at sea, Artie presents Homer and Marge with a proposal—he will give Homer one million dollars if he can have Marge for the weekend. Marge refuses, but Homer's snoring condition becomes unbearable and she realizes that they could use the money for Homer's operation. Homer lets Marge go once Artie agrees that he will not try any funny stuff with her. Later, after talking to the guys at Moe's, Homer has second thoughts. Fearing that Marge might leave him for a life of luxury with Artie, he races to Artie's mansion to retrieve his wife. Meanwhile, Artie attempts to win Marge back by recreating the entire prom night. When Homer arrives, he finds Marge kissing Artie. Homer is

SHOW HIGHLIGHTS

"Oh, Jar Jar, everyone hates you but me."

Marge arrives on Patty and Selma's doorstep:
Patty: *Hmm? Overnight bag? No husband in sight! It's happened!*
Selma: *She left Homer? I'll get the Champale!* (She exits.)
Patty: *And let's get that ring off!* (She grabs bolt cutters and goes for the ring.)
Marge: *Whoa, whoa, whoa, Delilah! I didn't leave Homer, and I never will! I just need one night away from his snoring.* (Selma returns with a bottle and opens it with a bottle cap remover.)
Selma: *Great, we'll have a girls' night!*
Patty: *No bras!* (She cuts her bra loose with bolt cutters.)

Scene from BHO's cable series "Nookie in New York":
(Four women eat at YUMÍ Ristorante.)
Cynthia Nixon-Type: *If I'm not having sex by the end of this goat cheese quesadilla, I'm going to scream.*
Kristen Davis-Type: *I also enjoy sex.*
Kim Cattrall-Type: *Since this morning I've had sex with a New York Knick, two subway cops, and a guy who works on Wall Street.*
Kristen Davis-Type: *Broker?*
Sarah Jessica Parker-Type: *Nah, she's just really sore!* (They all laugh, as does their waiter.)

Marge e-mails Artie Ziff with a little "help" from Patty:
Marge: *Dear Artie.*
Patty: (typing) *"Dear Hottie!"*
Marge: *Congratulations on your recent TV appearance.*
Patty: *"I wanna sex you up! Your love slave, Marge."*
Marge: *Gasp! You can't use the word "sex" on the Internet!*
Patty: *Watch me!*

Artie's Modem Noise-Converter song:
(to the tune of "Georgy Girl")
Hey, computer geek,
You will be connected in no time!

"Unguarded breakfasts! The sweetest taboo!"

THE STUFF YOU MAY HAVE MISSED

Comic Book Guy sleeps in pajamas adorned with Chewbacca's picture. In his bedroom is an inflatable Jabba the Hutt chair, a bed shaped like a land cruiser, a stormtrooper standee, hanging models of a TIE fighter and the *Millennium Falcon*, a dewback with stormtroopers action figure set, a light saber, a model of the Death Star, a poster for the original *Star Wars* movie, and a copy of the rare *Revenge of the Jedi* poster. On the wall are two autographed photos of Mark Hamill—one as he appeared in *Star Wars* (1977) and one in his *Return of the Jedi* (1983) costume.

As Marge tries to get some sleep on the front porch, she is hit by a newspaper with the headline, "Sleep Important, Say Experts" and the sub-headline, "Slow News Day Grips Springfield."

Marge says "Whoa, whoa, whoa, Delilah" to Patty, which is a lyric from the Tom Jones song "Delilah" about a man who killed his love because he could not take her cheating ways. In "Marge Gets a Job" (9F05), Tom Jones is named as Marge's favorite singer and Mr. Burns arranges to have her serenaded by him.

Artie's yacht is christened *PaZIFFic Prince*. Pictured aft is Artie in a sailor cap, holding a glass of wine.

Marge returns home from Artie's via a taxi from the Just Take Me Home Cab Co.

One of the dolls Homer uses to dramatize Marge kissing Artie is Funzo, introduced in "Grift of the Magi" (BABF07).

Homer and Lenny travel to West Springfield on the Suck-U-Busline.

The one-armed boss is smoking while leaning against a "No Smoking" sign.

Grampa's memory of Homer bowling a 300 game took place in "Hello Gutter, Hello Fadder" (BABF02).

According to the map, Springfield and West Springfield combined form the shape of Texas.

"You can't spell 'party' without 'Artie!' If you misspell 'party'... *(weakly)* or 'Artie.'"

Artie: *Homer, Marge, I have a rather delicate proposition.*
Homer: *Spill it, moneybags.*
Artie: *Heh-heh heh-heh. Yes, I do have everything. But yet I often wonder what life with Marge would have been like.*
Homer: *It's like being married to my best friend, and he lets me feel his boobs!*

Making beautiful music:
Marge: *I'll get used to the snoring, just like I got used to saying "Courtney Cox-Arquette!"* (sexily) *Besides, I like some of the noises you make in bed.*
Homer: *Oh ho ho!* (knowing chuckle) *One "Squeaking Spring Symphony" coming up!*

Homer defends his actions to the barflies: **"I didn't sell her! I just rented her...to an old boyfriend."**

Homer confuses the consequences of Marge's actions: **"Oh no! If Marge marries Artie, I'll never be born!"**

Homer drowns his sorrows at Moe's Tavern:
Homer: *Oh, guys, it was horrible! I saw Marge kissing a far superior man.*
Moe: *Eh, well, if it makes you feel any better, he's probably doin' her right now.*
(Homer sobs and Lenny gives Moe a dirty look.)
Moe: *Oh, yeah. Make me the bad guy.*

Homer's new plan:
Homer: *My life here is over. Lenny, how would you like to leave town with me and never come back?*
Lenny: *Sounds like a plan!*
Homer: *Then it's settled! We leave Springfield forever!* (They leave. Carl comes out of the men's room.)
Carl: *What'd I miss? Anything good?*

Homer overcomes the technical difficulties of videotaping: **"Marge, If you're watching this, then it means I've figured out how to work the camera."**

PROPOSAL

Episode DABF04
ORIGINAL AIRDATE: 02/10/02
WRITER: Tim Long
DIRECTOR: Lauren MacMullan
EXECUTIVE PRODUCER: Al Jean
GUEST VOICES: Jon Lovitz as Artie Ziff

heartbroken and is unaware that Artie tricked Marge into kissing him.

Marge is outraged at Artie's behavior and leaves the mansion. Back at home, she finds a videotaped message from Homer saying that he is leaving her and that she will never see him again. Homer, along with Lenny, takes a bus to West Springfield, where they both take dangerous jobs on an oil rig. After some investigating by Bart and Lisa, Marge enlists Artie's help by using his helicopter to find Homer and Lenny. They arrive just in time to save Homer and Lenny from a ferocious oil rig fire. At first, Homer refuses to climb to safety because Marge is with Artie, but Artie explains that Homer owns her heart, something he could never buy. Artie also solves Homer's snoring problem by inventing a device that masks Homer's snores with music. However, Artie uses the device, equipped with a small camera, to spy on Marge.

TV Moments:
As Marge flies away in a helicopter to be with Artie Ziff, the "Theme Song from M*A*S*H (Suicide is Painless)" plays. In a nod to the television show's final episode, Homer spells out in rocks a final message to Marge ("Keep Your Clothes On"), whereas B.J. Hunnicut's final message to Hawkeye Pierce was "Goodbye."

"Nookie in New York" is a parody of the HBO series "Sex and the City," starring Sarah Jessica Parker.

Homer's videotaped message:
Homer: *I'm leaving you, Marge. The next time you see my name will be in the hobo obituaries. Don't worry about the kids. I'll drop them off with Patty and Selma.*
Bart: (off camera) *Patty and Selma? Screw that!*
Homer: *Just run the camera, you little...!* (He charges the camera, knocking it over.) *D'oh!* (Through the upended camera, we see Homer sobbing as he chokes Bart.) *Goodbye, my darling.* (He sobs some more and continues to choke Bart.)

On the bus with Lenny:
Homer: *It's no good. Everything reminds me of Marge.* (He looks out the bus window and sees cacti and clouds shaped like Marge.)
Lenny: *I know what you're going through. We're coming up on Mount Carlmore.* (Lenny looks out the window and sees a mountain with Carl's face carved into it.) *I carved that one wonderful summer.*
Homer: *What did Carl think?*
Lenny: *You know, we've never discussed it.*

"Roughnecks Wanted—Dangerous Work, Free Burial":
Homer: *Do you have any jobs for a man who wants to die? Something indoorsy.*
Lenny: *Close to a bathroom.*
One-Armed Man: *I'll put you on rig thirteen, as soon as they burn off the corpses.*
Homer: *This job will be perfect. I'm gonna leave this world the way I entered it—dirty, screaming, and torn away from the woman I love.*
Lenny: *Ho, ho. Quick and pointless, that's the death for me.*

Slavering slave to lust:
Artie: *I hope we can always be friends.*
Marge: *Of course.*
Artie: *With privileges?* (He ogles her body, his tongue hanging out. He stops when Marge frowns at him.)
Marge: *Does that work on anyone?*
Artie: *No. But when it does...Hello!*

Love conquers Artie:
Artie: *Listen to me, Homer. You've won. You own Marge's heart. And that's something I could never buy.*
Homer: *Woo-hoo!*
(Homer starts to climb up the helicopter rescue ladder. He looks back and sees a despondent Lenny on the rig.)
Lenny: *There's nothing on that helicopter for me.*
(Carl leans out of the helicopter.)
Carl: *Don't be so sure.*
Lenny: *Gasp! Carl Carlson!*
(He hurries up the ladder.)

Homer: *Artie, thanks for saving my life. Now, I believe there's a little matter of the million dollars?*
Marge: *We can't take his money!*
Homer: *Oh bu–! I can't take his money. I can't print my own money. I have to work for money. Why don't I just lie down and die?*

Artie's Snore-Converter song:
(to the tune of The Eurythmics' "Sweet Dreams (Are Made of This)")

*He's a loser, Marge, dump him!
I've traveled the world and the seven seas,
I am watching you through a camera!*

Movie Moments:
The entire premise of the episode is based on *Indecent Proposal* (1993), in which millionaire Robert Redford offers Woody Harrelson $1 million to sleep with his wife, Demi Moore.

Dr. Nick drives while Dr. Hibbert hits mailboxes with a golf club in a sequence similar to Kiefer Sutherland's baseball bat-wielding, mailbox-smashing joyride in *Stand By Me* (1986).

As Homer runs around the grounds of Artie Ziff's estate looking for Marge, guitar riffs are played that are similar to the ones played by Simon & Garfunkel in *The Graduate* (1967) when Dustin Hoffman is attempting to prevent Katherine Ross from getting married.

Homer and Lenny's bus trip echoes the final moments of Joe Buck and Ratzo Rizzo's ill-fated journey to Florida in *Midnight Cowboy* (1969), complete with a harmonica-tinged variation on Harry Nilsson's "Everybody's Talkin'" theme song.

Homer's attempt to leave his old life behind in the rigorous oil fields is based on the similar plight and flight of Jack Nicholson in *Five Easy Pieces* (1970).

After returning home from a disappointing appointment with Dr. Hibbert, Homer is heard snoring just like Curly Howard in several "Three Stooges" films.

Music Moment:
At the beginning of the episode, The Everly Brothers' "All I Have to Do Is Dream" plays while the town of Springfield serenely slumbers.

THE BART WANTS WHAT

The Simpsons flee in their car while being chased by Olympic authorities in a black helicopter. Homer has stolen the Olympic Torch because he is sick of his favorite shows being preempted for a month every four years. Marge angrily takes the torch from Homer and tosses it to the Olympic officials, who accidentally crash the copter and extinguish the flame. Homer is unhappy and bored until he spots a fair being held at a local preparatory school for rich kids. As the family and other Springfield residents enjoy the fair, Bart rescues a student named Greta from annoying bullies. Soon afterward, Bart is surprised to learn that Greta is the daughter of movie star Rainier Wolfcastle.

Greta and Bart become good friends. Bart spends a lot of time at the Wolfcastles' mansion, and Rainier even hangs out with Homer so their kids can be together. Bart is oblivious that Greta is falling in love with him. Greta is overjoyed when Bart promises to go to the school dance with her, but he stands her up. Instead, he and Milhouse choose to heckle Principal Skinner, who is performing stand-up comedy at a local club. Lisa confronts Bart about his callousness, so he decides it is best to break up with Greta, which leaves her heartbroken.

Bart goes over to Greta's house to apologize and is shocked to discover that she has replaced him with Milhouse. Bart despairs over leaving Greta, but Lisa is convinced he just wants Greta because he cannot have her. Bart follows Milhouse and Greta around, spying on them, and he calls her, trying to win her back. Greta tells Bart that she is going to Toronto, where her father is making a movie, and that there is no hope for reconciliation. Bart talks his parents into taking him to Toronto, but before he can talk to Greta, he is waylaid by Milhouse. Bart and Milhouse fight until Greta tells them that she does not want to be with either one of them. In fact, they have put her off dating for a long while. Bart and Milhouse make up, and in the end find out how incredibly easy it is to become members of the Canadian Olympic Basketball Team.

SHOW HIGHLIGHTS

Lisa: *Springfield Preparatory School? Dad! You told me there were no private schools in Springfield!*
Homer: *But knowing about it would make you want to go here.*

Marge: *This campus is so lush and verdant!*
Headmaster's Wife: *Yes, you probably recognize it from the film, Calling All Coeds.*
Marge: *Oh! Is that where Boozer drank the pee?*
Headmaster's Wife: *It's one of the places.*

Marge samples the rich food at Springfield Preparatory School:
"Mmm! All this food is so froo-froo! Ooo! Fabergé egg salad!"

The Crepes Crusader:

Cletus: *Look, Brandine! It's Wolfgang Puck! Mr. Puck, you make the only grub what satisfies my gut worm. I swear.*
Wolfgang Puck: *Try my Rice Krispie squares! They are wasabi-fused with a portabello glaze. And you can buy them at the airport!*
Marge: *I make mine with M&Ms.*
Wolfgang Puck: *With M&Ms? Now, that's what I call fusion! I could sell them on the Internet! (He kisses her.) To the Puckmobile!*

A lesson in bullying:

Greta: *You were so brave to take on all those bullies.*
Bart: *Those weren't bullies. That's a bully!*
(He points to Nelson, who's forcing a butler to smack himself.)
Nelson: *Hey, butler, stop butling yourself!*
Butler: *Would that I could, sir.*

Rainier Wolfcastle: *Time to go, Greta. Your mother's custody starts at 1800 hours.*
Bart: *Your dad's McBain?*
Rainier: *Hah hah hah! I play many characters—McBain, Officer Nick Vengeance, Sergeant Murder, and I was a voice on the "Frasier."*

"Here's my advice on women: don't give them nicknames like 'Jumbo' or 'Boxcar' and always get receipts. Makes you look like a business guy."

Rainier's ride:

(Rainier Wolfcastle drives his earth-shaking Humvee up the Simpsons' driveway.)
Marge: *That car's as big as all outdoors.*
Homer: *Wow, what kind of mileage does it get?*
Rainier: *One highway, zero city.*
Marge: *Ooooooooh!*
Rainier: *Mm-hm.*

Bart's play date gets off to a rough start:

Rainier: *Bart, your little tie makes me smile.*
Bart: *Excuse me, but you don't sound as tough as you do in the movies.*
Rainier: *(turning around menacingly) If you don't shut your big yap, I will rip off your face and use it as a napkin! (The momentary tension is broken when Rainier laughs. Bart and Greta join in until Rainier stops abruptly.) Laughing time is over!*

Having the Wolfcastles over for dinner:

Marge: *I hope you enjoy these German sausages. I've been grinding all day, so I'm not sure what organ meat is in what intestinal casing.*
Lisa: *Bratwurst, sauerbraten, donderblitzen? Oh, Mom, isn't there anything vegetarian?*
Rainier: *Ha ha ha! Homer, I see your daughter is one of those whale-kissing, Dukakis-hugging moon maidens.*
Homer: *Ha ha! Yeah, one time she...oo! She's looking at us! Be cool.*

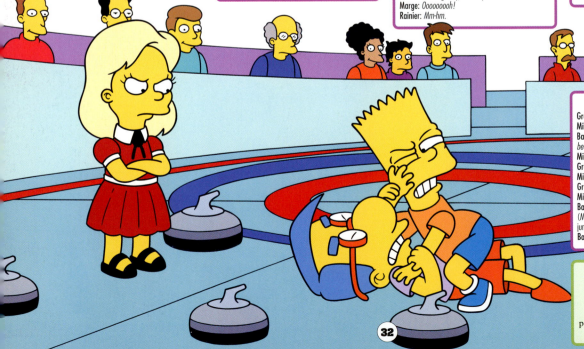

The third wheel:

Greta: *Hi, Bart.*
Milhouse: *Wha'zzzuuuup?!*
Bart: *Yeah, this is Milhouse. He's my best friend, because...well, geographical convenience, really.*
Milhouse: *I'm wearing my bathing suit under my pants.*
Greta: *Um, you wanna go swimming?*
Milhouse: *Okay, but you have to watch me dive.*
Greta: *Fine.*
Milhouse: *(crossing his arms) Do you promise?*
Bart: *Just go!*
(Milhouse throws off his outer clothing, and is heard jumping in the pool and laughing wildly.)
Bart: *(chuckles) He'll sleep tonight.*

Music Moment:

When the elephant is eating Scratchy during "Circus of the Scars," "Baby Elephant Walk" by Henry Mancini plays. Homer rises to prominence performing his routine to the same song in "Dancin' Homer" (7F05).

IT WANTS

Episode DABF06
ORIGINAL AIRDATE: 02/17/02
WRITER: John Frink & Don Payne
DIRECTOR: Michael Polcino
EXECUTIVE PRODUCER: Al Jean
GUEST VOICES: Wolfgang Puck as Himself

THE GIVING TREE IS NOT A CHUMP
THE GIVING TREE IS NOT A CHUMP
THE GIVING TREE IS NOT A CHUMP

GRETA WOLFCASTLE

Daughter of:
Mega-movie star Rainier Wolfcastle

Target for:
Old money bullies

Hobbies include:
Playing with dolls, swimming, and co-producing her father's action movies

No slouch when it comes to:
Thumb wars

How she expresses affection:
Through words on a Scrabble board

Early romantic entanglements include:
Bart Simpson and Milhouse Van Houten (on the rebound)

Firm believer in:
Community property

Floppy's "Open Mic Night—Pity Laughs Welcome":

Krusty: *That was the prop comedy of the Sea Captain. More like "Thar he blows!"*
(The audience laughs.)
Captain McCallister: *Yar. I'm...so sorry.*
Krusty: *All right, let's keep this train wreck movin'!* (looks at card) *Principal Skinner? I know him. He's not funny. Well, enjoy!*

"I only lied because it was the easiest way to get what I wanted."

A simple experiment:

Bart: *I was an idiot. Now I'll be alone forever. Why did I break up with her?*
Lisa: *Oh Bart, it's human nature. You only want her because someone else has her.*
Bart: *Prove it, using examples from this room.*
Lisa: *All right, look. Maggie is not playing with this ball right now, but look what happens when I take it.* (She takes the ball from the playpen. Maggie starts to reach for it.) *See?*
Bart: (reaching for ball) *Gimme the ball! Gimme the ball!*
Lisa: *Sigh!*

Geographically challenged:

Bart: *Just hear me out!*
Greta: *Bart, forget it! I'm leaving in ten minutes. My dad's shooting a movie in Toronto.*
Bart: *Gasp! You're going to Spain?!*

The Simpsons make travel plans:

Bart: *...so to win Greta back, I have to go to Toronto.*
Homer: *Canada? Why should we leave America to visit America Junior?*
Bart: *This is for love, Dad. Someday you'll feel what I feel.*
Marge: *It's only fair. We went to Europe when Lisa lost her balloon.*

TV Moments:

Wolfgang Puck's Puckmobile, the music, and the swirling pizza scene change hearken back, of course, to the 1960s "Batman" show.

Principal Skinner's stand-up comedy setting and the background music pay homage to Jerry Seinfeld's routines at the beginning and end of many episodes of "Seinfeld."

THE STUFF YOU MAY HAVE MISSED

Rich people whose children attend the prep school include Kent Brockman and Dr. Hibbert.

Bart uses the Mercedes hood ornament on his bumper car to target another child for bumping. The child he hit has an airbag in his car.

Milhouse's "Wha'zzzuuuup?!" catchphrase comes from a series of Budweiser beer commercials.

While playing Scrabble, Greta spells out "boyfriend," "kiss," "adore," "romance," "love," "desire," and "us." Bart spells out "oblivious."

Maggie is playing with a Bongo plush doll. Bongo is the one-eared rabbit from Matt Groening's "Life in Hell" comic strip.

When Greta talks to a jealous Bart on the phone, Milhouse is seen sitting on her bed, brushing a doll's hair.

Seen getting off the bus in Toronto, Canada: a mountie, a hockey player, and Bigfoot.

Lisa is seen entering the "Dodgers of Foreign Wars" building while visiting Toronto.

Rainier Wolfcastle is filming at "Paramountie Studios" in Canada. The logo looks like the Paramount Studios logo with a mountie hat instead of a mountain.

The last time Bart and Milhouse got into an all-out brawl was in "Worst Episode Ever" (CABF08) when they fought over how to run a comic book store...their first love. They also fight to the same "fight theme music" in both episodes.

The curling competition is being filmed for a show called "Curling for Loonies."

Marge meets Canada: "It's so clean and bland. I'm home!"

Marge's misdirection:

Marge: *Oh, I see you drive on the left up here!*
Tram driver: *No, ma'am. I'm drunk.*

Movie Moments:

Greta's room is decorated with huge prop items from her dad's film, *The Incredible Shrinking McBain.* There were several films that used such props, such as *The Incredible Shrinking Man* (1957), *The Incredible Shrinking Woman* (1981), *Honey, I Shrunk the Kids* (1989), and one television show, "Land of the Giants" (1968-1970).

When Rainier Wolfcastle says to a piece of pie, "Remember when I said I'd eat you last? I lied," it is a parody of an Arnold Schwarzenegger line in the action film *Commando* (1985).

Quitters never win and winners never quit:

Homer: *There she is, boy.*
Bart: *I dunno, Dad. What if she's still mad at me?*
Homer: *Listen to me, son. No one loves a quitter, so you go over there and win her back!*
Bart: *But she might say "no"!*
Homer: *Oh, I quit! There's no convincing you! I'm gonna take a nap.*

The exciting world of championship curling:

Host: *Well, we've seen some wild sweeping here today.*
Female Host: *Yes, the broom-handling has been truly dazzling!* (Bart and Milhouse roll down the stands and onto the ice.) *What's this? Two young Yankee Doodles have turned this match into a dandy!*
Host: *Ha ha ha. Both our viewers must be thrilled.*

Greta: *Sorry, Milhouse. I thought Canada would save our relationship, but it only made it worse.*
Milhouse: *You're breaking up with me? Why?*
Greta: *I guess I was just looking for someone more...masculine.*
Milhouse: *I told you, I don't know how that scrunchie got in my hair!*

Music Montage Moments:

"She Used to Be My Girl" by The Manhattans plays over the montage of Bart spying on Greta and Milhouse. And when the Simpsons go to Toronto, Geddy Lee's song "Take Off" performed for the Bob and Doug McKenzie comedy album *Great White North* is heard.

YOU TWO HAVE PUT ME OFF DATING FOR AT LEAST FOUR YEARS.

Guest Voice:
Reese Witherspoon as Greta Wolfcastle

BUCK MCCOY

His rip-roarin' reputation:
Old-time western film and television star

His high-falootin' character flaw:
He's a dedicated alcoholic

His yippie-ki-yi-yay résumé includes:
Gunfight at the Museum of Natural History

His bronco-bustin' bag of tricks includes:
A calming technique effective on dogs and David O. Selznick

His six-shootin' swan song:
Written out of his TV show so it could become a hippie sitcom

TO THE LAUNDRY ROOM! YEE-HAW!

Guest Voice
Dennis Weaver as
Buck McCoy

Bart is having a lucky day. He catches a baseball hit out of the Duff Stadium, finds two shiny new dimes, and is given a free ice cream cone. Things take a turn for the worse, however, when a vicious dog decides it wants to tear Bart into bits. It chases Bart wherever he goes, making his life miserable. No one takes Bart's concerns seriously because the dog is nice to everyone but him. One day, Bart is trying to get to school safely, when he is forced to climb the tall gates of a driveway to get away from the vicious dog. Bart believes he is safe behind the gates until he turns around to see several wild animals staring back at him.

Most of the animals turn out to be movie props, and Bart finds himself on property belonging to old-time western movie and TV star Buck McCoy. Although Bart has never heard of Buck before, he is impressed by the old cowboy, especially after Buck shows Bart how to calm the vicious dog down. Bart is so taken by Buck, he starts a new Western "craze" at his school. Later, Bart and Lisa manage to get Buck a guest appearance on "The Krusty the Clown Show." Unfortunately, Buck is so nervous about appearing on "live" TV, he starts drinking. By the time he makes his entrance, Buck is so drunk he accidentally shoots Krusty.

Bart is disillusioned to learn that his new hero is an alcoholic, and he sinks into a depression. Marge and

SHOW HIGHLIGHTS

Excuses, excuses:
Bart: *Mom! A dog ate my clothes!*
Marge: *Nice try, but we're still going to "Riverdance."*
Bart: *D'oh!*

Lisa gossips to Janey Powell about Ralph Wiggum: **"You know that new baby brother Ralph's been bragging about? It's just a pine cone!"**

The family watches TV together:
Homer: *Eh, I'm sick of this Tarzan movie.*
Lisa: *Dad! It's a documentary on the homeless!*
Homer: *Oh, right.*

Pecking order:
Milhouse: *Bart's a goner. Anyone want to be my new best friend?*
Ralph: *I will!*
Milhouse: *Great! Finally, I'll be the dominant one!*
Ralph: *Be quiet!*
Milhouse: *(submissively) Yes, sir.*

Bart fends the vicious dog off with a textbook: **"Eat my short stories!"**

Down at the McCoy homestead:
Bart: *Wow! It's like you live in a steak house.*
Buck McCoy: *Well, thank you! Most people just mutter that.*

Bart: *Is that horse vacuuming?*
Buck: *If you can call it that. He soils as much as he cleans. Frank the Wonder Horse was in twenty-four of my pictures. (The horse stomps twice with his hoof.) And directed one. (The horse stomps again.) And he got the "Film by" credit.*

Movie Moment:
The segment when Buck McCoy goes on "The Krusty the Clown Show" is reminiscent of Peter O'Toole, playing aging drunken swashbuckler Alan Swann, appearing "live" on King Kaiser's "Comedy Cavalcade" in *My Favorite Year* (1982).

"Buck McCoy? He was the greatest of them all! He was bigger than opium!"

History lesson:
Bart: *What's this lunch box made of?*
Buck: *Well, back in my day we had a thing called metal. Everything was made of it— lunch boxes, cars, you name it!*
Bart: *Met-tal.*

Homer: *Hey, boy, where'd you get that hat?*
Bart: *Buck gave it to me. He's just about the greatest guy who ever lived. I wanna grow up to be just like him.*
Homer: *(hurt) No kidding. Hey, speaking of achievers, they're thinking of spraying your old man's work space for ticks!*
Bart: *(patronizing) That's great, champ. I know you've been wanting that.*

Dinner invitation:
Marge: *Thanks for coming, Mr. McCoy. We cooked your favorites—rattlesnake meat, varmint kabobs, and refried whiskey.*
Buck: *I like the sound of that last one!*
Grampa: *Don't listen to 'em, Buck! It's an ambush! They're tryin' to jump your claim!*
Marge: *Take him outside.*
(Bart and Lisa push Grampa out the door.)
Grampa: *I love you, Buuuuuuck!*

Watching films of yesteryear:
Buck: *In the '50s I did a TV show. It only lasted a year, but we did 360 episodes—all of them great! I did the commercials myself.*
Buck: *(on screen) Remember kids, "Drunken Cowboy" brand whiskey is smooth as milk!*
Marge: *I'm not sure I approve of selling whiskey to children.*
Buck: *Well, that was aimed at children who were already heavy drinkers.*
Marge: *Ooooh.*

TV Moment:
The "McTrigger" sequence is a parody of guest star Dennis Weaver's real-life '70s show "McCloud," about a small-town western sheriff who comes to New York to fight crime.

Kent Brockman: *This is Kent Brockman here at Springfield Elementary, where a new western craze is sweeping the campus.*
Lisa: *I'm Annie Oakley!*
Nelson: *I'm Kevin Costner in one of his western roles.*
Ralph: *I'm a gulch!*
Kent: *So, I guess you could say this barely qualifies as news! I'm Kent Brockman.*

THE STUFF YOU MAY HAVE MISSED

The book that Bart throws at the dog is *America's 2nd Best Short Stories*. One of the stories in the book, judging from the torn pages, is a parody of "The Lottery" by Shirley Jackson.

While chasing Bart through a dog show tent, the vicious dog wins a "Most Vicious" award ribbon.

The dog biscuit Marge makes for the vicious dog is shaped like Bart.

When he was a child, Grampa signed his Buck McCoy Junior Buckaroo 2nd Class card "Little Grampa Simpson."

The picture on the metal lunch box shows Buck shooting two bad guys while they lay in their bed rolls next to a campfire.

In the "McTrigger" clip, characters from Gilbert Shelton's underground comic strip "Fabulous Furry Freak Brothers" are among the hippies Buck McCoy shoots.

The TV show "McTrigger" is billed as a Quinn Martin production. Quinn Martin produced many TV shows of the '50s, '60s and '70s, including "The FBI," "The Fugitive," and "The Invaders."

There's a hitching post with a horse tied to it and a wagon wheel outside the Kwik-E-Mart.

Homer creates a picture of himself in a bathing suit that mimics the famous Farrah Fawcett pinup poster from the '70s.

One of Snake's bank robbing cronies is Jimmy the Scumbag, who made his first appearance in "Lisa's Date With Density" (4F01).

IN THE WEST

Episode DABF07
ORIGINAL AIRDATE: 02/24/02
WRITER: John Swartzwelder
DIRECTOR: Bob Anderson
EXECUTIVE PRODUCER: Al Jean
GUEST VOICES: Frank Welker as The Vicious Dog

Homer vow to help Buck quit the booze and become Bart's hero again. Buck attempts to stop drinking but finds it too hard, telling Homer and Marge to mind their own business. Homer refuses to give up. When he sees a news bulletin on television reporting that Snake and his cronies are robbing a bank, he talks a reluctant Buck into stopping them. Buck foils the robbery, and he does it without drinking. Bart's faith in him is renewed. Once more the hero, Buck rides off into the sunset, bidding Bart farewell, and asking the boy to never bother him again. The vicious dog returns and begins to chase Bart.

Homer

A Kwik-E-Mart sing-along:

Apu: *Oh, give me land, lots of land, under starry skies above!*
Kids: *Don't fence me in!*
(Homer enters the store, desperate to go to the bathroom.)
Apu: *Sir, you cannot pee, unless you are an employee!*
Homer: *Can't keep it in!*

Buck McCoy's filmography includes:

Gunfight at the Museum of Natural History, Texas Rangers, Wyatt Earp Meets the Mummy, Six Brides for Seven Brothers, Six-Gun Lullaby, and *The Wild Lunch.*

At Krustylu Studios:

Bart: *Krusty, how do you feel about putting Buck McCoy on your show?*
Krusty: *Pass.*
Lisa: *We also represent Billy Joel.*
Krusty: *Who's the first one again?*
Bart: *Buck McCoy.*
Krusty: *Forget it! I'm not putting some western star on my show just 'cause it's the flavor of the month. I want my show to have a timeless quality.*
Writer: *Here's your "hanging chad" sketch, Krusty.*
Krusty: *(laughs while reading) Oh, good! You worked in Judge Ito.*

Buck comes out of retirement:

Buck: *I ain't goin' on some clown show! I'm retired.*
Lisa: *No one expects you to do anything difficult. They understand you're too old.*
Buck: *Listen, missy, the last two city slickers who used reverse psychology on me are pushin' up daisies!*
Bart: *They're dead?*
Buck: *No, they just got lousy jobs.*

"We've got such a great show tonight! I won't be doing a monologue because my feet hurt."

Krusty takes a shot at Buck, after Buck shoots Krusty:

Krusty: *This is horrible! My spit-takes all have blood in 'em!*
Buck: *Look, I'm really sorry.*
Krusty: *Sorry don't suture my colon!*

At the John Ford Center:

Buck: *Well, that's it. This place ain't for me.*
Marge: *Well, we're not giving up! We're going to cure you of drinking!*
Buck: *Look, I worked long and hard, got rich, and now I'm retired. Why shouldn't I be able to drink all I want?*
Marge: *Well, I don't know. I just naturally assumed it was some of my business.*
Buck: *I don't see how it is. Nobody's even told me your name yet.*

"I'm still not giving up on Buck! There must be some harebrained, half-assed way!"

Bart's long list of heroes:

Bart: *Buck, you're my hero again.*
Homer: *Ain't you forgetting someone?*
Bart: *Well, there's Krusty, Itchy, Scratchy, Poochie, America's firefighters...and then you, Dad!*
Homer: *Heh, heh, heh. And don't you forget it.*

NO:
CHECKS
CREDIT CARDS
FOOD STAMPS

Music Moments:

The song that Apu and the kids are singing, "Don't Fence Me In," was written and originally sung by the most famous of all western movie and TV cowboys, Roy Rogers. And as Buck rides into the sunset, the theme from *The Magnificent Seven* by Elmer Bernstein is heard.

THE OLD MAN AND

Marge receives a disturbing phone call from the Springfield Retirement Castle claiming that Grampa has died. Upset, the Simpsons go to the facility, only to find a mistake has been made and Grampa is very much alive. The deceased's room is already being rented out, and Grampa is happy to discover that the new resident is a sexy elderly woman named Zelda. Grampa attempts to woo Zelda, but she is only interested in men who can still drive. He begs Homer to help him get his revoked license back, but Homer refuses. After Grampa throws a tantrum, Marge agrees to help him. After taking driving classes, he receives a new driver's license at the DMV.

Grampa wants to borrow Homer's car so he can take Zelda out. Homer refuses but agrees to Marge's suggestion that they double date. After proving his ability to drive safely during the double date, Grampa is entrusted with the car and has a few exciting nights out with Zelda. One evening, however, he stays out all night with Zelda, and Homer takes away his driving privileges. Grampa is further upset when Homer and Marge remark that Zelda is a loose woman and no good for him. Grampa is restricted to only driving Homer's car to the store and only for a few minutes, but when a gang of elderly Latin men challenge Grampa and his pals to a death race, he cannot refuse. Unfortunately, he totals Homer's car in the race, and Homer forbids him to ever drive again.

Zelda has planned a trip to Branson, Missouri, but when she finds out that Grampa has no car, she dumps him for Zack. Zack has a car and a license, and so she goes on the trip with him. Determined to win her back, Grampa steals Marge's station wagon, taking Bart with him, and follows Zelda to Branson. Hopping on a bus, Marge, Homer, Lisa, and Maggie pursue them. When

SHOW HIGHLIGHTS

(Homer excitedly sits on the couch waving an "XFL" pennant.)
Marge: *Honey, I've got some bad news for you.*
Homer: *Not now, Marge. I'm waiting for the new XFL season! Who will win this year's million-dollar game? Who? Who?!*
Marge: *Honey...*
Homer: *The X stands for "X-treme"!*
(Homer holds up his index fingers crossed to form an "X.")
Marge: *There is no XFL this year. The league folded.*
Homer: *(speechless, he removes his XFL cap) Who told you?*
Marge: *Last year's MVP. He sweeps up toenails at the beauty parlor.*

(The phone rings.)
Marge: *Hello?*
Automated Phone Voice: *(recording) Hello. This is the Springfield Retirement Castle. Your parent...*
Grampa: *(recording) ...Abraham Simpson...*
Automated Phone Voice: *...is dead.*
Marge: *Oh, my God!*
Automated Phone Voice: *He died from...*
Grampa: *...complications of a medical nature. (reading) The-nur-sing-home-was-not-re-spon-si-ble. (The recording beeps. Marge hangs up the phone.)*
Marge: *Homer. Your father's dead!*
Homer: *(sobbing) And he never even lived to be a vegetable!*

Grampa: *What's got into you punks?*
Marge: *The home told us you were dead.*
Grampa: *Me? I ain't dead. It was Stimson down the hall. So much for Mr. "I can button my own shirt!" (He laughs.)*
Homer: *(hugging him emotionally) Aw, Dad! We've got what people never get—a second chance.*
Grampa: *(touched) Yeah, there's so many things we can...*
Homer: *Yeah, yeah, yeah, yeah. We'll call you...or send you some fruit.*

Grampa tries to impress Zelda: **"If you're lookin' for somethin' with a big back seat and a lot of gas, I'm your man!"**

Homer and Bart mix up their board games:
Bart: *B-6.*
Homer: *You sunk my Scrabble ship!*
Lisa: *This game makes no sense.*
Homer: *Tell that to the good men who just lost their lives! (He salutes a toy ship.) Semper Fi!*

"Give Grampa a chance. Statistics show that old people drive at least as well as sleep-deprived apes."

Donor conversation:
Chief Wiggum: *You know, it's kind of ironic. These old people are being kept alive by the organs of the young people they ran over.*
Officer Lou: *Makes you think, huh, Chief?*
Wiggum: *Not really.*

Marge takes Grampa to the DMV:
Patty: *Next!*
Marge: *Grampa's here to get his driver's license.*
Patty: *Okay, look at the eye chart and cover your left eye.*
Grampa: *That's my seein' eye. The right one's my winkin' eye. (He winks at her and chuckles.)*
Patty: *I'll give you your license if you never do that again.*
Grampa: *Aw! Everything's the last time I do everything!*

Watching the film *Dude, Where's My Virginity?*:
(A scene at a frat house beer party.)
Jock: *Woo! This is the best party of my life! (He fills up a cup from a beer tap and takes a swig.)*
Black Best Friend: *Bro! You tapped the septic tank! (The jock spits out what he drank. Marge and Homer comment on the scene.)*
Marge: *Dude sure got his comeuppance.*
Homer: *(chuckling) In real life, he would die.*

"Movies were better in our day. For a nickel, you got two movies, a cartoon, a bag of popcorn, and a whuppin'! Kept your mind on your business."

Movie Moment:
Grampa's aqueduct death race with Los Souvenir Jacquitos is similar to Danny Zuko's race with Leo, the leader of the Scorpions, in *Grease* (1978).

Homer shows his concern when Grampa comes home late: **"Do you have any idea what you put us through? I called the police, the hospital, my bookie, the kennel—okay, this isn't about who I called!"**

The concerned children of a troubled parent:
Homer: *I just don't know what to do.*
Marge: *He used to be such an angel. Maybe you should give him another chance.*
Homer: *No! He's got to learn, Marge—the way my Dad made me learn.*
Marge: *He is your dad.*
Homer: *(thinks for several seconds) Cosmic.*

Music Video Moment:
As Grampa and Zelda peel out and speed away from the Retirement Castle, the ZZ Top song "Sharp Dressed Man" plays. Simultaneously, three old guys with long beards make the same circular hand motion ZZ Top made in many of their videos.

THE KEY

Episode DABF09
ORIGINAL AIRDATE: 03/10/02
WRITER: Jon Vitti
DIRECTOR: Lance Kramer
EXECUTIVE PRODUCER: Al Jean
GUEST VOICES: Bill Saluga as Ray Jay Johnson

Grampa and Bart get to Branson, they spot Zelda and her new gentleman friend going into a theater. Grampa and Bart are backstage when they realize Homer and the rest of the family have caught up with them. Grampa figures he had better do something quick before he is taken home, and so he interrupts the show and asks Zelda to come up on the stage. Once there, Grampa berates her for being a fickle floozy. Zelda runs off crying, and Grampa asks Homer to come up on the stage so he can apologize. Homer says he forgives his father for the things he has done—at least while they are in public.

THE STUFF YOU MAY HAVE MISSED

The preppies at the Springfield Retirement Castle have a banner that proclaims they're from the class of '16.

A sign on the door of the room where Senior Driver's Education class is held reads, "Must Clean Up Own Mess."

Playing at the Springfield Drive-In is *Dude, Where's My Virginity?* starring Bridget Fonda, Jr., and Judd Nelson as Dean Probationly.

Much like a teenager, Grampa runs into a bedroom, slams the door, and starts playing music full blast—except, in his case, he plays the classic Glenn Miller swing tune "In the Mood."

Grampa's shopping list is on stationery that says, "From the desk of Homer Simpson" and features a picture of Homer. The listed items to buy, ostensibly "for the baby," are: milk, pretzels, and martini olives.

The jackets worn by Los Souvenir Jacquitos gang members are from Planet Hollywood Orlando, Jurassic Park, Warner Bros. (with the Tasmanian Devil in a Looney Tunes logo), and Hard Rock Cafe.

The transition music from the Kwik-E-Mart to the aqueduct is a riff on the Jets gang theme from *West Side Story*.

Snake's girlfriend, Gloria, makes a silent appearance at the death race. Earlier in the season, Gloria got back together with him in "A Hunka Hunka Burns in Love" (CABF18).

During the death race, the English subtitles don't match the words spoken in foreign languages.

Signs seen in Branson, Missouri: "Wilfred Brimley in 'The Angina Monologues,'" "Andy Williams presents Glen Campbell," and "Glen Campbell presents Andy Williams."

When the Simpsons go up onto the stage in the Branson theater, the orchestra plays "The Simpsons" theme song.

Apu and the octogenarians:
Apu: *Gentlemen, the new "Scratch-n-Win" tickets are out today!*
(He waves the tickets.)
Grampa: *I'll take one, Achoo.*
Apu: *No, not "choo." "Pu."*
Old Jewish Man: *I got trouble with both.*

Fighting words at the Kwik-E-Mart:
Hispanic Gentleman: *Pardon me, sir...your scrapings have landed on my jacket from Planet Hollywood—Orlando.*
Grampa: *So what if it did?*
(The Hispanic Gentleman is joined by one of his sidekicks.)
Sidekick: *So, it is very thoughtless. I should cut you like I cut sodium out of my diet.*
Grampa: *You don't scare me with your dignity and your subtle cologne.*
Hispanic Gentleman: *Then perhaps you should be taught a lesson by us, Los Souvenir Jacquitos.* (The two men are joined by two more as they turn their backs together and reveal their souvenir jackets.)
Jasper: *Bring it on!* (He strikes a defensive pose with his cane.)

At the death race with the members of Los Souvenir Jacquitos:
Snake: *Whichever car makes it through that tunnel first is the winner.*
Grampa: *But it's only big enough for one car.*
Hispanic Gentleman: *What are you scared of, old man?*
Grampa: *Everything—dogs, Dutchmen, the gathering darkness!*

TV Moments:
Homer is disappointed when he doesn't get to see Grampa Munster of "The Munsters." He starts stomping his foot and saying, "Darn! Darn! Darn!" until plaster is shaken loose from the ceiling and falls on his head, much like Herman Munster would do on the same show.

The entire closing credits, including the music, the sustained waving, and Lisa saying, "This has been a Gracie Films presentation" with a Southern accent, parody those of the '60s situation comedy "The Beverly Hillbillies."

Historical facts:
Grampa: *During the war, Eleanor Roosevelt was the voice of Scratchy.*
Bart: *The lady knows funny!*

Marge: *First he wrecks your car, then he steals mine. Your father's out of control.*
Homer: *Oh, sure! When he does something bad, he's my father!*

Homer: *Here we are! Branson, Missouri!*
Man: (Charles Bronson voice) *No, pally, this is Bronson, Missouri.*
(Looking around, they see that everyone in town looks, talks, and acts like Charles Bronson.)
Lisa: *Well, how do we get to Branson?*
Woman: (Charles Bronson voice) *Number ten bus.*
Kid: (Charles Bronson voice) *Hey, Ma! How 'bout some cookies?*
Woman: *No dice.*
Kid: *This ain't over.*

Hot-wire helper:
Bart: *Hey, Grampa! Stealin' Mom's car?*
Grampa: *Yeah, it's the only way to win back Zelda. And if I go to prison, I'll get better food and more hugs.*
Bart: *Uh, it's actually blue wire to yellow wire.*
Grampa: *It is?* (He tries Bart's suggestion and the car starts.) *Hot diggity Dodge! Next stop—Branson, Missoura!*
Bart: *Can I tag along?*
Grampa: *Sure, why not? School ain't helpin' ya.*

Bart the lookout:
Grampa: *Okay, keep an eye peeled for Zelda.*
Bart: *Is that her?*
Grampa: *No.*
Bart: *Is that her?*
Grampa: *No.*
Bart: *Is that her?*
Grampa: *No.*
Bart: *Is that her?*
Grampa: *No! Wait. It was the second one.*

Bart spots his family: **"It's Captain Bringdown and the Buzz Killers!"**

ZELDA

Chosen calling:
Stone-cold hoochie

Known to:
Make old men change their final wishes to "Do resuscitate"

Favorite getaway:
The Grits-Carlton Hotel in Branson, Missouri

Her perfect man must have:
High pants, a fast car, a valid license, and a pulse

I PUT THE "ASS" IN ASSISTED LIVING.

Guest Voice:
Olympia Dukakis as Zelda

PROLOGUE

Homer receives a notice from the library that a book is way overdue. Lisa finds the book, titled *Classics for Children*. Homer checked it out ten years earlier when Bart was born so that he could read to Bart every day. He never managed to get around to actually reading to Bart, and so at Lisa's urging he begins to read it aloud to the family.

THE STUFF YOU MAY HAVE MISSED

One of the bills in the mail that the Simpsons receive has "I Kill You!" scrawled on it in blood.

SHOW HIGHLIGHTS

Homer: *Hmm. Homer's Odyssey. Is this about that minivan I rented once?*
Lisa: *No, Dad. It's an epic tale from ancient Greece.*
Homer: *(reaching for a frame photograph) That minivan had the biggest cupholders! And change slots for every coin—from penny to quarter. (He touches the picture lovingly.)*
Bart: *Dad, I loved it too, but it was seven years ago.*
Homer: *Fine. (He throws the framed picture over his shoulder. It shatters on the ground.)*

D'OH, BROTHER WHERE ART THOU?

At the end of the Trojan War, the Greek hero Odysseus (Homer) cleverly uses the gift of a large wooden horse to the King of Troy (Ned Flanders) to get his men inside the city gates and then attacks the city. Odysseus refuses to make an animal sacrifice to the gods in gratitude for his victory, thus displeasing Zeus (Mayor Quimby). Zeus orders Poseidon (Captain McCallister) to take care of Odysseus, who then blows their ship off course. Odysseus and his men are lured by an entrancing song to an island occupied by sirens (Patty and Selma). However, when they get one look at the women, they flee in terror. Back on course, the gods once again misdirect them to an island where they encounter Circe. Odysseus's crew drinks a liquid from Circe's bubbling cauldron and are transformed into swine. Odysseus, not realizing the swine are his crew members, eats them all. Alone, Odysseus must travel through Hades crossing the River Styx to return to the loving arms of his long-suffering and patient wife Penelope (Marge) in Ithaca, where she is courted by many suitors. When he returns, Penelope asks Odysseus to regale her with stories of his adventures for the past twenty years. Feeling smothered, Odysseus quickly walks out, saying he is going to Moe's.

SHOW HIGHLIGHTS

At the mighty walls of Troy:
King of Troy (Ned): *Hi, O-diddily-ysseus!*
Odysseus (Homer): *(to himself) Stupid King of Troy!* *(to the king) I think I speak for all the Greeks when I say this war has gone on for too long.*
King: *I'll say. I'd really like to go out and get the mail. (He gestures down to the mailbox outside the wall, which is massively overstuffed and spilling over.)*
Odysseus: *Anyway, over torture, one of your soldiers mentioned you collect giant wooden animals. We hope you don't have a horse.*
(The king looks over his shoulder at several large wooden animals in the courtyard: a Scottish Terrier, a pig, and two horses.)
King: *Well, I don't have one from you.*

"Now throughout history, when people get wood, they'll think of Trojans!"

Asking for trouble:
Odysseus: *Now I can return to Ithaca and my sweet wife, Penelope.*
Apu (Soldier): *(holding out a sheep) Odysseus, do not forget to thank the gods for our victory with an appropriate animal sacrifice.*
Odysseus: *Forget it! Sacrificing animals is barbaric! Now, have the slaves kill the wounded.*

On Mount Olympus:
Zeus (Mayor Quimby): *No sacrifice? We'll teach that mortal to trifle with the gods.*
Dionysus (Barney): *I got it. (He grabs one of Zeus' lightning bolts and throws it earthward. We hear an explosion.)*
Zeus: *You fat lush! You just destroyed Atlantis!*
Dionysus: *You used to be fun. Where's the Zeus who used to turn into a cow and pick up chicks?*
Zeus: *He grew up. Maybe you should too. (to Poseidon) Poseidon, you take care of Odysseus.*
Poseidon (Captain McCallister): *Yarrr, I'll send him farrrr...off course.*

THE STUFF YOU MAY HAVE MISSED

Outside the devastated city of Troy, on the sign that says, "City of Troy Pop. 12,801," Odysseus crosses out the old number and writes "0."

Mayor Quimby wears a sash in this segment that reads "Zeus." Later, in "Hot Child in the City," he wears one that reads "King of France."

During the storm at sea, we can see that Odysseus has no shorts under his toga.

On the ancient map, Odysseus' ship is seen passing images of a minotaur rowing a boat, a sea serpent, a three-headed mermaid sinking a ship, another mythical sea monster, and a giant squid. The ship comes to a stop near a location called "Crazy Islands."

PUBLIC DOMAIN

Episode DABF08
ORIGINAL AIRDATE: 03/17/02
WRITER: (Pt. 1) Andrew Kreisberg, (Pt. 2) Josh Lieb, (Pt. 3) Matt Warburton
DIRECTOR: Mike B. Anderson
EXECUTIVE PRODUCER: Al Jean

Music Moment:
As Homer crosses the River Styx, we hear the '70s band Styx's song "Lady." Dead people all dance and sway with the music. One holds his fire-tipped thumb up, which looks much like a concertgoer holding a cigarette lighter in the air, and some flash the devil sign. One lost soul is playing the air guitar, and a lady skeleton sitting on another skeleton's shoulder is exposing her skeletal chest.

"Greece is the word!"

Patty and Selma's Siren Song:
(to the tune of Barry Manilow's "Copacabana")

On the island, Island of Sirens,
Our hot sex will leave you perspirin'.
The feta is cheesy.
The Sirens are easy.
On the island, we'll sex you up.
Island of Sirens!

Odysseus finishes eating all of the pigs (his crew):

Odysseus: Oh, I'm still hungry.
Circe: Didn't you eat enough of your friends?
Odysseus: Gasp! Those were my friends?!?
Circe: Yes! I've been saying that for hours!

Helen of Troy (Agnes Skinner), channels Phyllis Diller: **"This is the face that launched a thousand ships–the other way! Ah-ha ha ha!"**

Cartoon Moment:
After knocking Homer's ship back off-course with a flick of his finger, the god Poseidon says, "Ain't I a stinker?" much like Bugs Bunny does in many of his Looney Tunes cartoons.

Cold reception:
Odysseus: Honey, I'm home!
Penelope: Well! Look who The Fates dragged in.

HOT CHILD IN THE CITY

Joan of Arc (Lisa) receives a message from God, directing her to lead the French army and win The Hundred Years War. Her family is skeptical, but when God makes a visitation at their dinner table, they believe Joan. On the battlefield, the French general (Chief Wiggum) and the other soldiers laugh at Joan's attempt to take over. Everyone is impressed, however, with Joan's innovative ideas and lust for battle as she attacks the English. Soon, the general and his soldiers follow her to victory. Joan is brought to the court of the Dauphin (Milhouse) where, after being tested, she is honored and hailed as a savior. Later, as the French continue to beat the English in battle, Joan is captured by an enemy soldier and brought before an English court. In her defense, Joan calls God as her witness. God appears, but then embarrassedly admits that he visited people on both sides and told them to fight in his name. The English decide to burn Joan as a witch, but before she dies, Marge interrupts the tragic story, hastily adds a happy ending, then tears the real ending out of the book and swallows it.

The call to arms:

God: Joan of Arc, I am your God.
Joan (Lisa): (pulling at her collar) Uh-heyyy!
God: I have chosen you to lead the French army to victory over the English invaders!
Joan: But I'm just a little girl!
God: (sarcastically) I know! I have three eyes! Now get cracking!

Lost in the translation:

Marge: God wants you to lead the French army to what?
Joan: Victory.
Homer: Victory? We're French! We don't even have a word for it.

At the French army's catapult:

French general (Chief Wiggum): All right, garçons! Troi! Deux! Un!
French soldier (Lou): Huh?
General: No, "un." You know, French for "one."
Soldier: Well, you keep switching back between French and English.
General: Just fire the damn thing.

SHOW HIGHLIGHTS

Homer tells the fairy-tale version of "Joan of Arc": **"This one takes place in a make-believe kingdom called France. The French were fighting the English in The Hundred Years War, which was then called 'Operation Speedy Resolution.'"**

THE STUFF YOU MAY HAVE MISSED

Marge mistakes hearing "Joan of Arc" for Joan Van Ark. Joan Van Ark is an actress, most famous for playing Val Ewing on the TV show "Dallas" and its spinoff, "Knots Landing."

Joan's mother speaks a few of the lines from the song "Frére Jacques," when she says, "Morning bells are ringing, morning bells are ringing!"

While praying, Joan asks for a blessing on Coco Chanel, the famous French fashion designer and cosmetics queen.

Reverend Lovejoy and Ned Flanders sit in judgment during Joan's witch trial.

The executioner who is tying Joan to the stake to be burnt is wearing an apron that says, "Kiss Ye Cook."

Royally skewered:
Dauphin (Milhouse): *Loyal subjects, let us drink to Joan of Arc, who'll conquer the English, and has already conquered my heart.* (He puts his hand on hers and makes eyes at her.)
Joan: *Uh, God says we should just be friends.*
Jester (Krusty): *I wouldn't say King Milhouse is a loser, but that's the twelfth girl he's struck out with this week!*
Dauphin: *Boil him in oil!*
Jester: (as he is dragged away) *So, no 10:30 show?*

"Let us kill the English. Their concept of individual rights could undermine the power of our beloved tyrant."

High tea in the English camp:
English Soldier 1: *They're attacking again.*
English Soldier 2: *I thought we had a truce.*
English Soldier 1: (testily) *Just because you keep saying it, doesn't make it so!*
(Both soldiers are shot in the chest by arrows, grimace, and fall to the ground.)
English Soldier 1: *Oh. My word.*

"I captured a wee girl! I'm the greatest hero in English history!"

At Joan of Arc's trial:
God: *I told this maiden to lead the French to victory.*
Groundskeeper Willie: *Wait a minute, ya two-timin' spot of light! Ya told me to lead the English to victory!*
Joan: *Gasp! Is that true, Lord?*
(God's light squirms nervously in the witness chair.)
God: *Uh, ha ha! Well, I never thought the two of you would be in the same room actually, eh...this is a little embarrassing. Goodbye now.*

Parental pleas:
Marge: *Don't burn her! She's just an innocent child!*
Homer: (holding up Bart) *Burn this guy! He lost the good bucket!*

Marge's happy ending: **(taking the book from Homer) Just then, Sir Lancelot rode up on a white horse and saved Joan of Arc. They got married and lived in a spaceship. The end."** *(She rips out the actual ending, sticks it in her mouth, hums as she chews it, and then swallows.)* **Well, it's easier to chew than that** *Bambi* **video.**

DO THE BARD, MAN

Hamlet (Bart) is visited by the ghost of his father, the former king (Homer). The ghost tells Hamlet that he was murdered by his brother Claudius (Moe), who is now married to his queen, Gertrude (Marge). The ghost commands Hamlet to avenge his death, but Hamlet is not sure the story is true. Hamlet decides to investigate further and uses Krusty's band of players to trick Claudius into confessing to the crime. Claudius all but admits that he did the deed. Armed with a sword, Hamlet invades Gertrude's bedroom bent on killing Claudius, but he stabs Polonius (Chief Wiggum) to death instead. With his dying breath, Polonius entreats his son Laertes (Ralph) to avenge his death. Meanwhile, Claudius is busy poisoning everything in the castle Hamlet might eat or touch. In the final showdown, Laertes idiotically kills himself, Hamlet kills Claudius, Hamlet slips on blood and dies, and Gertrude avoids having to clean up the mess by dispatching herself with a mace.

SHOW HIGHLIGHTS

Ghost (Homer): (appearing to Hamlet) *Hamlet! Avenge me!*
Hamlet (Bart): *Dad?*
Ghost: *Yes! I have returned from the dead!*
Hamlet: *Looks like you've returned from the buffet.*
Ghost: *Why, you little...*

Flashback on Hamlet's father's fate:
Ghost: *As I slept, your Uncle Claudius poured poison in my ear—poison most foul! So he could marry your mother and become the king!*
Hamlet: *Yeah, that was quite a weekend.*
Ghost: *Now you must avenge me! Avenge me!*
Hamlet: *How?*
Ghost: *I dunno, surprise me.* (spooky voice) *Surpriiiise meee!*

Hamlet's father's ghostly warning: **"It's cold outside, you'll need a sweater. (spooky voice) A sweeaaateeerrr!"**

"And if your idea of a first date is burning down her village, you just might be...a viking!"

PUBLIC DOMAIN

On the rebound most foul:

Gertrude (Marge): *I love these jesters! They're exactly what I need to forget about my first husband.*
Claudius (Moe): *Yeah, I really miss the old guy. It was all I could do to put on his jewels and score with his wife every night.*

Actor (Krusty): *Now we would like to warn you, our performances tend to make audience members blurt out hidden secrets.*
Claudius: *(worried) Ho-boy.*
Hamlet: *(aside) Aha! Methinks the play's the thing, wherein I'll catch the conscience of the king!*
Claudius: *Catch my conscience? What?*
Hamlet: *You're not supposed to hear me. That's a soliloquy.*
Claudius: *Okay, well, I'll do a soliloquy too. (clears his throat) Note to self: Kill that kid.*

Ophelia will not be upstaged:

Ophelia (Lisa): *Oh great, now Hamlet's acting crazy. Well, nobody out-crazies Ophelia! (singing nonsensically) Hey, nonny, nonny, with a hoo and a haw and a nonny, nonny, hey...(As she sings, she jumps onto a table, kicks an apple out of a roasted pig's mouth, dances crazily about, and kicks flowers out of a vase. She then cartwheels off the table, across the floor, and out a window, falling to her death. A splash fountains up to the window, soaking two onlookers.)*

Laertes: *I'm gonna kill Hamlet. Here's my mad face! Hrrr!*
(Claudius uses a brush to apply poison.)
Claudius: *Uh-heh. Cute kid. But, just in case you don't kill Hamlet, I put some poison on the food, on the drapes, even on Rosen-Carl and Guilden-Lenny here.*
Guilden-Lenny: *If Hamlet touches either of us, he's dead.*
Rosen-Carl: *Boo-yeah!*
(They high-five one another, then fall over dead.)

Outrageous misfortune:

(Hamlet enters Gertrude's bedchamber.)
Hamlet: *(running in with sword) Eaaagh!*
Gertrude: *(startles and sits up) Hamlet! What'd I tell you about running with swords?*
(Hamlet sees the closed curtains move.)
Hamlet: *Someone's behind the curtain! It could be Claudius! Only one way to find out... (He stabs at the curtain.)*
Polonius (Chief Wiggum): *Ow! Ow! (Polonius emerges, falls to the ground, and holds his stomach.) Ow!*
Hamlet: *Polonius? What are you doing behind the curtain?*
Polonius: *(bleeding profusely) I hide behind curtains because I have a fear of getting stabbed.*
Laertes (Ralph): *(pointing) Daddy's stomach is crying!*

All's well that ends...well?:

Lisa: *And that's the greatest thing ever written.*
Bart: *Are you crazy? I can't believe a play where every character was murdered could be so boring.*
Homer: *Son, it's not only a great play, but also became a great movie...called Ghostbusters. (The whole family dances to the Ghostbusters theme song.)*

THE STUFF YOU MAY HAVE MISSED

The poster on Hamlet's bedroom wall says, "Danes Do It Melancholy," and there is a pennant that reads, "Feudalism."

Krusty's viking joke is a parody of the "redneck" jokes made famous by comedian Jeff Foxworthy.

Sideshow Mel's prop ear poison has the warning "Do Not Get In Eyes."

As Hamlet's father's ghost passes through the castle wall, he leaves a residue of green ectoplasm, just like Slimer in the movie *Ghostbusters* (1984).

RONALDO THE ORPHAN

Former residence:
Orfanato Dos Anjos Imundos (Filthy Angels Orphanage)

Current occupation:
Flamenco Flamingo character on Brazilian children's TV show "Teleboobies"

How much money he makes:
As much as Malcolm in the Middle

Upside to being an orphan:
Because he has no parents, his earnings remain unstolen

How very sweet he is:
To the monkeys that bite him, he is like sugar

BECAUSE OF YOUR GENEROSITY, I BOUGHT STURDY SHOES THAT WILL LAST FOR A THOUSAND SAMBAS!

Marge is shocked to discover that the family's phone bill includes an expensive call to Brazil. She and Homer go to the phone company to try and sort things out, but Homer manages to get their service cut off. As the family commiserates, Lisa reveals that she is the one who ran up phone charges to Brazil, trying to locate a poor orphan boy she sponsors. The boy, Ronaldo, appears to have gone missing, and Lisa is very worried. After watching a videotape of Ronaldo, and seeing how adorable he is, the rest of the family decide to help Lisa find him, and they make plans to travel to Brazil.

The Simpsons arrive in Rio de Janeiro, and begin their search for Ronaldo. A visit to the orphanage proves to be unhelpful, so they split up and look through the streets. Though momentarily distracted by the beaches, the risqué dance studios, and the exotic outdoor shops, the family remains determined to find the orphan. Unfortunately, Homer ignores warnings and gets into an unlicensed taxi, whereupon he is immediately kidnapped.

Homer's kidnappers take him deep into the Amazon jungle. From there, Homer is allowed to call Marge and tell her of their demands—they will release Homer unharmed for $50,000. Marge is only able to raise a fraction of that amount, and Homer's calls to others for help prove fruitless, as does Marge's visit to the Rio

SHOW HIGHLIGHTS

Lindsey Naegle: Hello! I'm your customer service rep, Lindsey Naegle.
Marge: We've met you many times, Miss Naegle. Why do you keep changing jobs?
Lindsey: I'm a sexual predator.
Marge: Oh.
Lindsey: Now, how may I best dispense with you today?
Marge: We've been charged with calls to Brazil that we didn't make.
Homer: (holding up the bill) We are not paying this bill!
Lindsey: Fine. I'll cut off your service! (She angrily types in her computer.)
Homer: Fine, I'll cut off your ponytail!
Marge: Homer!
Homer: (aside) Marge, it's called negotiating.
Marge: Hrmm.

Homer springs into action:
Homer: That's it! They have awoken a sleeping giant!
Marge: (warily) Homer, what are you gonna do?
Bart: (praying and crossing his fingers) Crazy scheme! Crazy scheme! Crazy scheme!
Homer: Get me tools and beer!
Bart: Yes!

Marge: That's it! We're just going to have to pay for that call to Brazil.
Lisa: (nervously) What call to Brazil?
Homer: The one I didn't make and Marge didn't make and Bart didn't make and, hence, no one in the house made.
Lisa: Uh-oh.
Marge: You made that call? But you're the good one!
Homer: Yeah, the one we both like.

Lisa: I've been sponsoring an orphan boy in Brazil.
Marge: Oh, aren't you sweet? Sharing your allowance with a poor Brazilian boy.
Homer: Don't you know the boys from Brazil are little Hitlers? I saw it in a movie...whose name I can't remember!

Marge's maternal instinct kicks in:
Marge: Can we have another baby?
Homer: No way! I still haven't lost the weight I put on from the last one!

THE STUFF YOU MAY HAVE MISSED

The title of this episode is a play on the film title *Blame It on Rio* (1984), a comedy that took place in Rio de Janeiro, starring Michael Caine, Joe Bologna, and Demi Moore.

The last time a long distance call was placed to a foreign country was in "Bart Vs. Australia" (2F13). Bart called collect, causing an international incident in the process.

As the Simpsons walk up to the phone company, its name is being changed from Comquaaq to Zovuvazz.

Homer is seen reading *Blue Pants Weekly* magazine.

The name of the orphan charity that Lisa donates to is *Li'l Writeoffs*.

On the plane, Lisa is reading *Who Wants to be a Brazilionaire?* Bart is learning Spanish from a tape series entitled *Español Para Dummies*, which pictures Bumblebee Man on the covers.

The Simpsons stay at the Rio Days-Inn-Ero.

The family dines at a restaurant called Churrascarias, which is a type of barbecued meal served in Brazil. One of the employees at the restaurant is a South American version of the Frank Nelson-Type character.

Homer is seen wearing a T-shirt that depicts Uncle Sam devouring the Earth, with the words "Try and Stop Us" printed below.

In order to avoid seeing Homer's butt in a Speedo bathing suit, a woman on the beach covers her face with a jellyfish.

As the taxi drives up, the door reads "Unlicensed Taxi," and when it pulls away with Homer inside, the sign atop lights up to read "Hostage."

Things in Homer's kidnapping scrapbook "Memories": A photo of Homer with his arms around the two masked kidnappers, a section titled "Remember...," a leaf that is captioned "toilet paper," a poem by Homer titled "My Teeth Hurt," a photo of Homer with one eye swollen shut, a splatter of blood, another poem by Homer called "My Nose Knows," more blood splatters, a photo of Homer with a bloody nose and popped-out, bloodshot eye, a photo of Homer on a torture table while a kidnapper approaches with a pair of pliers, a photo of Homer running from a swarm of bats, a cigarette butt, a haiku to torture, a drawing by Homer of a kidnapper with lit cigarettes used for torturing, a photo of Homer smiling, a photo of Homer with the cinnamon bag over his head, and a piece of the cord his hands were bound with.

On the way to Brazil:
Lisa: Okay, here's some travel tips: only drink bottled water, don't get into an unlicensed taxi, and, remember, they have winter during our summer.
Homer: Wait wait wait wait! So in August, it's cold?
Lisa: That's right.
Homer: And in February, it's hot?
Lisa: Mm-hmm.
Homer: So it's Opposite Land! Crooks chase cops! Cats have puppies!
Lisa: No, Dad. It's just the weather.
Homer: So hot snow falls up?
Lisa: (giving in weakly) Yes.
Homer: Woo-hoo!

Bart: Get ready, Brazil. I now speak fluent Spanish.
Marge: Well done, Bart, but in Brazil they speak Portuguese.
Bart: Ay caramba, que mujer tonta! Veinte horas estudiar por nada!

Fly the friendly skies:
Pilot: This is your captain speaking. The local temperature in Rio de Janeiro is hot, hot, hot! With a 100% chance of passion.
Co-pilot: Bernardo, you make that joke every time!
Pilot: It was that joke that made you fall in love with me.

Lisa: Look! It's the giant statue of Christ on Corcovado!
Homer: Wow! It's like he's on the dashboard of the entire country!

ON LISA

Episode DABF10
ORIGINAL AIRDATE: 03/31/02
WRITER: Bob Bendetson
DIRECTOR: Steven Dean Moore
EXECUTIVE PRODUCER: Al Jean

police. As luck would have it, Marge and Lisa find Ronaldo when they leave the police station and get caught up in a Carnival parade. Ronaldo is now a performer on a popular children's TV show and has enough money to spare $50,000 for Homer's safe return. Marge, Lisa, and Bart make the exchange with the kidnappers while on passing Sugarloaf Mountain skyway trams. Unfortunately, when Homer hops from the kidnapper's tram to the tram containing Marge and the kids, their cable snaps. Luckily, the Simpsons survive their tram rolling down the mountain and crashing at the bottom. They briefly celebrate Homer's safe return, only to find that Bart has been swallowed by a giant boa constrictor.

Movie Moment:
When Scratchy hits the Man in the Moon in the eye during the Itchy and Scratchy cartoon, it is reminiscent of the rocket ship landing in the silent film *Le Voyage dans la Lune* (*A Trip to the Moon*) (1902), created by imaginative French director and master magician Georges Méliès.

TV Moment:
The Brazilian children's show "Teleboobies" takes its name from the British import "Teletubbies," aimed at very young children, and its content from the short-lived Brazilian import "Xuxa."

Marge: *What a charming neighborhood!*
Lisa: *Mom! These are slums. The government just painted them bright colors so the tourists wouldn't be offended.*
Marge: *Works for me!*
Bart: *Yeah! Check out the rats.*
(Hundreds of multicolored rats swarm past.)
Homer: *Ooo! They look like Skittles!*

Lisa: *Excuse me, we're looking for this little boy?*
(She hands a picture of Ronaldo to a nun. The nun sets her broom aside.)
Nun: *Ah yes, Ronaldo. He went off months ago, and we haven't heard from him since. Every day we light a candle for him.*
Bart: *Have you tried looking for him?*
Nun: *That's Plan B.*

Getting away from it all:
Bart: *Have some meat on a sword, Lisa! It'll cheer you up.* (tearing the meat off with his teeth) *Mmmmm-mn!*
Lisa: *You know I'm a vegetarian.*
Homer: *But you're on vacation, honey. I'm not wearing my wedding ring.*
Marge: *Homer!*

Homer's Copacabana Beach song
(to Peter Allen's "I Go to Rio")

I'm in Rio,
And I'm walkin' on the beach.
I'm in my Speedo!
Hee hee hee!

Taxi Driver: *My American friend, I'm afraid that this is a kidnapping.*
Homer: *So, that means I don't have to pay the fare?*
Taxi Driver: *I-I suppose, eh...*
Homer: *Woo-hoo!*

Homer: *Listen, I really need a rest stop.*
Kidnapper: *Again?*
Homer: *I have a bladder the size of a Brazil nut.*
Taxi Driver: *Eh, we just call them "nuts" here.*

A phone call for help (Part 1):
Mr. Burns: *Ahoy-hoy?*
Homer: (sheepishly) *Mr. Burns? It's Homer Simpson. I've been kidnapped, and I need fifty thousand dollars.*
Burns: *Hmmm! Well, I'm high on sheep embryos, so I am feeling charitable. How about I advance you the money and you work it off?*
Homer: (angrily) *No deal!*

A phone call for help (Part 2):
Moe: *Moe's Tavern, home of The Stinkiest Rag in America!*
Homer: *Hey, Moe.*
Moe: *Oh, Homer! Listen, I need fifty grand. Don't ask me why.*
Homer: *No, no! I need fifty grand!*
Moe: *I asked you first.*
Homer: *Fine! I'll send you fifty grand.*
Moe: *Thanks.*

A phone call for help (Part 3):
Homer: *Hello, Flanders? I need a hundred grand!*
Ned: *Well, I don't really have that much. But, uh, if you need it that bad, you'll be in my prayers.*
Homer: *Go suck a Bible!*

"It's Carnival!":
Marge: *Oh, your father would have loved this. The drunkenness, the ambiguous sexuality...Gasp! I've got to get out of here!*
(A man dressed in a toucan costume walks up.)
Man: *You cannot run from Carnival! Because even running is a kind of dance!*
(A second man covered in flames joins them.)
Second Man: *I am on fire, and I dance!* (He dances away.)
Marge: *I'll just dance and worry at the same time.*

Hope floats:
(Ronaldo unzips himself from his costume.)
Lisa: *Ronaldo!*
Ronaldo: *Yes, I am "Flamenco Flamingo." And it all started with the dancing shoes you bought me.*
Lisa: *Why didn't you tell me?*
Ronaldo: *I tried to write, but I didn't know what state you lived in.*
Lisa: *It's a bit of a mystery, yes. But if you look at the clues, you can figure it out.*

Music Moment:
As Homer and Bart walk along the Copacabana Beach, the song "Brazil" plays.

"Memories":
Homer: *Listen, um...*(pulling out a book) *I made a little scrapbook to remember the kidnapping. I'm still working on it, but as you can see, I've...aw, look! This is the cigarette butt you burned me with!*
Taxi Driver: *You slept like a baby that night.*
(Homer and the kidnappers laugh.)
Homer: *I remember that, yeah!*

Marge serves genetically enhanced vegetables for dinner, but when Lisa's potato eats her carrot, Marge decides to grow her own vegetables. It does not take long for crows to hone in on Marge's vegetable patch, so she builds a scarecrow. After Homer mistakes the scarecrow for an intruder and destroys it, the crows become Homer's friends, accompanying him everywhere. Their friendship goes awry, and when Homer attempts to get rid of the crows by shooing them off, the crows attack him.

The crow attack leaves Homer with punctured eyeballs and Dr. Hibbert prescribes medicinal marijuana to ease the pain. Homer is at first reluctant to use the drug but soon becomes a habitual user. Marge is concerned for Homer's well-being, but he is perfectly happy smoking pot. He even gets promoted to executive vice president at the power plant when he is so stoned he impresses Mr. Burns by laughing at his terrible jokes. The anti-drug lobby in Springfield launches a political campaign to repeal the use of medicinal marijuana, and Homer quickly organizes a rally, featuring the rock group Phish, to encourage voters to keep medical marijuana legal. During the rally, prescription pot supporters suddenly become aware that the vote was taken the previous day and that medical marijuana has been outlawed.

Going cold turkey is hard for Homer, but he promises Marge and the kids he will stop smoking dope. Later, when completely sober, Homer is called in to listen to the speech Mr. Burns plans to give to investors. It is vitally important to Burns that his speech be humorous, but Homer can no longer find Burns funny. After threatening Homer and Smithers, Burns retires to take a bath saying that someone had better laugh at his jokes when he returns, or else. Homer

SHOW HIGHLIGHTS

Marge attempts to get rid of the crows: **"I tried heckling them, I tried jeckling them. It's time I made myself a scarecrow."**

The names of some of Homer's crow-nies: Russell Crow, Cameron Crow, Crow Diddley, Hume Crow-nyn, and Gregory Peck

Homer: *Say, doctor, can you do something about my (spasming) searing pain?*
Dr. Hibbert: *There is a medication, although it is a little controversial.*
Homer: *Does it go in the butt?*
Hibbert: *I'm talking about medicinal marijuana. Prescription pot. Texas THC.*
Homer: *Look, man, I don't do drugs.*
Hibbert: *Homer, for your eyes, the best tonic is chronic.*

 "For me, the '60s ended that day in 1978."

Homer follows the instructions for his medical marijuana: **"Okay, let's see. 'Toke as needed. Caution: Objects may appear more edible than they actually are.'"**

Clearing the air:
Marge: *What's that billowing down the stairs? Gasp! It's smoke!*
Lisa: *It smells like the art teacher's office.*

Homer's version of "Smoke on the Water" by Deep Purple:
They burned down the gambling house,
It died with an awful sound,
I am hungry for a candy bar,
I think I'll eat a Mounds!

(Homer calls Marge from work.)
Marge: *(on the phone) Hello?*
Homer: *(on the phone) Marge! I just realized, I'm the "ow" in the word "now."* (threatening) *And if you tell anyone...*
Marge: *Honey, I like it when you call, but we just talked five minutes ago.* (beep) *Hang on. I've got call waiting.* (click) *Hello?*
Homer: *Hey, it's me. I've got Marge on the other line, and she is totally bumming me out.*
Marge: *Hrmmm.*

A visit from Ned Flanders:
(Flanders is at the door holding a clipboard.)
Flanders: *Hi-diddly-hey, Homer!*
Homer: *Oh, my God! This dude does the best Flanders! You have the mustache, and the "diddly." Okay, now do Wiggum.*
Flanders: *(laughs nervously) Homer, i-i-it's me. Ned.*
Homer: *Oh-ho-ho-ho, right. The God dude. Hey, I've got a question for you.* (He pulls a crumpled piece of paper out of his pocket and reads from it.) *Could Jesus microwave a burrito so hot that he himself could not eat it?*
Flanders: *Well, sure. Of course, he could, but then again...Wow. As melon-scratchers go, that's a honey-doodle!*

Homer: *Oops! I thought this was the can, man.* (He laughs.)
Mr. Burns: *Well, you're a happy Homer. What's your name, young man?*
Homer: *You just said it!* (laughing harder)
Burns: *Well, if you like that, listen to this: working hard or hardly working?*
(Homer laughs uncontrollably.)
Burns: *Heh-heh-heh. Smithers, you could learn a thing or two from this braying moron. Heh-heh-heh.* (to Homer) *Young man, I'm making you my executive vice-president.*
Smithers: *Sir, I believe that position was informally promised to me.*
Burns: *Oh, Smithers! I would have said anything to get your stem cells.* (to Homer) *Now, welcome aboard!*
Homer: *(touching Burns' face) You're covered with a very fine fuzz.*

Fighting the Reefer-endum:
Homer: *We've got to get out and stop that initiative! Marge, I'm gonna need ten thousand veggie burritos!*
Otto: *No "guac" in mine.*
Marge: *Goodnight, Homer.* (She leaves.)
Otto: *Dude, your mom is hot!*

 "Whether you suffer from glaucoma, or you've just rented *The Matrix*, medical marijuana can make things fabulous. Medically."

TV Moment:
When Dr. Hibbert says, "I'm talking about medicinal marijuana. Prescription pot. Texas THC," it parodies the opening song of vintage TV show "The Beverly Hillbillies," specifically the lines, "...when up from the ground came a bubbling crude. Oil that is. Black gold. Texas tea."

BURNSIE'S

Episode DABF11
ORIGINAL AIRDATE: 04/07/02
WRITER: Jon Vitti
DIRECTOR: Michael Marcantel
EXECUTIVE PRODUCER: Al Jean

GUEST VOICES: Phish (Trey Anastasio, Jon Fishman, Mike Gordon, Page McConnell) as Themselves

hatches a quick plan—he still has a joint in his pocket and recommends that Smithers smoke it to get the giggles. Smithers agrees, gets stoned, and becomes involved in a long conversation with Homer. Smithers suddenly realizes that Burns has been in the bath for an hour. Racing to the bathroom, they are horrified to discover that Burns has drowned in the tub. Twenty minutes later, when the investors' meeting begins, Homer takes the podium, and Smithers manipulates Mr. Burns' lifeless body from above the stage as though he were a marionette puppet. The investors start asking difficult questions, and Smithers distracts them by having Burns perform a big dance number. The investors are satisfied, and, as luck would have it, the dancing revives Mr. Burns.

THE STUFF YOU MAY HAVE MISSED

Marge plants "Dirty Hoe" brand seeds in her garden.

Marge makes a scarecrow while interesting facts pop up, à la the hit VH1 series "Pop-Up Video." Each pop-up features a picture of Comic Book Guy with an appropriate popping sound. The pop-ups are "Lisa's jersey from 'Lisa on Ice,'" "Bart's jockey pants from 'Saddlesore Galactica,'" "Jack-o-lantern from 'Treehouse of Horror III, IX-XII" and "Grampa's hat from 'Who Shot Grampa's Hat?'" The jack-o-lantern from the "Treehouse" episodes is a stretch, but the episode "Who Shot Grampa's Hat?" is completely fictitious.

When Homer asks the crows to do his bidding, they bring him a mug of beer, a sandwich, a donut, a bag of chips, and a *Playdude* magazine.

After Marge leaves the bed, four crows get under the covers next to Homer to take her place.

Sgt. Scraps, the drug-sniffing, crotch-grabbing police dog from 1978, should not be confused with Officer Scraps, the bloodhound that went in search of Homer in "The Computer Wore Menace Shoes" (CABF02).

As Homer gets ready for work while stoned, the animation takes on a distinctive style similar to the work of popular sixties artist Peter Max.

As Kent Brockman delivers the news about the possible recriminalization of medical marijuana,

the picture of the pot leaf in the background is captioned "Reefer-Endum."

The signatures on the petition to make medicinal pot illegal include: Scott Christian, Waylon Smithers, Abraham Simpson, Herschel Krustofski, Kirk Van Houton, Edna Krabappel, Barney Gumble, Reverend Timothy Lovejoy, Rainier Wolfcastle, Luann Van Houten, Patty Bouvier, Birch Barlow, Agnes Skinner, Moe Szyslak, Apu Nahasapeemapetilon, Seymour Skinner, Captain McCallister, and Helen Lovejoy.

At the rally, pro-pot protest signs say, "Save Medical Marijuana," "Weed Us Our Rights" and "Keep Off The Grass (Get It?)" Someone has placed a Cat in the Hat hat on the statue of Jebediah Springfield. One person is dressed in a marijuana leaf costume.

Seen in the rally audience are aging hippies Seth and Munchie, first introduced in the episode "D'oh-in' in the Wind" (AABF02), and Mr. Mitchell, the blind stoner from "The Canine Mutiny" (4F16). Also seen: Otto, Hans Moleman, Snake, and Disco Stu.

For some reason, there's a newspaper dispenser on Phish's stage at the rally.

Mr. Burns almost drowned in his bathtub once before in "Burns' Heir" (1F16).

Attendees at Burns' investors' meeting include: Dr. Nick Riviera, Lindsey Naegle, Mr. Costington, the Blue-Haired Lawyer, and the Rich Texan.

Movie Moment:

The title of this episode and the closing act antics of Smithers and Homer, are a take on *Weekend at Bernie's* (1989), a film comedy starring Andrew McCarthy and Jonathan Silverman as two men who trick everyone into believing a dead man is still alive so they won't get accused of murdering him.

Music Moments:

Marge assembles her scarecrow to the tune "If I Only Had a Brain" from the movie musical *The Wizard of Oz* (1939).

Homer trips out to Strawberry Alarm Clock's "Incense and Peppermints" after taking the first hit off his marijuana joint. The song was also heard in "D'oh-in' in the Wind" (AABF02). Other drug culture music heard in the episode includes: "Smoke on the Water" by Deep Purple and "Wear Your Love Like Heaven" by Donovan.

Phish plays "Run Like an Antelope" at the medical marijuana rally.

Homer's solution:

Homer: *(pulls out a joint) This stuff can make anything funny—even that show that follows "Friends." But I promised my family I wouldn't smoke it anymore.*
Smithers: *Well, I've got to do something.*
Homer: *Start inhalin', Waylon.*

"Oh, man! We killed Mr. Burns! Mr. Burns is gonna be so mad!"

At the pwer plant investors' meeting:

Bill Clinton: *...so when somebody says I was an embarrassment to the country, I say it depends on what the meaning of "was" is...jerk! (laughs) You owe me two hundred thousand dollars! Good night, everybody!*
(The investors applaud.)
Homer: *Bill Clinton, everyone! He's Jimmy Carter with a Fox attitude!*

Homer: *It's been three days and my mind is clearer. My sperm count is up, and I'm able to recognize simple shapes and patterns.*
Lisa: *Dad, you just said that three minutes ago.*

Marge: *Homer, it's over. I want you to look at your children and promise them you'll never do drugs again.*
Homer: *All right. I'll do it for my kids.*
Bart: *As long as you're doing things for me, could you tie up your bathrobe when you walk around the house?*
Homer: *Never!*

"Going cold turkey isn't as delicious as it sounds."

Back with the boys at Moe's Tavern:

Moe: *(to Homer) Look, I'm really glad you're off the wacky tobacky.*
Lenny: *Yeah, you were getting all spacey and everything. We were gonna have an intervention.*
Carl: *Yeah, but, at the planning party, I got alcohol poisoning. Heh. I nearly died.*
(Moe, Carl, and Lenny laugh.)
Moe: *I was already makin' excuses not to go to your funeral!*
(They laugh some more.)

THE CROWS

Enemy:
The scarecrow

Alpha crow:
Homer Simpson

Eager to:
Do his bidding...whatever it may be

Tendency to:
Envelop

Gather together in:
A murder

Most recent victim of said murder:
Barney Gumble

Not very receptive to:
Ground rules, separation, or the word "Shoo!"

Drink of choice:
Sweet, sweet eye juices

KANG AND KODOS

Who they are:
Aliens from the planet Rigel 7

Their relationship to each other:
Brother and sister

Where you may have seen them:
Old Navy commercials

Their planet's crowning achievement in amusement technology:
Pong

Interesting biological fact:
They vomit through their eyes

How to recognize the males of their species from females:
You don't want to know

> I AM ACTUALLY SPEAKING RIGELLIAN. BY AN AMAZING COINCIDENCE, BOTH OF OUR LANGUAGES ARE EXACTLY THE SAME.

GUMP

While Homer sits on a bus bench waiting for Marge and the kids to pick him up, he is joined by Chief Wiggum. As they talk, Homer recalls his earliest years, from when he was forced from the womb, through years without a mom under the uninterested parentage of Abe, to when he first met Marge, and later adventures with the kids as a family. Finally, Marge and the kids arrive to take Homer to a surprise event. Homer is blindfolded until they arrive at their destination—the Springfield Friars Club, where Homer is to be roasted by his family, friends, and colleagues.

Krusty the Clown hosts the roast, and Homer is surprised that the event features jokes at his expense. Lisa and Bart are first up, relating some of the enjoyable shenanigans they have shared with their dad, from Christmastime hijinks to their misadventures in Japan. Mr. Burns is introduced and recalls many times when Homer's incompetence almost destroyed the town. Abe Simpson and Agnes Skinner take the podium next to provide the senior citizen perspective on Homer's misadventures. By this time, Homer has consumed far too much alcohol, prompting him to speak out angrily to the assembly, then pass out drunk.

Ned Flanders and Reverend Lovejoy's homage to a revived Homer is interrupted by the sudden appearance of space aliens Kang and Kodos, who crash their flying

SHOW HIGHLIGHTS

Homer: (Gump-ishly) *Want a chocolate?*
Chief Wiggum: *Hold it right there, Forrest Plump! This town has laws against impersonating movie characters.* (Cut to Moe, who is dressed as Austin Powers.)
Moe: *Oh, behave!*
(Officers Lou and Eddie grab Moe and stick him in a paddy wagon. Dr. Hibbert is already in the wagon dressed as Darth Vader.)
Dr. Hibbert: *Luke, I am your father. Ah hee hee hee.*
Moe: (dully) *Eh...shagadelic.*

Homer on life in the womb:
"Things started out great! I ate what my mother ate, and my mother loved chili."

Homer: *Don't you have criminals to catch?*
Wiggum: *Hey, I'm workin' on it!* (confidentially) *We, uh, we got an undercover guy who's infiltrating the mob. Oh, there he is now* (yells) *Hey, Pete! Pete! They fixed the Coke machine!*
(Pete, standing next to Fat Tony across the street, looks uncomfortable all of a sudden. Fat Tony removes his sunglasses and eyes Pete suspiciously. Pete laughs nervously.)

"Then came the day that changes every couple forever—the day we got our elephant."

Marge: *Now, before we get there, you have to put this blindfold on.*
Homer: (tying on the blindfold) *Gasp! All my other senses are getting sharper! Sniff! Sniff! Bart, you had pizza for lunch. Sniff! Lisa, you're extremely depressed.*
Lisa: (laughing nervously) *As if!*

Krusty: *Hey, Homer! Do you remember this voice?*
Homer: (blindfolded) *Kathleen Turner! Brrreow!*
Krusty: *No, it's me, Krusty!* (removes Homer's blindfold) *And you're at the Springfield Friars Club... where tonight we're roasting you...Homer Simpson!* (The audience applauds)
Homer: (frowning) *Are the proceeds going to charity?*
Krusty: *Pfft! Hell, no!*
  Homer: *Woo-hoo!*

THE STUFF YOU MAY HAVE MISSED

The sign at the roast with Homer's picture says, "Man of the Hour" and "Friars Club." The outside marquee reads, "Homer Simpson Roast Tonight" and "Milhouse Roast Tomorrow."

The Friars Club is a historic landmark in old Hollywood, where people were roasted as part of a time-honored tradition many years before Dean Martin began hosting celebrity roasts on television.

Bart puts on glasses to read the podium teleprompter.

Agnes Skinner is wearing a revealing dress similar to the controversial one Jennifer Lopez wore to the Grammy Awards in 2000.

Agnes Skinner responds to Grampa with a Phyllis Diller-like laugh. Phyllis Diller was a staple of the "Dean Martin Celebrity Roasts." Agnes also uses the laugh in "Tales from the Public Domain" (DABF08).

Kang and Kodos make a rare, non-"Treehouse of Horror" appearance in this episode.

Apparently, Kang and Kodos practice a religion very similar to Christianity.

The probe the aliens use on Maggie is a "Hello Probie" probe, which resembles a Hello Kitty product. The cat pictured on the probe, however, only has one eye.

Celebrities seen at the People's Choice Awards include Brad Pitt, Jennifer Aniston, Drew Carey, Harrison Ford, Julia Roberts, Garth Brooks, Tom Arnold, Mel Gibson, Pierce Brosnan, Bette Midler, Whitney Houston, Jason Alexander, Burt Reynolds, and Michael Jeter.

The picture of Homer on water skis, jumping over a shark, relates to the phrase "jumping the shark," which refers to a television show that has peaked and is in creative decline. The phrase originated from the time Fonzie jumped over a shark tank with his motorcycle on "Happy Days," which many fans consider the show's turning point.

Krusty: *We're all here for one reason—to keep Homer away from the buffet!*
Hibbert: *Ah hee hee hee.*
Nelson: *Haw haw!*
Mr. Burns: *Excellent!*
Homer: *Gasp! That was at my expense! What kind of roast is this?*

The montage of Homer's violent outbursts against Bart and barbeques includes clips from:

"Mom and Pop Art" (AABF15), "Like Father, Like Clown" (8F05), "Secrets of a Successful Marriage" (1F20), "Radio Bart" (8F11), "So It's Come to This: A Simpson Clip Show" (9F17), "The Parent Rap" (CABF22), "Last Tap Dance in Springfield" (BABF15), "Miracle on Evergreen Terrace" (5F07), "A Tale of Two Springfields" (BABF20), and "Children of a Lesser Clod" (CABF16).

Krusty: *Now I'd like to read some telegrams from people who couldn't make it. First, we have Mark Spitz!*
Lisa: *Who's Mark Spitz?*
Bart: *What's a telegram?*
Krusty: *Aw, forget it! I gotta get to the hot wings before the Comic Book Guy.*

Burns: *I stand here to expose the criminal ineptitude of Homer J. Simpson.*
Homer: *Gasp!*
Burns: *Again and again, he's brought this town to the brink of annihilation.*
(The audience laughs.)
Burns: *Why are you laughing? His bungling has shortened your lives and mutated your children!*
(The audience laughs harder. Kent Brockman falls over backwards in his chair.)
Burns: *Just look at all his catastrophic nincompoopery!*
Carl: (laughs) *Poop!*

46

ROAST

Episode DABF12
ORIGINAL AIRDATE: 04/21/02
WRITER: Deb Lacusta & Dan Castellaneta
DIRECTOR: Mark Kirkland
EXECUTIVE PRODUCER: Al Jean

GUEST VOICES AND APPEARANCES: Ed Asner as the Lifeways editor; Alec Baldwin, Kim Basinger, Stephen Hawking, Ron Howard, Elton John, Lucy Lawless, Joe Namath, *NSync (Lance Bass, J.C. Chasez, Joey Fatone, Chris Kirkpatrick, Justin Timberlake) as Themselves; Elizabeth Taylor as Maggie; U2 (Bono, Adam Clayton, The Edge, Larry Mullen) as Themselves.

saucer through the ceiling. They, too, have come to roast Homer, but for entirely different reasons. The aliens explain that they have been watching Earth for some time and have come to pass judgment on the planet based entirely on the actions of the epitome of the human race—Homer Simpson. After reviewing some scenes of Homer's brutish behavior, Kang and Kodos decide to obliterate the Earth. Lisa speaks up, asking the aliens to judge instead the world as seen through the innocent eyes of Maggie Simpson. Maggie's memories of the Simpsons' run-ins with celebrities intrigue Kang and Kodos, and they finally agree to leave the Earth alone if they can be invited to the People's Choice Awards and the Daytime Emmy ceremony.

Krusty: Now, here's a couple that's been dating—carbon dating! Ha ha ha! Grampa Simpson and Agnes Skinner!
(The audience applauds.)
Grampa: (to Agnes) Sweet Toledo! What's keeping that dress on?
Sideshow Mel: (from the audience) The collected will of everyone in this room!
Hibbert: Ah hee hee hee.
Nelson: Haw haw!
Burns: Excellent!
Agnes Skinner: You fruits wouldn't know what to do with me!

"I first met Homer in 1927, in a bar in Brooklyn. Little did I know he would soon become Mrs. Joe DiMaggio."

Grampa: Now, everyone knows Homer loves his family...
Homer: (belligerent and drunkenly) I'm sick of your lies! Secrets and lies! It's always secrets and lies!
Marge: Homer, these people are professional roasters. Don't give them fodder.
(Homer passes out in a compromising position, snoring loudly.)
Homer: (in his sleep)...secrets and lies...

(A spaceship crashes through the ceiling. Kang and Kodos, armed with ray guns, are beamed onto the stage.)
Kodos: Silence!
Kang: Cease all quips and comebacks!
Krusty: Look, you weren't in dress rehearsal, so you're not in the show!
(Kodos zaps Krusty with ray gun, shooting him full of electricity.)
Krusty: Yaaaaaah! This can't be good for my pacemaker.

TV Moments:
The entire episode is structured like one of the popular "Dean Martin Celebrity Roasts" that aired periodically as specials in the 1970s and 1980s.

The routine performed at the roast by Reverend Lovejoy and Ned Flanders hearkens back to Tommy and Dick Smothers' comedy bits on "The Smothers Brothers Comedy Hour."

Movie Moment:
The beginning of this episode parodies the opening moments of *Forrest Gump* (1994), when a feathers floats through the sky, landing next to Forrest Gump sitting on a park bench with a box of chocolates on his lap while waiting for a bus.

Marge: What are you doing here?
Kang: Our planet has been observing your puny species since your planet was created...five thousand years ago...by God. (Kang and Kodos cross themselves and lower their heads.)
Kodos: (mumbling) In the name of the Father, the Son, and the Holy Ghost. (to audience) And now humanity must be judged. The fate of your planet rests on one human being—Homer Simpson!
Bart: Why him?
Kodos: Because his is the fat, selfish epitome of modern man!
Moe: (checking note cards) Hey, he stole my bit!
Kang: Now we shall probe you to see if you are worthy! (Kang places a helmet on Homer's head.)
Moe: (pulling out a ramshackle probe helmet) Yep. Word for word!

Kang: Your species is brutish and primitive!
Kodos: Do you have anything to say before we obliterate your planet?
Lisa: Wait! What about Maggie's memories? Surely the innocent soul of a child will redeem mankind.
(Kang and Kodos laugh raucously.)
Kodos: (quickly) Sure, let's give it a shot.

Music Moments:
The clip-show montage song "They'll Never Stop the Simpsons" parodies Billy Joel's 1989 hit, "We Didn't Start the Fire."

When Mr. Burns is introduced at the roast, the "Imperial March (Darth Vader's Theme)," from the soundtrack of *The Empire Strikes Back* (1980) is played.

At the People's Choice Awards:
Kodos: Ooo! Burt Reynolds and Michael Jeter!
Kang: Could an "Evening Shade" reunion be in the works?
Kodos: Gasp! There's Shannen Doherty! Didn't you have a thing with her?
Kang: Don't go there!

"They'll Never Stop the Simpsons" stills and clips include:
"Simpsons Roasting on an Open Fire" (7G08), "Life on the Fast Lane" (7G11), "Oh Brother, Where Art Thou?" (7F16), "Radio Bart" (8F11), "When Flanders Failed" (7F23), "Whacking Day" (9F18), "Marge vs. the Monorail" (9F10), "Mr. Plow" (9F07), "Deep Space Homer" (1F13), "Cape Feare" (9F22), "Lisa's Wedding" (2F15), "A Fish Called Selma" (3F15), "Marge Be Not Proud" (3F07), "King-Size Homer" (3F05), "Homer's Phobia" (4F11), "The Itchy & Scratchy & Poochie Show" (4F12), "Trash of the Titans" (5F09), "The Cartridge Family" (5F01), "D'oh-in' in the Wind" (AAF02), "Viva Ned Flanders" (AABF06), "30 Minutes Over Tokyo" (AABF20), "Eight Misbehavin'" (BABF03), "New Kids on the Blecch" (CABF12), "Lard of the Dance" (5F20), "Alone Again, Natura-diddily" (BABF10), "She of Little Faith" (DABF02), "Weekend at Burnsie's" (DABF11), and "Whot Shot Mr. Burns? (Part Two)" (2F20). The sequence is framed by contrasting images of the Simpsons sitting on the couch, first as they appeared in the early shorts and then as they appear today.

D isappointed with the caliber of speakers on Career Day, Principal Skinner goes to the Springfield Speakers Bureau to find a good motivational speaker. At Lisa's urging, Skinner enlists Geoff Jenkins, a famous cartoon creator, to speak at the next school assembly. The cartoonist does little to satisfy the principal's requirements for a guest, but the students are inspired nonetheless. Afterwards, Bart tries drawing a comic himself. Impressed with his own work and sure that he could make money, Bart tries to sell his comic art to Comic Book Guy. Comic Book Guy has nothing positive to say about Bart's drawings, but comic legend Stan Lee, who has stopped by the Android's Dungeon, is very encouraging. With renewed interest, Bart goes home to think up a new character to star in his comics. After watching Homer get into a furious fight with a lawn chair outside, Bart comes up with his new cartoon creation—Angry Dad.

Angry Dad proves to be very popular. The Comic Book Guy racks Angry Dad comics in his store, and soon Bart is doing an autograph session at school. An Internet company convinces Bart to let them make a series of animated cartoons of Angry Dad for the World Wide Web. Angry Dad Internet cartoons are a hit, and Homer happens to see one on a computer at work. He is furious with Bart for humiliating him by turning him into a cartoon character and rushes home to confront him. On the way, he is accosted by fans of the cartoon, who try to drive him into a fit of rage. Homer escapes from them, and when he arrives at home, he attacks Bart. The family forces him to admit he has a problem with anger. Seeing the light, Homer denounces his raging ways and vows to stop being angry.

Homer works very hard to relax and keep his temper, despite daily annoyances that almost get the best of him. He even puts up with Ned Flanders. However, he is barely able to suppress his rage. He internalizes it, causing boils to erupt on his neck. Bart starts to get antsy because Homer is no longer providing him

SHOW HIGHLIGHTS

Principal Skinner: *Welcome to Career Day! Here to tell you about his job is Bart's friend's dad, Kirk Van Houten.*
Kirk: *How many of you children have gone out to your car and found a flyer on the windshield?*
(Cut to Kearney, Nelson, and Jimbo in the audience. Jimbo is asleep and snoring.)
Nelson: (bored) *Are you the guy that puts 'em there?*
Kirk: *No, I'm his assistant. But one time he was sick and he let me do it.* (ashamed) *I totally screwed it up.* (backing up and sitting down) *Ah, em, that-that's it.*
Skinner: *I see.* (Skinner checks his watch and approaches the podium.) *Well, we, uh, still have fifty-six minutes left. Any questions?*
(There is no response, but someone coughs.)
Milhouse: *Do you know Mom's getting remarried?*
Kirk: (upset) *What? But she...ah, um...I think we should probably talk about that later, son.*
Skinner: (looking at his watch) *No, you might as well talk about it now.*

In the principal's office:
Skinner: *That was one lousy Career Day.*
Mrs. Krabappel: *If we can't get better speakers, we'll have to go back to teaching. And I can't stare at those lifeless fish-eyes anymore!*
Lisa: *As head of the Student Activities Committee, I have an idea.*
Skinner: *I was wondering what she was doing here.*
Lisa: *The speakers are poor because we're letting just anybody do it. Groundskeeper Willie, Groundskeeper Willie's enemy Seamus...*
Skinner: *Ah, yes, Seamus. Ninety minutes of watching a man drink in a bathtub.*

Battle of the groundskeepers:
Skinner: *Seamus, uh, we won't need you to speak anymore.*
Seamus: *What?! Ah, this is your doin', Willie! I'll turn your groin ta puddin'!*
Groundskeeper Willie: *Oh, ya speak like a poet, but ya punch like one, too!*

Excerpt from "The Danger Dog Easter Special":
Mayor: *Danger Dog! Neuterville needs you!*
Danger Dog: *I hope this is important. I've got a hot date tonight—with Sarah Jessica Barker.*
Mayor: *Nice! Anyway, your archenemy, Molly Ringworm, has threatened to destroy the city with her puke-ray!*
(The mayor is struck by puke-ray that comes through the window. He vomits into a wastepaper basket.)
Danger Dog: *The mayor's barf is worse than his bite!*

The cartoonist has all the answers:
Geoff Jenkins: *Are there any questions?*
Martin: *What state does Danger Dog live in?*
Jenkins: *Michigan. Next?*
Bart: *Why does Danger Dog mean more to me than school or church?*
Jenkins: *Because those things suck.*
Kids: *Yay!*

The influence of Danger Dog:
Nelson: *I'm comin' up with my own cartoon character. He's called Danger Cat!*
Milhouse: *Mine's called Trouble Dog!*
Ralph: *I'm called Ralph!* (He draws on his face.)
Bart: *Mine is Danger Dude...but he's a dog.*

Contructive comic criticism:
Stan Lee: *Let's see what you've got, son.*
Bart: *Gasp!*
Stan Lee: (looking at Bart's comic) *My Spidey-Sense is tingling.*
Bart: *It's that good?*
Stan Lee: *Whoa! Did I say "spidey"? I meant stinky. 'Nuff said.*

Words of encouragement:
Bart: *So you're saying I should keep trying?*
Stan Lee: *Absolutely! And if you fail, you can always open a comic book store.*
Comic Book Guy: *Stan Lee insulted me! But in Bizarro World, that means he likes me!*

The classic character "Angry Dad" is born: As Homer attempts to unfold a lawn chair, he first becomes trapped, then manages to set himself on fire, saying, "Oh, I hope no one's drawing this."

Comic inspiration:
Lisa: *Bart, this is just Dad.*
Bart: *It's a composite character. Your dad, my dad, a little of Maggie's dad...*
Lisa: *No, it's just Dad.*
Bart: *Maybe Angry Dad needs a sidekick—Know-it-all Sister.*
Lisa: *Gasp! Can she have a pony? And the last line in the scene?*

"...and in a gutless act of political correctness, 'Pizza Day' will now be known as 'Italian-American Sauce Bread Day.'"

Comic Book Guy gives a rare compliment: **"Your penciling is sub-Ziggy, and the main character is off-model in every frame. However...I deem this rack-worthy."**

(YELLOW)

Episode DABF13
ORIGINAL AIRDATE: 04/28/02
WRITER: John Swartzwelder
DIRECTOR: Chuck Sheetz
EXECUTIVE PRODUCER: Al Jean
GUEST VOICES: Stan Lee as Himself

with material for Angry Dad, so he designs an elaborate trap in the backyard to guarantee that Homer will lose his temper. Bart visits the Internet company to let them know another Angry Dad adventure will be written shortly, but to Bart's dismay, the company has gone bankrupt and will no longer be producing Angry Dad cartoons. Meanwhile, Homer falls into the trap, wherein he is covered in green paint and his clothes get torn. Homer becomes so enraged, he goes on a rampage through the town. The police subdue Homer and take him to the hospital. When the family comes to visit, Dr. Hibbert informs them that Bart did a good thing for Homer by allowing him to release pent-up rage that might have overwhelmed him. In gratitude, Homer takes Bart on a fishing trip, where Bart spends his time getting Homer mad for the sake of his health.

GEOFF JENKINS
ANIMATOR

His claim to fame:
Creator of hit cartoon "Danger Dog"

His signature touch:
Abundant animated barfing

One of his "freeze-frame" moments:
The chunks of barf are actually pictures of the show's animators and their friends

His educational background:
Constant doodling during class

What his career lacks:
Hard work and buckling down

Still in the Android's Dungeon:
Stan Lee: Hold it, son. Wouldn't you rather have an exciting action figure?
Database: But only Batman fits in my Batmobile.
Stan Lee: Are you nuts? The Thing fits in there perfectly. (He starts shoving The Thing figure into the Batmobile model, breaking it.) Look, he's fitting right now.
Bart: Stan Lee came back?
Comic Book Guy: Stan Lee never left. And I'm starting to think that his mind is no longer in mint condition.
Database: (crying) Aaah-ha-ha-ha! You broke my Batmobile!
Stan Lee: Broke...or made it better?

Empty promises:
Todd Linux: Now Bart, we can't pay you salary, but we can give you stock.
Lisa: How's your company going to make money? Do you have a business model?
Linux: How many shares of stock will it take to end this conversation?
Lisa: Two million.
Linux: It is done!

Krusty checks out the competition:
Krusty: Whoa, that's funny! There's only one way my show can compete with this! (into the intercom) Book that animal that always chomps on my groin.
Assistant: (over intercom) Susan Anton?
Krusty: No, the lemur!

Worldwide celeb:
Homer: That guy's hilarious. I especially like his white shirt and blue pants. Gasp! Wait a second! Angry Dad is me!
Lenny: Yeah, didn't you know? You've been world-famous for an hour now.
Carl: You're the Internet's number-one non-porno site.
Lenny: Which makes you ten trillionth overall.

Lisa: Dad, I'm no fan of Bart's cartoon, but you have a real problem with anger.
Homer: I'm just passionate...like all us Greeks.
Marge: No, you're angry. Look, you're punching the cat right now.

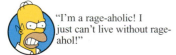
"I'm a rage-aholic! I just can't live without rage-ahol!"

THE STUFF YOU MAY HAVE MISSED

The title of this episode is a play on the movie title *I Am Curious (Yellow)* (1967), but the plots bear no resemblance.

Chuck Garabedian, the motivational speaker from "30 Minutes Over Tokyo" (AABF20), Kent Brockman, the Rich Texan, Lindsey Naegle, Dr. Joyce Brothers, Maya Angelou, and Governor Mary Bailey from "Two Cars in Every Garage and Three Eyes on Every Fish" (7F01) can be seen on the wall of photos at the Springfield Speakers Bureau.

"The Danger Dog Easter Special" has nothing to do with Easter.

Stan Lee goes through the comic shop putting Marvel comics in front of other brands. He places an X-Men comic featuring Wolverine in front of a DC Superman comic.

"The Boring World of Niels Bohr" refers to the famous Danish theoretical physicist (1885–1962). Bohr is best known for the investigations of atomic structure and also for work on radiation, which won him the 1922 Nobel Prize for physics.

Comic Book Guy racks the Angry Dad comic next to a Power Person comic. He also places the comic in front of a Bongo comic. The same comic, featuring the character Bongo from Matt Groening's weekly syndicated strip "Life in Hell" was also seen in "Worst Episode Ever" (CABF08).

The Batmobile model that Stan Lee destroys is the version designed and built by George Barris for the 1960s TV show.

Stan Lee is heard humming the theme from the 1960s Spider-Man animated series while moving comics around the comic book rack.

The Internet company that turns Angry Dad into a cyberspace animated series is named BetterThanTV.com. The company resembles a start-up Internet animation company called icebox.com, which suffered a similar demise.

In an Angry Dad cartoon, Angry Dad's newspaper's headline reads, "You Suck, Angry Dad." The cartoon is designated as a "Bartoon Presentation" in association with "Ay Carumba Entertainment."

The brand name of Homer's horse tranquilizers is "Churchill Downers." The picture on the bottle is of a horse in a nightcap, sleeping in a bed.

Homer relaxes in the bathtub: **"I gave up anger forever. From now on, I'm into candles, soft music and horse tranquilizers."**

A refreshing walk in the neighborhood:
Homer: Ah! Nothing can make me mad out here! (He walks down the street whistling.)
Paperboy: (off screen) Paper boy! (Homer is hit in stomach with a newspaper.)
Milkman: (off screen) Milkman! (Homer is hit in head with milk bottle. It bounces off and crashes to the ground)
Piano Lady: (off screen) Piano lady! (A piano lands on Homer's foot.)

"I'm not a nerd, Bart! Nerds are smart."

Homer: Homer mad! Homer smash! Get revenge on world!
Lenny: Look, it's The Incredible Hulk.
Homer: Gaaarrgh!
(Chief Wiggum, Lou, and Eddie subdue him.)
Stan Lee: (looking on) He can't be the Hulk. I'm the Hulk. Rroww. (tearing at his clothes) Rrrowwlll!
Comic Book Guy: Oh, please. You couldn't even change into Bill Bixby.

A blessing in disguise:
Marge: Bart, your prank cost ten million dollars in damages!
Bart: I know. I'm sorry.
Dr. Hibbert: Sorry for what? Saving your father's life?
Marge/Bart/Lisa: What?
Dr. Hibbert: It's true. You see, these boils on Homer's neck are pent-up rage. If Bart's trap hadn't set Homer off, the anger would have overwhelmed Homer's system.
Marge: You mean I shouldn't punish Bart at all?
Dr. Hibbert: Why, if anything, he should punish you.

I SPEND MOST OF MY TIME EATING CANDY AND GOING TO R-RATED FILMS.

ANNETTE THE SQUISHEE LADY

Her job:
Measuring syrup levels and supplying all the Kwik-E-Mart's Squishee needs

Her pleasure:
Supplying a certain Kwik-E-Mart clerk's needs

Her special talent:
Can spell "Do me" out of red licorice rope with her tongue

How to satisfy her itch:
Scratch and Win

Especially attractive to Apu because:
She has had less than eight kids

HOW'S LIFE, HANDSOME?

Homer drops by the Kwik-E-Mart to pick up a keg of beer for the annual reenactment of the Second Battle of Springfield during the Civil War. While Homer makes his purchase, Apu laments over how the romance has gone out of his marriage. Apu's wife, Manjula, will no longer allow him to touch her. Much later that day, after a rousing and chaotic Civil War reenactment, Homer returns an empty and battered beer keg to the Kwik-E-Mart. Apu is nowhere in sight, prompting Homer to investigate the unusual sounds he hears coming from the back room. To his utter shock, Homer catches a glimpse of Apu having intimate relations in the storeroom with Annette, the lady who delivers Squishee syrup.

When Marge finds out about Apu's affair, she is very upset. She talks Homer into having a chat with Apu about his infidelity. Confronted by Homer and Marge, Apu is ashamed and promises the hanky-panky with the Squishee lady will end. But the next time Annette comes into the Kwik-E-Mart, she and Apu have relations again. Manjula begins to get suspicious since Apu is no longer pressuring her for sex. She views the store's security tapes and discovers Apu's extracurricular activities. Apu is very apologetic, but Manjula forces him to leave their apartment and live somewhere else. Marge tries to get them back together by inviting them both to dinner. However, at the dinner Manjula serves Apu with divorce papers.

SHOW HIGHLIGHTS

(The octuplets wreak havoc through the Kwik-E-Mart.)
Apu: *Manjula, why did you bring the octuplets to work? This is supposed to be our special time together.*
Manjula: *Some special time! I get to stand around watching you sell fatty poisons to overfed Americans!*
Comic Book Guy: *(squirting cheese on his nachos) You'd think that would deter me, but no! (He adds chocolate-covered mini-donuts to the mound of nachos, then more cheese.)*
Apu: *Look, please. Can you just take the children home? The porno magazine buyers are too embarrassed to make their move.*

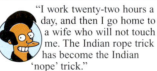

"I work twenty-two hours a day, and then I go home to a wife who will not touch me. The Indian rope trick has become the Indian 'nope' trick."

19th-century put-down:
Lisa: *Come on, guys! We're going to be late!*
Homer: *Okay, okay. Don't go Mary Todd on us.*

Movie Moment:
During the Civil War reenactment, Professor Frink arrives in his gigantic steam-powered robot spider, much like the one created by Dr. Arliss Loveless (Kenneth Branagh) in *Wild Wild West* (1999).

Seymour Skinner, serving as reenactment historian and referee:
"The 2nd Battle of Springfield was fought by the North...the South...and the East...to keep Springfield in, out of, and next to the Union, respectively. Now, the actual battle was fought over there, where that man is standing...but he won't move, so we'll do it here."

Dixie fever:
Skinner: *Oh, this battlefield is rife with inaccuracy! You dead people stop playing cards! And Stonewall Jackson, stop roller-blading!*
(Disco Stu, dressed as Stonewall Jackson, skates through the battlefield and brandishes a sword.)
Disco Stu: *The South will boogie again!*

"The Grumpiest Generation":
Tom Brokaw: *We are gathered here this Memorial Day to once again honor you World War II veterans. Truly, you are "The Greatest Generation."*
Grampa: *Keep it coming, Brokaw!*
Tom Brokaw: *A lot of your legacy is a labor of love.*
Old Jewish Man: *You're damn right it is! You can't thank us enough!*
Grampa: *Every generation stinks but ours!*

Playing badminton:
Manjula: *Oh, Apu! You keep scoring while my back is turned.*
Homer and Marge: *(grabbing at their collars) Guh-ooo!*
Manjula: *Are you sure you're not cheating?*
Homer and Marge: *(grabbing at their collars again) Guh-ooo!*
Apu: *Now, Manjula, do you want me to find another partner?*
Marge: *No, no! No, no! Let's just keep playing! (nervous laugh) What's the score?*
Homer: *Dirty love...I mean, 30-love...I mean, anyone for penis? (flustered) I'll just get the shuttlecock! Ulp!*

(Marge watches Apu and Manjula's wedding video and begins to sob.)
Homer: *Marge! Why are you crying? You're not in any physical pain—the only kind of pain a man can understand.*
Marge: *We have to do something to save that marriage. Maybe I should just tell Manjula. Or you could talk to Apu.*
Homer: *He already knows. (getting an idea) Let's tell Krusty.*
Marge: *What would that accomplish?*
Homer: *That guy's hilarious. His reaction would be priceless.*

[Moe offering drink]
Moe: *Hey, Marge! Uh, you care for a tropical drink?*
Marge: *Sure. (sniffing the drink) Is that Windex?*
Moe: *It's Windelle. I can't afford Windex.*

James Lipton: *Welcome back to "Inside the Actor's Studio." We've met Rainier Wolfcastle—actor, novelist, barbecue sauce spokesman—now, can we meet...McBain?*
Rainier: *Let me get into character. (He closes his eyes, concentrates, and when he finally speaks, he does not look or sound different at all.) Okay, I'm McBain. (The audience applauds enthusiastically. Rainier pulls out two big guns.) All right, Mendoza! I'll give you the Maxwell circuit, if you put down my daughter!*
James Lipton: *Ooo! Ha-ha! Uh...*
(Rainier fires his guns, and James Lipton falls to the floor.)
James Lipton: *(in pain) Oh! It's a pleasure eating your lead...good sir!*

Dinner disaster:
Manjula: *I know you have all gone to a lot of trouble to meddle in my affairs, but you cannot change my mind with one night of blasphemy and store-bought tandoori...or should I say, "bland"-oori?*
Marge: *Gasp!*
Apu: *Marge, please! I have known we were meant to be together ever since my mother forced me to marry you!*

Manjula meets with a divorce lawyer:
Manjula: *I have to warn you. Apu does not have very much money.*
Divorce Lawyer: *Are you absolutely sure? Because legally, I am allowed to shake him by the ankles and see what falls out. It's established in the case of "Lawyers vs. Justice." (chuckling evilly) That was a wonderful day for us.*

"The face of divorce is not as beautiful as I had hoped."

"When will you humans learn that your 'feelings,' as you call them, can stand in the way of big cash payoffs?"

APU

Episode DABF14
ORIGINAL AIRDATE: 05/05/02
WRITER: John Swartzwelder
DIRECTOR: Matthew Nastuk
EXECUTIVE PRODUCER: Al Jean
GUEST VOICES: James Lipton as Himself

As the divorce moves ahead, Manjula begins to have second thoughts. Taking Marge's advice, Manjula decides to reconcile with Apu if he completes a list of difficult tasks that she sets down. Since Apu is near suicidal with grief, he welcomes the chance at redemption. The list of tasks is difficult, but Apu attacks the challenges with relish and soon accomplishes them all. True to her word, Manjula accepts Apu back into her home and her bed. The reunion is awkward at first, and Apu and Manjula agree to take things slowly—but that night they are soon intimately reunited.

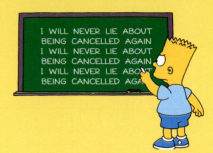

I WILL NEVER LIE ABOUT BEING CANCELLED AGAIN
I WILL NEVER LIE ABOUT BEING CANCELLED AGAIN
I WILL NEVER LIE ABOUT BEING CANCELLED AGA

The octuplets first words:

Poonam: *Mommy...*
Sashi: *will...*
Pria: *you...*
Uma: *let...*
Anoop: *Daddy...*
Sandeep: *come...*
Nabendu: *back?*
Gheet: *Cookie.*

Marge's idea of revenge is a list best served cold: **"When Homer does something wrong, I make a list of ways he can make it up to me. Then I shred the list and put it in his food."**

Bart: *Uh-ooo! This Squishee is awful!*
Apu: *I only sell Smooshies now. Squishees reminded me of my misdeeds.*
Milhouse: *My Smooshie tastes like a shopping bag!*
Lisa: (gagging) *Mine tastes like dog fur!*
Apu: *Yes, but look at the delivery man. He is hideous!*
Smooshie Delivery Man: (flirty) *Ooh, a challenge!*

Apu's Reincarnation Chart (in order of existence): **Tiger, snake, clod (picture of Alfred E. Newman), a goat with a hat, Apu, tapeworm, assistant to Lorne Michaels.**

Manjula's list of tasks for Apu:

1) Break up with squishee girl.
2) Lose weight.
3) Get cartoon published in *The New Yorker.*
4) Legally change name to 'Slime Q. Slimedog.'
5) Wear nametag that says same.
6) Fix carburetor.
7) Eat lightbulb.
8) "My Fair Lady" performed with all-octuplet cast.

Manjula: *Apu, you have completed the list. You may now move back in with your family and your never-ending disgrace.*
Homer: *Wait...wait! You forgot to eat a lightbulb.*
Apu: *Thank you very much, you big, fat blabbermouth...Sorry, sorry...it's been a rough month.*
Homer: (handing him a lightbulb) *Here ya go!* (aside) *Don't worry, I soaked it in the toilet to soften it up.*

THE STUFF YOU MAY HAVE MISSED

At the Civil War reenactment, Cletus is on the "South" side, playing "Dixie" on a banjo.

The small group of Civil War reenactors that make up the "East" are dressed in plaid and stand around the parking lot looking slightly confused.

Homer finds the word "eunuch" in the dictionary after "unique" and "unite" even though it actually starts with an "e."

On the video of Apu and Manjula's wedding, Homer is seen singing Italian-like gibberish while accompanied by Indian musicians, a previously unseen part of the wedding that took place in "The Two Mrs. Nahasapeemapetilons" (5F04).

While stalling for time at Moe's before bringing up the subject of Apu's infidelity, Homer has apparently explained several verses of "99 Bottles of Beer on the Wall" to Apu. (53 to be exact.)

A sign at the Springfield Bachelor Apartments reads, "Our Beds Are The Murphiest."

The statue out in front of the Divorce Law Specialists is of a lawyer separating a bride and a groom.

TV Moment:

Similar to Moe and Mesmerino in "The Blunder Years" (CABF21), Apu pays tribute to a Johnny Carson bit when he says, "Mmm...that's good adultery!" Coincidentally, all three characters are voiced by Hank Azaria. In another "Tonight Show" reference, Homer responds to one of Apu's jokes by saying, "Hi-yo!" à la Ed McMahon, Carson's longtime second banana.

LITTLE GIRL IN THE

Lisa is failing gym class at Springfield Elementary, so it is decided that she needs a private coach. Marge and Homer take her to see Lugash, a tough and explosive gymnastics instructor. At first she is reluctant to join the gymnastics class, but after slipping and knocking herself out, Lisa is visited in a dream by President John F. Kennedy, who explains to her the importance of physical fitness. Lisa makes new friends at the gym, a pair of college girls named Tina and Carrie. Wanting to hang out with Tina and Carrie, Lisa fibs, saying she is also in college. Meanwhile at Krusty Burger, Bart is bitten by a mosquito that came all the way from China inside a Laffy Meal prize. Bart gets sick and needs to be taken to the hospital.

Dr. Hibbert explains that Bart has a rare virus that is contagious. He must spend a week quarantined inside a plastic bubble. Bart has trouble living inside the

bubble at first, but he soon becomes comfortable with it, and even uses it to his advantage against bullies. At the same time, Lisa has started going to college and manages to fool everyone into thinking she is old enough. She really enjoys her charade, experiencing the academic life of a college student in the afternoons and hanging with the college kids at a local café in the evening, but her double life proves to be exhausting. Milhouse becomes curious about Lisa's after-elementary school activities and with Martin and Database follows her to a college classroom. When the instructor asks Milhouse and company to leave the classroom because of their age, Milhouse asks why Lisa is allowed to stay, since she is just a kid, too. Her true age revealed, Lisa is shunned by her college friends and flees the classroom in tears.

Forced back into her real world, Lisa is miserable. Her parents are mad at her

SHOW HIGHLIGHTS

Principal Skinner confers with Brunella, the gym teacher, about Lisa's failing P.E. grade: **"Are you mad, Brunella? You can't fail Lisa. She's the only child keeping this school accredited. Without her, we'd have to release these children back into the forest."**

Lisa: Who wants to put on a leotard and get screamed at?
Homer: Well, hookers and Spider-Man.

Marge: My little munchkin bumped her pumpkin.
Homer: Are you okay, Lisa?
Lisa: I'm more than okay. Ich bin ein gymnast!
Homer: Aw, she must have dreamt about Hitler again.

Grampa: Skeeter bites are good luck. Scratch it and you get a wish.
Bart: Ooh! I don't feel so good. Can you take me to the hospital?
Grampa: Finally, we're doin' somethin' I wanna do!

Lisa on the balance beam:
Coach Lugash: Just relax...think of floor as full of snakes...you fall, they kill you! Relax...relax...(Lisa composes herself by exhaling) and snakes!

Lugash: Bravo, little girl. Great progress! You deserve reward. (He pulls Snowball II from out of his sweat suit.) Here is your cat back—good as new.
Snowball II: Meow!
Lisa: Oh, thank you! Do you think I'll pass gym this term?
Lugash: Is no problem. God give you greatest gift—big head, like beach ball made of bone. Gives you perfect balance.

Music Moment:
Lisa clandestinely transforms from elementary school student to college undergrad to Henry Mancini's "The Pink Panther Theme."

Lugash: You girls were all great. Cats back for everyone!
Tina: I had a dog.
Lugash: Is cat now.

Movie Moment:
When Lisa appears in the bubble, flying through the air with the sun behind her and "Thus Spake Zarathustra" playing, we are reminded of the starchild in his womb flying through space at the end of Stanley Kubrick's masterpiece *2001: A Space Odyssey* (1968).

Homer's "Knocked Down" song:
(to the tune of "Tubthumping" by Chumbawamba)
I get knocked down, I get knocked down again,
You're never gonna knock me down!
I take a whiskey drink, I take a chocolate drink,
And when I have to pee, I use the kitchen sink!
I sing the song that reminds me I'm a urinating guy!

Dr. Hibbert: Hmm. Now you're sure you haven't been to China? There's no shame in it.
Bart: No, I told you! A mosquito came out of my Laffy Meal and bit me!
Marge: What's wrong with him, Doctor? It can't be mange. I just had him dipped.
Hibbert: Your son is exhibiting classic symptoms of Panda Virus. Here, take a look. (He hands Marge a magnifying glass. In the glass, Bart's bite looks like a pink panda bear.)
Marge: Gasp! I knew it was serious when he said he didn't want ice cream.
Bart: I did want ice cream.
Marge: Well, your father ate it all!

Hibbert: Now don't worry. These pills will take care of everything. But for a week, Bart will be highly infectious to others. Ah hee hee hee.
Bart: Contagious? Outrageous! I got me some teachers to lick!

Hibbert: While you're infectious, you will lead a normal life full of normal social interaction.
Bart: I don't like how many times you said "normal."
Hibbert: You'll be living in this bubble. It's clear plastic so the world can see how normal you are.

(Lisa is thrilled to be on a college campus.)
Tina: Lisa, where've you been?
Lisa: In heaven! (She dances away.)
Carrie: I love her! She's a total free spirit.
Tina: She'd have to be where she lives. That place had a Manson Family vibe.
Carrie: Yeah, well, I live in a dorm without a DSL line.
Tina: Freaky.

BIG TEN

Episode DABF15
ORIGINAL AIRDATE: 05/12/02
WRITER: Jon Vitti
DIRECTOR: Lauren MacMullan
EXECUTIVE PRODUCER: Al Jean
GUEST VOICES: Robert Pinsky as Himself

for running off to college each day, and her elementary school chums chide her for being smarter than they are. Lisa confides in Bart, who comes up with a plan for her to win back the friendship of the kids at school. A celebration is being held the next day to honor Principal Skinner for his many years of service. Skinner answers questions at the new parking annex dedicated to him, while standing in a white suit next to a huge chocolate cake. Bart pushes Lisa, who is in the bubble, off the top of the building that looms over the precedings. Lisa and the bubble smash into the chocolate cake, splattering icing all over Skinner and winning her the adulation of the kids at school.

THE STUFF YOU MAY HAVE MISSED

Seen in Lisa's gym class are Allison Taylor, first introduced in "Lisa's Rival" (1F17), and Francine, introduced in "Bye Bye Nerdie" (CABF11). According to Brunella's roll sheet, Francine's last name is Rhenquist, and three of the Spuckler (Delroy) children—Brittany, Tiffany, and Heather— are also in Lisa's gym class.

The sign outside of Lugash's Gym reads, "I make you star. I am Lugash."

At the Krustyco Sweatshop in China, there's a banner that reads, "Today: Force Your Daughter to Work Day."

Carrie keeps a bottle of College-Strength Tylenol in her car.

Nelson runs around an entire block so he can laugh twice at Bart in the bubble.

Lisa has a Happy Little Elf figure on her backpack.

Outside Café Kafka, there is a banner that reads, "Now with Hegel's Bagels," referring to Georg Wilhelm Friedrich Hegel (1770–1831), the German/Romantic idealist philosopher. The café is decorated with paintings of cockroaches, a nod to the plight of protagonist Gregor Samsa in Franz Kafka's "The Metamorphosis."

The roadie at Café Kafka tests the microphone by reciting a bit of the greeting card sentiment "Roses are Red" and the opening phrase of "The Waste Land" by T.S. Eliot.

Bart's "When nerds are in trouble…" oath is an altered version of the animated canine superhero Underdog's pledge. Underdog was the superheroic identity of the humble and lovable Shoeshine Boy and was voiced by Wally Cox.

To pass as a college student, Lisa removes a sticker from her bike that says, "I am an Honor Student at Springfield Elementary," and replaces it with one that says, "U.S. Out of Everywhere!"

The college class where students study Itchy & Scratchy cartoons is "Anthropology 101: Passive Analysis of Visual Iconography."

Other objects Homer has apparently used to free Bart and his bubble from the tree appear to be a hockey stick, a brick, and an oil funnel.

Ralph Wiggum, to a passed-out Lisa: **"You're like my mommy after her box of wine."**

Schoolyard semantics:
Kearney: *Give me your lunch money!*
Wendell: *But it's after lunch.*
Kearney: *It's just an expression. Like, "kick your butt" could involve no kicking whatsoever.*

Interpreting "Itchy & Scratchy":
Professor: *So what does this cartoon mean?*
Tina: *It shows how the depletion of our natural resources has pitted our small farmers against each other.*
Professor: *Yes, and birds go "tweet." What else?*

Tina: *Lisa, did you lie to us?*
Lisa: *Well, I just wanted to belong! For once I felt I was with intellectual equals.*
Carrie: *I can't believe I cheated off an eight-year-old!*
Lisa: *I guess we won't be biking through Italy! (She runs out, sobbing.)*
Carrie: *She's worse than that eighty-year-old who pretended to be a freshman.*
Hans Moleman: *I just wanted a place to sit down.*

Homer: *What the—?! You earned how many credits without our permission?*
Lisa: *Sixteen.*
Homer: *Oh!*
Marge: *College is no place for a young girl…with those quadrangles, and study carrels, and syllabi!*
Lisa: *Doogie Howser went to college when he was my age.*
Homer: *Against my wishes.*

College vs. Kitchen:
Lisa: *But the atmosphere there was so stimulating. It was a bustling marketplace of ideas.*
Marge: *Oh? And this kitchen isn't?*
Lisa: *Well…*
Marge: *I put those "Cathy"s on the fridge for you. I don't even like them. They've gotten so smutty.*

(Homer repeatedly throws a Frisbee into the branches of a tree.)
Lisa: *What are you doing?*
Homer: *I was trying to throw Bart over the roof and he got stuck in this tree.*
(The camera pans up to reveal Bart in his bubble caught in branches. Homer throws the Frisbee again and it gets stuck as well.)
Homer: *D'oh! Marge! Where's my pellet gun?*
Marge: *(from house) In the tree!*
Homer: *Right. (He starts shaking tree. The pellet gun falls out, hits ground and fires, hitting him in the rear.) Ooooow! Oh, no! Not the good cheek!*

Lisa: *Poor Bart. I know just how you feel—isolated, alone, cut off from everyone.*
Bart: *Are you kidding? This little baby has made me more popular than ever!*
(Lenny and Carl walk down the street and see Bart.)
Lenny: *Hey, Bubble Boy! Looking good!*
Carl: *Call me!*

Superintendent Chalmers: *In recognition of your twenty years as interim principal, I hereby dedicate the "Seymour Skinner Parking Annex."*
(A musical flourish is played and the audience applauds. Chalmers reveals a plaque with Skinner's profile and the words "Seymour Skinner 1953–2010" written on it.)
Principal Skinner: *Did they have to guess the date of my death?*
Chalmers: *Can't you be a team player just once?*

Skinner: *I will now take pre-approved questions from Honor Roll students.*
Agnes Skinner: *(knocking a student out of her way) I got a question! How dare you wear white? I hear what you do at night.*
Skinner: *Security!*

Skinner poses for Martin Prince, reporter for the *Daily Fourth Gradian*: **"Now, normally, I wouldn't go near a giant chocolate cake in my dress polyester, but with Bart Simpson safely encapsulated, I'd be delighted to pose."**

"Look up there! It's Lisa, and she's winning us back."

BRUNELLA POMMELHORST GYM TEACHER

Her mission:
To make sure students are physically fit or else designated as failures

Grading system:
Check plus or check minus

Her philosophy:
"Faster, higher, better!"

Has sworn an oath to:
Xena

Living proof that:
The red marker is mightier than the sword

GYM ISN'T JUST ABOUT ENCOURAGING FITNESS, IT'S ALSO ABOUT EXPOSING WEAKNESS!

FRANK NELSON-TYPE

Recognizable by:
His penchant for saying, "ee-Yesss?"

Past occupations include:
Dinner theater maître d', department store manager, South American waiter, ice cream vendor, and prison guard

Amazing ability:
Can tell how much money is in a basket by feel alone

His downsides:
Beady eyes, a creepy vibe, and a tendency to be a little too enthusiastic

His upsides:
Known to give away free ice cream, bilingual, and can tie a lovely present bow

THE GOVERNOR SAYS HE HOPES YOU'RE A TWITCHER. OH EE-YESSS!

Homer buys Marge a koi pond as an anniversary present, but the peacefulness of the meditative pond is ruined when a rare caterpillar, known as a screamapillar, moves in. The screamapillar screams constantly, and when Homer decides to stop the noise by stepping on it, he is thwarted by a scientist from the Environmental Protection Agency. The EPA scientist tells the Simpsons that the screamapillar is an endangered species and that they are legally required to protect it. The family does their best to care for the needy and vulnerable insect, but one night while reading it a story, Homer accidentally crushes the screamapillar with a book. Homer buries the dead screamapillar but is caught by the EPA scientist. Luckily, the screamapillar turns out to be alive after all; however, Homer must still go before a court for attempting to kill the insect. Homer is sentenced to 200 hours of community service. He is assigned to a Meals on Wheels program that he hates, but it appears to be much worse than he thought when an old lady shut-in advances on him with an ax.

It turns out the old lady, Mrs. Bellamy, is not trying to kill Homer. She merely uses the ax to cut her steaks. Homer and Mrs. Bellamy sit and have an enjoyable talk. Before he leaves, Mrs. Bellamy asks Homer if she can call him if she ever needs help. Homer agrees, but Mrs. Bellamy starts calling all the time, asking Homer to do things for her. Marge goes to complain to Mrs. Bellamy but soon finds herself doing chores for the old woman as well. Marge and Homer become Mrs. Bellamy's domestic

SHOW HIGHLIGHTS

Bar talk:
Lenny: If you ask me, Muhammad Ali in his prime was much better than anti-lock brakes.
Carl: Yeah, but what about Johnny Mathis vs. Diet Pepsi?
Moe: Oh, I cannot listen to this again!

The joy of koi:
Homer: Guys? I just ordered my wife the greatest anniversary present—a koi pond!
Carl: A koi pond?
Moe: Yeah, a meditative lily pond with big, beautiful fish that fry up really good.
Carl: Oh, that's the perfect gift.
Lenny: Yeah, you don't even have to feed the fish, 'cause squirrels drown in it.

Carl: You got this husband thing down, Homer.
Lenny: Yeah, you must be some kind of marriage super-genius. How about a few tips?
Homer: Certainly, Lenford. Make every day a celebration of your love. Surprise her with a pasta salad! Put a mini-beret on your wang!
Lenny: Ooh! This stuff is gold!
Carl: Happy marriage, here I come!

Endangered species:
EPA Scientist: You are now legally responsible for the safety and well-being of this screamapillar. Everything you need to know is in this pamphlet.
Lisa: "Screamapillar Care Tips." Wow! Look at all this stuff. "Without constant reassurance, it will die. It's sexually attracted to fire..."
Homer: Are you sure God doesn't want it to be dead?

"Homer Simpson, for attempted insecticide and aggravated buggery, I sentence you to 200 hours of community service!"

Homer: Meals on wheels? Eat it up, or I go to jail!
Old Jewish Man: Didn't these meals used to have a cobbler?
Homer: Uh, they discontinued the cobbler.
Old Jewish Man: You smell like cobbler!
Homer: Now, let's not get into who smells like what.

Homer: ...so I threw the super ball so hard it hit the ceiling twice, then broke a lamp!
(Homer and Mrs. Bellamy laugh.)
Mrs. Bellamy: Oh, Homer! I feel like I'm talking to Bennett Cerf!
Homer: Yeah, I've gotten a lot of compliments about my talking.

Mrs. Bellamy: Oh my, you're as strong as you are handsome!
Homer: And I can ride my bike real fast!
Mrs. Bellamy: Aren't you a wonder? Can I call you the next time I need a muscular he-man?
Homer: Hey! I'm not running an employment service, you old b—Oh-ho-ho-ho! You mean me! I'd be delighted.

Marge: I am so sick of doing her dirty work! She's taking advantage of us, Homer.
Homer: (sheepishly) The Mrs. prefers you call her Simpson.

Scare tactics:
Chief Wiggum: Well, I'd like to thank you both for cooperating with our—(accusingly) Did you do it?!?
Marge: Chief Wiggum! Homer and I are innocent!
Wiggum: I'm sorry, Marge. I can't believe I tried to trick you with such an underhanded—(accusingly) Did you do it?!?
Marge: No!
Homer: Now, if you'll excuse us, we'll just be—(accusingly) Does that ever work?!?
Wiggum: No. No, it never does.

Marge: Oh, dear! Now everyone will think Homer and I did it. The real killer is the man with the braces.
Bart: (chuckling) Yeah, if Dad killed anyone he talked about killing, would any of us be here?
Homer: You'd be dead a million times!
(The family all laughs.)

Carl: Do you really think Homer could be a killer?
Lenny: I just can't believe a man we sat and drank with all these years could do such a horrible thing!
Moe: Well, we've all got that voice inside our heads telling us to kill. You just have to drown it out! (covers ears and sings to himself) "I've been working on the railroad, all the livelong day!" Ah! Yeah, that's better.

Homer: Oh, man! What a day! I'd kill for a beer!
Barney, Lenny, and Carl: Gasp!
Moe: Gasp! Uh, right away, sir! I-I-I don't want no trouble! (Moe gives Homer a beer, placing it on the bar nervously.)
Homer: Hmm! (slyly) I'd stab somebody for a pickle. (Moe takes Lenny's pickle and gives it to Homer. Homer happily bites into the pickle.)
Homer: Give me some peanuts!
Moe: Up-bup-bup! You didn't say you'd kill me!
Homer: Sigh! I'll kill you, if you don't give me some peanuts.
Moe: H-h-here ya...here you go, mister!

At the First Church of Springfield:
Rev. Lovejoy: Today's readings come from Matthew, Mark, Luke, and John. (Homer from the pews clears throat threateningly.) Or maybe just Matthew and Mark. (Homer clears his throat again and makes a throat-cutting gesture.) Amen! (Lovejoy runs out and off-screen can be heard getting in his car and driving away.)

Otto, entrepreneurial bus driver:
"Next on the Springfield Death Tour is the home of Marge and Homer Simpson...also known as H-Diddy and his murder ho."

Brief search:
Marge: This is ridiculous! You've been through my delicates, my silkies, my dainties, and my unmentionables!
Wiggum: (holding one of Marge's bras) I insist on searching every inch of this home, personally!
Homer: (holding out his drawer) Here's my underwear drawer.
Wiggum: Where's that robot?

"I hope you're not suggesting that I would take that necklace as a bribe! Think again, dirt bag! Because I can just swipe it later from the evidence locker!"

Homer learns how to play the prison game: **"Don't worry, Marge. I'll cut us a deal by becoming a jailhouse snitch. I know who stopped up the toilet!"**

GAME

Episode DABF16
ORIGINAL AIRDATE: 05/19/02
WRITER: John Swartzwelder
DIRECTOR: Michael Polcino
EXECUTIVE PRODUCER: Al Jean
GUEST VOICES: Carmen Electra as Herself, Frances Sternhagen as Mrs. Bellamy

servants. Things go from bad to worse when Marge and Homer discover a burglar, a mysterious man with braces, stealing a necklace and leaving behind a wounded Mrs. Bellamy. When Mrs. Bellamy dies, the police are suspicious of Marge and Homer because all the evidence points to them. Soon everyone in town believes that Marge and Homer killed Mrs. Bellamy and is afraid of them. When her diamond necklace is discovered in Maggie's room, they are arrested.

The Simpson kids are placed in foster care, and Marge and Homer go on trial, are judged guilty, and sentenced to death. On death row, Homer cannot bear Marge's grief, so on the eve of the execution he confesses to acting alone in the murder so that her life will be spared. Homer's execution proceeds, and the governor refuses to pardon him. But when the prison guard throws the electric chair switch, the murder and execution are revealed to be a fabrication. It is all an elaborate hoax for a new Fox reality game show called "Frame Up." Mrs. Bellamy is not really dead. She is actually starlet Carmen Electra in disguise. Everyone is relieved, and the family is reunited. Homer makes a point to chide Carmen Electra about the terrible deception, even as he ogles her impressive bosom.

Bart and Lisa meet their foster folks:

Cletus: *Young 'uns, meet your new brother and sister. They's worth five dollars a day, county money.*
Bart: *I'm Bart and this is Lisa.*
Cletus: *Them's city names. From now on, you're Dingus Squatford, Jr. and Pamela E. Lee.*
Lisa: *But I like my old name.*
Brandine: *You hesh up, Dingus!*

Judge Snyder: *Does the defense have any closing remarks?*
Gil: *Well, eh, not at this time, your Honor.*
Judge Snyder: *This is the only time.*
Gil: *Oh well, eh, eh, then no.*

Judge Snyder: *Mr. Foreman, have you reached a verdict?*
Jury Foreman: *Verdict? Is that what we were supposed to do?*
Judge Snyder: (sputtering) *Well in all my years on the bench—*
Jury Foreman: (smiling and waving a slip of paper) *'Cause that's what we did!* (laughs)
Judge Snyder: *Oh-ho-ho-ho. You juries!* (chuckling) *You're gonna be the—*(wiping a tear away then back to business) *How do you find?*

Homer to his lawyer, Gil: **"Can't you do anything? Surprise witnesses? Evidence tampering? Play the race card! Play it!"**

Chief Wiggum with a not so encouraging word: **"Chin up, Homer. We gotta put an electrode there to ground the brain stem."**

Starstruck:

Wiggum: *So, wait a minute, wait a minute! You tied up the judicial system, costing the city millions of dollars, just for a TV show?*
Carmen Electra: *Yes!*
Wiggum: *And I'm gonna be in the show?*
Carmen Electra: *Yes!*
Wiggum: *Can Eddie and Lou have producer credits?*
Carmen Electra: *Yep!*

Movie Moment:

As Homer is led to the electric chair, he passes a big man in overalls who says, "Give me your hands, boss," much like Michael Clarke Duncan's character John Coffey did in *The Green Mile* (1999).

Homer: *Well, I'm glad everyone's all right,* (to Carmen Electra) *but I think you should be ashamed! Toying with a human life for TV ratings!*
(Homer stares at Carmen Electra's cleavage.)
Carmen Electra: *Uh, Homer, my face is up here.*
Homer: (unchanging) *I've made my choice!*

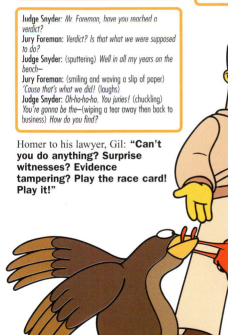

POPPA'S GOT A BRAND

An intense heat wave hits Springfield. The power plant is operating at maximum capacity and all the citizens are miserable. None more so than the Simpsons, whose tiny fan in the family room provides little comfort. Homer decides a touch of winter would help his family keep their minds off the heat, so he plugs in an electric Santa Claus. The Santa adds just enough of a power drain to cause a blackout throughout the entire city. Covered in the darkness of night, Springfield's heat-crazed citizenry go on a looting rampage, and the rule of law completely breaks down.

The next morning, Springfield is in shambles from the rioting the night before. A town meeting is quickly assembled for the citizens to express their outrage, despite the fact that they were the ones who did all the looting. Mayor Quimby patronizingly pledges to take action to ensure a more efficient police force, and the citizens leave appeased by the empty promise. At the Simpson house, Marge

is still not satisfied, nor does she feel comfortable with Chief Wiggum in charge of the police. Meanwhile, Lisa is upset because someone has stolen her Malibu Stacy collection during the looting, and Homer vows to catch the person responsible. Homer proves to be an effective detective and returns Lisa's dolls to her shortly thereafter. Prompted by a suggestion from Marge, Homer decides to start his own security company, SpringShield, and hires Lenny and Carl as officers. SpringShield proves to be such a popular police unit that Mayor Quimby fires the inept Wiggum and puts the town's security in Homer's hands.

One of Homer's first efforts as the top lawman in town is to bust an illegal ferret/French poodle operation being conducted by Fat Tony's mob. Later, over the radio, Fat Tony threatens to kill Homer if he is not out of town by noon the next day. Homer pleads with the townspeople to assist him in his impending fight against the mobsters, but everyone is too afraid. Since Lenny and Carl will

SHOW HIGHLIGHTS

At the morgue:

Dr. Hibbert: (sadly looking at bodies covered with sheets) *Ah, the old folks. It happens every heat wave.* (sternly) *Okay, people. Out of my freezer.*
(Grampa, Jasper and Old Jewish Man get up grumbling)
Grampa: *But we're hot and elderly!*
Hibbert: *I'm sorry, these are reserved for the recently deceased.*
(The old men file out, followed by Hans Moleman. Dr. Hibbert sizes him up.)
Hibbert: *Hmm. Don't you go too far. Ah hee hee hee.*

Mayor Quimby: *Gentlemen, our city's sucking down the juice like my wife at an open bar. Mr. Burns, can your plant handle it?*
Mr. Burns: *No problem. We've siphoned off extra power from the orphanage. Who are they going to complain to? Their parents?*

"Our town has dodged disaster, and I've come out smelling like guest-room soap."

After crashing into Costington's:

Lenny: *I don't hear an alarm. Let's take stuff.*
Carl: *Eh, whoa! Isn't that stealing?*
Lenny: *No! It's just looting.*
Carl: *Sweet! Let's go nuts!*

At the town hall:

Captain McCallister: *Yarr. The looters stole me glass eye.* (He pulls a sphere out of his eye socket.) *Ooo. This be a super ball.* (Then he bounces it off the floor and against the wall and catches it back in his eye socket.)
Agnes Skinner: *In my day, we had people who stood up to ruffians. We called them men!*
Sideshow Mel: *I agree with the hideous crone!*
(The townspeople agree.)
Apu: *She is ugly!*
Drederick Tatum: (with a black eye and arm in a sling) *I think I speak for myself, Comic Book Guy, and Bumblebee Man when I say I blame Chief Clancy Wiggum.*
(The townspeople agree again.)
Wiggum: *You know, it's not just my fault. You were the ones doing all the looting.*
Cletus: (dressed in a tuxedo and top hat) *Oh, sure! Blame the victims. Throw some Nikes at his head.*
Brandine: (holding up bag full of shoes) *What size?*

Marge: *I don't care what they say! I won't feel safe in this town until we have better police.*
Homer: *Pfft! Yeah! Wiggum couldn't catch cooties at Milhouse's birthday party!*
Bart: (elbowing Homer) *Dad...*
(Homer notices Milhouse sitting next to him on the couch.)
Homer: *Oh!* (to Milhouse) *Seriously, everybody says your parties rock.*

Movie Moment:

The final act of this episode is a parody of the classic Gary Cooper western, *High Noon* (1952). As a side note, *High Noon* was later remade as the science-fiction film *Outland* (1981), starring Sean Connery as a deep space marshal who wore a uniform very similar to Homer's in this episode.

Homer: (shaking Jimbo Jones) *Did you steal dolls from my daughter?*
(Lisa's dolls and doll furniture fall out of the bully's clothes.)
Jimbo: *Uh, I think they demean women.*
Homer: *Well, think again, son. You're going to Juvie!*
Jimbo: *But, I just got out of Juvie.*
Homer: *Good, 'cause I need directions.*

Music Moments:

The citizens of Springfield loot and riot to the sounds of The Lovin' Spoonful's "Summer in the City."

Homer's résumé: **"You know, I've had a lot of jobs—boxer, mascot, astronaut, imitation Krusty, baby-proofer, trucker, hippie, plow driver, food critic, conceptual artist, grease salesman, carny, mayor, grifter, bodyguard for the mayor, country-western manager, garbage commissioner, mountain climber, farmer, inventor, Smithers, Poochie, celebrity assistant, power plant worker, fortune cookie writer, beer baron, Kwik-E-Mart clerk, homophobe and missionary—but protecting Springfield...that gives me the best feeling of all."**

NEW BADGE

Episode DABF17
ORIGINAL AIRDATE: 05/22/02
WRITER: Dana Gould
DIRECTOR: Pete Michels
EXECUTIVE PRODUCER: Al Jean
GUEST VOICES: Joe Mantegna as Fat Tony

not help, Homer must face the gangsters alone. As the clock strikes noon on the designated day, Homer faces Fat Tony and some additional muscle from New Jersey. As the hoods prepare to fire on Homer, shots ring out from above, wounding and disarming the mob. Homer gives the job of top law officer back to Chief Wiggum, when he suddenly appears on the scene. Homer and Marge thank him for his rescue, but the policeman claims that he is not responsible. Wondering who saved him from certain death, Homer and Marge fail to see Maggie retreating from her bedroom window with a rifle in her hands. The couple go inside to check on the "sleeping" Maggie, unaware that she has hidden the rifle under her crib mattress.

THE STUFF YOU MAY HAVE MISSED

Students who return to Springfield Elementary to take advantage of the air conditioning include Jughead (from Archie Comics), Bill Cosby's Fat Albert, and "Happy Days" alum Arthur "Fonzie" Fonzarelli.

Settings on Groundskeeper Willie's thermal air conditioner are "Glasgow Winter," "Well-Digger's Bum" and "Witch's Teat."

The screen behind Kent Brockman reads, "Time to Panic" as he reports on the riot.

During the rioting, Otto is seen carrying the *Guernica* by Pablo Picasso down Evergreen Terrace.

When Drederick Tatum says, "I think I speak for myself, Comic Book Guy, and Bumblebee Man when I say I blame Chief Clancy Wiggum," it is a bit of an inside joke, since Hank Azaria does the voice for all those characters.

A sign in Moe's gambling den reads, "Tonight in Moe's Attic: Paul Anka!"

Johnny Tightlips was last seen in "Insane Clown Poppy" (BABF17).

Marge: *If you like protecting people, you could make that your job! You know, start a security company.*
Homer: *Gasp!* (Homer kisses Marge.) *Finally, a way to combine my love of helping people with my love of hurting people!*

Homer: *Fellas, I'm starting my own private police force. Will you join me?*
Carl: *Well, who would my partner be?*
Homer: *How about Lenny?*
Carl and Lenny: (pointing at each other) *Him? No way!*
Homer: (firmly) *You'll do as I say, or I'll have your badges...once I make and give you your badges.*

The SpringShield slogan: **"Have no fear! SpringShield's present!"**

TV Moments:

The sequence as Fat Tony and his mob drive to confront Homer, while the Alabama 3 song "Woke Up This Morning" is played, parodies the opening credits of the HBO show "The Sopranos." Furthermore, the Jersey muscle that joins Fat Tony resembles "The Sopranos" characters Christopher, Silvio and Paulie "Walnuts."

Otis, the lovable town drunk, resembles the character of Otis Campbell (as played by Hal Smith), who always found himself inside a Mayberry jail cell on "The Andy Griffith Show."

Homer's visit to the Woolly Bully hat shop, specifically the questioning of the hat salesman and the accompanying music, parodies the classic Jack Webb detective show "Dragnet."

Marge: *Homie, to honor Springfield's newest hero, I made you your favorite dinner. All three courses are dessert.*
Homer: *Even dessert?*
Marge: *Dessert is three desserts!*
(She reveals a Jell-O mold with assorted desserts suspended in it.)

Mayor Quimby, standing behind Springfield's boys in blue: **"Behind these doors are the finest cops ever to wriggle into size 46 pants!"**

Homer: *Now that I'm the law, I'm gonna make a lot of changes around here. First, I'm gonna cut overhead by freeing Otis, the lovable town drunk.*
(He unlocks the cell.)
Otis: *You can let me go, but I'll just keep exposing myself at the mall.*
Homer: (chuckling) *What a character.*

Bart: *Cool, a lie detector.* (He puts on a headband with wires attached.) *Lisa is a dork! Lisa is a dork!*
Lisa: *Dad! Make him stop!*
Homer: (looking at the printout) *Well, according to this, he's telling the truth.*

The Simpsons listen to the radio:

Bill: (on the radio) *It's Bill and Marty on the line right now with Springfield's very own Fat Tony!*
Fat Tony: (on the radio) *I wish to announce that my associates and I will gun down Homer Simpson if he has not left town by noon tomorrow.*
(The family gasps with alarm.)
Marty: *Wow! That's quite a threat! Do you have a song request?*
Fat Tony: *"Radar Love."*

Excuses, excuses:

Homer: *What about you, Dr. Hibbert?*
Hibbert: *Oh, uh, well, I'd love to help you, Homer, but I have too darn much to live for. I just discovered Thai food.*
Comic Book Guy: *I'd help you, but have yet to kiss a human girl.*
McCallister: *And I've got a TiVo full of unwatched "Dharrr-ma and Gregs."*
Barney: *Sorry, Homer. I'm a coward now, just like all recovering alcoholics.*

Fat Tony: *Is your husband at home?*
Marge: *Fat Tony, how can you do this?*
Fat Tony: *Sorry, but this is the business we've chosen.*
Marge: *But you're just perpetuating a negative Italian-American stereotype. I mean, you could be a pizza man, organ grinder, uh, leaning tower maker, and, uh...did I say pizza man?*
Fat Tony: (wiping tear away) *You are listing my broken dreams.*

Showdown on Evergreen Terrace:

Fat Tony: *Any last words, Simpson?*
Homer: *Yeah! You can kill me, but someone will take my place. And if you kill him, someone will take his place...and that's pretty much the end of it. The town'll be yours.*
Fat Tony: *All right! Let's do it!*
Louie: *Dibs on the crotch!*
Other gangsters: *Aw!*

JOHNNY TIGHTLIPS

Who he is:
A mobster who can keep his mouth shut

Where he is from:
Jersey

Demeanor:
Vague and unhelpful

Has a tendency to:
Get shot

Has a distaste for:
Pasta sauce that comes from a can

I AIN'T SAYIN' NOTHIN'.

SEASON 13

CHARACTER DESIGNS

ROUGH

LM ROMAN
TALES FROM THE PUBLIC DOMAIN
DABF08

313   ENGLISH SOLDIERS 30F5   KM

ACT III

DABF13   ACT 11
SEA CAPTAIN AS
MARIE ANTOINETTE
9·12·01   JOC

C.U. 9·21·01   SEP 18 2001

TUNK
HAS FLIP FLOP
PATTERN ON IT.

DABF02 / A
"JASPER DRESSED
KEVIN N.

DABF14 / ACT I
"BARNEY DRESSED AS U.S. GRANT"
KEVIN N.

DABF02 / ACT III
JEWISH MAN DRESSED AS WISEMAN
KEVIN N.   APR 25 2001

DABF02 / ACT III
"GRAMPA DRESSED AS WISEMAN"
KEVIN N.
APR 25 2001

DABF14 / ACT I
CARL IN UNION UNIFORM
KEVIN N.

PLEASE CHOOSE:

DABF13 ACT II
MRS. KRABAPPLE —
VOODOU PRIESTESS
·13·01   — JOE
·21·01
SEP 18 2001

·SHIRT
PATTERN

DABF04 /ACT II
"WIGGUM IN 70'S CLOTHES"
KEVIN N.
(OPTION #1)

DABF17   ACT II
MARGE IN CURL
AND MUD MASK
10·23·01   JO

DABF13 ACT III
HOMER / HULK,
STAGE 1

DIRECTORS
APPROVAL CA

RED TINGE
ON NOSE?

ENAMORED

PEEVED

ROUGH

CABF19 ACT I
LEPRECHAUN NOV 1
                — JO
DIRECTORS
APPROVAL JM   C.U. 12·2

"DABF10 /ACT 3
GIRL IN PARADE"
KEVIN N.

ROUGH
DABF07 ACT II
MR. TEENY IN
GINGHAM DRESS
+ BLONDE WIG
                — JOE
C.U. 7·13·01

DABF14 /ACT III
WART HOG (RESEMBLING HOMER)
KEVIN N.

" DABF08 /ACT I
MOE AS PIG "
KEVIN N.
DIRECTORS
APPROVAL MA

ROUGH
DABF08 ACT
OTTO AS A MINSTREL
KEVIN MOORE

DABF08 /ACT I
" CARL AS PIG "
KEVIN N.
DIRECTORS MA

DABF08 /ACT I
BARNEY AS DIONYSUS "
KEVIN N.
DIRECTORS MK
APPROVAL   JUL 17 2001

ACT I
ODYSSEUS "
(ITY OF TROY)
KEVIN N.

ACT I
ODYSSEUS
(ITY OF TROY)
KEVIN N.
JUL 19 2000

DABF08 /ACT
DEAD SOULS #
KEVIN N.

JUL 25 2000

DABF08 /ACT I
MRS. SKINNER AS HEL
KEVIN N.
DIRECTORS
APPROVAL MA

EPIS: DABF17 POPPA
SCENE #   DESCRIPTION:
SCARY MONSTER.

184

ROUGH
DABF17 ACT 2
KEVIN MOORE

HOMER

DABF08 /
CLOPS (COMIC
KE
DIRECTOR
APPROVA
JUL 17

DOROTHY LOOK FROM
"WIZARD OF OZ" (IN DRAG)

ROUGHS

DOGS ARE SIZED
IN RELATION TO
EACH OTHER.

SPANIEL
SCOTCH TERRIER
YORKSHIRE TERRIER
TUXEDO-PRINTED
T-SHIRT
RAINBOW CAPE
BOSTON TERRIER
BORZOI
STD. POODLE

DIRECTORS
APPROVAL NK

DABF05 ACT 1
FLAMBOYANT DOGS
6·5·01   -JOE/NANCY
C.U. 9-26-01
JUN -6 2001

HOMER

SEASON 14

PRODUCTION ART

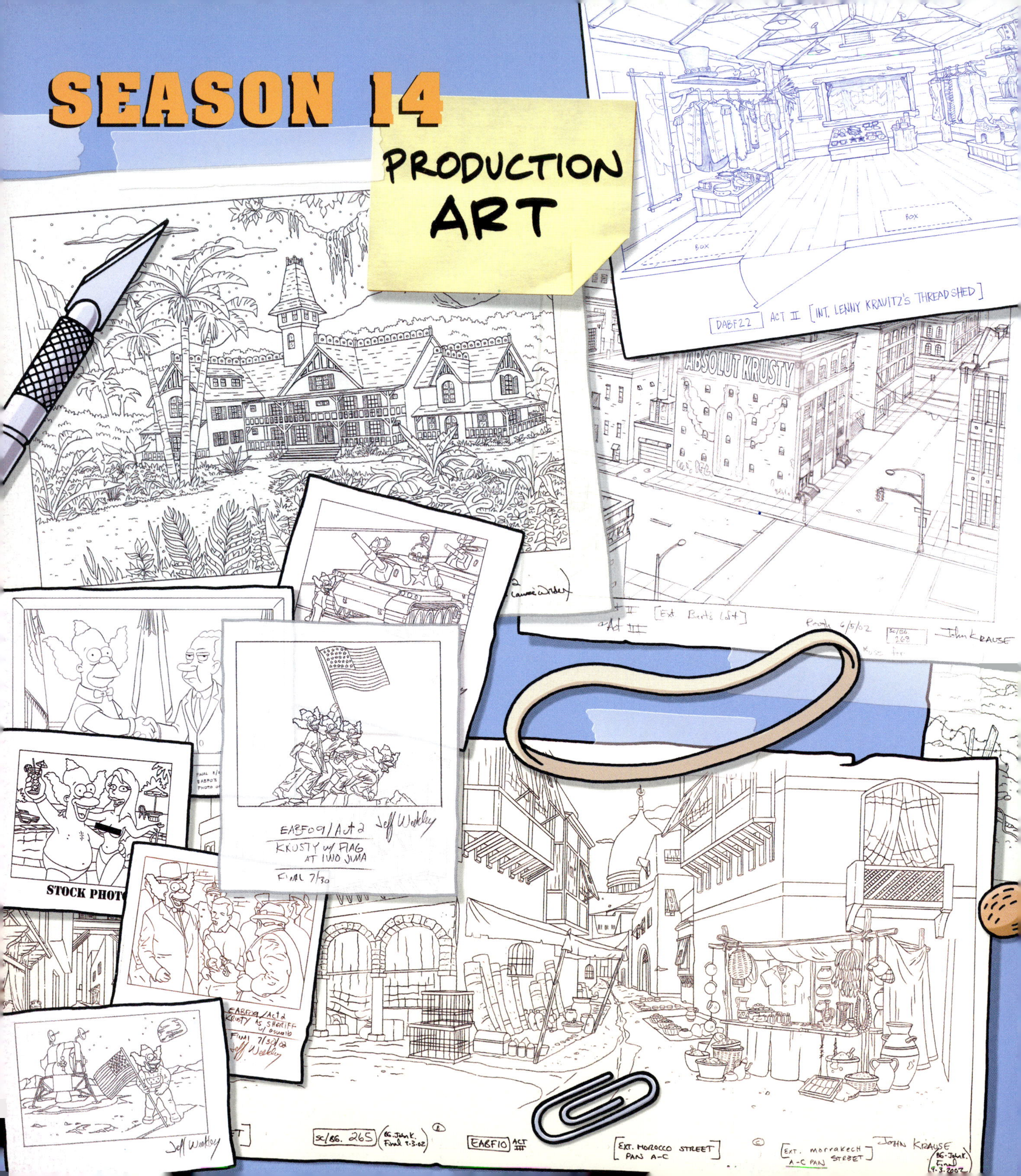

BOX
BOX
DABF22 ACT II [INT. LENNY KRAVITZ'S THREAD SHED]
ABSOLUT KRUSTY
[Ext. Bart's Loft]
Act III
John KRAUSE
EABF09 / Act 2
KRUSTY w/ FLAG AT IWO JIMA
FINAL 7/30
STOCK PHOT
EABF09 / Act 2
KRUSTY AS SHERIFF w/ oswald
FINAL 7/30/02
sc/86. 265
EABF10 ACT III
[EXT. MOROCCO STREET PAN A-C]
[EXT. marrakech A-C PAN STREET]
JOHN KRAUSE

BG: HUGH MACDONALD

EABF02] ACT I [ON IMAX SCREEN, THE GRANDIEST OF ALL CANYONS

THE ROLLING STONES' ROCK N' ROLL FANTASY CAMP

FINAL 9/10/02
EABF07 ACT 2
GRANDPA'S LARK SCOOTER
KEVIN MOORE

FINAL VERSION:
DIRECTOR HAPPY. I CAN GO HOME.
DABF22] ACT II [ENTRANCE TO "ROLLING STONES FANTASY CAMP"] BG: HUGH MAC

GRANDPA'S FLASHBACK —
WWI BATTLE FIELD   BG: HUGH MACDONALD

DABF22 ACT II [EXT. CABIN, "INDIANS CROWD THEORY"] ROUGH: HUGH MACDONALD

FINAL 12/4
EABF15 ACT 1
OCTOPUS IN PLASTIC BAG
KEVIN MOORE

EABF07 / Act III   Lisa's Dream / Greek Island Paradise
1 of 2

SEVEN SISTERS

EABF07/Act III   Lisa's Dream / Detail of Greek Island
Finalize

Opening Sequence

Marge and her family convince Ned Flanders to participate in a Halloween Night seance so that he may contact his departed wife, Maude. Ned reluctantly agrees, and when Marge begins the seance, Bart appears dressed as Maude. Everyone screams—but not at Bart. The specter of the former Mrs. Flanders appears, at first ghostlike but as she appeared in life, and then transforming into a hideous demon. The demonic Maude challenges the company to hear this episode's Halloween tales, then she pulls out a tome that is titled *The Simpsons Treehouse of Horror 13*. As the haunting theme music swells and the opening credits are displayed, we hear Homer screaming in terror.

THE STUFF YOU MAY HAVE MISSED

When originally aired, a TV13 box appeared in the left-hand corner of the screen at the same time Ned says that a seance sounds "a little PG-13."

Marge has dressed as a gypsy for the seance.

Bart's Maude wig is made from a mop.

SHOW HIGHLIGHTS

Ned: *Maude! You still look as pretty as the day I buried you.*
Homer: *Rrrrrowl!*

Demon Maude: *Are you ready for tales that will shatter your spine and boil your blood?!*
Lisa: *Well, duh.*

SEND IN THE CLONES

When Homer buys a new hammock, the peddler warns him it is evil. Soon, Homer discovers the nature of the hammock's evil—by spinning in it, he is able to clone a slightly dumber copy of himself. At first this seems like an ideal situation. Homer's first clone, however, meets an unfortunate demise. When Homer realizes he needs help moving the dead clone, he comes up with the idea of making another clone. Homer creates several clones to do all his chores and unwanted duties, such as clothes shopping with Marge, visiting Grampa at the nursing home, and playing ball with his children. In no time, Homer has created dozens of clones, but after one of them kills Ned Flanders, Homer realizes he must get rid of them. He drives them far into the country and leaves them there after shooting the ones who know how to find their way home. Unfortunately, Homer jettisons the evil hammock at the same site, and the clones soon create an army of Homer clones. The Homer horde eats everything in its path, causing the military to take action. At Lisa's suggestion, helicopters with giant donuts lure the Homers to Springfield Gorge, where they all fall to their deaths. Later, Marge discovers that the only remaining Homer is really a clone and that the original Homer is dead. Since he offers to give her a back rub, however, Marge decides to make the best of the situation.

SHOW HIGHLIGHTS

"Now to spend some quality time away from my family."

Hammock Peddler: *The price is ten dollars. But, I must warn you, this is no ordinary hammock. Its webbing is a mesh of comfort...and evil.*
Homer: *You had me at "comfort"!*

Homer breaks in the new hammock: **"Mr. Hammock, say hello to Madam Ass."**

Homer, checking out the physical attributes and endowments of his clone: **"Hmmm...no belly button... (checking below the belt) shuttle's in the hangar!"**

HORROR XIII

Episode DABF19
ORIGINAL AIRDATE: 11/03/02
WRITER: (Pt.1) Marc Wilmore, (Pt.2) Brian Kelly, (Pt.3) Kevin Curran
DIRECTOR: David Silverman
EXECUTIVE PRODUCER: Al Jean

"...then after World War II, it got kinda quiet 'til Superman challenged FDR to a race around the world. FDR beat him by a furlong! Or so the comic books would have you believe. The truth lies somewhere in between."

Clone: *Me good dad!*
Lisa: *(aside to Bart) Hmm. Does Dad seem a little dumber than usual?*
(Bart and Lisa watch Homer beat on his car with a baseball bat.)
Bart: *Me not notice.*

"Like comedy clubs in the late '80s, these ravenous clones are everywhere. They've destroyed every building in town, except for Moe's Tavern, which is reporting record business."

Fool me thrice:
Homer: *It would take three clones to beat the original Homer!*
Three Clones: *(having a thought) Hmmm!*
Homer: *(nervously) Gasp! I mean four.*
Three Clones: *Oh.*
Homer: *(runs inside) Suckers.*

Ned: *Say, Homer, I was, uh, I was wondering if I could borrow that chain saw you, uh, stole from me?*
Homer: *Yeah, but you have to leave a credit card.*

Music Moment:
Marge's decision to settle for the back-scratching Homer clone is accompanied by Stephen Stills' "Love the One Your With."

Movie Moments:
The war room setting is very similar to the one in *Dr. Strangelove (or How I Learned to Stop Worrying and Love the Bomb)* (1964), including the presence of a general who looks and sounds like George C. Scott.

The idea of making clones that happen to be slightly dumber than the original was also seen in *Multiplicity* (1996), starring Michael Keaton.

Lisa: *Dad, is there something you'd like to tell us about this horde?*
Homer: *You'd think so, but no.*
Marge: *They look like you, they were rude to Patty and Selma, and the horde has been described as very gassy.*
Homer: *Yeah, it's a good group.*

Marge: *The horde is almost dead! There's still some writhing and twitching, but that should stop by morning.*
Homer: *Good news.*
Marge: *Hmm. (They cuddle and kiss.) One handsome hubby is all I need. (She kisses him, then looks down at Homer's exposed belly.) Gasp! No belly button? You're a clone! Then the real...*
Homer/Clone: *First over cliff.*

THE STUFF YOU MAY HAVE MISSED

Four of the chores on Marge's list are "Change Floodlight," "Clean Downspouts," "Write Wedding Thank You Notes," and "Mow Lawn."

When the clones start duplicating themselves in the country, one of them fills in for a tree, hanging the hammock rope around his neck.

Included in the horde of Homers is a Homer with an extra-high forehead, a Homer with thick glasses, a Homer without a face, the morbidly obese Homer from "King-Size Homer" (3F05), Peter Griffin from the TV series "Family Guy," and Homer as he appeared in the original Simpsons shorts, who says, "Let's all go out for some frosty chocolate milkshakes."

Many clones fall into Springfield Gorge, bouncing off the cliff walls in much the same manner as Homer did in "Bart the Daredevil" (7F06).

THE FRIGHT TO CREEP AND SCARE HARMS

While burying her pet goldfish, Lisa is inspired by a hopeful anti-gun plea carved on the gravestone of a victim of gun violence, William H. Bonney, in Springfield Cemetery. She speaks out against guns and convinces the town to ban them. When Springfield is completely weapon-free, the undead William H. Bonney (a.k.a. Billy the Kid) returns along with other zombie outlaws from the Old West to take over the defenseless town. To fight back, Professor Frink creates a time machine, and Homer travels back in time to warn the town not to ban guns. Homer leads the citizens with their guns to the graveyard, where they shoot up the gravesites of the dead outlaws. The western zombies emerge from their graves and head for the hills. Suddenly, another Homer from the far distant future arrives with a warning to ban all their weapons in order to save the Earth, but Moe shoots him and uses the time machine for his own purposes.

SHOW HIGHLIGHTS

"I Dream of a World Without Guns":
Lisa: *If not for guns, poor William Bonney might have become a doctor, or a senator...*
Moe: *Or a frustrated novelist!*
(Moe holds up a transcript of his own book My Troubled Mind.)
Lisa: *(laughing nervously) Sure. The point is—let's stop the madness and ban guns now!*
(The citizens cheer in agreement.)
Rich Texan: *Yee-haw! The girl's right! (He dances and fires his guns into the air, then stops amidst the townspeople's glares.) I'm sorry. I can't live without passion.*

Lisa: *(counting guns from a box)...twenty-eight, twenty-nine...there's one missing!*
Homer: *Not Mr. Blasty! (He pulls out a pistol and tearfully caresses it.) It's okay, boy. You'll be shooting angels in Heaven. (He gives up the gun and runs off sobbing.)*

(Snake turns in his shotgun in exchange for cash.)
Chief Wiggum: *Well, well. Not so tough without your gun, are you, Snake?*
(Snake slugs him in the face.) Ow! I guess you are. (rubbing his jaw) That's what I like about this job. You learn stuff.

THE STUFF YOU MAY HAVE MISSED

Protest signs carried by people in the crowd say, "Conceal Love, Not Firearms," "Let's Murder Gun Violence" and "Fire Gil, Not Guns."

As the townspeople line up to turn in their guns, the Simpsons have three boxes of guns labeled "Homer's Guns," "Bart's Guns," and "Maggie's Guns."

The name of the "Hole-in-the-Ground Gang" is inspired by Butch Cassidy's real-life Hole-in-the-Wall Gang.

Part of Professor Frink's time machine is a mantelpiece clock.

Concealed weapons:

Chief Wiggum: (disarming himself) *Well, boys, now it's our turn.*
(Officers Lou and Eddie follow suit.)
Officer Lou: (looking at his gun) *It's always made me feel like a man, you know? Now all I've got are my enormous genitals.*

"I proudly declare our town…utterly defenseless!"

Zombie Billy the Kid, potential NRA spokesman: **"Looks like the only guns left are in my cold, dead hands!"**

Wanted—Dead or Undead:

Zombie Billy the Kid: *Now, I'd like you to meet The Hole-in-the-Ground Gang—Frank and Jesse James! The Sundance Kid!*
Comic Book Guy: *What happened to Butch Cassidy?*
Zombie Sundance: (mimicking) *"What happened to Butch Cassidy?" We're not joined at the hip, ya know!*
Zombie Billy: *And the most evil German of all time…Kaiser Wilhelm!*
(The townspeople are confused by the kaiser's inclusion.)
Zombie Frank: *He ain't no cowboy!*
Zombie Kaiser: *Sure I am! Yippee, whippee! Whippee!*
Zombie Frank: *Okay, he's in.*

"Now let's rob the bank, give the money to the poor, then rob the poor, and shoot the money!"

Bart and Lisa's saloon song:
(at gunpoint, to the tune of "Skip to My Lou")

Bart: *Calf's in the field, so you sneak up slow,
Grab 'im by the tail and go, man, go!*
Lisa: *Break into the bank and snatch that dough!*
Bart and Lisa: *Please don't hurt our family!*

Homer: (playing piano) *Marge, let me do a solo! This could be my big break!*
Marge: (playing cello) *I very much doubt that, Homer. These are horrible ghouls from the past.*
Homer: *Hey, so are the Grammy judges.*

Professor Frink: (having yanked Homer by the collar) *Pardon the grabbing, but I've perfected a device that could save us all. A time machine! We can go into the past and save our guns.*
Homer: *Gimme!* (He grabs the time machine and disappears.)
Professor Frink: *Oh, for flavin out loud, I hope he doesn't do anything to ruin the space-time continuum! That's all–* (He looks at his hand, and it is now an eggbeater.) *Oh, dear.*

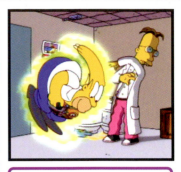

Sideshow Mel: *Another tragedy prevented by gun violence!*
Lisa: *I guess guns really are the answer.*
Far-Future Homer: (materializing) *Hear me, people of Springfield! I come from yet another distant future, where gun violence has destroyed the very Earth itself!*
Moe: *What is this, open mic night?* (He shoots Far-Future Homer and grabs the time machine.) *Ha! Now to get me some caveman hookers!* (He disappears.)

THE ISLAND OF DR. HIBBERT

The Simpsons take a vacation on The Island of Lost Souls and stay at a resort run by Dr. Hibbert, who is rumored to have gone mad. While things in the lush paradise seem somewhat normal at first, a curious Marge decides to investigate while the rest of the family sleeps. In the dark jungle, Marge is waylaid by Dr. Hibbert, who transforms her into a half-panther/half-woman creature. Homer is shocked to discover Marge has been transformed, although he does not realize it until after a night of passionate jungle sex. Homer vows to get to the bottom of Hibbert's island secret, only to discover most of Springfield has also been transformed into animal hybrids. Although his first reaction is to fight, Homer thinks about the benefits to living as an animal, and decides to let Hibbert transform him into a manimal, too.

SHOW HIGHLIGHTS

Hibbert: *Willie, help them with their bags.*
(Groundskeeper Willie enters, looking and acting dog-like.)
Willie: *Duuuh…*(Willie grabs their suitcases, as the Simpsons gasp and recoil.) *Grrrr!*
Hibbert: *Now, he may try to slobber on your crotch.*
Homer: *Hey, I've been around Scotsmen.*

Marge: *Dr. Hibbert, this is a top-notch resort! Can you recommend some activities?*
Hibbert: *Well, one activity you might enjoy is not asking questions. Ah hee hee hee hee hee hee hee.*
Lisa: *But man's inquisitive nature is what separates us from the animals.*
Hibbert: *And why must we be separated, damn it?! Think of what Shakespeare might have accomplished if he'd had the eyes of an eagle or could spray stink on his critics!*

Turkey Frink is on the menu: **"Hoy-lid! Nooo! Wait a minute now. Guess what, I'm dying. Wh-hy-hy? With the basting and the butterballing and the chestnut stuffing in my pupik! Gobble, gobble, gobble…death!"**

Marge: *Homie, something very creepy is going on here.*
Homer: *You mean they're gonna try to sell us timeshares?*
Marge: *I think I'm going to do a little sleuthing.*
Homer: *Bring back some ice!*

"Why am I always so funny when no one's around?"

Homer and Marge share a night of jungle love: **"What's up, honey? You want a little lovin'? Woo-hoo, quite a tiger, there…easy, easy! Ooh, I guess it has been a while…okay, okay! That hurts more than it tickles!"**

Jungle love:

Homer: *Isn't vacation sex always the best?*
Marge: *Growwwl-rowwwl.*
Homer: *Marge, you were like a wild beast—so voracious and prowly! And I've never seen you use your tail like that!*

TV Moment:
The Simpsons arrive on the island in much the same way guest stars did on "Fantasy Island," starring Ricardo Montalban and Hervé Villechaize. Later, a variation of the show's theme music plays as all the animals recline poolside at the end of the segment.

Homer: *I've got to find a way to change Marge back—and replace the M&Ms I took from the mini-bar.*
Ned: *Hey, Homer!*
Homer: *Flanders?! Oh, a perfect vacation ruined!*
Ned: *Hate to be a "needy Neddy," but could you do me a favor? (He reveals himself as a half-cow/half-man.) Milk me-e-e-e!*
Homer: *Uh, I really don't want to do that, Ned.*
Ned: *Aw, c'mon, Homer, all I'm askin' is for you to yank my teats and harvest my milk.*
Homer: *(exasperated) Fine! (He starts milking Flanders.)*
Ned: *Ooooo! That's nice! You're actually quite gentle when you want to be.*
Homer: *You know, you're not helping!*

THE STUFF YOU MAY HAVE MISSED

Simpsons regulars and their animal transformations: Groundskeeper Willie/shaggy dog, Professor Frink/turkey, Marge/panther, Ned Flanders/cow, Mrs. Krabappel/hyena, Jasper/ billy goat, Selma/elephant, Patty/lion, Snake/skunk, Krusty/lion, Apu and the octuplets/opossums, Lou/cheetah, Eddie/dog, Squeaky-voiced Teen/donkey, Reverend Lovejoy/coyote, Ralph Wiggum/peacock, Comic Book Guy/ram, Grampa/rooster, Mayor Quimby/panda, Sideshow Mel/lemur, Manjula/antelope, Superintendent Chalmers/bear, Hans Moleman/turtle, Moe/toad, Cletus/sloth, Otto/camel, Rich Texan/buffalo, Clancy and Sarah Wiggum/pigs, Smithers/flamingo, Luigi/guinea pig, Bart/spider, Maggie/anteater, Lisa/owl, Rainier Wolfcastle/rabbit, Captain McCallister/alligator, Dr. Nick/squirrel, Judge Snyder/hippo, Mr. Burns/fox, Bumblebee Man/bumblebee, Disco Stu/shrew, Kent Brockman/rhino, Martin Prince/sheep, Agnes and Seymour Skinner/kangaroos, Nelson/wolf, and Homer/walrus.

According to Kang and Kodos, the Rigellian number "4" is shaped like a skull.

Literary Moment:
The entire story is a take on H.G. Wells' horror fantasy *The Island of Dr. Moreau*, which has been made into several films, most recently in 1996 starring Marlon Brando and Val Kilmer.

Homer's jungle song (while riding Cow Flanders):
In the jungle,
The creepy jungle,
Homer rides a freak...

Comic Book Guy: *(as a ram) Hear me, accursed brethren! I understand that some of you are still wearing tattered pants. Please! Throw them on the bonfire and embrace your animal essence.*
Chief Wiggum: *(as a pig) Okay, but I'm keeping the tattered vest. I still have my dignity. Hey, slops! (He dives in and starts to eat.) Ooo, a toenail! Ha ha!*

"You guys are nuts! All you can do is eat and sleep and mate and roll around in you own filth and mate and eat—where do I sign up?"

Lisa: *So, how do you like being a walrus, Dad?*
Homer: *It's great! I haven't been this skinny since high school.*

ROCK STARS

What they need never do:
Apologize

What is expected of them:
Reckless and destructive conduct

What they are celebrated for:
Behavior that would land normal people in jail

What most people don't know:
They're caring, sensitive, do yard work, and have a ton of paperwork

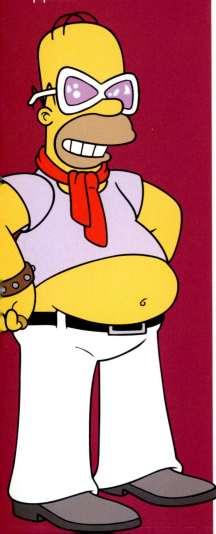

Homer does not have any money, and Moe will not give him free beer, so he looks for other ways to alter his consciousness. After breathing thin air, licking toads, and giving blood, Homer returns to Moe's quite wasted. Once there, Moe relents and gives him a free beer. Moe does not want Homer to drive in his intoxicated condition, so he puts Homer in a cab and sends him home. The next day, the Simpsons are watching a TV show called "Taxicab Conversations." Hidden cameras secretly recorded Homer during the previous night's cab ride home. On the show, he confesses that his dreams of being a rocker or *Playboy* photographer were ruined by marrying Marge and having the kids. This revelation comes as a shock to his hurt and angry family.

Just as Homer is getting off work the next day, Marge and the kids pull up and tell him to get into the car. They have packed a suitcase for him, and Homer gets increasingly worried the farther out of the town they travel. Homer's fears are unwarranted, however, when his family reveals that they have decided to send him to a rock 'n' roll fantasy camp. The camp is run by The Rolling Stones and other rock stars and features instruction in all the things you need to know to be a successful rock 'n' roll personality. The week flies by, and Homer and other

SHOW HIGHLIGHTS

Carl: *You wouldn't serve Homer just 'cause he didn't have money?*
Lenny: *(chastising) What happened to you, Moe? You used to be about the booze.*
Moe: *Uh, yeah. I guess I got caught up in all the glitz and glamour.*
(He looks down at the bar top and sees a rat chewing on a pretzel.)

Homer: *(drunkenly) I'm outta here!*
Moe: *Hey, we can't let our friend drive like this! I'm liable, here.*
(Outside of the bar, Homer staggers off-balance. Moe, Lenny, and Carl join him.)
Homer: *Ahhh...*
Moe: *Get his keys!*
(Homer plays keep away with his keys.)
Homer: *Hey, you want my keys?* (He throws the keys in sewer.) *Get 'em now, jerks.* (He laughs and gets in the car.) *So long, jerks!* (He pretends to drive away, making car sounds, then sees his friends in rearview mirror.) *Running after the car, huh? Let's see if you can follow this!* (He makes skidding noises.)
Moe: *Oh, that's it!*
(Moe, Lenny, and Carl get Homer out of his car. Moe hails a cab and puts Homer in it.)
Cab Driver: *Where to, pal?*
Homer: *Moe's Tavern!*

Lost weekday:

Homer: *Good morning, everybody!* (He kisses Marge.) *What's for breakfast, cutie?*
Marge: *Homie, it's 5 P.M. We're having dinner.*
Homer: *What? Wait a– That can't be right. Wait! Was last night the night we set the clocks ahead eight hours?*
Bart: *No, it was the night you got loaded at Moe's and the car had to be towed home.*

"Taxicab Conversations":

Cab Driver: *So, what do ya do for a living?*
Homer: *(drunk) Aw, you know, I'm a guy at a place. How'd you get such a crappy job? You a convict or a junkie?*
Cab Driver: *A little of both. You got a family?*
Homer: *Oh, yeah. A wife and two or three kids.*

Homer's drunken confession: **"One minute you're a carefree teenager, with dreams of being a rock star or a photographer for *Playboy*, then BAM! some babe gets her claws in ya, and BOOM! you got a buncha kids that always need LOVE. So WHAMMO! you get stuck in some boring job where they don't let you play guitar or take pictures of naked women, and all you can do is watch yourself get bald and fat and kiss your dreams goodbye."**

Lisa: *Have you always resented us, Dad?*
Homer: *Oh, I don't resent you, sweetheart. What I was trying to say, and maybe I didn't use the right words, was that...marriage is like a coffin, and each kid is another nail. But, as coffins go...*
Lisa: *(horrified) Please don't say any more!*

Marge: *We had a family meeting, and decided that even though what you said about us was incredibly thoughtless, and hurtful...you had a point.*
Homer: *Damn straight.*
Marge: *You work a job you don't like so I'm able to be home with the kids.*
Lisa: *And you take me places you hate, like museums, plays, and the Olive Garden.*
Bart: *And even though you knew I ratted you out to the IRS, you never busted me on it.*
Homer: *You what?*

Mick Jagger: *Welcome to Rock 'n' Roll Fantasy Camp, where you'll experience the complete rock 'n' roll lifestyle, without the lawsuits and STDs.*
Homer: *Woo! STDs!*
Keith Richards: *Now, you're all here for one reason.*
Homer: *To rock!*
Keith Richards: *(angrily) Who said that?* (Homer points at Otto.) *That's right, Otto. We're here to rock!*
Mick Jagger: *So, get a good night's sleep and remember rule #1—there are no rules!*
Campers: *Yeah!*
Mick Jagger: *Rule #2—no outside food.*

Music Moments:

The rock 'n' roll soundtrack for the episode includes: Elvis Costello's "Pump It Up," Lenny Kravitz's "Are You Gonna Go My Way," Jerry Leiber and Mike Stoller's "Hound Dog," Tom Petty's "The Last DJ," and The Rolling Stones' "Start Me Up," "She's So Cold," and "Rip This Joint."

THE STUFF YOU MAY HAVE MISSED

Homer's new favorite TV show is "MTC Monkey Trauma Center."

Although Homer does not remember anyone telling him he was going to be on TV, he drinks from a coffee cup that reads, "I Was on Taxicab Conversations."

As Homer's family takes him on a mystery trip, he becomes increasingly fearful of getting dumped at a mental institution, then a slaughterhouse, and finally at Santa's Village.

Lenny Kravitz runs the camp's "Thread Shed." Inside we see Kirk Van Houten in platform shoes, Gil in an S&M leather harness, and Homer dressed exactly like Lenny Kravitz.

Classes at The Rolling Stones camp include: "Intro to Guitar Slinging with Brian Setzer," "Lyrics Workshop with Tom Petty" and "Escape from the Limo" taught by Prof. Keith Richards.

Mick Jagger's diploma from the London School of Economics hangs in his camp office.

During his workshop, Tom Petty flips his acoustic guitar over, and there is an electric guitar on the other side of it. His hot rod also has the words "Improve Public Schools" on the driver's door.

The Springfield concert the rock stars are performing at is a benefit to support Planet Hollywood.

Standing in line outside the men's room at the benefit concert are Otto, Kirk Van Houten, Moe, Cletus, "The Simpsons" executive producer Mike Scully, and re-recording mixers R. Russell Smith and Bill Freesh.

STRUMMER VACATION

Episode DABF22; ORIGINAL AIRDATE: 11/10/02;
WRITER: Mike Scully; DIRECTOR: Mike B.
Anderson; EXECUTIVE PRODUCER: Al Jean;
GUEST VOICES: Elvis Costello, Mick Jagger,
Lenny Kravitz, Tom Petty, Keith Richards and
Brian Setzer as Themselves

campers from Springfield have a terrific time. Homer is heartbroken when camp is over and his family comes to take him home.

When Homer becomes despondent over leaving the camp, the rock stars take pity on him and invite him to join them onstage at their benefit concert in Springfield. Homer invites all his friends, but it comes as a big disappointment when he is informed by the rock stars that he is the honorary roadie and only allowed to do the preshow sound check. Deflated, Homer takes to the stage to test the equipment, but knowing his friends and family expect him to perform, he refuses to disappoint them. He sings and plays guitar, angering the rock stars. The rockers attempt to chase Homer off the stage, which results in a fiery stage prop explosion and an ensuing riot. Afterwards, the rock stars apologize to Homer for their behavior and ask him to perform with them on stage for real at another benefit. Homer politely declines, saying he would rather rock out at home with his family as his backup group.

Homer: *Are you ready...to receive professional training in rock?!*
(He slides across the cabin floor on his knees, striking a guitar chord and rock 'n' roll pose.)
Chief Wiggum: *Have you been awake all night?*
Homer: (speedily) *I am so excited, I couldn't fall asleep! I even took some pills I found on the floor, and still nothing.*
Apu: *You took pills you found on the floor?*
Homer: (speedily) *Uh-huh. Now I'm afraid that if I stop talking, I'll die. Isn't Mick cool? I thought he'd be all like, "I'm a rock star! Aren't I great?" But he's just like you, or me, or Jesus over there!* (He points to an empty corner.)

Elvis Costello: *Come on, who'd like to be a bass player?*
Homer: *Out of my way, Nerdlinger!* (Homer knocks off Elvis' hat and glasses, then jumps over the counter.)
Elvis Costello: *My image!*

Apu: *May we talk about, uh, accentuating the... (embarrassed sound) masculine area?*
Lenny Kravitz: *Did you hear that, people? Apu asked about crotch-stuffing. Now, I don't do it. Kenny Loggins does.*
(Kenny Loggins appears at the window.)
Kenny Loggins: *I trusted you!* (Kenny runs away, embarrassed and sobbing.)

TV Moment:
"Taxicab Conversations" is a spoof of the HBO reality show "Taxicab Confessions," featuring real people who are secretly videotaped while riding in the back of cabs.

Brian Setzer: *Now, a guitar has many, many nicknames. An ax, a git box...uh, I guess that's it. Anyway, we're gonna start with the fundamentals—playing a burning guitar with your teeth.*
Campers: *All right!*
Homer: *Mr. Seltzer?*
Brian Setzer: *Setzer.*
Homer: *No, I think it's Seltzer.*

Mick Jagger: *And no matter where you are, always say it's the wildest town in the whole damn world!*
Wiggum: *So when you said it in Springfield last year, you didn't mean it?*
Mick Jagger: *Yeah, sure I did. But only because Springfield really is the wildest town in the whole damn world!*
Campers: *Yeah!*
Wiggum: *I knew it! I knew it!*
Homer: *Springfield!*

Tom Petty: *Lyrics are the hardest part of song writing. But, when you come up with something meaningful and heartfelt...*
Homer: *Boring!*
Tom Petty: *Will you stop saying that?*
Homer: *But rock stars are supposed to be about drinking, and getting drunk, and boozing it up.*
Apu: *And girls that have legs and know how to use them.*
Otto: *And why I can't drive fifty-five!*
Tom Petty: *You just want mindless generic rock?*
Homer: *Precisely!*

Tom Petty's semi-mindless, semi-generic, but still meaningful and heartfelt rock song:
See that drunk girl speedin' down the street?
She's worried 'bout the state of public schools.
She likes to party, she likes to rock,
She prays that our schools don't run out of chalk!

Homer: (to Marge) *What the hell are you doing here?*
Mick Jagger: *Camp is over, Homer.*
Homer: *It's been a week already?*
Marge: *I'm glad you had fun, but it's time to come home.*
Tom Petty: *Your mother's right, Homer.* (Marge frowns.) *Gotta get back to the real world.*
Mick Jagger: *Yeah, we've all got to get home. My lawn's not gonna mow itself.*
Keith Richards: *And I've got to put up the storm windows. Winter's coming.*

Homer's roadie song:
Test...test, test, you're testin' my love for you.
Check, check, you're checkin' to see if I'm true.
Test one, test two, test three, test four!
You test me like the water in El Salvador!

"Wow, Homer, I ain't had front row seats since my Moonie wedding."

Bart: *Did you know it was gonna turn into a riot, Dad?*
Homer: *Oh, yeah. When you've been in as many as I have, you can sense them coming.*
Marge: *Did they ever find Tom Petty's toe?*
Homer: *What am I, the Lost and Found?*

Mick Jagger: *We're doing a gig tomorrow to benefit the victims of tonight's gig, and we'd consider it an honor if you'd join us.*
(Mick holds up a tour jacket that reads "Guitar Hero.")
Homer: *Well, you're very sweet, Mick, but the only rocking I want to do is in my living room chair, surrounded by the world's greatest backup group, my family.*

ired of the programs the main television networks have to offer, the Simpsons purchase a home satellite dish. With hundreds of new shows to watch, Homer and Bart are glued to the set for days. Lisa is not interested in the new channels and reminds a preoccupied Bart of the upcoming and very important school achievement test. During the test, Bart begins to hallucinate due to his excessive TV watching. Later, during an assembly, Principal Skinner announces that Lisa is going to be advanced to the third grade since she did so well on the test. Conversely, Bart does so poorly that he is sent back to the third grade. Lisa and Bart are horrified to find out they are going to be in the very same class.

Lisa has a hard time adjusting to the third grade, but Bart breezes along with the memory tricks he used to pass the first time. Lisa cannot stand that Bart succeeds by cheating, and she gets penalized for tattling on him. The third-grade teacher seems oblivious to Bart and Lisa's animosity towards one another and continually pairs them together, causing more friction. When the class goes on an overnight field trip to Capital City, things reach a boiling point. In response to a class assignment, Lisa designs a new state flag to present to the governor. Bart tampers with it, altering its slogan and embarrassing Lisa in front of the governor and the whole class.

Outside the state capital building, Lisa angrily attacks Bart. Fighting and choking each other, the Simpson siblings tumble down a hill and out of sight. The school bus leaves without them, and they soon manage to get lost in the woods. Time passes, and Bart and Lisa are neither rescued nor manage to find their way back, so they are forced to sleep in the forest. That night, Bart and Lisa

SHOW HIGHLIGHTS

Homer: *Oh, I hate reality shows!*
Marge: *A year ago, you said they were the greatest thing that ever happened to us.*
Homer: *I've grown, you haven't.*

Lisa: *Networks love reality shows because they don't have to pay writers or actors.*
Homer: *Stupid writers and actors, priced yourselves right out of the business. Nice going, geniuses.*

Homer points out a throbbing lump in his neck: **"If I wanted reality, I'd finally have this lump looked at."**

Bart: *Hey, let's get one of those home satellite dishes! Then we can stop suckling on the six network teat!*
Marge: *Get back, honky cat! Those systems are too expensive.*
Homer: *Marge, we can't pinch pennies on the machine that's going to be raising our children!*

At the Boob Tubery:
Cashier: *Okay, now all we have to do is install your satellite dish. Can you be home from 8 A.M. Monday morning through...June?*
Homer: *No problem.*

Homer: *Hey, Flanders, check out my new satellite dish!*
Ned: *(whistles) Boy, that's jim dandy roof candy! I'd love to come over sometime and watch that Church Channel.*
Homer: *I bet you would.*
Ned: *Oh, you'd win that bet. Seems like I'm spendin' all my money on religious pay-per-view, or as I like to call it, "pray-per-view."*
Homer: *Damn your sparkling wordplay!*
Ned: *And bless your humble home.*

Bart turns on the satellite TV: **"And the Lord said, 'Let there be crap.'"**

A scene from the Japanese "Friends":
Japanese Chandler: *Do you like my new shirt? It says "Reggae Hairstyle Rock 'n' Roll." Could I be more Japanese?*
Japanese Phoebe: *You are the emperor of last year!*
Japanese Chandler: *Your comeback shames me.*

Bart: *How about The Clock Channel?*
TV announcer: *Coming up on The Clock Channel...six o'clock!*
Bart: *Wait a minute. I saw this one.*

"No pressure, children, but these test results will follow you the rest of your life and beyond the grave."

The bland, informative rap of M.C. Safety and the Caution Crew:

M.C. Safety: *Yo, yo, yo! Y'all feelin' cautious?*
I say cross, walk,
A-cross-a-the-walk,
And you don't stop crossin'
'Til you're on the next block.
First you look both ways,
Then you walk, not run.
Obeyin' safety rules
Is acceptable fun.
Break it down now!
Caution Crew: *Just walk, don't run,*
Drink juice, yum-yum!

Mrs. McConnell: *Lisa, I want you to stick close to your big brother until you catch up.*
(She moves Lisa's desk next to Bart's then puts a clamp on them.)
Lisa: *Aah!*
Nelson: *Haw haw!*
Mrs. McConnell: *Young man, you're not in this class! What are you doing here?*
Nelson: *Laughin' at jerks.*

Bart's mnemonic devices:
Quiet **N**erds **B**urp **O**nly **N**ear **S**chool (The four original provinces of Canada: Quebec, New Brunswick, Ontario, Nova Scotia)
Dogs Eat Barf Solely on Wednesday, Mabel (Their principal exports)
Clowns Loves Haircuts; So Should Lee Marvin's Valet (Canada's Governors General)

Lisa: *What's this weird mark next to my A?*
Mrs. McConnell: *That's an A-minus.*
Lisa: *Minus?*
Mrs. McConnell: *(handing Bart his test) Nice work, Bart.*
Bart: *An A? Copacetic!*
Lisa: *You did better than me?*
Bart: *Nah, I took this test last year. The answer key never changes. (reciting by heart) B, C, B, C, A, A, B, B, C, C, D, False, False, True, William Jennings Bryan.*

Mrs. McConnell gives her students a tour of the capitol in Capital City: **"Now children, if you look up at the capitol dome, you'll see a mural of our state bird, the Pot-bellied Sparrow, eating our state pasta, bow-tie."**

THIRD GRADE

Episode DABF20
ORIGINAL AIRDATE: 11/17/02
WRITER: Tim Long
DIRECTOR: Steven Dean Moore
EXECUTIVE PRODUCER: Al Jean
GUEST VOICES: Tony Bennett as Himself

have a heart-to-heart talk and make peace with each other. The next morning, they awaken to find themselves surrounded by mountain folk pointing guns at them. When the mountain folk learn that Bart and Lisa have gotten lost on a field trip, they take pity on the siblings, since that is how they came to be in the woods, too. Bart and Lisa are returned to Capital City and their waiting parents. Principal Skinner, realizing that it is important to maintain the status quo, places Bart and Lisa back in their original grades.

Senate Chairman: *Order! Order! Order!* (He bangs his gavel.) *The chair recognizes the esteemed representative from Capital City.*
Bart: *The Capital City Goofball?*
Mrs. McConnell: *That's right! To win, he spent eighty million from his own pocket.*
Goofball: *Mr. Speaker, the time has come to redesign our state flag. This Confederate symbol is an embarrassment, particularly as we are a Northern state.*

Lisa's call home to Marge from Capital City: **"Well, Bart's being his usual jerky self...but, Mom, I'm really excited about this new flag design. Oh, and the hotel gives you a free *USA Today* outside your room...No, I'm sure it's free...Okay, I won't touch it."**

Bart desecrates Lisa's redesigned state flag: **"When I get through with that flag, it's gonna be a Bart-mangled banner!"**

Bart: *Ha ha! They left without you!*
Lisa: *They left without you, too, you idiot.*
Bart: *If I'm such an idiot, how come I'm the smartest kid in the 3rd grade?*
Lisa: *Because you've already done it once!*
Bart: (thinks a bit) *You've lost me.*
Lisa: *Oh, forget it!*

Lisa: *Hey, how do we get back?*
Bart: *No problem! We'll just circle around like those kids in The Blair Witch Project.* (He strides ahead and out of the frame, then suddenly appears walking up behind Lisa, disheveled and out of breath.) *I must be getting close! I recognize that girl!*

Principal Skinner: *Bart and Lisa are lost in Capital City and presumed crying.*
Marge: *My poor babies!*
Skinner: *I'm so sorry. Lisa's a very special little girl, and we'll spare no expense in finding her.*
Homer: *But what about Bart?*
Skinner: *We're looking, but, in the meantime, the Class Clown Pro Tem will take his place.*
(Milhouse enters.)
Milhouse: *Cowabunga!*

So beautiful, so fragile.

Forest confessions:

Lisa: *Bart, you're my big brother. You should act like it more often. You know, protect me from the bad things in the world.*
Bart: *As far as nerdy little sisters go, you're the coolest.*
Lisa: *Thanks, Bart.*
Bart: *And I'm sorry I sabotaged your flag.*
Lisa: *I'm sorry I got us lost out here.*
Bart: *Oh! And I'm sorry I sawed the heads off your Malibu Stacy dolls. Okay, now you go.*
Lisa: *I don't think I've done anything else.*
Bart: *Okay, I'll go again. Remember when your bike was mangled by "gypsies"?*
Lisa: *Yes?*
Bart: *Yeah, funny story. One day I was really bored, and Dad had left a steamroller idling in the driveway...*

Homer: *This is where the kids were last seen.*
Marge: *Gasp!* (picking up an object) *The plastic casing from the tip of Bart's shoelace.* (Homer looks skeptical.) *A mother knows!*
Homer: *Well, he's not gonna get very far without that!*

Lisa: *Listen, we're really sorry. We got lost on a field trip from Springfield Elementary.*
Mountain Man: (sputtering) *Lost on a field trip? Heck, why didn't you say so! That's how grandpappy wound up in these parts.*
Grandpappy: *They wuz takin' us to Capital City to see th' Nutcracker, an' I wandered away from the group, married a bear, an' I started up my family.*
Mountain Woman: *I told you, I ain't a bear!*
Grandpappy: (good-naturedly) *Roar roar roar!* (laughing) *No one understands you, she-bear!*

Skinner: *Well, if this episode has taught us anything, it's that nothing works better than the status quo. Bart, you're promoted back to the fourth grade.*
Bart: *Yaaay!*
Skinner: *And Lisa, you have a choice. You may continue to be challenged in third grade, or return to second grade and be merely a big fish in a small pond—*
Lisa: *Big fish! Big fish!*
Everyone: *Aw...*
Homer: (dreamy) *The status quo.*
(Milhouse enters.)
Milhouse: *The status quo? Ay carumba!*
Skinner: *That's just sad.*

THE STUFF YOU MAY HAVE MISSED

Marge's exclamation, "Get back, honky cat," is a lyric from the Elton John song "Honky Cat," from his album *Honky Chateau.*

Homer buys his satellite dish from The Boob Tubery.

Bart's TV hallucination features Bender the robot from "Futurama," Pikachu from "Pokémon," a crazy clown, a clock-faced man, the robots from "Robot Rumble," Tom Brokaw, and the cast of the Japanese "Friends."

M.C. Safety's bling-bling necklace is a traffic signal.

Bart's fanny pack says "Lisa's Brother" and Lisa's says "Bart's Sister."

On the school bus, Lisa is reading *Love in the Time of Coloring Books.*

On their field trip to Capital City, the class stays at the Second-Best Western Hotel.

Governor Mary Bailey beat Mr. Burns in the gubernatorial race that took place in "Two Cars in Every Garage and Three Eyes on Every Fish" (7F01).

When Principal Skinner attempts to trick Marge and Homer into waiving their right to sue, Homer mentions that he cannot be fooled because he is from the "Learn to Fart" state. "Learn to Fart" is the motto Bart puts on Lisa's flag.

AUDREY MCCONNELL 3RD GRADE TEACHER

Has high praise for:
The buddy system

Has little praise for:
Mrs. Hoover and Mrs. Krabappel

Curriculum of choice:
Logic questions and field trip homework

Does not care for:
Tattling, moaning, or sobbing

Raises students grades:
For spite

Has a tendency to join together things like:
Desks, hands, siblings, and buddies

Biggest field trip security risk:
Saying your buddy's name out loud

IF THE BUDDY SYSTEM CAN FAIL, I DON'T KNOW WHAT TO BELIEVE IN.

DR. VELIMIROVIC
PLASTIC SURGEON

His favorite procedures:
Ten-minute suck and tucks

What he discusses with nurses during surgery:
Patients' genitals size

Nasty habit:
When examining an extremely ugly patient, he whistles the sound of a bomb dropping

Where he practices:
Stomach Staples Center

Why he keeps a soldering iron handy:
To cauterize pesky te, teardruct leakage

NOW WE SEE IF YOU GO ON MY WALL OF FAME, OR MY BLOOPER REEL.

Marge worries that Homer is no longer attracted to her when she witnesses what appears to be Homer flirting with a pair of single women. She confides in Apu's wife, Manjula, who has had experience with a cheating husband. Manjula suggests that men cheat when their wives lose their figures, so Marge goes to a plastic surgeon for liposuction. Unfortunately, the plastic surgeon makes a mistake, and Marge awakens from her operation with breast implants.

The plastic surgeon tells Marge that he can remove the implants after two days, so she goes home and tries, unsuccessfully, to hide her enhanced bosom from her family. Once Homer discovers Marge's new figure, he wants to show her off. He takes the family out to dinner, where Marge receives a lot of praise from the men of Springfield. In fact, a modeling agent suggests Marge become a model for trade shows. Meanwhile, Bart and Milhouse pull a prank they learned from watching Krusty on TV. A group of concerned citizens protest the clown's antics, and soon Krusty finds himself in hot water.

Krusty is forced to clean up his TV show and to inspire kids to do positive things like learn about safety. Krusty's kinder and more instructive approach to comedy upsets his fans. Bart and Milhouse decide to help Krusty regain his credibility. They come up with a scheme to cause a riot at the Shoe Expo, wherein Krusty will save Milhouse

SHOW HIGHLIGHTS

(Homer is vigorously painting a wall at a "Domiciles for the Destitute" building project.)
Lisa: Dad, you're getting paint on your wedding ring.
Homer: Huh? Oh, right! Can you hold it? (He removes ring, and gives it to Lisa.)
Lisa: This is a Band-Aid wrapped in tin foil!
Homer: (shamefully) My real ring's inside a turtle.

Cookie Kwan, realtor, on the make: **"I could move you into a beautiful new home...mine. Sign here...sign here...kiss me here...initial there."**

Marge's politically correct sense of humor: **"That's good satire—it doesn't hurt anyone."**

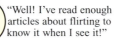

"Well! I've read enough articles about flirting to know it when I see it!"

Milhouse and Bart have a sleepover:
Milhouse: Bart, remember when I was crying at recess? I think I'm finally ready to tell you why.
Bart: (changing the subject) Let's see what's on TV.

Milhouse: Sweet Valley High! Krusty played a Batman villain?
Bart: Well, sure. He was also Uncle Velderschmoink on "Bewitched."

"Doctor, my assistant is as flat as ever. Where are the new knockers the taxpayers paid for?"

Marge reacts to her new enhancements: **"Aaagh! What on earth have you done?! My McGuppies became bazongas!"**

Marge: Accidentally giving me breast implants is not a "simple misunderstanding!" My surgery was botched!
Dr. Velimirovic: "Botched." What is that, the word of the day?
Marge: You had no right to make my bosom this ample!
Velimirovic: Look, just come back in forty-eight hours, I can remove the implants.
Marge: Oh, I'll come back all right, and I'll bring my husband to do a little malpractice on you!
Velimirovic: (sarcastically) Yes, your husband. I'm sure he's going to be furious.

Marge: Now, don't get too used to these. That awful doctor said he'd take them out in a couple of days.
Homer: Yeah, he truly is a monster. Hey! Let's go out to dinner tomorrow—just you, me the kids and the twins! What do you say?
Marge: (getting out of bed and admiring her shape in the mirror) Hmm...they do make my neck look thinner. Oh, all right, let's do it!

Lisa: Mom! What happened?! Your endowment's bigger than Harvard's.
Homer: Well, that cinches it. Lisa gets the prize for the best off-the-cuff response.
Lisa: Actually, I saw them earlier, and I was working on it in the hall.

Kiki Highsmith: (enters clapping) Kiki Highsmith, Highsmith Modeling. (She hands Marge a card and sits down.) Honey, I like your look!
Homer: Forget it, Kiki! You're not putting your brain into her body!
Kiki: That's not why I'm here. I could offer your wife a lot of modeling work. Trade shows to start, then who knows?
Homer: No dice! Take your fun and adventure outside.
Marge: Now wait, Homer!
Homer: Wait for what? Confirmation of my attitude?

Homer: Gentlemen, say hello to Springfield's newest super-model!
Lenny: You're a lucky man, Homer.
Carl: Yeah! This is the longest I've ever gone without looking at Lenny.
Marge: Don't make a fuss over me, boys. Just pour me a beer in a clean glass.
Moe: Whoa, whoa, whoa! You said "no fuss."
(Marge sits at the bar and reaches for some peanuts.)
Uh, I wouldn't eat them peanuts. They're, uh, they're spit-backs.

THE STUFF YOU MAY HAVE MISSED

As the camera pans down a cross-section of the house from Homer and Marge's bedroom to Milhouse and Bart in the family room, we see baby dinosaurs being hatched from eggs under the floorboards.

As Bart clicks through TV channels, he stops momentarily on a Frankenstein film starring Humphrey Bogart.

On the 1960s "Batman" TV show, Clownface's henchmen are Hoo, Hah, and Hee.

Joan Rivers can be seen behind the Comic Book Guy at the plastic surgery clinic with a big frozen grin on her face.

Dr. Velimirovic first appeared in "Pygmoelian" (BABF12).

The marquee at the Oven Mitt Convention reads, "If the Mitt Don't Fit, We Will Remit," a parody of Johnny Cochran's famous O.J. Simpson trial admonition: "If the glove doesn't fit, you must acquit."

In the Simpson's living room, there's a framed cover of Convention Digest magazine, featuring a picture of Marge holding a huge dog biscuit; and a framed oven mitt award that reads, "Presenter of the Month."

The peeping Toms in the window ogling Marge are Barney, Moe, Bill Clinton, Surly (one of the Seven Duffs), Groundskeeper Willie, Comic Book Guy, and Jasper.

Booths seen at the Shoe Expo are "Fat Tony's Cement Shoes—The Last Shoes You'll Ever Need)," "Shoes for Jesus," "Drederick Tatum Footwear," "Global Shoehorn," "Let's Make a Heel," "Assassins" [featured in "Bart's Dog Gets an F" (7F14)], and "The Keds Are All Right."

Stampy, the elephant that is endorsing shoelaces at the Shoe Expo, was first seen in "Bart Gets an Elephant" (1F15).

MARGE

Episode DABF18
ORIGINAL AIRDATE: 11/24/02
WRITER: Ian Maxtone-Graham
DIRECTOR: Jim Reardon
EXECUTIVE PRODUCER: Al Jean

GUEST VOICES: Baha Men (Patrick Carey, Omerit Hield, Marvin Prosper) as Themselves, Jan Hooks as Manjula, Burt Ward as Robin, and Adam West as Batman

from a marauding elephant (actually Bart's former pet elephant Stampy). Once the plan is set in motion, things go awry. Krusty cannot remember the elephant's safety word, and the pachyderm threatens Milhouse, Bart, and Homer's lives. Marge, now a popular trade show model who happens to be working at the same show, distracts the police from shooting the elephant by exposing her breasts. Inspired by the sight of Marge's ample bosom, Krusty remembers the safety word and saves the day. His reputation is restored. Marge returns to the plastic surgery clinic, reversing the operation, and Homer assures her that he is still very much attracted to her.

TV Moment:
Bart and Milhouse watch an episode of the 1960s "Batman" featuring Krusty the Clown as the painted Pagliacci of perfidy...Clownface. In dynamic dual cameos, Adam West and Burt Ward are reunited and reprise their roles as Batman and Robin.

Music Moment:
The Baha Men have a little fun with their hit song "Who Let the Dogs Out?" by singing two alternative versions: "Who Left the Milk Out?" on Marge's car radio and "Who Let Her Jugs Out?" over the end credits.

Krusty's new approach to entertainment:
Sideshow Mel: So, Krusty, are you ready to shoot this apple off my head?
Krusty: Well, if by "shoot" you mean "teach," and by "my head" you mean "safety"...then yes!
(Bart and Milhouse watch at home.)
Bart: Oh man, now they won't let Krusty do anything fun!
Milhouse: Teletubbies get away with more than this!

Bart: Hey, we got Krusty into this, we'll get him out! We just have to make him a hero again.
Milhouse: Maybe if we cut his foot off, people will feel sorry for him.
Bart: It didn't help your dad get your mom back.

In the Springfield Friars Club sauna:
Bart: Hey, Krusty.
Krusty: How'd you get in here?
Bart: The doorman died.
Krusty: Oh, no! He was my agent!
Bart: Listen, I have a plan that will make the world fall in love with Krusty the Clown again!
Krusty: It's too late. I've given up.
Bart: The Krusty I know didn't get where he is by giving up.
Krusty: No, I got where I am by naming names in the '50s.

Pachyderm performance:
Bart: Okay, here's the drill: a rogue elephant, played by my old friend Stampy, is about to crush sweet, young Milhouse. Then you run up and save the day by saying Stampy's safety word, "Mogumbo!"
(Upon hearing the word, Stampy drops and rolls playfully onto his side.)
Krusty: Whoa! He's as big as Brando, but he takes direction!

Chief Wiggum: Aim for the big hose coming out of his face!
Lou: You mean his trunk?
Wiggum: Easy there, college boy.

Marge saves the day, by dropping her dress straps: **"Hey, cops! Check out this all-points bulletin!"**

Short Film Moment:
As former U.S. presidents Jimmy Carter, George Bush and Bill Clinton fight and squabble while building a house, they emulate the antics of The Three Stooges—Larry, Moe and Curly—in one of their several short films, *The Sitter-Downers* (1937).

"I came out of the elephant's mouth, right? 'Cause I already showered once today."

Marge: You're the only man I want ogling me.
Homer: Oh, we're going to do a little more than just ogling.
Marge: Oh, Homie.
Homer: Let's go get fried chicken!

A s compensation for getting hurt at work, Homer is given skybox seats for a hockey game. While the rest of the family enjoys the plush accommodations of their skybox, such as portrait painting, a hot tub, a masseuse, and sushi, Lisa watches the game with the regular fans. After she yells a suggestion to a Russian hockey player and he scores a goal, the player gives a delighted Lisa his hockey stick. Later that night at home, rare Russian termites eat their way out of the hockey stick and begin to rapidly devour the Simpsons' house. An exterminator is called in, and he informs them that their house must undergo fumigation for six months.

The Simpsons have a hard time finding a place to stay—all the motel rooms are booked, and living with friends proves to be very uncomfortable. They decide to

participate in a new reality TV show, living for free in an old Victorian house as people did in 1895, while being constantly monitored. Homer and his family find the going tough at first, but soon settle into their nineteenth-century lifestyle. In fact, they get so accustomed to their living conditions, their TV audience gets bored and the ratings slip. To pick things up, the network adds a "new" member to the family—Squiggy from the 1970s TV sitcom "Laverne and Shirley," but his addition does little to improve ratings. After watching other TV shows for inspiration, the producers come up with a new strategy to attract viewers. While the Simpsons sleep late at night, a helicopter picks up their house, and whisks it away.

The family awakens the next morning to find their house floating rapidly down

SHOW HIGHLIGHTS

Marge: *Can't beat a skybox! All the excitement of being in the sky, with the security of being in a box.*
Bart: *Oh-ho-ho! This is gonna be the coolest basketball game ever!*
Lisa: *Actually, it says here we're gonna see hockey.*
Homer, Marge and Bart: *Noooo!*

Moe tries to build a human ladder to the skybox seats: **"Otto! What are you waitin' for? Get your ass on my neck!"**

Lisa: *This is a joke. You'll find me down with the real fans, standing ankle-deep in beer and blood.*
Homer: *Fine, watch your stupid Eagles concert.*
Lisa: *It's a hockey game!*
Homer: *Whatever.*

"Well, cock-a-diddily-doo! What a Marge-alicious way to start my Flander-rific day."

Exterminator: *These are no ordinary termites. What you got here are Russian No-wood-niks.*
Marge: *Can you save our house?*
Exterminator: *Okay, but, in order to kill these bugs, I've got to live like a bug, think like a bug, become a bug!*
(He gets on his hands and knees and starts gnawing on the coffee table.)
Marge: *(to Homer) Why do you always hire the cheapest guy?*
Homer: *(referring to the "A Bug's Death" logo on the exterminator's van) I go by how funny the sign is.*

Homer: *I know. We'll stay with my very best friend in the whole world...Lenny.*
(The Simpsons are now at Lenny's front door. They ring the buzzer.)
Lenny: *Hey, Simpsons!*
Homer: *That's Lenny?! Oh, I wanted the black one!*

Barney: *You know, I heard of a new reality show where they let you live in a home for free.*
Carl: *Oh yeah. The gimmick is, it's a house from 1895, and you gotta do everything like they did back then.*
Homer: *1895? Forget it! We'd be too late to save Lincoln and too early to save Kennedy.*
Moe: *You could save McKinley.*
Homer: *It's not a time machine, Moe.*

At The Reality Channel:
Female Executive: *Well, this family looks pretty interesting.*
Mitch Hartwell: *But isn't the dad Bill Cosby?*
Bill Cosby: *Ya see, I gotta get back on the TV, 'cause with the Osbournes and the soft-core porns, and the dogs poopin' and nobody scoopin', and the vee-tha-vul hah-hah hah!*
Female Executive: *We need a family that hasn't been on TV forever. Let's try the Simpsons!*

Music Moment:
Scenes in the 1895 house are introduced with a rendition of Scott Joplin's ragtime classic "The Entertainer."

THE STUFF YOU MAY HAVE MISSED

The Simpsons watch a hockey game at the Gee Your Hair Smells Terrific Arena.

While the Simpsons enter the arena through the red-carpeted Skybox Entrance, everyone else enters through the Shnook Entrance.

The cologne containing ground-up whale spritzed on Homer by a skybox attendant is called "Blowhole."

In the skybox, Bart gets a shave from Jake the Barber, first seen cutting Homer's newly grown hair in "Simpson and Delilah" (7F02).

The Springfield professional hockey team is named the Ice-O-Topes. They are playing the Shelbyville Visitors.

The logo for A Bug's Death Exterminators looks very similar to the logo for the Disney/Pixar CGI-animated film *A Bug's Life* (1998).

The "King of the Hill" sequence features Homer drinking a beer as sanitation workers pick up the garbage, a telephone repairman goes up and down a telephone pole, Grampa drags an old couch over to where the trash cans are, Kirk Van Houten stops his truck and loads the old couch, Patty and Selma change a flat tire on their car, Ned Flanders passes by on his tractor-mower, Santa's Little Helper enters, and Milhouse rides circles on his bike around the dog several times before riding away.

Comic Book Guy refers to the Simpsons as "Our Favorite Family"—a common appellation for "The Simpsons" coined by fans and online aficionados.

Other shows that are produced for The Reality Channel besides "The 1895 Challenge" include: "Sucker Punch," "Mystery Injection" and "Tied to a Bear."

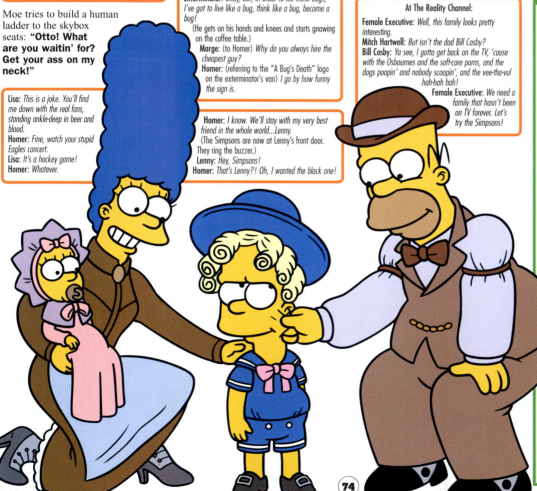

SHELTER

Episode DABF21
ORIGINAL AIRDATE: 12/01/02
WRITERS: Brian Pollack & Mert Rich
DIRECTOR: Mark Kirkland
EXECUTIVE PRODUCER: Al Jean
GUEST VOICES: Larry Holmes as Himself, David Lander as Himself

the Amazon. Realizing the producers have turned their show into a survival contest, the Simpsons flee to safety just before their house is destroyed. They are stranded in the middle of nowhere, and the producer and camera crew will not share food with them. While foraging for food, the Simpsons meet forgotten outcasts from another reality series. They join these outcasts in overpowering the TV crew and seizing their helicopter. Once back in their now termite-free home, the Simpsons try to return to a normal life, but they soon determine that the plethora of reality-based programming and poorly scripted dramas make TV unwatchable.

Mitch: *Welcome to your home for the next six months.*
Bart: *Oh, man, I can't wear this. I look like Buster Brown...whoever that is.*
Homer: *Oh-ho-ho, you look adorable (Homer pinches his cheek)...Lisa.*
Marge: *Your school chums are going to be so jealous of your little outfit.*
(Outside the window, the bullies look inside. Jimbo punches a fist into his other hand.)
Jimbo: *God, I wish I had that little outfit.*
Kearney: *Yeah, those golden curls are to die for.*

Homer: *Wow! They had an army helmet under every bed? (He puts the pot on his head.)*
Mitch: *Mr. Simpson? That's a chamber pot. You're supposed to go to the bathroom in it.*
Homer: *Befoul an army helmet? You'd like that, wouldn't you? Hippie!*

Mitch: *Behind this door, you'll find the one piece of twentieth-century technology in the whole house.*
Marge: *Oh! Please be a melon baller, please be a melon baller!*
Mitch: *(opens door to reveal closet with camera and stool inside) This is your video confessional. You come in here to express your deepest feelings and darkest secrets.*
(Marge rushes in and closes the door.)
Marge: *(to camera) Uh...(laughing nervously) my hair isn't really blue. (looking around) Gasp! (She reaches for the camera.) I need that tape!*

TV Moments:

The opening credits of fellow Fox animated program "King of the Hill" are lampooned as the Simpsons stand still outside of their tented home and life moves around them in time-lapse photography.

Several reality shows are spoofed during the episode, including "Survivor" and "The Surreal Life," but the main inspiration for the "The 1895 Challenge" is the UK mini-series "The 1900 House."

"Law & Order: Elevator Inspector Unit" is a friendly poke at the popular NBC franchise. When this episode aired, there were only three "Law & Order" shows, there have since been four.

Bart: *Good morning, ladies!*
(Lisa and Marge are exhausted and covered in flour.)
Lisa: *What's so good about it?*
Marge: *It takes six hours to make breakfast now.*

Shopping at the General Kwik-E-Mart:

Apu: *By orders of The Reality Channel, I must make sure you only buy items available in 1895! Oreos? Sorry, these are from 1896. Non-scarring toilet paper? Ho! Dream on! Urkel O's. Delicious, but forbidden.*
Marge: *I'll just take these tampons.*
Apu: *(looking through an 1895 Almanac) I don't believe they had those in 1895.*
Marge: *Yes they did! Look closer! (Marge slams almanac on Apu's face) Twenty-three skidoo! (She exits.)*

Homer tries some old-fashioned "dirty talk" on Marge: **"You know, it's 6:15, and Maggie's in her cage. Maybe I could wuther your heights."**

In the confessional:

Bart: *This has been the worst week of my life! I miss my toys, my video games. (He holds up newspaper funnies to the video camera) "Mutt and Jeff" comics are not funny! They're gay. I get it!*
(There is a knock at the door.)
Homer: *(from outside) You've been in there over an hour, boy! Other people have to confess, too, ya know! Oh! I can't hold it in...I hate this house!*

Lisa: *Huh. Bread tastes like clothes.*
Bart: *I'm so cold.*
Marge: *All of you stink so much!*
(The camera pulls back to reveal the residents at the Springfield Retirement Castle watching the Simpsons on TV.)
Old Jewish Man: *This is great television.*
Grampa: *Yeah! I can't wait to see which one of 'em dies first!*

"Look, we can't give up! We're on TV! And when you're on TV, you dig in your claws and you never let go...just like Bill Moyers!"

The Simpsons and Squiggy eat dinner:

Lisa: *Why is the guy from "Laverne and Shirley" living in our house?*
David Lander (Squiggy): *'Cause nobody's watching you clowns! If you was to ask me, you're all too calm and happy. The essence of drama is conflict. That's why they gave me this taser.*
(He shocks Homer with the taser.)

Red seal of approval:

Homer: *You monsters! You turned this show into a "Survivor" clone!*
Mitch: *Mr. Simpson, your contract allows us to do anything we want to you.*
Homer: *I would never sign that, unless there was a red sticker that says "Sign Here"!*
Mitch: *Uh-huh. That's what we used.*
Homer: *Where do you get those things, anyway?*

Homer: *I can't remember the last time I cried like this!*
Lisa: *When you put your T-shirt on backwards?*
Homer: *(breaking down) Aaah-ha-ha-ha-oh, yes! The tag chafed my throat!*

Homer: *TV was the one good thing in my life, and now I can't enjoy it anymore!*
Marge: *I guess we'll have to find a new way to entertain ourselves.*
Lisa: *What about books?*
Marge: *Yeah! If we read books, we could form a club.*
Homer: *If we formed a club, we can serve drinks!*
Bart: *Hey, Dad! Why don't we watch you drink from a hose?*
Homer: *Good idea, Lisa!*

**MITCH HARTWELL
THE REALITY
CHANNEL PRODUCER**

Creator of:
"The 1895 Challenge"

Where he got the idea for the show:
He saw it on Dutch television and tweaked the title

How he adds excitement to his show:
By bringing in the biggest, most famous star from a 1970s sitcom whose phone hasn't been disconnected

His idea of original thinking:
Flipping through other TV channels

What really puzzles him:
Why it's so hard to get cocktail sauce in the Amazon

I HAVE AN IDEA. IT'S CRAZY, BUT IT JUST MIGHT WORK...LIKE IT DID LAST WEEK...ON ANOTHER SHOW.

THE GREAT

JUNIOR (A.K.A. FRANK GRIMES, JR.)

Murderous son of:
Frank Grimes (a.k.a. Homer's Enemy)

His pastimes include:
Repairing cars and plotting revenge on Homer

His secret shame:
Came to be because his father happened to like hookers

Special abilities:
Tuning parade float engines to whisper-quietness and running on stilts

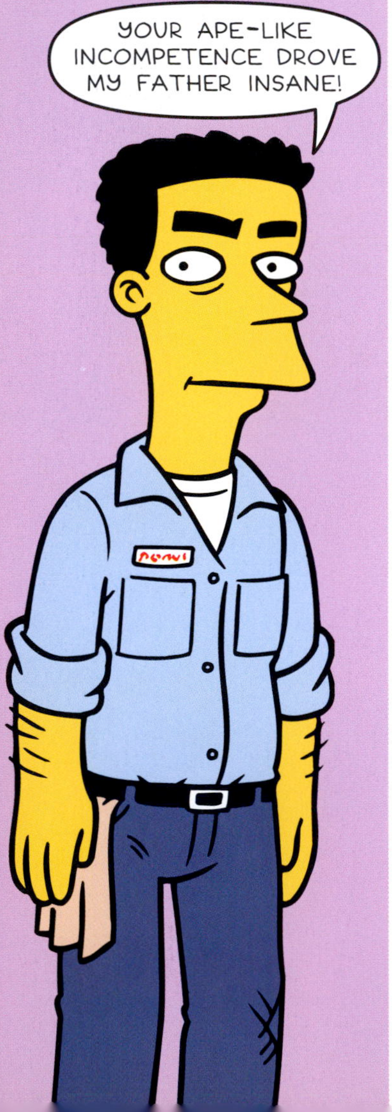
YOUR APE-LIKE INCOMPETENCE DROVE MY FATHER INSANE!

The Simpsons take advantage of a surprise mail offer to spend a free weekend at a spa-resort in the desert. While the whole family takes advantage of the spa's amenities, Homer spends time in the steam room. Soon, a mysterious figure outside turns up the temperature and braces the steam room door shut. The extreme heat quickly overcomes Homer. Luckily, Krusty happens by and frees him. Realizing someone is trying to kill Homer, the Simpsons go to the police for help. Chief Wiggum suggests they enlist the aid of Sideshow Bob to catch the culprit.

Bob agrees to help—provided he can have 24-hour-a-day access to the Simpson family. Homer and Marge agree, despite Bart's misgivings, and Bob is released to the Simpsons and manacled with a shock garter. With Bob on the case, the Simpsons return to their normal lifestyle. There are several possible suspects, but the Simpsons are sure that none of them want Homer dead. Soon, another attempt on his life is made at Moe's Tavern. Unable to ascertain the would-be killer, Bob suggests Homer stay out of sight until the assailant is captured. Homer agrees to do so until he is voted King of Mardi Gras, where he will be highly visible while riding on the king's parade float.

Sideshow Bob tries to convince Homer that his assailant stuffed the ballot box to make him king, but Homer is

SHOW HIGHLIGHTS

Homer: (reading the mail) *"Your family is invited to a free weekend at Stagnant Springs Spa."*
Marge: *Ooh, that place is famous! It's where J-Lo hit P. Diddy upside the head with Gary Coleman!*

In the sauna with Rainier Wolfcastle:
Homer: (thinking) *Oh, my God! A naked celebrity! Be cool. Don't stare at his famous wang!*
Rainier Wolfcastle: *Ha, ha, ha! Go ahead, look! The whole world already saw it in* Nudist Camp Commandant. (à la Sgt. Schultz on "Hogan's Heroes") *I wore nothing!*

Marge: *You have to do something to protect my husband!*
Chief Wiggum: (sarcastic) *Where on my badge does it say anything about protecting people?*
Officer Lou: *Uh, second word, Chief.*
Wiggum: *Thanks, Princeton Pete.*

Bart: *Wait. Wait. Wait. Bob can't stay with us. This man has tried to kill me so much it's not funny anymore.*
Wiggum: *Don't worry, son, we have ways of making him compliant.*
Bart: *Dad! I can't believe you're putting my life at risk to save your own!*
Homer: (calming) *You'll understand someday when you have kids.*

Chief Wiggum secures Sideshow Bob: **"Now, if he even looks at you funny, this shock garter will set him straight! *(to Bob)* And don't try taking it off, because it's taped to your leg hair, and that really hurts!"**

Sideshow Bob: *Homer, think carefully. Of all the people you have known, who might have reason to do you ill?*
Homer: *Hmmm...well, there's Mr. Burns, Fat Tony, the emperor of Japan, ex-President Bush...*
Marge: (chiming in) *The late Frank Grimes...*
Homer: *...PBS, Stephen Hawking, the fat little Dixie Chick...*
Marge: (chiming in again) *And the state of Florida!*
Bob: *How can one ordinary man have so many enemies?*
Homer: *I'm a people person...who...drinks.*

THE STUFF YOU MAY HAVE MISSED

On the front of the George Foreman Mail Sorter, there's a picture of George saying, "I Like Money!" Sorted into the "bad" file are a Visa bill, a jury summons, and an invitation to Patty and Selma's party.

The Stagnant Springs Health Spa sign directs patrons to "Follow the Smell." Below the sign is a steer skeleton in a reclining pose on a beach chair, wearing swim trunks and holding a cocktail.

In the Dr. Mas-Seuss room, Thing #1 and Thing #2 from *The Cat in the Hat* by Dr. Seuss are applying mud packs to Lisa's face. Nearby stands a large dandelion, reminiscent of the one featured in Dr. Seuss' book *Horton Hears a Who.* The masseuse working on Bart wears a Cat in the Hat tie and hat.

Chief Wiggum has an unsolved Rubik's Cube puzzle on his desk.

Sideshow Bob is incarcerated in Campbell's Chunky Soup Maximum Security Prison. He is so well shackled, even his dreadlocks have manacles attached to them.

The warden's office door has a sign that reads, "Shhh! Backroom Deal in Progress" and depicts a guard making a quieting gesture.

The copy of *Jugs and Ammo* magazine that Homer plans to buy features a sexy girl in camouflage pants on the cover, wearing a bandoleer and carrying a machine gun. The cover also states that it is "A Larry Flintlock Publication."

Junior's tow truck can be seen for a moment through the swinging door of Moe's Tavern after Junior tries to shoot Homer.

The mustachioed and cigar-smoking Mardis Gras drag queen is wearing a Marilyn Monroe wig and *Seven Year Itch* white dress.

Junior reaches a dead-end at a high brick wall with a sign on it that reads, "Sanderson's High Brick Walls - No One Builds 'Em Higher."

Junior is the son of Frank Grimes, whose difficulty coexisting with Homer led to his madness and shocking demise, as chronicled in "Homer's Enemy" (4F19).

Bob: *Ah yes, the Kwik-E-Mart! I haven't been here since I robbed it, dressed as Krusty—my one successful crime.*
Apu: *You were quite the gentleman. Today's robbers, they are all smash and grab. You understood the dance.*
Bob: *Our time is passing, old friend.*
Homer: *Uh, if you two country hens are finished clucking, I'd like to buy a copy of* Jugs and Ammo.

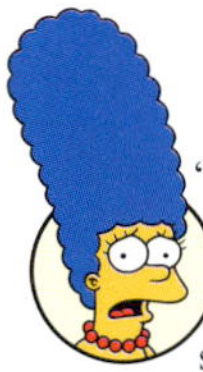

"These are Homer's friends and family. They don't want him dead! They just want him to suffer."

Movie Moments:

Bart's planned prank of floating a Baby Ruth candy bar in the mineral bath hearkens back to the pool-emptying scene in the film *Caddyshack* (1980).

When Sideshow Bob sings to Bart about how he's grown accustomed to his face, he emulates Rex Harrison's singing soliloquy in *My Fair Lady* (1964), which first graced the stage as a Broadway musical in 1956.

Carl: *Say, Bob—how come you were never able to kill Bart?*
Moe: *Yeah, kids should be real simple to kill.*
Lenny: *I'd just come up behind him with a knife and slit his throat real quick-like.*
Homer: *Guys! Bob is my only hope. Back off and give him some room to think!*
Bob: *Homer, if I can write haikus while skinheads beat me with soap, I can concentrate anywhere.*

LOUSE DETECTIVE

Episode EABF01
ORIGINAL AIRDATE: 12/15/02
WRITER: John Frink & Don Payne
DIRECTOR: Steven Dean Moore
EXECUTIVE PRODUCER: Al Jean

GUEST VOICES:
Kelsey Grammer as
Sideshow Bob,
additional vocals by
Sally Stevens

determined to appear nonetheless. When the day of the Mardi Gras Parade arrives, someone sabotages Homer's float by cutting the brake line. Homer goes careening down a hill on the float, and Bob comes to Homer's rescue. He also determines that Homer's auto mechanic, Junior, is behind the murder attempts. Together, Bob and Homer capture Junior. Junior reveals himself to be Frank Grimes, Jr., the son of the deceased man who considered himself Homer's enemy. With Junior in custody, Bob is tranquilized and incapacitated by the police. That night, however, Bob appears in Bart's room with a plan to kill the boy. However, with Bart totally at his mercy, Bob realizes he cannot bring himself to do it. Sideshow Bob leaves Bart alive and steals away into the night, promising they shall meet again.

Bob: *Homer, it's a trap. You only won because somebody stuffed the ballot box with these.* (He rifles through a sheaf of Mardis Gras ballots with "HOMER SIMPSON" written in identical handwriting on each one.)
Homer: *Nonetheless, the people have spoken.*

TV Moments:

The yoga master does an imitation of Johnny Carson from "The Tonight Show," including Johnny's trademark golf swing pantomime.

Sideshow Bob watches "That '30s Show" a parody of the long-running "That '70s Show" and the short-lived "That '80s Show."

As Homer and Sideshow Bob chase Frank Grimes, Jr. on stilts, the theme music from the 1970s crime show "The Streets of San Francisco" is heard. The theme song was heard previously in "Separate Vocations" (8F15) when Bart goes on a ride along with Officers Lou and Eddie, and they end up pursuing Snake.

"The killer is out there. I stake my entire fortune of cigarettes on it."

Lisa: *Dad's heading straight for the Museum of Swordfish!* (Several swordfish are on display, their sharp protuberances primed for impaling.)
Marge: *That museum has been nothing but trouble since it opened.*

Bart: *Dad, I'm really glad you're still alive.*
Homer: (sweetly) *Yeah, it's every parent's dream to outlive their children. Goodnight, son.*

(Homer and Bob drop from the Duff blimp gondola onto Jimbo and Kearney, who are walking on stilts.)
Homer: *Your king needs these stilts!*
Jimbo: *Jesus is our only King.*
Homer: *Not anymore!*
(They shove the bullies off the stilts.)

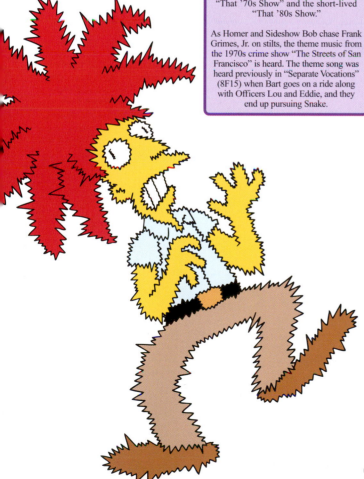

Wiggum: *That's nice work, Bob!* (to Officer Lou) *Now, give him the rhino trangs.* (Officer Lou shoots Bob with a tranquilizer gun. Bob babbles incoherently.) *If I can trang-out just one freak on stilts, I know I've done my job.*
Lou: *You're living the dream, Chief.*

Music Moment:

Moe relives memories with his precious pickled eggs jar to the strains of a Barbra Streisand-esque version of "The Way We Were." The imitation Streisand vocals are provided by Sally Stevens.

Bart procrastinates for several weeks on his class research paper about World War I. At the last minute, he puts together a paper from a story Grampa tells him, padded with a few advertisements, and gets an "F" for his efforts. He is forced to stay after class and do the paper over with his teacher, Edna Krabappel. While detained, Bart learns of Edna's romantic troubles with Principal Skinner. It seems that Skinner's mother is constantly getting in the way of their relationship. To cheer Edna up, Bart submits her name for a Teacher of the Year Award competition. The nominating committee is impressed with Edna's record, and chooses her as one of the nominees.

Edna is delighted by the nomination, but when Skinner tries to congratulate her publicly at a press conference, his mother interrupts again. Edna is saddened by

Skinner's lack of attention to her but is still excited about going to the award ceremony, which is being held at EFCOT Center in Orlando, Florida. Since Bart nominated Edna, he and his family get to join her at EFCOT Center, where they enjoy many rides and exhibitions. Meanwhile back at Springfield Elementary, Skinner becomes worried that Mrs. Krabappel may find another man on her trip, so he rushes to Florida to be with her. Unfortunately, Skinner brings his mother, and Edna tells him that she is sick of sharing him and storms off in a huff.

Skinner realizes that if Edna wins the Teacher of the Year Award, she might quit Springfield Elementary, and he might lose her forever. He decides to ruin her chances at the award ceremony. The principal enlists Bart's help and gets him to

SHOW HIGHLIGHTS

Academic suicide:
Martin: *May I type my report? It'll be easier on teacher's eyes.*
Mrs. Krabappel: *Yes! In fact, why doesn't everyone type their paper? Great idea, Martin.*
Martin: *(suddenly appearing with a black eye and a bloody nose, wearing his underpants on his head, and looking woozy) Can the paper be ten pages... minimum?*
Mrs. Krabappel: *Well, I was gonna say five, but okay. Thanks again, Martin...Martin?*
(Martin has disappeared and his underwear floats slowly down onto his desk.)
Nelson: *(dusting off hands) He's gone now, but you gotta admire his spirit!*

Bart, proficient in procrastination: "**Okay! Time to start this paper! 'World War I.' 'WWI.' Eh, that's a good start. Time to watch wrestling!**"

Principal Skinner: *Oh, I must have the wrong classroom! I was looking for my girlfriend...not Pam Dawber. Heh-heh. (Edna giggles.) Are you ready for a little "After School Special"? Y— (noticing Bart looking at them) Eyes front, Simpson! (His cell phone rings.) Hello? Mother? Sigh. I'll be right there. (hanging up) Now she wants to get out of the tub.*
Edna: *You've got to stop putting your mother ahead of me! We have a date!*
Skinner: *I'll be back in three hours. (sexily) Maybe less! (soberly) But almost certainly more.*

Edna Krabappel, on how it feels to be nominated for Teacher of the Year: "**I can't believe it! This, after I accidentally showed the R-rated *Romeo and Juliet*. I thought that nipple would haunt me forever!**"

Skinner: *Willie, you're no stranger to the inner workings of the female mind.*
Groundskeeper Willie: *Aye. Willie's sent many a Vermont Teddy Bear.*
Skinner: *Well, I'm a little worried that, uh, with all this attention, Edna might meet someone better.*
Willie: *Darn straight she will, ya brunch-eatin' popinjay! Your woman's in Orlando, man! You can't take two steps there without fallin' into a Tunnel of Love!*

Movie Moment:
One of the tapes viewed by the Teacher of the Year Nominating Committee is of an instructor who is using humor to reach his students in a Robin Williams-esque fashion à la *The Dead Poets Society* (1989), the story of a teacher who uses comedy to help students learn and "seize the day."

Skinner: *Edna Krabappel, please report to the principal's arms!*
Edna: *Oh, you came!*
Skinner: *Heh. I took a personal day.*
(They kiss and fireworks explode in the sky.)
Agnes Skinner: *(from the balcony above) Seymour! Bring me some ice! My fanny is baboon-red after that car ride! (She throws an ice bucket at Skinner, hitting him on the head.)*
Skinner: *Ow! Mother! We were sharing an open-mouth kiss!*
Edna: *You brought your mother?*
Skinner: *Ha, ha. Well, technically, since she's paying for the room...she brought me.*

Principal Skinner on his relationship with his mother: "**This woman carried me for nine and a half months! I was...out for two weeks, then went back in.**"

TEACHER'S PET

Music Moment:
The Turtle's "Happy Together" (1967) plays during Eastern Airlines' "World of Tomorrow" attraction as giant robots whip the enslaved masses and also over the episode's closing credits.

EDNA

Episode EABF02
ORIGINAL AIRDATE: 01/05/03
WRITER: Dennis Snee
DIRECTOR: Bob Anderson
EXECUTIVE PRODUCER: Al Jean
GUEST VOICES: Little Richard as Himself

pretend he cannot read in front of the judging panel. Even though his plan to humiliate Edna is succeeding, Skinner cannot bear to go through with it. Instead, he makes his way onstage and proposes marriage to her, despite his mother Agnes' attempts to interfere. Edna ends up losing the Teacher of the Year Award, but she is happy that Skinner stood up to his mother. Skinner and Edna sneak off for a romantic encounter inside one of the out-of-date attractions, and Homer braves the security measures to escape EFCOT Center and break into Disney World.

THE STUFF YOU MAY HAVE MISSED

The men Bart considers as potential boyfriends for Mrs. Krabappel are Barney, Captain McCallister, Mr. Burns, Waylon Smithers, Snake (holding a gun), Gil (holding open his empty wallet), Grampa (asleep), Kirk Van Houten, Milhouse, the Squeaky-Voiced Teen (wearing a Krusty Burger uniform and holding a tray of food), Kang, Surly (one of the Seven Duffs), Moe (holding a bouquet of flowers), Hans Moleman, Comic Book Guy (eating a caramel apple), Kearney, George Meyer (a writer on "The Simpsons"), Otto (flashing a peace sign), and Mr. Teeny (on roller-skates).

Agnes Skinner is shaking her fist angrily in the picture Edna has in her three-portrait, heart-shaped locket.

The picture of Mrs. Krabappel that Bart sends to the Teacher of the Year Nominating Committee shows her sitting at her desk, smoking and drinking coffee. There is a red apple on her desk.

Cletus, the Slack-Jawed Yokel, is a reporter for a newspaper called the Outhouse Times Picayune.

When Principal Skinner gets paged during the press conference, the pager plays music from Beethoven's Fifth Symphony. The text message from his mother is "Fridge Too Loud."

The marquee outside EFCOT Center says, "When Everything Else Is Booked."

Lisa describes the Future Sphere at EFCOT Center as a place depicting what people in 1965 imagined life would be like in 1987. The ride Lisa and Marge go on inside the Future Sphere is presented by Eastern Airlines, predicting their innovations of flying cars, a best-selling cola, and world-dominating super-robots. (Eastern Airlines went out of business in 1991.)

The whipping of the masses in the nation's capital by Eastern Airlines robots evokes memories of Kang and Kodos' world domination tactics in the "Citizen Kang" segment from "Treehouse of Horror VII" (4F02).

The Springfield Shopper newspaper's front-page story about Mrs. Krabappel's nomination is followed by a story at the bottom about the Comic Book Guy bearing the headline "Closed Pistachio Stymies Fatso."

Homer and Bart get covered with green slime at an EFCOT Center attraction called "Honey, I Squirted Goo on the Audience."

The roller coaster called "Enron's Ride of Broken Dreams" has a track that resembles a stock market growth chart. The coaster car climbs a steep incline, takes a steep dive, recovers a bit, then plummets all the way down into the Poor House. At the end of the ride, a voice is heard imitating Johnny Carson and saying, "Mmm...that's good satire!"

Outside the Teacher of the Year Awards, there's a sign that reads, "Tickets Very Available." Inside, most of the seats are empty.

Skinner: (thinking) *I feel terrible! But, this is the only way I can win Edna without upsetting Mother.* (Skinner smiles and pats Agnes on the back.)
Agnes: (thinking) *He has the tiny hands of a chimp!*

Bart: *I'm sorry. I can't read. Mrs. Krabappel never taught me to read!*
(The audience gasps.)
Little Richard: *Is this true, Edna?*
Edna: *Sigh!*
Skinner: *Oh God, I've created a Prankenstein. Wait! That boy is lying! He's not illiterate!*
Marge: (chiming in) *And he's good around the potty, too!*

Skinner: *Edna Krabappel, will you marry me?*
Edna: *Gasp!*
Skinner: *Now, I must warn you, two month's salary only bought me the ring box.*
Little Richard: (offering her a ring) *Oh here, honey! Take one of mine! Whoooooooo!*

Edna: *Seymour. Of course I'll marry you.*
Agnes: *Oh, great. Three in a bed.*

"What Do I Think?":
Homer: *Boy, those pies look good.*
Waitress: (feeding him a forkful of pie) *Open your gullet, you human blob!*
Lisa: *Well, what do you think?*
Homer: (singing) *What do I think of the pie? What do I think of the pie? Goodness gracious, it's delicious. That's what I think of the pie! Because...*(He marches off.)
Edna: *Should we follow him?*
Marge: *I'm on vacation.*

Fun Fact:
Dan Castellaneta's spot-on impression of Robin Williams was honed and previously heard when he filled in for the actor/comedian as the genie in Disney's first straight-to-video *Aladdin* (1992) sequel, *The Return of Jafar* (1994).

In "The Bedroom of Tomorrow" attraction:
Lisa: *Mom? Is that Principal Skinner sleeping in the Bed of Tomorrow?*
Robot Mom: (to robot boy in bed) *Rise and shine, sleepy-head! You'll be late for the next rocket to the moon!*
Skinner: *He's never going to get up. He's got no legs.*
Marge: *What are you doing here?*
Skinner: *Ah, well, since Edna dumped me, I've been wandering around this park all night. It's educational and offers mild thrills...just like Edna.*

Bart: *All right, I'm in. I'll humiliate the love of your life. Because I like you, I'll even do it pro boner.*
Skinner: *It's pro bono!*
Bart: *I know what I said.*

Announcer: *And now to present our final award, for Teacher of the Year—Little Richard!*
Little Richard: *I love teachers! In fact, I'm a teacher. I taught Paul McCartney to go "Whooooooo!"*
Homer: (from audience and holding up a lighter) *Purple Rain!*
Little Richard: *Shut up!*
Homer: (excited) *Michael Jackson just told me to shut up!*

"Good lord! I may lose Edna forever. I've got to stop her from winning. Then she'll be broken, miserable...and mine."

TEACHER OF THE YEAR AWARD NOMINATING COMMITTEE

Primary duty:
To select nominees for the Teacher of the Year Award competition

Not to be confused with:
Substitute Teacher of the Year Award Nominating Committee

Other responsibilities include:
The administration of urine tests to make sure nominees are not taking teaching-enhancing drugs

Prize they award to the Teacher of the Year:
Enough money to ensure the winner never has to teach again

Up until now:
Believed Bart Simpson ("The Devil in the Blue Shorts") was an urban legend

THIS IS THE MOST DIFFICULT ONE-DAY-A-YEAR JOB IN THE WORLD!

DEXTER COLT PRIVATE EYE

General Description:
Pistol-packing, hard-boiled detective who sounds a lot like Robert Stack

Modus Operandi:
Strong-arming, breaking and entering, blackmailing, making threats, framing the innocent, paper-stapling, and overcharging

Habits:
Chain-smoking, playing solitaire, and entering bake-offs

Known associate:
The Flying Giuseppe (The Human Cannonball)

> FROM THE MOMENT YOU WALKED INTO MY OFFICE, I HAD A FEELING I'D KILL YOU IN A HALL OF MIRRORS.

THE DAD WHO

Lisa wants a new security-enhanced diary for her birthday. Homer and Bart go in search of the "Turbo Diary" at the mall. Homer is sidetracked by the free samples at the food court, and when he arrives at the toy store, someone else has just purchased the last diary. Homer impulsively buys a custom-made videotape, featuring Lisa, at a nearby kiosk. When Lisa opens her present, she is not only disappointed she did not get the diary she wanted, she is angry and hurt because all the information Homer supplied for the video is completely inaccurate. Lisa accuses Homer of not knowing anything about her and runs to her room in tears.

The next morning, Homer tries to make up with Lisa, but she is still angry with him for not taking the time to get to know her. Acting on a tip from his bar buddies, Homer hires a private detective named Dexter Colt to gather information on Lisa. Colt soon delivers a full report on all of Lisa's likes and dislikes. With the information in hand, Homer treats Lisa to a wonderful father-daughter day doing things Lisa enjoys, which includes participating in an animal rights protest at a local laboratory. Homer's feeling of success is short-lived, however, when he gets Colt's exorbitant bill. When Homer refuses to pay the bill, the detective threatens revenge. Soon, Lisa is framed for a break-in at the animal testing lab, where all the animals have been stolen. Homer and Lisa flee the city with the police on their trail.

SHOW HIGHLIGHTS

After watching the "Turbo Diary" commercial:
Lisa: Hey, I could really use one of those.
(Bart is revealed, reading Lisa's diary.)
Bart: No arguments here. Man, I really come off like a jerk in this thing.

"A girl should have her own private diary. I had to share mine with my uncle."

At the toy store:
Homer: One Turbo Diary, please.
Toy Store Employee: (rubbing Bart's head) Tryin' to keep those crushes secret, eh, Romeo?
Bart: It's not for me! I'm not a girl like you.
Employee: Well played.

Naughty plush:
Employee: Sir, I can offer you this "Tickle Me Krusty"—the most popular toy of 1999. (He squeezes the doll.)
Tickle Me Krusty: I'm anatomically correct. Go ahead, take a peek! (The clerk squeezes the doll again.) I wonder what Mommy's medicine tastes like?

Bart's gift to Lisa:
Lisa: A laser pointer! Thanks, Bart.
Bart: It's really cool. You can point a red dot at people's crotches from really far away.
(He points it out window, and far away, Principal Skinner notices a red dot on his pants.)
Principal Skinner: Hmm. There appears to be a red dot on my trouser front. I'd better lower them. (He does so.) Ah! The dot also appears to be on my underpants. Well, down they go! (He drops shorts.)
(Chief Wiggum pulls up in his police cruiser, sounding his siren.)
Chief Wiggum: Hey, buddy! You better get that red dot checked out! My uncle died of crotch dot.

"Children don't remember bad birthdays, do they?"

THE STUFF YOU MAY HAVE MISSED

During the opening credits of the "Padz" television show, Rainier Wolfcastle is seen in his weight room, bench-pressing his butler.

On Krusty's wall at home, we see pictures of him with Bette Midler, Richard Nixon, Sideshow Mel, and by himself at Muscle Beach. A gold record and a Clown College diploma hang there, as well.

While punching Krusty, actor Elliot Gould names his physical blows to the clown after the title characters in his film *Bob & Carol & Ted & Alice* (1969).

The Springfield Mall sports a banner declaring it to be "Now Disney Store-Free!"

As they walk through the mall, Homer and Bart pass a kiosk that offers to "Put a Swear Word on a Hat." Choices of swear words seen are "Hell" and "Damn." Also seen are "Mug on a Mug," "Another Damn Candle Cart" and "Kumbersome Key Chains" kiosks.

Dexter Colt's office is across the street from the Hard Luck Café and Hangover Hamlet, a joke at the expense of the chain restaurants Hard Rock Café and Hamburger Hamlet, respectively.

On Colt's office door glass, it reads, "Dexter Colt Private Investigator —Please, No Set-Ups."

Homer gives his e-mail address as chunkylover53@aol.com. If one sends an e-mail to that address, a guy named Homer does, indeed, respond.

According to Colt's report, Lisa's favorite parent is "Mother."

Homer and Lisa hide out at "The Three Seasons Motel."

The lab test monkeys are put in a circus sideshow cart that reads, "See the Amazing Smoking Monkeys." The makeup-slathered pigs are in a cart that reads, "Sultry Sows of the South Seas."

Dexter Colt shoots a man out of a cannon, right into Homer's belly, and Homer gets up unhurt, proving that he still has the skills exhibited in "Homerpalooza" (3F21), where cannonballs were shot at him as part of the rock concert freak show.

Homer: Look, Lisa, I'm still trying to get to know you. (The school bus pulls up, honking its horn.) Who's your favorite Traveling Wilbury? Is it Jeff Lynne?
Lisa: (getting on the bus) Dad, you've had eight years to get to know me. It's too late.
(The bus pulls away and Homer calls after it.)
Homer: But, I'm full of questions! What's your favorite cigar size? Is it robusto? Is it?!

Music Moments:
Homer's free sample binge at the mall takes place to The Chantay's classic surfing instrumental "Pipeline" (1962).

Homer and Lisa wear adoring T-shirts and watch TV together while The Winston's "Color Me Father" (1969) plays.

Homer: Oh! My daughter hates me because I don't know anything about her.
Moe: Unh...well, whenever I gotta know something about a broad, I use this guy. (handing Homer a business card) This detective is unbelievable! He can learn more about a chick by digging through one garbage can than you could from years of intimacy.
Carl: He found out who was cobbling shoes for me at night. Turns out I have severe schizophrenia.

Dexter Colt: What can I do for you?
Homer: My name is Homer Simpson, and I desperately need your help.
Colt: Let me guess. It's about a girl.
Homer: Gasp! How did you know?!
Colt: It's always a dame, usually with gams that don't quit...'til they get to the shoes. And then they're only napping.

KNEW TOO LITTLE

Episode EABF03
ORIGINAL AIRDATE: 01/12/03
WRITER: Matt Selman
DIRECTOR: Mark Kirkland
EXECUTIVE PRODUCER: Al Jean
GUEST VOICES: Elliot Gould as Himself

Homer and Lisa hide out in a motel to avoid arrest, but Homer is forced to admit to Lisa that he hired Dexter Colt to get information on her and that the detective framed her. Once again, Lisa is angry with her father. The police discover their location, and Homer and Lisa escape into the forest. They come upon a traveling circus and find the stolen test animals locked up as sideshow attractions. Dexter Colt, who sold the animals to the circus, suddenly appears and threatens to shut them up forever. Colt chases Homer into a hall of mirrors and shoots him in the arm. Lisa comes to the rescue and blinds Colt with the laser pointer she received as a birthday gift from Bart just as he is about to kill Homer. As the police take Colt away, Homer and Lisa are friends again, especially when Homer tells her he released the test animals into the wild.

Colt: You're late, Muntz.
Nelson: Get bent, shamus. I got what you were looking for. (He gives him Lisa's book report on The Secret Garden.)
Colt: Nice. Very nice.
Nelson: Now give me back what's mine! (Dexter Colt hands him a framed photograph.) Aah! My picture with Snow White!
Colt: You know, she's just an actress.
Nelson: Shut up! Some of us prefer illusion to despair.

Ralph: Lisa Simpson is a girl at my school.
Colt: (frustrated) Yes, yes! You said that already! What else do you know?
Ralph: I once picked my nose 'til it bled.
Colt: About Lisa!
Ralph: Lisa Simpson is a girl at my school.
Colt: Someone's already worked this guy over.

TV Moment:
The show "Padz" parodies the MTV reality program "Cribs," where viewers were allowed to see inside the fabulous homes of the rich and famous.

Lisa: Is that Miles Davis' "Birth of the Cool"?
Homer: You should know! It is your favorite album.
Lisa: So you know one thing about me. Big Deal.
Homer: (consulting the report on Lisa) Wait! Wait! I thought you might like to go to an animal rights protest today.
Lisa: (pleased) Well, maybe.
Homer: On the way home, we could stop and get your favorite treat! (consults the report) Ice...(turns the page) cream!

Colt: I believe there's still the matter of my expenses. (He hands Homer a bill.)
Homer: Oh yes. Well, let's take a look and see—A thousand dollars? How did you spend a thousand dollars?!
Colt: It's itemized.
Homer: (reading) A forty-dollar steak?!
Colt: Yeah, but if I'd eaten the whole thing, it would have been free.
Homer: You've been living like a king on my dollar! Super-unleaded gas...silver bullets?!
Colt: Early on, I was working under the theory that your daughter was a werewolf. It didn't pan out.

Movie Moment:
Homer's encounter with Dexter Colt in the Hall of Mirrors is inspired by the climactic sequence from Orson Welles' *The Lady from Shanghai* (1947), in which he starred with his then wife, Rita Hayworth.

"I can't believe a man who agreed to follow my daughter around—for money—would turn out to be a dirt-bag!"

Kent Brockman: Breaking news at the Screaming Monkey Research Labs, where hundreds of test animals have been freed by unknown activists. Chief Wiggum, uh, do you have a statement?
Chief Wiggum: Uh, yes, yes I do, Kent. This is a horrible crime, one that...(gets distracted and laughs) Cut it out, Lou! I—he's making funny faces.
Officer Lou: Sorry, Chief. One of these monkeys has the same name as my ex-wife.

The Big Frame:
Kent Brockman: Chief, do you have any suspects at this time?
Chief Wiggum: Well, we do have several promising clues. Ah, let's see—there's a Malibu Stacy scrunchie, a saxophone reed, and a book report on The Secret Garden by Lisa Simpson.
Kent Brockman: Well, what does this tell you, Chief?
Chief Wiggum: (paging through the book report) Well, apparently, there's a secret garden in all of us, and that Lisa Simpson is guilty!

Ralph Wiggum, a boy sent in to do a chief's job: **"Can Lisa come out with her hands up?"**

Hiding incognito:
Motel Clerk: Names, please?
Lisa: Lady Penelope Ariel Ponyweather.
Homer: Uh...Rock Strongo.
Motel Clerk: Your real name?
Homer: Uh...Lance Uppercut.
Motel Clerk: Thank you! Sign here, Mr. Uppercut.

Homer: The man who framed you is a crooked detective...who I hired!
Lisa: Why did you do that?
Homer: To find out everything about you so I'd seem like a good father.
Lisa: How could you?
Homer: Well, all the childless drunks at Moe's thought it was a great idea.

At the circus:
Lisa: Those are the test animals! The detective must have sold them to the circus.
Homer: We'll just tell the police, and then I'm back to being plain, old Rock Strongo.
Colt: You're not telling nobody nothing! (pointing a cannon at them) Make one move, and you'll get a bellyful of The Flying Giuseppe.
The Flying Giuseppe: (poking his head out of the cannon) How ya doin'?

Homer sums it all up about the defeated Dexter Colt: **"How ironic! Now he's blind, after a life of enjoying being able to see."**

Brandine: Cletus, if I find pig lipstick on your collar again, I'm not gonna let you sleep in the sty no more.
Cletus: Duly noted.

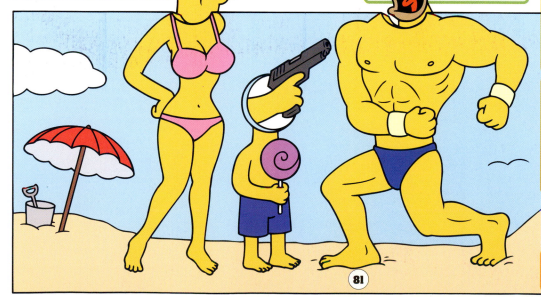

81

Homer buys so much stuff at Rainier Wolfcastle's bankruptcy sale that there is no room for him in the car. He hitches a ride with Rainier, and Marge takes the kids home in the car by herself. On the way home, Maggie soils her diaper, and Marge must make an emergency stop at the Kwik-E-Mart to change her. Apu reluctantly allows Marge to use a restroom that is accessible through the alley outside the store. When Marge and Maggie emerge from the restroom, a mugger with a gun is waiting. The only thing Marge has of value is her necklace, so the mugger takes it and runs off. Marge is left traumatized by the experience.

Marge feels vulnerable, develops agoraphobia, and cannot leave the house without becoming anxious. Despite Homer and the kids' attempts to reintroduce her to the outside world, Marge's condition worsens. She decides to start living in the basement, where she feels the safest. As time goes by, Marge gets bored. To occupy herself, she starts working out with weights that Homer bought from Rainier Wolfcastle. Within a few week's time, she has built up some muscle and confidence—so much so, she goes outside and does not even notice it. Marge joyfully jogs around town telling everyone she sees that she is no longer afraid. As luck would have it, she runs into the mugger and soundly beats him to a pulp.

Soon after, Marge spots Ruth Powers, her old neighbor, working out with bodybuilders at the beach. Ruth has been in prison and now has an extremely muscular body. She advises Marge to enter bodybuilding competitions and turns her on to steroids. Marge bulks up on all sorts of chemical concoctions, but the

SHOW HIGHLIGHTS

"Eye on Springfield":

Kent Brockman: I'm here with actor Rainier Wolfcastle who, surprisingly, has filed for bankruptcy. Rainier, what went wrong?
Rainier Wolfcastle: Three divorces in three months. What can I say, Kent? I'm a romantic.
Kent: But, this personal tragedy translates into a good old-fashioned bankruptcy sale.
Rainier: Yeah, everything must go. (He pulls out picture of woman wielding a tommy gun.) Even the painting of my Nana. This was done on her wedding day—or should I say..."deading" day?

Ned Flanders: Now, Rainier, I really don't thinks it's right to sell these Playdude centerfolds. (The camera pans over to four giggling bikini-clad models. Moe enters the picture.)
Moe: Zip it, Holy Joe. (He buys the centerfolds from Rainier and escorts them away.)
Centerfold: Are you taking us to another mansion?
Moe: Ah, yeah. (He takes them to his car and opens the trunk.) Ah, Miss September? I think you're gonna have to get into the trunk.
Miss September: Ooo!

Lenny: Hey look, a cyborg hand! This could really come in useful. (He scratches his rear end with it.)
Carl: Well, well. Look who's gone Hollywood.

(Homer rummages through Wolfcastle's dresser drawers.)
Rainier: Do you need some assistance picking over the tattered remains of my life?
Homer: No, I'm good. Hey, your early porno movies! Are any of these "hetero"?
Rainier: What's there is there.

Homer: Do you think you can give me a lift home?
Rainier: Sure, I'll carry you in this giant snuggly. I used it to carry Rob Schneider in the movie My Baby Is an Ugly Man.
(Rainier lifts Homer into the baby harness, and Homer rests his head on Rainier's chest.)
Homer: Your heartbeat is so soothing.
Rainier: Shhh. Time for sleep, little fatso.

Bart: Ewww! Mom! I think Maggie fudged her Huggies!
Marge: Bart, don't say it like that, you'll hurt her feelings. (She sniffs then gags.) Geez Louise! How did you turn cinnamon applesauce into that? (Maggie points at Lisa.)
Lisa: Don't try to pin this on me, sister! (Maggie crosses her arms and takes a suck on her pacifier.)

Video Game Moment:
Homer packs the car with his bankruptcy purchases to the music and in the fashion of the game Tetris.

At the Kwik-E-Mart:
Apu: Hello, Mrs. Homer.
Marge: Apu, where's your bathroom?
Apu: The bathroom is not for customers. Please use the crack house across the street. (Marge holds the smelly infant up to Apu's face.) Sniff! Goh! That is the most pungent thing I have ever smelled, and I am from India!

In the Kwik-E-Mart parking lot:
Marge: Okay, Marge, you can do this. You've done it a thousand times before.
Ralph: (approaches the car) Hi, Mrs. Simpson! (Marge sprays Ralph in face and he begins to cough.)
Marge: Oh, no! I pepper-sprayed Ralph!
Ralph: (coughing) Even my boogers are spicy. (He runs away crying.)

TV Moment:
The mailman goes to read the *Twilight Zone Magazine* only to discover his glasses are broken. "The Twilight Zone" theme follows, and the hapless mailman finds himself reliving Burgess Meredith's nightmare in the classic episode "Time Enough at Last."

Lisa: Mom, you didn't get the milk.
Bart: And you parked on top of the mailman.
Mailman: (from underneath the car) It's okay, all part of the job! Can you believe I get paid to wear short pants?

Dr. Hibbert: Marge, I'm afraid you've developed agoraphobia, a fear of leaving the house. I recommend watching this Lifetime Channel movie. It's called, The Woman Who Died in Her Home. Ah hee hee hee hee hee hee.
Marge: Oh my God! Isn't there anything I can do?
Dr Hibbert: Marge, I suggest you slowly desensitize yourself to the fear of going outside. Create controlled situations where you can leave the house without pain or panic.
Marge: What if I can't feel comfortable outside again?
Hibbert: Then, I hope you like throwing dinner parties.
Marge: I do!
Hibbert: No one wants to eat dinner at a crazy lady's house! Get real.

Marge declares her freedom:
Marge: Ned, I'm not afraid!
Ned Flanders: Well, aren't you a super-duper recouper!
Marge: Grampa, I'm not afraid!
Grampa: Then you're not payin' close enough attention.

Marge: (to the mugger, after beating him up) You've just been Marge-inalized!
(The townspeople cheer.)
Homer: Marge! That was amazing! It's like I'm married to Shaft.
Officer Lou: Hey, Chief, I think that's the guy who mugged her.
Chief Wiggum: Yeah, looks like she caught her own criminal. (to the townspeople) Unlike the rest of you lazybones! You're not gonna find those criminals looking at your feet, people!

THE MA

Episode EABF04
ORIGINAL AIRDATE: 02/02/03
WRITER: Carolyn Omine
DIRECTOR: Pete Michels
EXECUTIVE PRODUCER: Al Jean
GUEST VOICES: Pamela Reed as Ruth Powers

side effects make her aggressive, which worries the family. One night, after she has won second place in a competition, Marge goes on a rampage at Moe's Tavern when Moe tells her she is no longer attractive. She tries to kill Moe and beats up everyone in the bar, including a group of sailors. Homer appeals to her softer side, wishing for the old Marge to come back, and she comes to her senses. Back at home, Marge decides to give up her bodybuilding ways. She disposes of the weights and carries Homer up the stairs for some less aggressive snuggling.

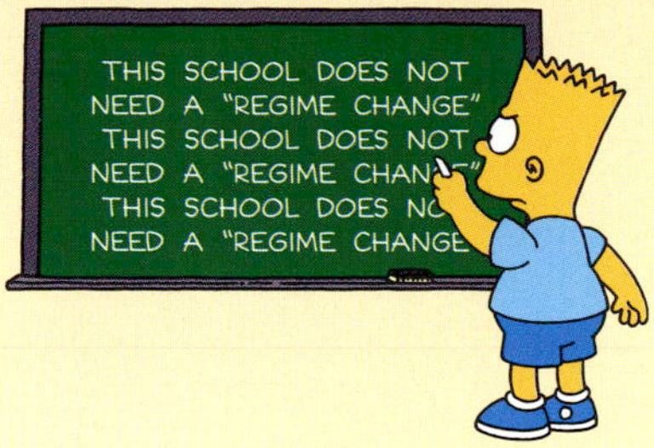
THIS SCHOOL DOES NOT
NEED A "REGIME CHANGE"
THIS SCHOOL DOES NOT
NEED A "REGIME CHAN
THIS SCHOOL DOES NO
NEED A "REGIME CHANGE

THE STUFF YOU MAY HAVE MISSED

At Rainier Wolfcastle's bankruptcy sale, there is a box labeled "Golden Globe Awards 50¢ a Pound."

Homer's many purchases include: a mounted deer head, a self-portrait of Vincent van Gogh, a bulk pack of Powersauce bars from "King of the Hill" (5F16), a bust of Rainier Wolfcastle as a *Terminator*-style android, and a People's Choice Award.

The neon sign in the crack house window reads, "Restroom for Crack Smokers Only."

Apu's key chain for the key to the Kwik-E-Mart's restroom is a miniature of the Hindu god Ganesh.

As Lisa pretends to be a magazine rack, the person on the cover of *US* magazine looks like "The Simpsons" creator Matt Groening.

Marge and Ruth Powers have drinks in a beachfront café named Let's Hear It For the Soy.

Marge drinks from the can of Ragin' 'Roids as the "Popeye" theme song plays. Grampa had a similar experience in "The Old Man and the Key" (DABF09) after taking his Viagra.

Anti-drugs bumper stickers seen on Marge's tailgate: "Moms Against Meth," "Just Say No," "I'm Anti-Crank And I Vote," "Talk to Your Kids About Huffing" and "D.A.R.E." (Marge's license plate number is EABF04, the same as the production code of this episode.)

Marquee at the bodybuilding contest: "Women's Bodybuilding Finals — First Two Rows May Get Oily."

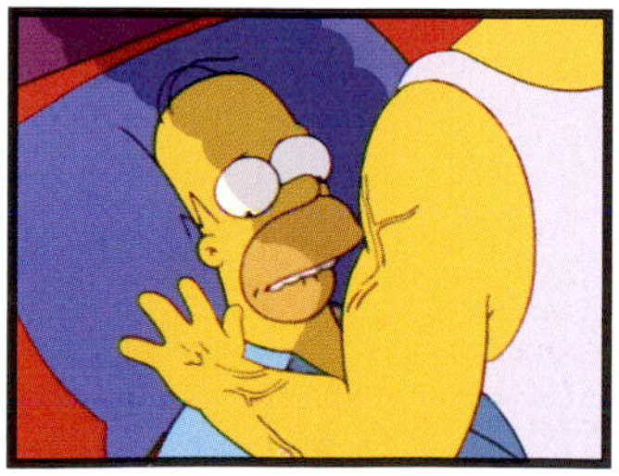

Movie Moment:

When Marge beats up the mugger in the street, she reenacts, in excruciating detail, the scene in *The Godfather* (1972) when Sonny Corleone (James Caan) pummels his wife-beating brother-in-law Carlo (Gianni Russo) with fists, feet, and trash cans.

Marge trains to the opening trumpet fanfare from *Rocky* (1976).

Ruth Powers: *You know, another four inches on your neck and you'd look pretty hot. Ever thought of competing?*
Marge: *I don't have those kinda muscles.*
Ruth: *Well, you could if you used these.*
(She puts a can marked "Ragin' 'Roids" on the countertop.)
Marge: *Steroids? I can't take drugs! I have so many anti-drug bumper stickers, I'd be making a liar out of my tailgate.*

Ruth Powers, advocate for steroid use: **"Steroids aren't drugs! They occur naturally in the body, like sweat...or tumors!"**

Marge's menu for muscles: **"A little of this and a little of that. Bulkenoids for my lats, mesomax for my delts, and estrogen blockers for that minty taste."**

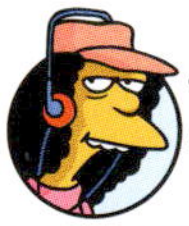

"Man! What am I smoking? Oh, yeah...pot."

Homer: *'Morning kids, I made your lunches. They're on the table.*
(Bart reaches into his lunch bag and finds a five-dollar bill.)
Bart: *Huh? Why didn't Mom make our lunch?*
Homer: *She had a lot of stuff to shave.*

Announcer: *...in second place, Marge Simpson!*
Bart: *Second place? Oh, man! This'll just encourage her.*
Lisa: *I'm tired of her criticizing my saggy glutes.*
Homer: *Quiet! Her muscular ears can hear us!*

Homer: *Oh, I'm so proud of you, honey. You bulked up, but managed to keep your femininity.*
Marge: (grabbing him by lapels angrily) *And that's why I didn't win!*
Homer: *Sorry, sir, sorry!*
Marge: *Starting tomorrow, I'm going to up my glyco-load, use a denser ripping gel...*
Homer: *Denser?*
Marge: *Damn straight! I didn't sacrifice my period for second place!*
(She pounds the bar with her fist. There is an uncomfortable silence in the bar.)
Marge: (laughing nervously) *I hear that!*

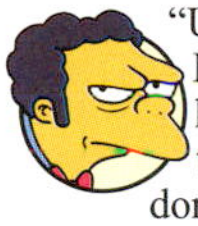

"Uhh...listen, Marge, um... how could I put this delicately? I don't got enough booze in this place to make you look good."

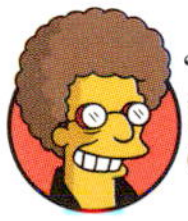

"Disco Stu should have Disco Duck-ed. Ow!"

Music Moment:

While beating up the men in Moe's Tavern, the jukebox plays Pat Benatar's "Love Is a Battlefield." Marge lifts the machine and hits Lenny and Charlie with it, changing the tune to Etta James' "At Last." After hitting Larry and another barfly with the jukebox the song changes to "Relax" by Frankie Goes to Hollywood.

Samuel Barber's elegiac "Adagio for Strings" plays as we survey the damage Marge has wrought upon Moe's Tavern.

(Marge holds a beaten Lenny over her head.)
Homer: *Marge! Somewhere in that sea of growth hormones is the sweet, wonderful girl I married—the woman who, instead of swatting a fly, will give it a bath and send it on its way. I'd sure like to go home and have Jiffy-Pop with her.*
Marge: *Oh my gosh! You're right!* (She tosses an injured Lenny on the ground.) *Steroids have turned me into everything I hate. Let's go home, sweetie.* (to Larry the barfly) *Club soda will get that blood out.*

THE MUGGER

Recognizable by:
His "Goofy" hat

Weapons of choice:
Surly attitude and a handgun

What he probably does with some of his loot:
Gives it to his cheap girlfriend

Favorite expression:
"Shut up!"

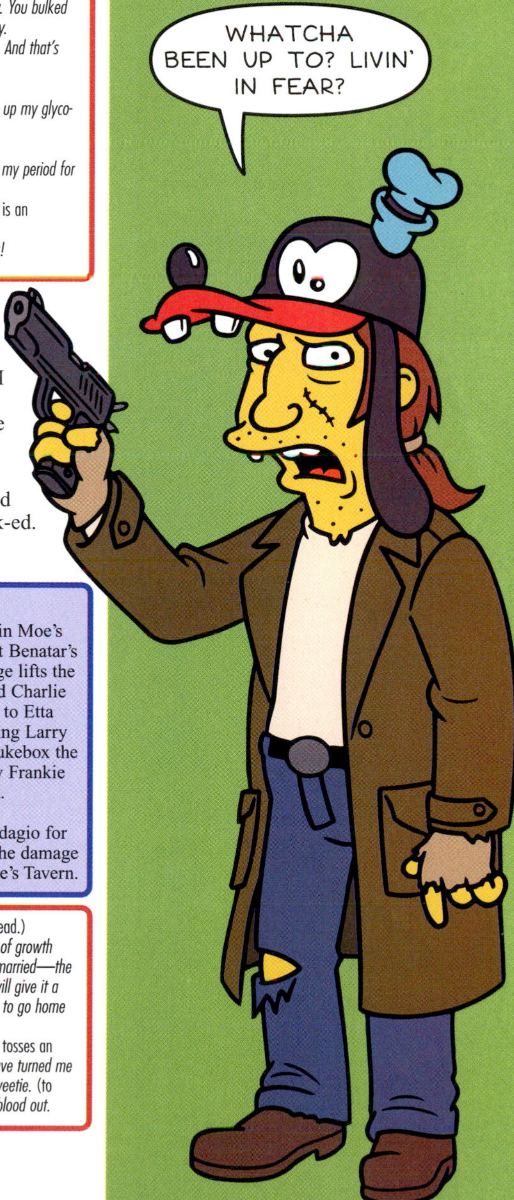
WHATCHA BEEN UP TO? LIVIN' IN FEAR?

LARRY H. LAWYER, JR.

Profession:
Personal injury lawyer

Talks like:
A TV commercial

Slogan:
"Slip and fall? Can't go back to work? I will work for you!"

Testimonial:
"He got me $60,000, and I was driving drunk in a graveyard!"
— Dr. Nick Riviera

Interesting fact:
Homer Simpson is his first client who is actually injured (according to "The Law"— that's a big plus)

I ALSO HABLA ESPAÑOL!

PRAY

The Simpsons attend a WNBA basketball game, where Homer witnesses Ned Flanders winning $50,000 for making a half-court basket, and then awarded another $100,000 for offering to donate the money to charity. After the game, Ned is allowed to drive home in the Wienermobile because his car is stuck in the parking lot. Homer comes to the conclusion that Ned's life is better than his own and asks Ned for his secret. Ned explains that he works hard and honestly, keeps himself clean, and prays for help. The only lesson Homer takes from the conversation is that prayer might be the secret to success. Later, Homer tries praying to God when he cannot find the remote control. Homer finds the remote, then prays for something to come about on a television show. Having both of his prayers answered instantaneously, Homer is convinced that there is real power in prayer.

Homer continues praying, and all his prayers are answered. Unfortunately, the family soon receives some bad news: their house is falling apart because of bad plumbing. Outside The First Church of Springfield, Homer prays for a solution to their house problems, but falls into a big hole and breaks his leg. A personal injury lawyer appears and convinces Homer to sue the church for damages. The court hearing does not go well for Reverend Lovejoy, and he is ordered to pay Homer one million dollars. Since Lovejoy does not have the money, he is ordered to give the church deed to the Simpsons. Homer and his family promptly move in, and Homer decides to throw a big housewarming beer bash. Meanwhile, Marge attends Lovejoy's service at his temporary church inside Barney's Bowlarama. The service is a disaster, so Reverend Lovejoy decides to leave town forever, believing there is no longer a place for him in Springfield.

SHOW HIGHLIGHTS

Lisa: *Dad, it's so enlightened of you to take us to a WNBA game.*
Homer: *Yeah, well, nachos are nachos.*

Announcer: *Now, here's something for the men to dribble over—our mascot Swish!*
(Swish, a large basketball-headed mascot, scantily clad with shapely legs, suggestively dances through the crowd.)
Lenny: *Ooh! I can see her logo and everything!*
(Swish sits on Moe's lap, teases his hair, and leaves.)
Moe: *A-heh-heh. Hey, come back! Hey, I love you!*
(Moe grabs Swish, knocking off half of the basketball head, to reveal Gil inside.)
Men in audience: *Aww!*
Gil: *Ah, darn it! Swish was everything I'm not!*
Moe: *Put the head back on.*

"I'm crazy as a crap-house rat for philanthropy! Yee-haw! Yee-haw!"

Squeaky-Voiced Teen: *(to Ned Flanders) I'm sorry, sir. Your car's still blocked in.*
Homer: *Well, I guess Flanders doesn't have all the luck.*
Squeaky-Voiced Teen: *So, we'll let you drive home in the Wienermobile!*
Ned Flanders: *Well, hot dog!*
Rod and Todd: *Yay!*
Flanders: *That cuts the mustard with me!*
Homer: *Oh, it's not fair! I always wanted to drive a food-shaped car.*
Flanders: *(from the Wienermobile cockpit) Heh-heh-heh! The steering wheel is a giant onion ring!*
Homer: *They thought of everything! (He breaks into sobs.) How come all the good things happen to Jesus H. Nice? (sobbing again) By which I mean Flanders! (He sobs some more.)*

Carl critiques the Monkey Olympics: **"Ooh, by the way, did you see the judging in the monkey figure skating? Whose banana you gotta peel to get a five point nine?"**

Homer prays again: **"Dear Lord, as I think of you, dressed in white with your splendid beard, I am reminded of Colonel Sanders, who is now seated at your right hand, shoveling popcorn chicken into thy mouth. Lord, could you come up with a delicious new taste treat like he did?"**

Homer: *Oh, heavenly God, my son is plagued with homework. With your vast knowledge of (looking at Bart's book) The Shore Birds of Maryland, I know you can help him.*
Marge: *Homer, God isn't some sort of holy concierge! You can't keep bugging him for every little thing.*
Homer: *Can and will! Now, to unstop this sink. Lord, please use your space-age clog-busting powers on this stubborn drain. Then, take some time off for yourself. Fly to France. Have a nice dinner.*

Homer: *Oh, Lord, I see thou art working through thy imperfect vessel, Marge. For thou art most wise...*
Marge: *You know, most people pray silently!*
Homer: *(pointing up) Marge, he's way the hell up there!*

"Homer, we can't sue the church! They'll poke fun at us in the church bulletin!"

Cletus: *We find for Mr. Simpson in the sum of one million dollars.*
Homer: *Woo-hoo! Can I get that in lottery tickets, please?*
Rev. Lovejoy: *Your Honor, we don't have that kind of money! We're not a synagogue!*
Judge Snyder: *In that case, I award Homer Simpson the deed to the church.*

Reverend Lovejoy hands the keys of the church over to Homer: **"The baptismal font tends to run–you have to jiggle the handle. Oh, and Wednesday is garbage day."**

"If it weren't for Alcoholics Anonymous, I'd still be sucking the juice out of glow sticks."

Homer closes down the AA meeting:
Homer: *I'm so sorry for all your horrible problems, but this is our dog's room now.*
Sideshow Mel: *Wherever shall we go?*
Moe: *(leans in the doorway wearing a fake mustache) You can come to my church.*
Sideshow Mel: *And what church might that be?*
Moe: *St. Paulie Girls' Cathedral.*

Music Moment:
Homer rocks out in The First Church of Springfield to " I Was Made for Loving You" by KISS.

Sermon at the bowling alley:
Rev. Lovejoy: *(preaching in bowling alley) As I was saying, if we keep our hearts pure, we can...Dr. Hibbert! Must you play the claw machine?!*
Dr. Hibbert: *I'll be right there. I've almost got me a kitty cat!*

Lenny: *Look at all this—the great food, the party, the sunshine—it's hard to believe one god came up with all this.*
Carl: *Oh, there's probably a lot of gods.*
Lenny: *Yeah, and some of them's gotta be chicks.*
Carl: *Yeah, with like a thousand boobs.*
Lenny: *Hoo-hoo! That's the god I'm gonna worship!*

All aboard Flanders' ark: **"Okay, I've got two of every animal. But only males! I don't want any hanky-panky...(to some of the off-camera animals) hey, hey, hey! Cut that out!"**

ANYTHING

Episode EABF06
ORIGINAL AIRDATE: 02/09/03
WRITER: Sam O'Neal & Neal Boushell
DIRECTOR: Michael Polcino
EXECUTIVE PRODUCER: Al Jean
GUEST VOICES: Lisa Leslie as Herself

Homer's housewarming party continues for days, and Marge begins to worry about Homer's mortal soul. Ned Flanders is worried about the whole town, as Homer's partygoers appear to be breaking all of God's commandments. Soon the sky darkens and rain clouds unleash thunder and lightning, leading to an unrelenting downpour. Springfield is quickly flooded, and its citizens are forced to the rooftop of the church. Homer prays to God for the rain to stop, but to no avail. Townspeople on the church roof threaten to tear Homer apart, but he is saved by a voice from above—it is Reverend Lovejoy in a helicopter. He prays to God for mercy, and soon the sun comes out and the waters recede. The Simpsons are unsure whether it was divine intervention that saved everyone, but Homer confesses to learning a lesson about God's anger and mercy.

TV Moment:

Moe's claim of preparing a Cornish game hen with chestnut stuffing, which he quickly amends to actually being a pigeon stuffed with Spam, and finally admits to really being a rat filled with cough drops, follows the pattern of Don Adams' "Would you believe" routines on the classic 1960s spy sitcom "Get Smart."

Homer the heretic:

Sideshow Mel: *This heretic has doomed us all!*
Moe: *Yeah, I say we skin him alive and set him on fire!*
Carl: *Yeah! That'll appease God!*
Moe: *Appease who, now?*

THE STUFF YOU MAY HAVE MISSED

The marquee outside of the Springfield Square Garden reads, "Tonight: WNBA Basketball - Courtside Seats 30 Cents."

Pictured on Homer's WNFL Cowgirls vs. She-gles ticket is a football getting a beauty shop treatment under a hair dryer and reading a magazine.

Ken Burns has a Springfield Isotopes banner on his wall.

Some of the sponsors of Monkey Olympics are Laramie Cigarettes, Omnitouch, and Fox.

The truck that crashes into the fudge tanker is full of Johnny Bench's Pre-Cooked Bacon. The logo shows the Hall of Fame catcher holding a large piece of bacon like a baseball bat.

When the plumber causes the drywall to break, the cracks form the shape of the famous painting of George Washington crossing the Delaware.

Homer falls into a hole dug for the future spot of the church's new nativity scene.

The church bulletin shows a picture of Homer asleep in a pew and reads, "Jesus Died for This?"

Larry H. Lawyer, Jr., is loosely based on Larry H. Parker, a personal injury lawyer who advertises with great frequency on television.

Marge's kitchen corncob drapes are seen hanging over one of the stained-glass windows of the church after the Simpsons move in. A basketball hoop is hung above the church entrance.

The file picture of Reverend Lovejoy used on Kent Brockman's broadcast is attributed to world-famous photographer Annie Leibovitz.

The Flanderses pray to a cross made from pool cues.

As always, God has four fingers and a thumb on each hand, unlike all the other characters in the Simpsons universe.

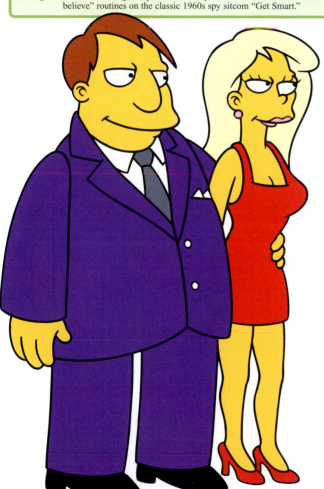

During Marge's annual spring cleaning, Bart and Lisa find a box of old videotapes in the garage. Later, while viewing the tapes, they discover a commercial Bart made as a baby selling bad breath patches for babies. The ad is particularly painful since Bart played a character called "Baby Stink-Breath." Bart asks his parents about his infant acting career, and Marge tells him he made a fortune. When Bart asks where the money is, Homer confesses that he spent it all. Bart is furious, and he and Homer have a falling out. Determined to punish his father, Bart goes to a lawyer seeking a divorce from his parents.

Bart's lawyer serves Homer with a subpoena, and the Simpsons find themselves in court in front of Judge Harm. The judge grants Bart emancipation from his parents, and Homer's paycheck is garnished in order to pay Bart for his financial loss. Bart sadly leaves his home, declaring that he cannot stay as long as Homer is there. Homer puts up an angry front, but he is devastated by Bart's departure. Bart rents a loft in the city, and, at first, he is very frightened being on his own. But he soon discovers that he is living in the same building as skateboarding legend Tony Hawk. Hawk always has a party going on, and Bart decides that his new life is perfect.

Bart's family pays him a visit in his new digs, and Homer tries to get Bart to come home. But Bart does not want to, especially since he has decided to join Tony Hawk on a skateboarding, rock-n-roll, and extreme sports tour. The tour stops in Springfield, where Homer asks Tony Hawk to help him look cool so he

SHOW HIGHLIGHTS

(Lisa awakens to the sound of Marge vacuuming her room.)
Lisa: *Oh, Mom, why did you wake me up? I dreamt I was at the Kennedy Center Honors!*
Marge: *Well, here's another low-rated annual event...* (holding up a rag and a spray bottle) *spring cleaning!*

"Homer and Marge Get Dirty":
(Bart and Lisa eat popcorn and watch a videotape.)
Marge: (from TV) *I can't believe you talked me into this.*
Homer: (from TV) *It's such a mess! Oh! Watch the teeth!*
Marge: (from TV) *Don't go telling your buddies at work about this.*
(On the television screen Homer and Marge are seen carving pumpkins, covered in pumpkin innards.)
Bart: (disappointed) *Every tape is pumpkin carving!*

The beginning of Bart's "Baby Stink-Breath" commercial:
(A woman pushes a covered baby carriage through the park. She approaches an old woman, who glances into the carriage at the unseen baby.)
Old Woman: *What a beautiful baby! Gasp! What horrible breath!*
Jingle Singers: *He's the baby whose mouth, Smells like death. Run for your life. It's Baby Stink-Breath!*
(Baby Bart pops up from the carriage and gives an evil laugh. A monstrous green cloud of halitosis comes out of his mouth.)

Bart, perplexed as he makes a show of eating a Butterfinger candy bar:
"Wait! I was in a commercial? I don't remember this at all!"

Bart: *How could you make me Baby Stink-Breath and not even tell me?*
Marge: *Honey, you did have a great time doing those commercials, and you made a lot of money.*
Bart: *I did? Where is it?*
Marge: *Your father invested it in a college trust fund which today must be worth a for—*
Homer: (covering his ears and singing) *La-la-la-la-la-la-la-la!*
Marge: *Hmm. Of course, the stock market has been down lately, but there must be some sort of—*
Homer: (singing louder) *La-la-la-la-la-la-la—nothing left—la-la-la...oh...la!*

Bart: *So my dad blew all the money I made from that embarrassing commercial. Promise me you won't tell anyone about it.*
Milhouse: *I won't. But these things have a way of getting out.*
Nelson: (riding by on a bike) *Haw haw! Baby Stink-Breath!* (He crashes into a tree, falling off the bike in pain.) *It was worth it.*

Bart: *I just wish there was some way to get back at my dad.*
Milhouse: *When my mom wants to get back at my dad, she uses her lawyer.*
Bart: *Does it make him cry?*
Milhouse: *More than normal.*
Kirk Van Houten: (enters) *Hey, son,* (sobs) *I've got tickets for the circus* (sobs some more).

Bart: *I want a divorce from my parents.*
Blue-Haired Lawyer: (startled) *You whaaa?!*
Bart: *I said, "I want a divorce from my parents!"*
Blue-Haired Lawyer: *Yes, I heard you. I was just calling my secretary. Uwa?* (His secretary appears at the door.) *Get me the standard "Child Divorcing Parent" form.*
Uwa: *Yes, sir.*

Blue-Haired Lawyer: (on the other side of the front door) *I am here to serve you with a subpoena.*
Homer: *Well, I'm not opening the door.*
Blue-Haired Lawyer: (pulling out a plate of bacon) *It comes with a side of bacon.*
Homer: *Is it crispy?*
Blue-Haired Lawyer: *Yeeesss.*
Homer: *But not too crispy?*
Blue-Haired Lawyer: *Nooo.*
(Homer opens the door, grunts, and takes both the plate and the subpoena.)
Homer: *I'll see you in court.*

Marge: *Bart, you're suing us?*
Bart: *Yes, I want to be emancipated.*
Homer: *Emancipated? Don't you like being a dude?!*

Blue-Haired Lawyer: *Bart, using this doll, tell the court where your father took money from you?*
Bart: (demonstrating) *Here and here.*
Blue-Haired Lawyer: *Let the record show that he pulled out the little pockets of the doll!*

"That boy's about as safe living with you as a crawdad in a gumbo shack!"

Judge Harm: *Bart Simpson, I declare you emancipated! Further, I hereby garnish Homer's wages until Bart is fully repaid.*
Homer: *Mmm...garnish.*
Judge Harm: *That means half your paycheck goes to Bart.*
Homer: *What the—?! Half goes to Bart! Half goes to my Vegas wife! What's left for Moe?*

Lisa: *Bart, where are you gonna live?*
Bart: *With the money Dad's paying me, I rented a loft downtown.*
Lisa: *Do you even know what a loft is?*
Bart: *No. I assume it has hay.*

OVER

Episode EABF05
ORIGINAL AIRDATE: 02/16/03
WRITER: Andrew Kreisberg
DIRECTOR: Matthew Nastuk
EXECUTIVE PRODUCER: Al Jean

GUEST VOICES: blink-182 (Travis Barker, Tom DeLonge & Mark Hoppus) as Themselves, Tony Hawk as Himself, Jane Kaczmarek as Judge Harm

can win Bart back. Tony agrees and gives Homer a technologically-enhanced skateboard that can make anyone look good in competition. Homer defeats Tony, but Bart still refuses to return home. It is not until Tony uses skateboard lingo to explain Bart's point of view to Homer that he understands the problem. Homer apologizes and promises to never take advantage of Bart again. Bart agrees to come back home, and Homer's impressive skateboarding moves lead to an endorsement deal that allows him to pay back Bart.

THE STUFF YOU MAY HAVE MISSED

The sign at the Kennedy Center in Lisa's dream reads "Kennedy Center Honors—Salute 'Em Before They Die."

The three law firms Bart has to choose from are: Badger, Haggle & Bill; Luvum & Burnham, Family Law; and Hackey, Joke & Dunnit.

There's a billboard painted on the side of Bart's building, which features a vodka bottle with Krusty the Clown's hair. The caption reads, "Absolut Krusty," parodying the popular Absolut Vodka ads.

Dia-Betty makes her second appearance at the Spuckler (Delroy) household in this episode. She was first seen in "Sweets and Sour Marge" (DABF03).

An elderly Nelson Muntz has appeared at Homer's gravesite once before, in Lindsey Naegle's computer simulation of Homer's financial ruin in "Homer Vs. Dignity" (CABF04).

Lisa: (tearfully) *Ooh...I'm gonna miss you.*
Bart: *Here's something to remember me by.* (He takes her arm.)
Lisa: *Ow! Indian burn!*
Bart: *Look at it.*
(There is a red mark on her arm in the shape of a heart.)
Lisa: *Aw, that's so sweet.*
Bart: *If I did it right, it's permanent.*

TV Moment:

When we first see an exterior shot of Bart's new downtown loft, the theme from "The Mary Tyler Moore Show" plays. Inside, Bart throws his lucky red cap up into the air, only to have it shredded by the ceiling fan.

Marge: *Please don't go, Bart! I'll let you swear in the house! Everything but the big three.*
Bart: *Sorry, Mom, I just can't.* (points at Homer, peeking out the window) *Not as long as he's here.*
Marge: *Aw, honey, I can't believe this is happening. I'll miss you so much!* (She smothers him with kisses.)
Cab Driver: *Either give me some of that, or let's get going.*

Bart's new and not so friendly neighbor: **"Be quiet in there! Some of us are trying to sell drugs!"**

Bart gets a ride to school...from Tony Hawk:

Bart: *Thanks for the lift, Tony Hawk! I gotta go now, Tony Hawk.* (to Milhouse) *Cool guy, Tony Hawk.*
Milhouse: *Bart! You know Tony Hawk?*
Bart: *Please, I'm trying to keep it quiet.* (shouts) *Catch ya later, Tony Hawk!*
Tony Hawk: *Stay cool, Brett.*

Outside Bart's building:

Marge: *I don't think this is a good place for a ten-year-old boy.* (She hands a bum some money.) *Here's five dollars. Buy yourself a suit and get busy.*
Bum: *I'll buy a suit...of drugs!* (He laughs maniacally.)

Bart: *I'm takin' off for six months to join the Skewed Tour!*
Lisa: *Skewed Tour?! The traveling festival of rock-n-roll, skateboarding, and extreme sports?*
Bart: *And nipple piercing!* (lifts shirt to show his chest amply adorned with rings)
(Marge screams.)
Bart: *Don't worry, they're clip-ons!*

Homer: *I just want to win my son back so badly.*
Tony Hawk: *I can relate. I'm a father myself. Ah, one day they're little shredders, and the next day they're grinding and gnashing their way to college.*
Homer: *Yeah, I make up words, too.*

Fun Fact:

Fox advertised this show as the 300th episode of the series. That dubious honor belongs, in fact, to "The Strong Arms of the Ma" (EABF04), which aired two weeks earlier. The two-episode difference is not lost on Marge, who mentions it during the episode.

Marge: *I can't count how many times your father's done something crazy like this.*
Lisa: *It's 300, Mom.*
Marge: *I could have sworn it was 302.*
Lisa: *Shhh!*

Bart: *Dad, you don't understand. This was never about being cool. It was about you not caring how I felt.*
Homer: *Aw, that's the dumbest thing I ever heard, you stupid little kid.*
(A battered Tony Hawk pulls himself up the side of the half-pipe.)
Tony Hawk: *Homer, you're heading for a parental face plant. Do a 180 emotional ollie.*
(Tony Hawk slides back down the half-pipe in pain.)
Homer: *Finally, someone explains it to me in words I can understand.*

Homer's "Viagrogaine" commercial:

(Homer and a model walk along the beach in their bathing suits. Homer wears a wig of thick hair.)
Kathy: *Oh, Steve, you're everything a girl could want. What's your secret?*
Steve (Homer): *Well, Kathy, I'll tell you. It's Viagrogaine. It gives you lots of hair and what you need down there.* (to viewer) *What are you waiting for...loser?*
Announcer: *Possible side effects include loss of scalp and penis.*

BABY STINK-BREATH

Who he is:
The baby with hellish halitosis

Who he really is:
Bart Simpson, infant actor

Where you'll see him:
In commercials for the "Baby-So-Fresh" Tri-patch System

What the patches do:
They alter a baby's DNA, while leaving the RNA untouched, giving babies the freshest of breath

Disclaimer:
"Not safe for babies under two."

BOOBERELLA

Spooky claim to fame:
Big-busted hostess of "Matinee of Blood and Commercials"

Weird times you can catch her act:
Weekend afternoons, during a plethora of commercial breaks from the movie

Creepy fare she will bring you:
Low-budget fright-flicks like 1983's *Frankenstein and the Harlem Globetrotters Meet the Mummy and the Washington Generals*

Strange turn of events:
Finds it necessary to appeal a temporary injunction in the middle of her show

NOW FOR THE FIRST OF OUR EIGHTY-TWO COMMERCIAL BREAKS. THEN YOU CAN SEE MORE OF MY BOOOOBS!

While watching a horror movie matinee on television, the Simpsons see a Krusty Burger commercial advertising the new Ribwich sandwich, and Homer is very enthusiastic about trying one. A few days later, school begins. For the first day's main activity, Principal Skinner has the students participate in an all-school spelling bee. Lisa is named school champ, to the cheers of her fellow students, and has the opportunity to participate in the State Spelling Finals.

Homer stops into Krusty Burger to try a Ribwich, and becomes instantly hooked on the addictive product. At the State Spelling Finals, Lisa again emerges as the winner. Afterward, Marge suggests that the family go to a movie to celebrate, but Homer bows out, saying he has important business to attend to. In reality, Homer is sneaking off to Krusty Burger for some more Ribwiches. But he receives bad news from the Krusty Burger employee—the Ribwiches were only offered for a limited time. Homer is very upset, but a stranger invites him to join the "Ribheads," a group of Ribwich fans who follow the Ribwich from test city to test city. The Simpsons travel to Calgary, to watch Lisa compete in the Spellympics. When Lisa makes it to the final three, Homer disappoints her again. He will not be able to stay in Calgary any longer because he plans to follow the Ribwich to San Francisco. Lisa's day gets worse. The master of ceremonies for the Spellympics, writer George Plimpton, asks Lisa to purposely lose the competition. It

---

SHOW HIGHLIGHTS

Apu's TV commercial: **"Hello, Springfield! Come to my 'Back to School Parking Lot Blow Out!' We've got first-rate school supplies at Third World prices. At the Kwik-E-Mart, where we believe in America! Please... don't beat me up anymore."**

The Ribwich commercial ("Tastes Like Liberty"):
(Hard working men are seen laboring in a factory similar to a steel mill.)
Singer: *Like a rib,*
It tastes like liberty!
Like a rib,
With a bun of sesame!
(The men throw a cow into a fiery hot furnace, then pour the molten processed contents into rib-shaped molds.)
Announcer: *We start with authentic, letter-graded meat...and process the hell out of it, 'til it's good enough for Krusty!*
(The resulting product is stamped and pressed by a huge machine. Krusty picks one up with a pair of tongs.)
Krusty: *Try my new Krusty Ribwich!* (placing the meat in a bun and eating it) *Mmm! I don't mind the taste!*

Principal Skinner: (sings to tune of Alice Cooper's "School's Out")
School's back in session!
Let's begin our lessons!
Groundskeeper Willie: (to himself while sharpening a knife) *This year, he gets it in the back!*
Skinner: *Willie, did you get the letter about your pay cut?*
Willie: *Aye, there'll be many a cut this year.*
Skinner: *Indeed there will...budget-wise, of course.*

Bart: *Nelson! How was your summer?*
Nelson Muntz: *Sucked.*
Bart: *What'd you do?*
Nelson: *Space Camp.*
Martin: *At ease, Cadet Nelson! Good to be back on terra firma, eh?*
Students: *Gasp!*
Nelson: *How 'bout I launch my foot into your butt?*
Martin: (incredulous) *I held your hair when you barfed in the simulator!*
Nelson: *Shut up!...Commander.*

Movie Moment:
When Homer first eats and becomes addicted to the Ribwich sandwich, with all the pupil-expanding, blood cell-rushing, slow-motion effects, we are reminded of similar scenes in the movie *Requiem for a Dream* (2000), directed by Darren Aronofsky.

Lisa runs through town wearing sweats while being tested on words by everyone she meets. She finishes her run at the top of the steps of a public building before a cheering crowd, parodying a memorable scene from *Rocky* (1976).

Skinner: *Welcome back, children. We've all had fascinating summers. I was the maître d' at the Springfield Country Club.*
Jimbo Jones: *My dad says you were a busboy!*
Skinner: *You mean your dad, the raging alcoholic?*

Skinner: *Um, we'd better get down to business. As this is a non-leap year, we're already a day behind.*
Bart: *C'mon, man, everyone knows the first day of school is a total wank.*
Skinner: *Well, if by "wank" you mean educational fun, then stand back...it's wanking time.*

Skinner: *Let's get the year rolling with an all-school spelling bee!*
Lisa: (gets up on her chair and cheers) *Woo-hoo!* (The other students are silent and stare at her.) *Sigh! I guess I won't be popular this year, either.*

Skinner: *Bart, your word is "imply."*
Bart: *Imply. I-M-P...*
Nelson: *Bart said, "I am pee." He's made of pee!* (The students laugh.)
Bart: *Well, I got my laugh. I'm out of here!*
Ralph: *I made Bart in my pants!*

Skinner: *Lisa Simpson, you're school champion!* (The students cheer.)
Lisa: *Wow! I'd better make the most of this!* (grabbing the mic) *FREE TIBET!*
Skinner: *There'll be time for that later.*

Skinner: *And here's your prize for today—a scale model of the planet Mars.*
(He hands her a red sphere.)
Lisa: *This is just a kickball with "Mars" written on it.*
Skinner: *Behold...the Red Planet!*
Students: *Yaaay!*

Lisa: *It was so exciting! I actually got applause for being smart.*
Homer: (looking at the kickball) *Mars, eh? Hmm...I see no evidence of water.*
Marge: *Well, this is very impressive, Lisa. I'm kicking this right onto the mantle!*

Rib-It: (man in a frog costume) *Hey! Hey! The Ribwich is back!*
Homer: *Gasp! The Ribwich! The commercials have come to pass.*
Rib-It: *Try the new Ribwich. It's so good, you'll croak!*
Homer: *You seem like an impartial observer, but I've been fooled by so many people in costume.*
Rib-It: *Try the sauce. I'm soaked in it!*
(Homer tastes the frog.)
Homer: *Ooh! I could lick you all day long.*
Rib-It: *And yet my children think I'm a failure.*

Homer, upon eating several Ribwich sandwiches: **"I have eaten the ribs of God!"**

Marge: *Lisa, I'm so impressed you're state champ.*
Bart: *Finally! A Simpson has a trophy without a bowling ball on it.*

Homer: *Three Ribwiches, please. And instead of a shake, I'd like a blended Ribwich.*
Squeaky-Voiced Teen: *I'm sorry, sir. The Ribwich was for a limited time only.*
Homer: *Not again! First you took away my "Philly Fudge Steak," and then my "Bacon Balls," then my "Whatchama-chicken!"* (sobbing) *You monster!*

TV Moment:
Booberella is a parody of monster movie matinee maven Elvira, Mistress of the Dark, the alter ego of actress and comedienne Cassandra Peterson.

FAST AS I CAN

Episode EABF07
ORIGINAL AIRDATE: 02/16/03
WRITTEN BY: Kevin Curran
DIRECTED BY: Nancy Kruse
EXECUTIVE PRODUCER: Al Jean
GUEST VOICES: George Plimpton as Himself

seems the sport of the spelling bee is teetering on the brink of extinction, and the Spellympics needs a younger, cuter student to win. Horrified, Lisa refuses, even though Plimpton offers her free college tuition and a hot plate.

In San Francisco, Krusty the Clown addresses the assembled Ribheads. He tells them that the Ribwich will be discontinued permanently, since the animal it is made from no longer exists. As a parting gift, Krusty throws the very last Ribwich into the crowd for them to fight over. Homer grabs it and hungrily prepares to eat it when he realizes he has exchanged Lisa's special day for a sandwich. He trades the Ribwich for another Ribhead's car, and hurries back to Calgary. He arrives just in time for Lisa's big moment in the Spellympics. Overjoyed that Homer does care about her, Lisa tells the crowd about the attempted bribe and proceeds to spell her word…incorrectly. Lisa loses the competition and the free tuition. In the car ride back to Springfield, her parents try to cheer her up, and when they arrive in Springfield, the whole town is waiting to celebrate her accomplishment. Being number two is good enough for Springfield, and to commemorate the event, they have had Lisa's image engraved on the side of a nearby mountain.

Kent Brockman, with another slow news day: **"And speaking of news stories, here's another. Springfield spelling phenom Lisa Simpson has qualified for spelling's answer to the Olympics: the Spellympics. In a related story, the Spellympics is being sued by the Olympics for the use of the suffix 'lympics.'"**

Cletus: *Hey, lookee! It's that youn'gun what sorts them squiggles into words. Can you spell "scabies"?*
Lisa: *S-C-A-B-I-E-S!*
Brandine: *(to their baby) Rubella, we got you a middle name!*

> **Fun Fact:** This episode marks Barney Gumble's return to drinking, as he is seen lying on the sidewalk guzzling beers.

George Plimpton: *Welcome…to the games of the 34th Spellympiad. I'm George Plimpton, founder of the Paris Review. I also played the evil dean in Boner Academy.*
Homer: *You monster! Why did you expel Boogerman?*
Plimpton: *He replaced my tennis racket with a rubber phallus.*
Homer: *(laughing) That was awesome.*

Music Moments:

The Ribwich jingle is inspired by "Like a Rock" (1986) by Bob Seger & the Silver Bullet Band, which has similarly been used to inspire people to buy GM trucks.

"I Put a Spell on You" by Screaming Jay Hawkins plays over the early round montage at the Spellympics and the closing credits.

George Plimpton acknowledges that the Spellympics fanfare is "an unlicensed knockoff of the Olympic anthem." The music heard is a variation of the Olympic theme "Bugler's Dream" composed by John Williams for the 1988 Olympics.

Homer represents for the Ribwich: **"It's not just a sandwich. It's about brotherhood. It's about freedom! It's about three days since I've had one! I'm getting the shakes, and I'm getting the fries!"**

 "Hey, don't Borgnine my sandwich!"

Krusty: *Look, about the Ribwich…there aren't going to be any more. The animal we made 'em from is now extinct.*
Homer: *The pig?*
Otto: *The cow?*
Krusty: *You're way off! Think smaller…think more legs.*
Crowd: *Eww!*
Krusty: *People, we went through something magical together—and it's not important who got rich off of whom, or who was exposed to tainted what. And because you believed in my dream, I want you to fight over the last Ribwich ever made. Here. (He tosses the Ribwich into the crowd.)*

Lisa: *My one chance for everyone to like me, and I blew it! (noticing the crowd in front of their house) Whaaa?!*
Principal Skinner: *Two cheers for Lisa! Hip-hip…*
Crowd: *Hooray!*
Skinner: *Hip-hip…*
Crowd: *Hooray!*
Skinner: *Now, deep breath and quiet.*
Lisa: *You mean you're all still proud of me?*
Mayor Quimby: *Lisa, with second place, you're the biggest winner this town has ever had. Before you, it was the woman who dated Charles Grodin.*

THE STUFF YOU MAY HAVE MISSED

We see Homer holding a Ribwich box with a captioned picture of Krusty saying, "Now without lettuce!" The caption on the Ribhead's Ribwich box reads, "Will cause early death!"

Under the Spellympic Village sign, there is another sign that reads, "A Place For Dorks."

During the Spellympics, Homer holds up a sign that reads, "**E**nglish **S**pelling **P**romotes **N**owledge." Besides having "knowledge" spelled wrong, the first letters of each word are written in red, spelling out the TV station call letters "ESPN."

George Plimpton's Detroit Lions jersey (#0), made famous in his book about his football training camp experiences, *Paper Lion*, is in a glass case in his office.

The hot plate George Plimpton tempts Lisa with is an official "The George Plimpton Hot Plate."

The banner the Springfieldians have hung on the Simpsons' house says, "2 Good 2 B #1."

89

The Simpsons go to the beach to attend the annual festival that welcomes back the migrating Stinging Red Jellyfish. That evening at The Jellyfish Cotillion, all the adults have a particularly romantic evening—that is, all except Ned Flanders. This is his first Jellyfish Festival without his late wife Maude, and he feels especially lonely. Since the ballroom dancing only adds to his forlorn mood, Ned decides to return to his Leftorium in the mall to work on his taxes. A very attractive female shopper enters the store, and eventually asks Ned out on a date. Ned hesitantly agrees and does not realize until she has left that the woman is a famous movie starlet named Sara Sloane.

Sara is in Springfield to film her new movie, *The Zookeeper's Wife*. Ned and Sara begin what becomes a whirlwind romance. Sara is smitten by Ned's lifestyle, protective nature, and honesty. Ned does not even seem to mind the obnoxious paparazzi that hound them constantly. On the set of her movie, Ned manages to convince the director to cut out Sara's nude scene. Later, when the filming is over, Sara asks Ned to return to Hollywood with her. However, Ned knows he could never withstand the pervasive evil of Hollywood, so he declines her offer. Sara proclaims she will stay in Springfield with Ned.

Despite locals still being starstruck by Sara's presence, she starts to settle in to life in Springfield. She goes shopping with Ned, joins Marge's book club, and falls deeper in love. One night when they attend a concert, Ned is particularly nervous about Sara's revealing dress. Sara seems sad at the concert and, upon Ned's inquiry, tells him she wants to have sex with him. Ned is torn, but he eventually gives in to his urges and makes love to Sara under the stars after the concert. The next morning, Ned expects Sara to marry him, but she is not ready to settle down. Reaching an impasse, Sara returns to Hollywood, leaving Ned behind. After hearing the news that Sara has entered into a quickie marriage/divorce, Ned remarks to Marge and Homer that he has suddenly become more attractive to women, now that he has dated a movie star.

SHOW HIGHLIGHTS

Dr. Hibbert's Daughter: *Daddy, why is everyone so happy the jellyfish are back?*
Dr. Hibbert: *Well, in the old days, people thought that the jellyfish venom had curative properties. Now we know it just makes things a whole lot worse.*
Dr. Hibbert's Son: *Like laser eye surgery?*
Dr. Hibbert: *Exactly!* (The Hibbert family laughs.)

Frugal fiancé:

Principal Skinner: *Mmm. This is as romantic as the night I proposed.*
Mrs. Krabappel: *Maybe we can have this band play at our wedding.*
Skinner: *I was kinda hoping we could use this audio cassette.* (He shows her a tape of "Free Wedding Songs.")
Mrs. Krabappel: *Seymour, we've got to have a band!*
Skinner: *Fine. But no cake!*

Ned: *Sigh! Well, Sea Captain, looks like you and I are sailing solo tonight.*
Captain McCallister: *Arr...you hitting on me? 'Cause I don't do that...on land.*

Ned: *Well, guess I might as well head back to my store. I've got a date with some twins—the state and federal tax forms.*
Marge: *Poor Ned! This is his first Jellyfish Festival alone.*
Homer: *I know! And it doesn't get any easier from here! There's the Tongue Kissing Festival, Cinco de Ocho, the Hobo Oscars...*(within Ned's range of hearing) *days just made for lovers! Not widowers! Lovers.*

"I gave up on L.A. when those TV people made that poor nun fly. All those Puerto Ricans looking up her dress. That's not right!"

Sara Sloane: *Are you for real?*
Ned: *I'm as real as the nose on your face.*
Sara: (sarcastically) *Yeah, real.* (She taps her nose, and it makes a metallic sound.)
Ned: *Well, it looks good. And it sounds pretty, too.*

Sara: *I'm here for a while, and I don't really know anyone. Would you like to have dinner tomorrow night?*
Ned: *A woman asking a man out? Well...well, why not? And maybe I'll eat my steak with a spoon!*

Ned's "A Girl with No Name" song:
(to the tune of America's "A Horse with No Name")

Well, I've got a date with a girl with no name.
It sure feels good to be back in the game.
At dessert, maybe I can ask her her name,
'Cause I can't pray for her without the right name!

"I used to worry Marge was too good for me. She was always thinking of ways to improve me. But then, part of her died and she doesn't try anymore. So we're all where we want to be!"

Lenny: *Eh, excuse me, Miss Sloane. May I have an autograph?*
Sara: *Sure.*
Lenny: *Oh, man! This is going right on eBay...I mean, my wall...which I will then sell on eBay!*
Sara: (to Ned) *Sad to say, this isn't the worst I get.*
Lenny: *Oh, oh!* (holding up a block of plaster.) *Can I just push this plaster cast onto one of your boobs?*
Sara: (to Lenny) *Okay, now you are the worst.*

Sara: (sentimentally) *You know, I grew up in a house like this. I didn't know there were people like you left in the world.*
Ned: (chuckles) *Yep! We occupy the useless mass of land between Los Angeles and New York called America.*

On the set of *The Zookeeper's Wife*:

Ned: *Whoa...whoa, whoa, whoa, whoa. This movie's turning into SpongeBob No-Pants!*
Director: (sighs) *Cut.*
Ned: *Sir, there's no reason Sara needs to do this scene in the altogether.*
Sara: *Sam, he's got a point. Katharine Hepburn never showed her breasts.*
Director: *There's still time.*
Sara: *I want a rewrite...with no nudity!*
Director: *All right, but you're going to have to kiss a woman.*
Sara: *Deal!* (excitedly) *Ned, we won!*
Ned: *Yep! Now, all we have to do is turn that woman into a fella, and that kiss into a game of Scrabble.*

Marge: *Miss Sloane, I loved you in Sleeping With Pinocchio and Honey, I Scotchguarded the Kids.*
Sara: *Thanks. I grew really close to the actress who played my daughter. I think she's in France or something.*
Marge: *Hmm. And, Ned, I haven't seen you this happy in years.*
Ned: *Mm-hmm. I haven't felt this good since we stole the 2000 election.*
Homer: *Hey, don't blame me. I voted for the green M&M.*

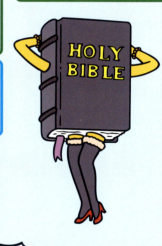

Bart: *Rainier Wolfcastle?!*
Sara: *My ex-boyfriend.*
Rainier Wolfcastle: *Sara, liebchen! Take me back. If tears could burst through my muscular ducts, I would cry like a baby who was just hit by a hammer.*
Sara: *Rainier, you're too jealous! You beat up Jon Lovitz just because he presented me an award.*
Rainier: *Oh, come on. Nobody misses a handshake that badly!*

"My libido has been terminated."

AGAIN

Episode EABF08
ORIGINAL AIRDATE: 03/02/03
WRITER: Brian Kelley
DIRECTOR: Michael Marcantel
EXECUTIVE PRODUCER: Al Jean

GUEST VOICES: Jim Brooks as Himself, Helen Fielding as Herself

CLANCY WIGGUM
Actor

Sara: Ned, I've never met a man like you. You're sensitive, you're in great shape, you have a mustache...and yet, you're not gay.
Ned: Oh, no way. I won't even eat vegetables over two inches long.

THE STUFF YOU MAY HAVE MISSED

On the cover of Lisa's *Modern Sandcastle* magazine is a picture of a little girl building a sandcastle that looks like the Sydney Opera House in Australia. On the cover of Bart's *Bad Boys' Life* magazine, we see a picture of a bad boy kicking down the same sandcastle as the little girl looks on in horror.

Marge applies Sunscreen SPF 1000 to Maggie.

Seen across the mall from Ned's Leftorium are the businesses I Can't Believe It's a Law Firm, Expensive Coffee in Little Cups, and Something Wicker This Way Comes.

The Sara Sloane movie advertised on the poster near Ned's store is titled *My Best Friend's Gay Baby*. The poster pictures a baby wearing a leather S&M outfit.

Marge is seen reading a celebrity magazine called *Envy*.

At Polystar Studios, there is a sign on the front gate that reads, "No Artistic Integrity Beyond This Point."

When Ned imagines himself in Hollywood, on the famous Walk of Fame, there are sidewalk stars honoring: Godlessness (for Film), Drug Abuse (for Music), and Adult Situations (for TV).

Even though James L. Brooks insists that Ned call him James L. Brooks during the episode, the closing credits list him as Jim Brooks.

Sara's license plate reads, "OS-CAR."

Ned takes Sara to an outdoor concert at Springfield Bowl where John Williams conducts the music of Itchy & Scratchy.

Ned: Sara, I'm sorry, but...I can't move to Hollywood. Heck, even Dollywood's too far-out for me. Too many people appreciating it ironically.
Sara: Well, then I'm staying in Springfield with you. For good.
Ned: Gasp! Oh, forgive my language, but, uh...I'm one happy camper!

Ned and Sara take a drive:
Otto: (calling out) Dude! What's it like kissing a movie star?
Comic Book Guy: (calling out) What's it like kissing a woman?
(Chief Wiggum pulls their car over.)
Ned: Well, what seems to be the problem, Officer?
Chief Wiggum: The problem is, I can't seem to get an agent. Could you give your girlfriend my head shot?

"Sure is nice to be shopping for a woman again. The last thing I bought for a lady was a casket."

Music Moment:
When the Stinging Red Jellyfish return to Springfield's beach, the song "Born Free," from the 1966 movie of the same name, plays.

The melancholic melody that accompanies Ned Flanders' plight through the episode is Claude Debussy's "Clair de Lune."

Apu: Sir, would you ask your sweetheart to sign her autograph for me?
Ned: Well, of course...Wait a minute, this is to adopt two of your kids!
Apu: Oh so it is! I've already dumped three on Mia Farrow. Sucker!

Marge: Today's book is Bridget Jones's Diary. Now, let's go around the room and analyze why we didn't read it.
Mrs. Krabappel: Cramps!
Agnes Skinner: All my friends are dead!
Luann Van Houten: Well then, I guess it's time for margaritas!

(A romantic instrumental of "The Itchy & Scratchy Show" theme plays.)
Ned: Sara, I love you, but, I– I get the feeling you're just not a Ned-head tonight. Is something wrong?
Sara: Sigh! Actually, there is something. The time we've spent together has been wonderful, but...I want sex! With you.
Ned: (flustered) Well...that's a...a-a mighty big kettle of, ah...(breathes deeply) premarital, uh, doodily. Heh-heh-heh.
Sara: I knew you'd say that! I need a glass of wine.

Flanders: This is quite a dil-diddly-lemma. I better talk this over with the big man. (He turns to Homer.) Homer, Sara wants us to have S-E-X.
Homer: Stupid Flanders. I'm not giving you any of my secret moves.

The morning after:
Sara: Whoa! Wow! That made me completely forget about Bob Balaban.
Ned: That's what Maude used to say.

Break-up call:
Sara: You...want to get married?
Ned: Uh-hmm. That's right. I'm like Baskin Robbins—you get one free taste, then you've got to buy the scoop.
Sara: Ned, I love you, but I'm not ready to be tied down.
Ned: I love you, too, and I always will. But, unlike The Bible, I guess this isn't going to have a happy ending. I'm sorry.

"Publicity Tonight":
Male Host: Screen siren Sara Sloane shocked Tinseltown last night with a midnight marriage to Gosford Park megahunk Bob Balaban.
Ned: Gasp!
Male Host: This was followed three hours later by a quickie divorce.
Ned: Sigh. I bet we would have lasted twice that long.

SARA SLOANE HOLLYWOOD MOVIE STAR

Filmography includes:
Sleeping with Pinocchio, Honey, I Scotchguarded the Kids, My Best Friend's Gay Baby, and *The Zookeeper's Wife*

Distinguishing features:
A nose that sounds like metal when you tap it

Her body:
Makes grown men drop their nachos and drool and young boys ask where babies come from

Ex beaux:
Every Tinseltown hunk from Affleck to Zmed (including Bob Balaban and Rainier Wolfcastle)

Lost love and fellow left-hander:
Ned Flanders

THE PUBLIC MIGHT NOT SEE ME NAKED, BUT **YOU** JUST MIGHT.

Guest Voice:
Marisa Tomei as Sara Sloane

COOKIE KWAN
RED COAT REALTOR

Claim to fame:
She is #1 on the West Side

Secret strategy:
Considers all of Springfield the West Side

Contact info:
555-DO IT

Special power:
Frightens lesser realtors

CALL ME! MY NUMBER'S ON THE BENCH.

The Simpsons appear to be experiencing an earthquake, but upon further investigation and after enduring a deafening roar, the family learns that a new airplane flight path goes directly over their home. The Airport Authority will do nothing to help them, and after several nerve-racking weeks they attempt to sell their house. No potential buyers will make them a decent offer once they find out about the noisy jets. The Simpsons decide to visit their elderly congressman. As luck would have it, the story of the Simpsons' plight upsets the old congressman so much, he dies from a heart attack. Then the family gets an idea—if they can convince Krusty the Clown to run for the now empty congressional seat, his celebrity status will make him a shoo-in, and he can help return the jet flight path to normal. Krusty decides to run for Congress aided and abetted by his friends from the Republican Party.

As his campaign begins, Krusty offends minority and special-interest groups with his uncouth personality, but with a little coaching from Lisa, he overcomes his initial character flaws, staying on message and capturing the hearts and minds of Springfield voters. With additional help from a biased news organization, demonizing his opponent, and his overly sentimental campaign commercials, Krusty is elected to Congress.

As his first order of business, Krusty tries to get his

SHOW HIGHLIGHTS

Marge, cussing up a storm after the swear jar breaks: **"Nutty fudgkins!"**

Airport Official: *Are you threatening a government official?*
Marge: *No!*
Airport Official: *Good, because we're the government. We make the laws, we print the money, and we breed the super-soldiers. So go home, learn to live with it, pay your taxes and remember: you didn't hear anything about the super-soldiers.*

Marge: *(frazzled) Homer, we haven't gotten a good night's sleep in weeks. The dog has eaten all of its hair. (Santa's Little Helper chews at his hairless body then coughs up a chunk of hair.) And the fixtures won't stay in one place.*
Grampa: *(sitting on a toilet that moves across the family room) I've had this dream before!*

Ralph makes an offer on the Simpsons' house:
Ralph: *I'll give you three crayons and my milk.*
Cookie Kwan: *It's a good offer. I advise you to take it.*
Homer: *Hmm. Make that a chocolate milk, and you've got a deal.*
Ralph: *I'm walking away.*

Krusty: *I could even tell the FCC to take a hike. (hands Bart a list) Look at this list of words they won't let me say on the air.*
Bart: *Aw...all the good ones. Hmm. I've never even heard of number nine.*
Krusty: *It's doing thirteen while she's eleven-ing your five.*
Bart: *Can I keep this?*
Krusty: *Sure! It's no twelve off my ass.*

At the Springfield Republican Party Headquarters:
Republicans: *We want Krusty! We want Krusty!*
Krusty: *Ah, just one thing. Are you guys any good at covering up youthful and middle-aged indiscretions?*
Mr. Burns: *Are these indiscretions romantic, financial, or...treasonous?*
Krusty: *Russian hooker. You tell me.*
Burns: *Oh, no problem! We'll say you were on a fact-finding mission.*
Krusty: *I did find out one fact...she was a guy!*

THE STUFF YOU MAY HAVE MISSED

The elderly Three Stooges movie is directed by Jules White III, presumably the progeny of Jules White, who produced hundreds of Three Stooges shorts, starting as early as 1930.

Attached to Fat Tony's private jet is a banner that reads, "Mafia Staff Jet—Keep-A You Hands Off," which is reminiscent of the "Mafia Staff Car" bumper sticker that was popular in the 1970s. Inside, Fat Tony wipes his nose with a piece of pizza as he tearfully watches a movie.

This episode signals the third shaving mishap by Homer over the course of seasons 13 and 14. He cuts himself psychedelically in "Jaws Wired Shut" (DABF05) and historically in "Helter Shelter" (DABF21).

A sign seen at the Airport Authority reads, "Complaint Department: Sarcastic Grief Counselors On Duty."

On Representative Horace Wilcox's office door, there is a sign that says, "Your Man Of Tomorrow Since 1933." During Kent Brockman's news report of the congressman's death, we learn he was a *Titanic* survivor.

The hat Krusty puts on Bart's head when he thinks he is a terminal patient reads, "Krusty's the Kure."

At the Springfield Town Hall, the marquee reads, "Big Debate Tonight — Kids Get Bored For Free."

The Fox News crawl during the episode and over the closing credits:...Pointless news crawls up 37 percent...Do democrats cause cancer? Find out at foxnews.com...Rupert Murdoch: Terrific dancer...Dow down 5000 points...Study: 92 percent of Democrats are gay...JFK posthumously joins Republican Party...Oil slicks found to keep seals young, supple...Dan Quayle: Awesome...Ashcroft declares breast of chicken sandwich "obscene"...Hillary Clinton embarrasses self, nation...Bible says Jesus favored capital-gains cut...Stay tuned for Hannity and Idiot...Only dorks watch CNN...Jimmy Carter: Old, wrinkly, useless...Brad Pitt + Albert Einstein = Dick Cheney...

Historical photos in Krusty's campaign commercial: Krusty plants a flag on the Moon, several Krustys plant the flag on Iwo Jima during WWII, Krusty stands in front of a Chinese tank in Tiananmen Square, and Krusty holds Lee Harvey Oswald as he's getting shot by Jack Ruby. A disclaimer and announcer come on saying, "Photographs have been modified to include Krusty."

On election night, Krusty and the Simpsons stay at the Second-Best Western Hotel.

One of the "gun nuts" in the crowd during Krusty's inauguration looks suspiciously like Charlton Heston, along with Meathook from "Take My Wife, Sleaze" (BABF05) and Jimmy the Scumbag.

Depressed Krusty boozes it up at a tavern called The Drinkin' Memorial. The logo features a tipsy Abe Lincoln, sitting in his memorial chair.

Reaching out to the League of Women Voters:
Krusty: *Let me say I was the first clown to put a woman in sketches. Miss Bada-Boom-Boom-Boom! She had more acting talent in one boob than most women have in their entire rack! (Some women raise hands to ask questions.) Yeah? You, with the million-dollar gams. (The women are shocked. One is heard walking out.)*
Marge: *Don't you see? He's pointing out how sexist men can be.*
Krusty: *Yeah! Listen to the tomato with the melons.*

"This is Kent Brockman with a special live report from the headquarters of Krusty opponent John Armstrong. How can I prove we're 'live'? Penis!"

Music Moment:
Krusty's campaign commercial song "When a Man Loves His Country" is inspired by Percy Sledge's "When a Man Loves a Woman" (1966).

TO WASHINGTON

Episode EABF09
ORIGINAL AIRDATE: 03/09/03
WRITTEN BY: John Swartzwelder
DIRECTED BY: Lance Kramer
EXECUTIVE PRODUCER: Al Jean
GUEST VOICES: Joe Mantegna as Fat Tony

airplane rerouting bill passed, but as a freshman congressman, no one will listen to him. He is placed on committees working on irrelevant issues. Krusty becomes disheartened, and the Simpsons find him licking his wounds in a bar. Initially disappointed with him, the family inspires Krusty to stick by his convictions. Krusty and the Simpsons enlist the help of the Capitol's janitor, who knows how to get things done. Under his tutelage, Bart blackmails one partisan congressman, and Homer gets another hopelessly drunk, rendering him unable to vote. Finally, Lisa paper clips the airplane routing bill to another, more popular bill, and it is voted into law. Krusty's faith in the congressional system is revived, and the Simpsons return to their home, now jet noise-free.

STOCK PHOTO

At the big debate:

Krusty: *Let me tell you all a story: when the network offered me fifty grand a week, I threw my caviar in their face...*
(Lisa coaches him from the audience.)
Lisa: (stage whisper) *Nooo! Connect!*
Krusty: *...because...I was thinking about the American family. One family in particular, who was stepped on by the government, and had nowhere else to turn.*
Homer: (from the audience) *Boring!*
Krusty: *I'm talkin' about the Simpsons!*
Homer: (from the audience) *Let him speak!*

Cletus: *I like that clown. He's really looking out for me—the average Joe Six-tooth.*
Brandine: *Where'd you get yourself another tooth?*
Cletus: *Sidewalk.*

Krusty stays on message:

Krusty: *People, tell me your problems—I'll fix 'em all!*
Moe: *The government wants to shut me down 'cause the pipes under my toilet don't lead nowhere.*
Krusty: *Elect me and I promise those pipes will lead to a better tomorrow!*

Krusty gets sworn in: **"I swear to uphold and protect the Constitution of these United States. So relax, gun nuts, I can't touch you!"**

At The Drinkin' Memorial:

Marge: *Krusty! We came to see how many campaign promises you've kept.*
Krusty: (drunkenly) *Uh, let's see...did I promise to be a slave to big oil?*
Marge: *No.*
Krusty: *Well, then none.*

Bart: *Krusty, I can't believe you're giving up. I thought you'd make a difference. That's why I voted for you.*
Krusty: *How could you vote? You're only ten.*
Bart: *This is not about me...or how many times I voted.*

Homer: *Krusty, you've let everyone down. And even worse, you've let down this sacred document!* (He holds up a piece of paper that looks like The Constitution.)
Krusty: *You're right. It's time I made a difference!* (He leaves.)
Lisa: *Dad! This is a kid's menu, where you have to help Yogi Bear get to the Washington Monument.*
Homer: *Stained with the blood of American patriots.* (She touches the stain with her finger.)
Lisa: *That's jelly.*
 Homer: *From the Unknown Toaster.* (He salutes.)

Krusty: *I came here for a reason! And I will not be silent until...hey, where is everybody?*
Congressmen: *No one usually shows up unless there's a vote.*
Krusty: *Well, then why are you here?*
Congressman: *I steal stuff when everyone's gone.* (taking some lamps) *My Christmas shopping's done!*

Janitor: *Now, Homer, that Southern congressman is your biggest obstacle. Your job is to drink him under the table so he misses the vote. You think you can do it?*
Homer: *Sir, I studied under Ed McMahon.*
(Homer approaches the Southern congressman.)
 Southern Congressman: *How 'bout a drinkin' contest, boy? Right after I vote on the latest bill.*
 Homer: *How 'bout before?*
 Southern Congressman: *Hah! You remind me of my high school drinking coach. Now enough talkin'. Let's drink!*

"The system works! I've become enchanted and illusioned with Washington."

Government in action:

Bart: *At last those planes are flying where they belong.*
Homer: *That's right—over the homes of poor people.*

C.E. D'OH

It is Valentine's Day, and Homer has done everything possible to assure that he and Marge have a romantic evening together. Marge, however, is too tired to make love and falls asleep. Depressed, Homer walks through Springfield at night, noticing that everyone and everything in town seems to be finding romance. A billboard for extension school classes catches his eye, and he decides to take a class that evening to improve his marriage. At first, he joins a class on "Stripping for Your Wife," taught by Dr. Hibbert, but he is thrown out for using up all of the body oil. Next, he tries "Successmanship 101," where the instructor gives him a more positive and aggressive outlook on life. Homer rushes home, barks commands at his kids, and demands sex from his wife, to which Marge willingly agrees.

Energized by the extension school instructor's book, *Megatronics*, Homer approaches the new day with vigor. At work, he follows the book's instructions, making a list of things around the plant that could use improvement and

presenting it to Mr. Burns. Burns is unimpressed, and dispatches Homer through a trap door. Homer is glum and has thoughts of getting revenge against his tyrannical boss. Later, Homer overhears a conversation between Burns and Smithers and discovers that Mr. Burns has made his pet canary the legal owner of the plant, so that he cannot be held personally responsible for any of the plant's wrongdoings. Homer has a brief crisis of conscience but then decides to get rid of the bird, setting it free. Burns finds out the bird is missing, and Homer uses that opportunity to trick Mr. Burns into believing that the Nuclear Regulatory Commission has arrived for a surprise inspection. Burns panics and makes Homer the new head of the power plant, filling the canary's position. Homer's first act as the new C.E.O. is to fire Mr. Burns.

At first, Homer enjoys the power that comes with running the nuclear plant. Soon, however, he realizes it is a lot of work and responsibility, and that there is little time for recreation. He begins to regret not being able to spend as much

SHOW HIGHLIGHTS

Homer: *So, kids, it's Valentine's Day, and you know what that means! You get to stay downstairs watching TV with the sound turned way up!*
Lisa: *What about you and Mom?*
Homer: *Oh, we'll be upstairs in the bedroom, making love...ly...rope ladders, in case there's a fire.*

Homer: *(sexily) Hey there, Little Red Riding Hood! I ate your granny, and now I'm in the mood for love.*
Marge: *(sleepily) Oh, Homie. I'm sorry. You know I usually bring my A-game to the bedroom, but tonight I just can't throw the heat.*
Homer: *But it's St. Valentine's Day! God wants us to do it!*
Marge: *(kissing him) You're so cute when you're begging for sex.*

Homer, left out in the cold: **"Shot down on Valentine's Day! That's supposed to be a gimme. Everybody's getting some but me!"**

Stark Richdale: *You see this watch? It's jammed with so many jewels, the hands can't move. What kind of watch do you have?*
Homer: *Uh, well, I drew it on. See?*
Richdale: *Uh-huh. You see that car out there? That's a Bentley Mark 12. They gave one to me, one to Steven Spielberg, then they shot the guy who made it!*
Lenny: *Wow, I'd hate to be in that union.*

Richdale: *Do you want to be the ultimate you?*
Homer: *Yes!*
Richdale: *Do you want to yodel at the top of the corporate mountain?*
Homer: *Yes!!*
Richdale: *Will you write me a check made out to "Cash"?!*
Homer: *God, yes!!!*

Literary Moment:
Mr. Burns' attempt to wall up Homer in his family mausoleum is inspired by Edgar Allan Poe's classic crime story "The Cask of the Amontillado."

Homer: *Listen up, life obstacles! From now on, nothing's gonna stand in Homer Simpson's way! (to Bart) Do your homework! (to Lisa) Don't do so much homework! (to Maggie) Learn to talk! (to Marge) You! Let's love! Now!*
Marge: *Sounds good to me!*
Homer: *(tries to carry Marge up stairs but runs out of breath) Go on ahead! I'll just slow you down!*

Homer: *All my life I've had one dream...to achieve my many goals. Mr. Burns has never given me a...thumbs-up or a..."way to be" or a..."you go, girl." No! He just steps all over everyone who works for him, taking pleasure in making us feel small.*
Marge: *Oh, Homie! Don't let it get you down. So Mr. Burns doesn't take you seriously—big whoop! Who gives a doodle? Whoopie-ding-dong-do!*
Homer: *Thanks for trying, but I'll be at Moe's.*
Marge: *So my husband goes to a bar every night—whoop-de-doo! Who gives a bibble? Gabba gabba hey!*

Movie Moments:
The Itchy & Scratchy short "Bleeder of the Pack" borrows the use of Bill Haley & His Comets' 1955 hit "(We're Gonna) Rock Around the Clock" as well as the roller-skating waitress and the motorcycle cop prank from George Lucas' *American Graffiti* (1973).

When Dr. Hibbert gives Homer a quarter to call his mother while at Springfield Extension School, he is echoing the words of John Houseman to Timothy Bottoms in *The Paper Chase* (1973), but in that film the professor is expressing his doubts about his student's prospects in law school.

Homer: *I gave Mr. Burns the best years of my life. And how much respect does he give me?*
Lenny: *Slim to bupkus.*
Moe: *Who's this Burns guy? Somebody you work with?*
Homer: *Moe...we've been complaining about him every night for eight years.*
Moe: *Well, if this guy's ridin' your rump, why don't you slap him some payback?*
Homer: *Revenge? On Mr. Burns?*
Lenny: *Yeah, send him magazine subscriptions he doesn't want.*
Moe: *Or give him some face time (holding up a brick) with sweet lady brick. Ha-ha! (He kisses the brick.)*

Mr. Burns: *So, when they come to put C.M. Burns in jail, it's the canary that does the time.*
Waylon Smithers: *Sir, can...can you do that?*
Burns: *Oh, yes! Tycoons have been doing it for years. Why, Standard Oil was once owned by a half-eaten breakfast.*

Episode EABF10
ORIGINAL AIRDATE: 03/16/03
WRITTEN BY: Dana Gould
DIRECTED BY: Mike B. Anderson
EXECUTIVE PRODUCER: Al Jean

time with his family as he used to. When Mr. Burns stops by, Homer asks how the old man kept up with all the work of running the plant. In response, Burns takes Homer to a graveyard to show him the people he never spent time with because he had to work so hard. Homer learns his lesson and is about to relinquish his top spot at the power plant, when Burns shoots him with a dart gun. Homer passes out, and Burns attempts to bury him alive inside his family mausoleum. But the enfeebled billionaire is too slow. Homer comes to, easily escapes the mausoleum, and gives the power plant back to Burns anyway. He opts instead to spend time with his family and friends at a barbecue in the park.

THE STUFF YOU MAY HAVE MISSED

Examples of everybody but Homer "getting some" on Valentine's Day are: Snowball II and a stray cat (their tails intertwine to make the shape of a heart), Professor Frink and a lady android (with a true-to-life "floivic"), cloud formations that look like a couple kissing, one jet refueling another, and Snake in the Springfield Penitentiary, seen in silhouette coupling with another prisoner. (In reality, Snake is choking a fellow prisoner for not waking him when the Bookmobile came by.)

The three billboards Homer notices while out walking are: "Suicide Hotline – Call 1-555-NO-KILL-U" (featuring a man hanging by a noose while on the phone), "Feeling Unattractive? Lose Weight At Chub Med," and "Find The Answers To Your Problems...At Springfield Extension School."

The sign on the door of the Extension School reads, "Orientation 7:30 Graduation 9:30."

The oil used in the male stripper class is named "Oil of Oh, Yeah!"

Near his workstation at the power plant, Homer covers a poster of The Swedish Bikini Team with one of The Swedish Efficiency Team, picturing three males in business suits posing provocatively.

On the authority flow chart of the Springfield Nuclear Power Plant, the canary is at the top, then Mr. Burns, then Smithers, then to several rows of employees (with Lenny and Carl on the bottom row), then the inanimate carbon rod from "Deep Space Homer" (1F13), and finally, Homer. The late Frank Grimes is also on the chart (next to Lenny), but his picture has a line drawn through it.

Once Burns is gone, there is a banner hanging between the power plant's two cooling towers proclaiming "Under New Management."

After Homer gives the plant back to Burns, he throws a barbecue, complete with a banner that says, "Homer's 305th Everything Is Back to Normal BBQ." (This may originally have been intended as a 305th episode in-joke, but this show actually marks the 306th episode.)

Hearing things:

Marge: Homie, what's wrong?
Homer: I have a plan to get to the top, but I'd have to do some pretty rotten things to get there. I'm not sure I could look at myself in the mirror or any highly-polished metal.
Marge: Well, if you don't know the right path to take, you have to be very quiet, and listen for that little voice inside that tells you what to do. (They both listen.)
Bart: (offscreen) Do it, Dad! You could get a less-crappy car.
Marge: Bart! You can hear us?
Bart: (offscreen) Oh, yeah. From my room, I can hear everything.
Lisa: (offscreen) Me, too. The walls are paper-thin. (She punches a hole in the wall and waves.) Hi!
Ned Flanders: (offscreen) And, it wouldn't hurt for you to get some curtains.
(They look out the window and see Ned Flanders sitting in an armchair staring at them. He puts his pipe in his mouth and turns out the light. Homer and Marge continue to see the glow of his lit pipe in the darkness.)

 "Now, a few more details about this year's company picnic—it's at the plant, no food will be served, the only activity will be work, and the picnic is cancelled."

Homer: Mr. Burns' reign of terror is over. (The workers cheer.) And today begins my reign of terr...(The workers gasp in fear.)...iffic management! (The workers sigh in relief.)
Lenny: I thought he was gonna say "terror."
Carl: Oh, I don't think he was going that way.
Homer: Unlike Mr. Burns, I will respect you, the working-class slob, because we are all equals! And now, as I ascend this crystal staircase to my office, I say—"avert your gaze!"

Music Moment:
The song heard playing on Maggie's tape machine is "Sex Bomb" (2000) by Tom Jones and Mousse T.

Mr. Burns, living the high life: **"Well, now that I'm forcibly retired, I feel I should give back to society and do some charitable work, but...first, I want to take a lot of opium."**

In the Marrakesh marketplace:
Smithers: (to shopkeeper) Uh, excuse me! Do you know where I can buy some, uh...(whispers) drugs?
Shopkeeper: (loudly) Drugs? Everything is drugs! Banana made of drugs! Monkey made of drugs! Look! All market made of drugs!
Smithers: (picks up a brick of hashish) I'd like to buy this.
Shopkeeper: Only American money! (whispers) Our money is made of drugs.

Lisa, award-winning student: **"I got a gold star at school today, for my exposé on toxins in gold star adhesive."**

"Bart's growing up without me. He won't be ten forever."

Burns: Knock! Knock!
Homer: Gasp! Mr. Burns! Where's Mr. Smithers?
Burns: He's doing eighty years on an opium bust. I never saw a man take to a Turkish prison so quickly.

Mr. Burns, on his lost love: **"This was my fiancée, Gertrude. I was working so hard, I missed our wedding, our honeymoon, and our divorce proceedings. She died of loneliness...loneliness and rabies."**

TV Moment:
As Homer and Bart roughhouse on a baseball field, the theme song to the late 1960s father/son sitcom "The Courtship of Eddie's Father," performed by Harry Nilsson, plays.

STARK RICHDALE

Author of:
Megatronics, The 48 Tips to Corporate Success

Published by:
Kinko's

What is Megatronics?:
The force that runs through the universe (formerly known as God)

He offers:
The secret to true success

He recommends:
Grabbing life, taking it by its little bunny ears, and getting in its face

He has the ability to:
Read the minds of losers

NOW, LIFE IS HARD, AM I RIGHT? WRONG! LIFE IS EASY! *YOU* SUCK!

DECLAN DESMOND

His profession:
Snooty documentary filmmaker

His impressive work thus far:
Lost Luggage, Shattered Lives, Upskirt Dreams, and Do You Want Lies With That?

His next great epic:
American Boneheads: A Day in the Life of Springfield Elementary

His stuffy ego:
Thinks famed documentary directors the Maysles brothers and Barbara Koppel are not good enough to wipe his lens

His unapologetic attitude:
Tearing down people's dreams makes him feel superior

AH, THAT'S GOOD NARRATION!

Guest Voice:
Eric Idle as
Declan Desmond

Documentary filmmaker Declan Desmond comes to Springfield Elementary to do an exposé on its students. Nelson and the other bullies humiliate Bart while he is being interviewed on camera. Bart's fellow students no longer perceive him as being cool, and Nelson soon becomes the most popular kid in school, mainly because he steals the hood ornament off someone's car and wears it around his neck. Principal Skinner is afraid the school is starting to look bad in Desmond's film, so he introduces the filmmaker to Lisa, presenting her as a typical Springfield Elementary student. Unexpectedly, Desmond does not think much of Lisa, calling her a dilettante without any path or objectives in life. This upsets Lisa greatly, and she sets off on a quest to bring meaning to her life. After visiting the Natural History Museum and finding herself in the planetarium, Lisa decides to become an astronomer.

Homer buys Lisa a telescope, but she soon learns she cannot use it anywhere near Springfield due to light pollution. She is particularly disappointed because she wants to see a spectacular meteor shower that is due to appear over Springfield during the next week. Lisa circulates a petition to turn down the town's lights at night. Meanwhile, Bart decides to top Nelson and regain his reputation by stealing his own automobile hood ornament. Lisa's petition passes, and the town's lights are turned low, enabling the bullies to steal more hood ornaments under cover of darkness. The only car that no one will touch is Mafia boss Fat Tony's. Bart realizes that stealing Fat Tony's ornament will restore his reputation, and he sets a plan in motion. It does not take long for the

---

SHOW HIGHLIGHTS

"Do You Want Lies With That?":
Declan Desmond: Aren't you ashamed to lend your likeness to substandard food?
Krusty: Look, I give people a meat-like burger and some kind of cola, and they still get change back from their fifty.
Desmond: Well, your customers might be shocked by my footage of you stapling together abandoned, half-eaten burgers.
(Footage of Krusty shows him in a Krusty Burger kitchen stapling burgers together.)
Krusty: (in the film) Hoo-Hoo-heh-heh-heh. Good as new!

Principal Skinner, naïve documentary film neophyte:
"Powerful work! And now he's going to make a documentary about Springfield Elementary, which I assume will be glowing and positive, unlike all of his other work."

Desmond: Now, everyone, while I'm filming, please be yourselves. I want to see troubled children brooding, bullies doling out what-for...
Milhouse: What about us cool kids? Should we just "chill out"?
Desmond: You're doing great! (aside to the cameraman) Stay with the dink.

Desmond: America is supposed to be a democracy, but in the schoolyard, cool rules. And Springfield's Machiavelli of the monkey bars is one Bartholomew Simpson. On today's royal agenda—digging up dirt clods to throw at his school chums.
Bart: I chuck 'em at nerds, girls I like, whatever. (Bart is hit by dirt clod himself.) Ow!
Nelson: Munch mud, Simpson! (Nelson and other bullies laugh.)
Bart: I'm telling! (He begins to cry, covers his face, and waves the camera away.) Oh, man!
Desmond: And, in a flash, Bart's glory has gone the way of England's masculinity.

Milhouse: It's a dangerous life being a hall monitor. When you leave home in the morning, you may be kissing your dolls goodbye for the last time.
Ralph Wiggum: My sash says "Ultraman!" (He starts doing martial arts movements.)
Principal Skinner: (interrupting the filming) I think we've seen enough. (leading Desmond away) You should know that our school is not all nitwits and Nelsons.

Skinner: Why, look! It's typical student Lisa Simpson.
Lisa: Oh, hello. I've just been listening to Bach, while reading at a sixth-grade level.
Desmond: Indeed?
Skinner: (laughing) Hitting it off already! I haven't seen such a natural pair since "Half-Sandwich" and "Soup of the Day!" I'll just leave you two alone. (whispering to Lisa) Remember, as far as he knows, we still teach Math.

Music Moment:
The planetarium's star enlightening and career-path guiding narration is accompanied by the "Jupiter" movement of Gustav Holst's The Planets.

The citizens admire the meteor shower to Don McLean's "Vincent."

Milhouse: Since Nelson nailed you with that dirt, no one thinks you're cool anymore. Even that kid that wears diapers is more popular, and he ain't popular.
Bart: So? I'll bounce back. I always bounce back—like after the time I accidentally called the teacher "Mom."
Milhouse: Even I beat you up that day...after you passed out.

Bart: Nelson steals a hood ornament, and now he's king of the school! All that's left for me is to become the biggest drunk this town's ever seen.
Homer: Pfft! Talking won't get you there! (taking a big gulp of beer) Lisa, what's bumming you out? They cancel a test or something? Heh-heh-heh-heh-heh.
Lisa: Dad, my life lacks direction!
Homer: (soberly) It's a concern. A serious concern.

THE STUFF YOU MAY HAVE MISSED

For supper, Marge serves her family "Dinnerables," a variation on the real-life all-in-one-box lunch product Lunchables, complete with the red plastic eating utensils.

The sign outside the Museum of Natural History reads, "Now with Multi-Ethnic Cavemen!"

Rigel 7, homeworld of Kang and Kodos, is referred to as the familiar blue planet within the Milky Way galaxy.

Homer and Lisa visit a hobby shop called Teenage Pasteland, and a product called Clay D'oh can be seen on the shelves.

Lisa learns about astronomy from a book called Ed McMahon's Star Searcher, which prompts her to exclaim "Hi-yo!" Ed McMahon hosted a talent show series called "Star Search" for many years.

Lisa's star gazing is interrupted, ironically, by illumination from the Starlight Hotel, which offers hourly rates and adult movies.

Miss Springfield appeared previously with Mayor Quimby at The Olde Off-Ramp Inn in "Mr. Spritz Goes to Washington" (EABF09).

Captain McCallister's scrimshaw signature on Lisa's petition pictures 19th-century whalers attacking a huge sperm whale.

The hood ornament on Fat Tony's car is shaped like an Emmy Award.

Signs held by anti-blackout protesters include "Darkness = Crime," "I'm Pro-Light," and "Lighten Up, Lisa."

The settings on City Hall's light control panel are "Low," "Normal," "Vegas," and "Perma-Noon."

Marge's crazy light-induced behavior includes ironing a phone book and carrying it around in a frying pan.

While Mr. Burns and Smithers are watching the meteor shower, Smithers does the old "yawn-and-stretch" trick to put his arm around Burns' shoulders.

MISS THE SKY

Episode EABF11
ORIGINAL AIRDATE: 03/30/03
WRITTEN BY: Dan Greaney & Allen Glazier
DIRECTED BY: Steven Dean Moore
EXECUTIVE PRODUCER: Al Jean
GUEST VOICES: Joe Mantegna as Fat Tony

townspeople to grow sick of the vandalism brought on by the reduced town lighting, so they pressure Mayor Quimby to turn the lights back up. Quimby overcompensates and turns the lights to their highest setting, which makes it seem like noon all night long. Lisa is frustrated, and Bart has the misfortune of having the lights come up just as he is attempting to vandalize Fat Tony's car.

After a week of constant daylight, some of Springfield's sleep-deprived citizens and animals start exhibiting odd behavior. Bart is still trying to get Fat Tony's hood ornament but finds it impossible with so much illumination. Realizing she and her brother have the same goal—to restore nighttime darkness to the town—Lisa and Bart sneak into the nuclear power plant with the help of a sleep-deprived and suggestible Homer. They turn the plant's main switch to overload, and when the lights all over town start to explode, Springfield is once again plunged into darkness. Those who are sleep-deprived immediately pass out from exhaustion, and those who are not quickly form an angry mob to hunt down Bart and Lisa. Just as the mob is about to capture them, Lisa points to the night sky. The brilliant meteor shower has arrived, and everyone becomes enthralled by it. Lisa is able to see the wonderful light show in the sky, Bart manages to steal his prized hood ornament, and Declan Desmond's documentary on Springfield Elementary debuts.

Prof. Frink: *What you are seeing is light pollution...light pollution. For astronomers like me, um hoyvin, this is a bigger problem even than, oh, I don't know, say, getting a date, which is difficult for the geeky people.*
Lisa: *We've got to do something. I know! Maybe we can get people to sign a petition.*
Frink: *Well, I'd like to help. I would. But if I leave this observatory, another astronomer will move right in. They're like hermit crabs. They really are quite–* (He spots movement in the distance.) *Oh, there's one now. I see you!* (He throws a microscope at an intruder.) *Hoy.*
Astronomer: (flees and yells at another astronomer) *You said he was out of microscopes!*

Luigi's New Valet Service:
Bart: *Buona sera, Fat Tony. I park-a your car, the way mama used to do.*
Fat Tony: *Why, thank you. And may I say, your mustache looks thick and hearty. Fully Italian.*
(Fat Tony gives his keys to Bart. Milhouse holds the door open for the boss and his gang.)
Milhouse: *Try-a the cheese-a pizza. It's greasy like-a you.*

Lenny: *Hey! What happened? It's bright in the middle of the night!*
Carl: *You know what this reminds me of? My Icelandic boyhood.*
Homer: *It's this new anti-crime dealie. The mayor turned the street lights way up. My daughter Lisa feels really strongly about it.*
Lenny: *Pro or con?*
Homer: *I dunno. What am I, Super Dad?*

Lisa: *Now we merely push this switch to "Overload."* (pausing) *Yet once we do, we'll be breaking the law. Can good truly come from civil disobedionco? Gandhi thought so...*
(Bart pushes past her and throws the switch.)
Bart: *But Gandhi also said "less talk, more rock!"*

Chief Wiggum: *Uh-oh! All the lights are out. We better get the entire force working on this.*
Officer Lou: *But, Chief, we are the entire force.*
Wiggum: *Okay, we gotta start recruiting, Lou.*

"I can't read porno by candlelight! Who am I? Abe Lincoln?"

Homer, on sharing his appreciation of the meteor shower: **"I wish God were alive to see this."**

Desmond: *Where do you think you'll be in seven years?*
Ralph: *I'm gonna live with underground grandma!*

"People of Springfield, I've heard your pleas! Whether you're an idealistic stargazer, like Lisa, or a faded Southern belle who needs the forgiving cloak of night to seduce naive young delivery boys with more pizza than common sense, I say Springfield will be the dimmest city in America!"

Kent Brockman: (anchoring) *Look out Matthew Modine and Charlene Tilton! There are new stars in town—sky stars! Now visible thanks to Springfield's latest cave-in to the astronomer lobby.*
Lisa: (being interviewed) *The best part is, next week we'll get to see the Deadly Meteor Shower.*
Kent: *Deadly Meteor Shower?*
Lisa: *Named after its discoverer, Professor Artemis Deadly, who was, ironically, killed in the shower of 1853.*

Grampa Simpson, on Springfield history: **"The last time those meteors came, we thought the sky was on fire. Naturally, we blamed it on the Irish. We hanged more than a few."**

Movie Moment:
The overloaded baseball field lights burst and shards of glass rain down on Groundskeeper Willie accompanied by dramatic music, much in the same way as the climactic home run pyrotechnics in the Robert Redford film *The Natural* (1984).

"Hoods Rob Hoods In 'Hoods":
Kent: *Springfield's pro-darkness policy has resulted in a spree of vandalism unmatched since the Detroit Tigers last made the playoffs over two centuries ago. The government has issued an orange alert, which, once again, means nothing.*

It is "Family Wednesday" at the Simpson household, and Marge brings out a giant jigsaw puzzle for the family to piece together. The puzzle is so big, in fact, that it takes them a week to finish it. Unfortunately, one of the pieces is missing, and they search the house to find it. During his hunt, Homer comes across Marge's memory box, collecting items that she kept from when she and Homer were dating. Inside, Homer finds a placemat on which a young Marge had expressed her doubts about their future together. On the night she wrote it, he mostly ignored her, then ended up in the hospital with alcohol poisoning. When Homer confronts Marge about what she wrote, she is forced to admit that Homer did, and still does, many things she dislikes. Homer is outraged and upset. He sleeps in Bart's room that night.

Although Marge tries to reconcile the next morning, Homer remains bitter. Finally, Homer decides to move out for a while to think things over. He moves

in briefly with Kirk Van Houten, but the loneliness and yearning of the divorced men at the singles apartment complex is more than he can bear. Homer considers returning home, but instead, he spots an ad for a roommate in the paper that sounds just right for him. Homer moves into a condominium located in Springfield's gay community. His two new roommates, Grady and Julio, are gay, and, surprisingly, this does not seem to bother Homer. In fact, Homer adapts well to living among gay men. Julio tolerates Homer, and Grady finds himself attracted to Homer, hoping his marriage will break up.

Marge, unable to express her feelings in words, hires "Weird Al" Yankovic and his band to serenade Homer. Homer is reluctant to come home, but he agrees to a date with Marge. On the night of the date, Homer is so nervous, he drinks several margaritas with Grady and Julio. He arrives late and drunk for the date, infuriating Marge. After Homer returns to the condo, he finds himself alone

SHOW HIGHLIGHTS

Lisa: *I wonder what Mom came up with for this week's Family Wednesday?*
Homer: *I hope it's as fun as Pictionary was last week!*
Bart: *Dad, we weren't playing Pictionary. That was an intervention to stop your drinking.*

Puzzle night:
Marge: *The box says it's the perfect way to spend a day. And why would a box lie to a person? (She empties an endless mountain of puzzle pieces on the coffee table and floor.) The first step is the funnest—turning all the pieces face-up.*
Bart: *Go crazy, dorks! I got better things to do. (He opens the front door, and Milhouse is there.)*
Milhouse: *(holding a rock tumbler) Hey, Bart! I fixed my rock tumbler! What do you say we turn this baby loose on some feldspar?*
Bart: *(closing the door on Milhouse) I'm in.*

At the Meaux's Tavern grand opening:
Homer: *(playing an arcade game while intoxicated) Marge, I need both hands for this game. Can you feed me nachos while I play?*
Marge: *Why don't you just stop playing?*
Homer: *Tell that to the brave crew of the S.S. Triangle! (He is playing Asteroids.) Evil rocks...take that!*
Marge: *Homer, I really don't want to feed you.*
Homer: *Come on! You're always saying we should do things as a couple.*

Ned Flanders: *Ooh...that's quite a thingama-jigsaw! But, it looks like you're missing a piece.*
Homer: *Looks like you're missing a wife.*
Flanders: *Heh-heh-heh. I walked right into that one.*

Marge: *I can't believe our family finished a project this complicated.*
Homer: *It's the only worthwhile thing I've ever made that wasn't Lisa. (Maggie gives him a dirty look. Homer challenges her.) Prove me wrong, Silent Bob!*

Homer: *Oh, so you don't like it when I drink? What other secrets have you been hoarding to use against me?*
Marge: *Homer, let it go! It's not always going to be perfect. We've been married for ten years.*
Homer: *Oh, I didn't realize you've been counting the years! Is it that horrible living with me?!*
Marge: *Well, this morning isn't a barrel of laughs!*
Homer: *It is to me! Marge, I can't live like this! I'm tired of walking around on eggshells!*
Marge: *Maybe if you didn't throw them on the floor!*
Homer: *(standing on scattered eggshells) Now you're just making up rules! Who made you Judge Judy and executioner?*

Lisa: *Dad, where are you going?*
Homer: *Kids, sometimes when a daddy learns that a mommy always hated him, he needs some time away to think.*
Bart: *But, you're not gonna get divorced like Milhouse's parents, are you?*
Homer: *Oh-ho no, no. This is nothing like Milhouse's parents. Now, if you need me, I'll be staying with Milhouse's father.*

Homer: *Are you trying to tell me that you guys are those guys that like guys?*
Grady: *That's right, Homer. We're gay!*
Homer: *You are? Hmm. Which will win out? My old-fashioned prejudices or the fact that I've already mixed my laundry with yours?*

Over a bowl of fruit salad:
Julio: *Uch. Where'd you buy this? From the guy at the exit ramp? This is disgusting!*
Homer: *Calm down, "Picky Ricardo." He made us a great breakfast, and you're just riding his butt...and not in a good way.*

Julio: *Grady, are j-ou sure j-ou want to live with him?*
Grady: *It's either him or that girl who put "Mother Earth" as a reference. And with a male roommate, we can walk around naked.*
Homer: *Way ahead of you! (Having dropped his robe, he exits.)*

Lisa: *Mom, I know Dad cares about you, but his feelings are really hurt. Why don't you just say you're sorry?*
Marge: *Lisa, marriage is a beautiful thing, but it's also a constant battle for moral superiority. So I can't apologize.*
Bart: *Couldn't you just say you're sorry and not mean it? I do it all the time! I don't think I've ever meant it.*
Marge: *Bart! That's not right!*
Bart: *(apologetically) Sorry, Mom. (snapping his fingers) See, it's that easy.*

CONDO

Episode EABF12
ORIGINAL AIRDATE: 04/13/03
WRITTEN BY: Matt Warburton
DIRECTED BY: Mark Kirkland
EXECUTIVE PRODUCER: Al Jean

GUEST VOICES: Ben Schatz as Himself,
"Weird Al" Yankovic as Himself

with Grady, who consoles him, and then gives him a tender and romantic kiss. Homer flees Grady and the condo, and ends up at Moe's. Homer wonders if his excessive drinking is to blame for his marital woes, but before he can explore this line of reasoning, Moe forces him to get so drunk that he winds up at the hospital with alcohol poisoning again. Dr. Hibbert reveals that he videotaped the last time Homer was there with alcohol poisoning—the same night Marge wrote the hurtful things that have upset Homer so much. Dr. Hibbert plays the video, and Homer hears the endearing and loving words she shared with him while he was unconscious. Homer realizes he has made a mistake doubting Marge's love for him. Just then, Marge arrives, and the couple reconciles.

THE STUFF YOU MAY HAVE MISSED

Bart's drawing of Homer's alcohol intervention pictures Homer happily drunk, holding a bottle of beer, while Bart, Lisa and Maggie cry and point at his drunken antics.

The "Concert in Golden Gate Park" jigsaw puzzle is labeled as an "Oprah's Puzzle Club" jigsaw.

Lonny suffers another in a series of eye injuries, chronicled in "Saddlesore Galactica" (BABF09) and "Homer Vs. Dignity" (CABF04).

When Homer is searching through a closet, his Mr. Plow jacket and Pin Pals bowling shirt are seen.

The fake business card Homer made to impress Marge when they were first going out says, "Homer Simpson, Quarterback" and pictures a football player about to throw a football.

The T-shirt Homer finds in Marge's memory box says, "Rolling Stones Last Tour Ever '89," poking fun at the fact that the Stones have had more than their fair share of farewell concert tours.

The placemat from the Moe's Tavern grand opening has "Moe's" spelled "Meaux's."

Outside Homer and Marge's bedroom, Patty and Selma have put up an image-changing billboard that reads, "Homer Out of Springfield - Vote Yes on 104." When the billboard changes pictures,

we see Patty and Selma kicking Homer over the city limits line, with a sign behind them that reads, "Now Leaving Springfield."

The sign outside Kirk Van Houten's apartment complex says, "Bachelor Arms - 3 Days Without a Suicide." A gunshot is heard, and the 3 is changed to 0.

In the gay section of Springfield, Homer is seen walking past such businesses as "Alternative Knifestyles," "Armistead's Mopeds" and "Fab Abs." Mr. Smithers skates out of the "Sconewall Bakery." Later, Homer, Grady, and Julio go shopping at "Victor/Victoria's - An Upscale Men's Clothing Store." At night, the three of them go dancing at "One Night Stan's."

When Grady educates Homer about gays on television, he first clicks on the original Dr. Tad Winslow, the character that "handsome" Moe replaced on the soap opera "It Never Ends" in "Pygmoelian" (BABF12).

To give himself a little stubble after shaving, Homer uses spray-on "Muzzle in a Can."

At Medieval Times, the marquee announces, "Jousting Contest - Henry VI versus Spider-Man." Later, Comic Book Guy is seen being hauled out of the arena, a jousting lance piercing his belly.

Movie Moment:
While searching in the closet, Homer says, "Puzzle piece, come out and play-aay!" mimicking David Patrick Kelly's memorable taunt, "Warriors, come out and play-aay!" from the cult-favorite flick *The Warriors* (1979).

A knight at Medieval Times: **"Who dares challenge ye Black Knight? Step forward if ye be free of lower back pain, heart conditions, and pregnancy. And please turn off thy cell phones and pagers!"**

"I've learned a lot living here. It doesn't matter what someone's sexual preferences are...unless they're a celebrity, in which case it's dish, dish, dish!"

Wasting time in Margaritaville:
Julio: *Homer, weren't you supposed to meet your wife half an hour ago?*
Homer: *D'oh! You guys don't have a gay time machine do you?*
Julio: *J-es. It's called Grady's shoe closet.*
Grady: *Hey, Julio? Ouch.*

Homer: *You know, Moe, I was just thinking. My problems with Marge started because I drink too much. And then tonight, alcohol only made things worse. Maybe all of my problems are actually caused by...*
Moe: *(shoving a beer bottle in Homer's mouth and pouring it down his throat.) Yeah, yeah, yeah. Take your medicine, ya lush ya.*

(Marge kisses Homer.)
Homer: *That is the best kiss I've had tonight!* *(thought) Or was it?*
Marge: *Homie? What are you thinking?*
Homer: *(quickly) Manly thoughts!* *(They kiss again.)*

Hooking up at One Night Stan's:
Woman: *I didn't think it was possible, but watching him makes me more lesbian.*
Hans Moleman: *(in an army uniform) Lesbian? This isn't my Army reunion.*
Large Gay Man: *(dressed in cut-off military garb) You're coming home with me.*
Moleman: *(saluting) Yes, Colonel.*

Homer: *"Weird Al" Yankovic?!*
"Weird Al": *Homer, Marge wrote me about what happened. And, as soon as her check cleared, I was on the first reasonably priced flight here.*
Homer: *Did you ever get the parody songs I sent you?*
"Weird Al": *Sigh! Yes.*
Homer: *Which one was better? "Living La Pizza Loca" or "Another One Bites the Crust"?*
"Weird Al": *They were pretty much the same, Homer.*
Homer: *(grumbling) Yeah, like you and Alan Sherman.*

"Weird Al's" reconciliation song: (to the tune of John Mellencamp's "Jack and Diane")
Little ditty 'bout Homer and Marge,
Her heart was as big as his stomach was large,
Oh yeah, they say love goes on,
Long after the grilled cheese sandwich is gone!
(Reprise over credits)
That's the story 'bout Homer and Marge,
Two folks I helped out for a nominal charge,
After Homer went gay, they patched up their schism,
But the dude never dealt with his alcoholism!
"Weird Al" say a ...
Oh yeah, the credits go on,
Long after the viewer's interest is gone,
Oh yeah, "Weird Al" had fun on this show,
Even if it was just a brief cameo!

Music Moment:
Pet Shop Boys' "West End Girls" plays over Homer's alternative lifestyle montage.

JULIO AND GRADY

Together they lead:
An active social life involving cocktails

Their cure for nerves:
Margaritas

Julio:
Prefers the *New York Times* to the *Springfield Shopper*; is disgusted by fruit bought from the guy on the exit ramp; changes his hair color constantly; and has a soft spot for eight-year-old girls

Grady:
Prefers to walk around naked; holds the key to the lotion cabinet; and has a strong theatrical "gay-dar," an outdated shoe collection, and a soft spot for Homer Simpson

HE'S SLEEPING IN THE PANTRY.

¡GASP!¡ MY SPICES!

Guest Voice:
Scott Thompson as Grady

LUKE STETSON
JUNIOR WRANGLER

Age:
13

Appearance:
Breathtaking

Interests:
Animal rights, cloud gazing, moonlight serenades, square dancing, and a free Tibet

Represents:
A kinder, gentler side of the West

History:
His family left Central Park West to avoid city slickers with chutzpah

> THIS HERE'S THE NEW WEST, WHERE WE RESPECT EQUINE AND BOVINE AMERICANS.

Guest Voice:
Jonathan Taylor Thomas as Luke Stetson

DUDE, WHERE'S

I t is Christmastime, and during their house-to-house caroling, the Blue-Haired Lawyer informs the Simpsons that they cannot sing the songs they are singing due to copyright laws. Homer decides to write an original Christmas carol, but after Ned Flanders interrupts him, Homer is inspired to write a song about how much he hates his neighbor. The song gets the attention of music star David Byrne of Talking Heads. Byrne produces a recording of Homer's song, and it soon becomes a big hit. Eventually, the Simpsons get sick of hearing it every time they turn on the radio. They decide to leave town, taking a vacation at a dude ranch until the song's popularity wanes.

At the dude ranch, everybody is having a good time except Lisa. She dislikes the way the ranchers treat animals and the local indigenous people, but she changes her mind about the vacation spot when she meets a young cowhand named Luke Stetson. Luke is environmentally friendly, he is cute, and he plays the guitar to accompany Lisa's sax. Lisa's affection for Luke has Marge worried. She thinks Lisa is too young to be falling so hard for a boy. Meanwhile, Homer and Bart decide to help the local Native Americans after they find out that beavers have built a dam and flooded the natives' land. Together, Homer and Bart attempt to dismantle the beaver dam, but the vicious creatures outsmart them and attack Homer. Later, as everyone prepares for a dance to be held that evening, Lisa gets a shock. She overhears Luke on the phone, inviting a girl named Clara to the dance.

Heartbroken, Lisa goes for a ride on her pony, and while

SHOW HIGHLIGHTS

The Simpsons: (singing) ...walkin' in a Winter Wonderland!
Mr. Burns: Exquisite, just exquisite! Makes me wish I hadn't released the hounds.
(The vicious guard dogs send the Simpsons family fleeing for their lives.)
Smithers: Shall I call them off, sir?
Mr. Burns: No, no! It's their Christmas, too.

The Simpsons: (singing to the tune "Hava "Nagila") Have a nice Christmas, have a nice Christmas, have a nice Christmas...
Lisa: Non-Christian friends!
Krusty: That's even worse than "I'm Dreaming of a Whitefish Christmas"!
Rabbi Krustofski: For this I tied my bathrobe?

Blue-Haired Lawyer: Cease and desist! You are forbidden to perform that song without paying royalties to the copyright owner.
Marge: Nobody owns Christmas carols. They belong to everyone, like grapes at the grocery store!
Blue-Haired Lawyer: Not true! But you are welcome to sing the many beloved public domain carols such as "O Tannenbaum," "Good King Wenceslas," "Jesu, Joy of Man's Desiring"...
Homer: Those suck. They're worse than nothing. I could write way better songs.
Blue-Haired Lawyer: Go ahead. But don't use A-flat or G-natural. Those notes are owned by Disney.
Homer: Oooh...
Blue-Haired Lawyer: That's A-flat.
Homer: (higher pitched) Oooh...
Blue-Haired Lawyer: That's better.

Homer's Christmas carol:
Christmas in December
Wow, wow, wow!
Give me tons of presents
Now, now, now!

Music Moment:
Maggie imitates the dance moves and soda endorsing savvy of Britney Spears to the pop star's "Oops!...I Did It Again."

David Byrne: Excuse me? I've been researching indigenous folk music of Springfield, and I couldn't help overhearing your delightfully cruel hate song.
Carl: David Byrne?
Moe: Singer, artist, composer, director, Talking Head?
David Byrne: And...I used to wrestle under the name "El Diablo."
Lenny: I thought that was Philip Glass?
David Byrne: Yeah, he wishes.

Marge: I am so sick of that song!
Homer: Ugh! Me, too! I've come to hate my own creation. Now I know how God feels.

The extended salsa version of "Everybody Hates Ned Flanders":
No nos gusta Flanders.
Es un hombre estupido.
No nos gusta Flanders.

David Byrne: Can you take me to the hospital?
Moe: Yeah, no problem.
(They pass Springfield General Hospital.)
David Byrne: Wasn't that the hospital?
Moe: Uh...you ever see the movie Misery?
David Byrne: Actually, no.
Moe: Then this'll all be new to you.

Movie Moment:
Cleanie, voiced by Andy Serkis, crawls out of the chuck wagon, slinks over to the picnic blanket, gathers up all the garbage, and says, "My precious! Gollum!" in a tip of the hat to the actor's gripping performance in the three *The Lord of the Rings* (2001–2003) films.

Moe's query to David Byrne about the movie *Misery* (1990) could not be more appropriate. The film, based on a Stephen King novel, is about a celebrity who is held captive by a deranged fan after being injured in a car accident.

Bart: I thought you guys lived off the land. How come you're selling junk to jerks like us?
Native American: We used to live and farm in a beautiful valley, then the river was dammed to make that lake by our ancient enemy—the beaver.
Marge: Why don't you just chase the beavers away?
Native American: Unfortunately, the beaver is also our god. In retrospect, it was a poor choice.

Homer: You poor people are guests in our country, and the beaver have no right to treat you that way! If I get back your land, will you promise to build a casino on it?
Native American: Sure! And when we do, your breakfast will be comped.
Homer: How many decks will your blackjack dealers use?
Native American: Eight.
Homer: Three.
Native American: Four.
Homer: Deal! (They hug.) My brother.

Homer, victim of a vicious beaver attack: **"No! I wanted to die choking on food!"**

Marge: Shucks, Lisa. You sure have taken a shine to that cowpoke.
Lisa: Mom, why are you talking like that?
Marge: Don't rightly know! I just soaked up the lingo like a biscuit in a bucketful of gopher gravy...I'll stop now.

 "We did it! Finally, man has triumphed over a small furry animal!"

Indian Chief: Thank you. You have restored our village and our way of life.
Brave: We would like to make you honorary members of our tribe.
Indian Chief: Drink deep from these cups. (Homer and Bart drink deeply.) The bear urine will make you strong. (Bart and Homer stare at him, and he laughs.) Actually, it's Fresca.
(Homer and Bart spit it out.)
Brave: Fresca?!

 100

MY RANCH?

Episode EABF13
ORIGINAL AIRDATE: 04/27/03
WRITTEN BY: Ian Maxtone-Graham
DIRECTED BY: Chris Clements
EXECUTIVE PRODUCER: Al Jean
GUEST VOICES: David Byrne as Himself, Andy Serkis as Cleanie

on the horse trail, she meets Clara, the girl Luke invited to the dance. Clara does not know the way to the dude ranch, so Lisa deviously gives her the wrong directions. The unwitting girl takes off into a dark, dangerous part of the forest. At the same time, Homer and Bart distract and outwit the wily and dangerous beavers, destroy the dam, and return the land to the grateful tribe. That night, the ranchers are having a great time at the dance, and Lisa is overjoyed to have Luke to herself. But Luke is worried that Clara has not arrived. That is when Lisa discovers that Clara is Luke's sister. Totally ashamed of herself, Lisa enlists Bart's help, and they go out looking for Luke's missing sister. They find her stranded on a rock in the middle of the newly flowing river. Since Clara cannot swim and the water is rising, Bart acts quickly and rescues her, tricking the beavers into knocking down a tree and giving Clara a way out of the river. The next day, the Simpsons are preparing to leave, and although Clara did not tell her brother what Lisa did, Lisa herself comes clean with Luke. Unfortunately, Luke is furious with her, and Lisa is crushed. On the way home, Marge explains to Lisa that romantic relationships can be hard. When they discover that Moe is Springfield's new "one hit wonder," they turn around and go back to the dude ranch for another week.

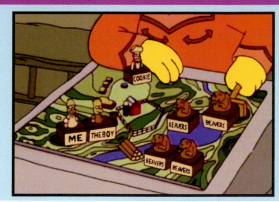

The square-dance caller's product placement:

Well...grab your partner and start swingin' 'em.
Don't forget the two-drink minimum.
Take your corner by the hand.
Get adult videos on demand.
Flash your teeth, let's see those smiles.
Pay with Visa, earn free miles. Yee-haw!

Luke: *Dang it! Clara should be here by now.*
Lisa: *I'm sure she's just running late. Or she's not coming because she doesn't understand how special you are.*
Luke: *That sure don't sound like my sister.*
Lisa: *Sister? You mean she's not your girlfriend?!*
Luke: *Hell, no! They outlawed that in this state two years ago.*

Lisa: *I'm sorry. I only sent you the wrong way because I thought you were Luke's girlfriend.*
Clara: (cross) *Well, that certainly justifies attempted murder! You know, there are more important things in this world than boys, and wh—*(to Bart) *Hellooo, handsome!*
Bart: *What's up, cootie breath?*

Homer: *Look at those stupid city slickers with their fur coats and pointy hats.*
Marge: *Homer, those are elk.*
Homer: *I still hate them.* (hollering) *Go back to Pittsburgh!*

Lisa: (sobbing) *Oh, I had my first crush, and all it did was make me do terrible things and then break my heart.*
Marge: *Lisa, welcome to love. It's full of doubt and pain and uncertainty. But then, one day, you find a man you love so much, it hurts.*
Homer: (suspiciously) *Who is he?!*
Marge: *You, Homie.*
Homer: *Woo-hoo! In your face, imaginary guy!*

The Moe Szyslak Connection's "Moe, Moe, Moe":
(to the tune "More, More, More")

Moe, Moe, Moe!
How do you like me?
How do you like me?
Moe, Moe, Moe!
Why don't you like me?
Nobody likes me...

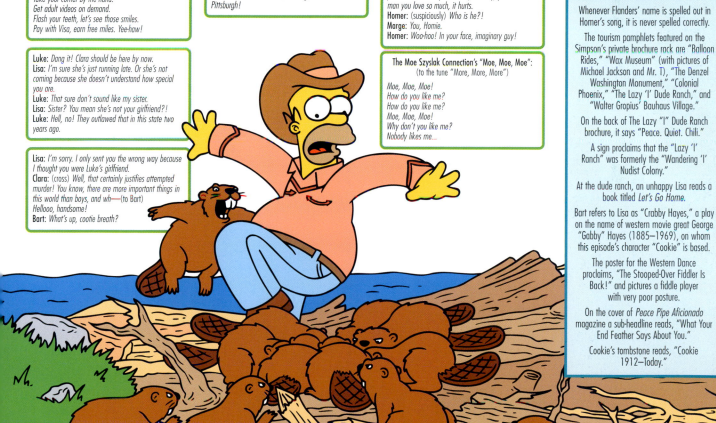

THE STUFF YOU MAY HAVE MISSED

Whenever Flanders' name is spelled out in Homer's song, it is never spelled correctly.

The tourism pamphlets featured on the Simpson's private brochure rack are "Balloon Rides," "Wax Museum" (with pictures of Michael Jackson and Mr. T), "The Denzel Washington Monument," "Colonial Phoenix," "The Lazy 'I' Dude Ranch," and "Walter Gropius' Bauhaus Village."

On the back of The Lazy "I" Dude Ranch brochure, it says "Peace. Quiet. Chili."

A sign proclaims that the "Lazy 'I' Ranch" was formerly the "Wandering 'I' Nudist Colony."

At the dude ranch, an unhappy Lisa reads a book titled *Let's Go Home*.

Bart refers to Lisa as "Crabby Hayes," a play on the name of western movie great George "Gabby" Hayes (1885–1969), on whom this episode's character "Cookie" is based.

The poster for the Western Dance proclaims, "The Stooped-Over Fiddler Is Back!" and pictures a fiddle player with very poor posture.

On the cover of *Peace Pipe Aficionado* magazine a sub-headline reads, "What Your End Feather Says About You."

Cookie's tombstone reads, "Cookie 1912–Today."

Bart and his friends are having a club meeting in his treehouse, and their first order of new business is to spy on Lisa and her girlfriends. Lisa discovers a tin can on a wire that the boys are using to bug her tea party, so she begins tugging on it. Her friends join in, as do the boys in the treehouse. Soon, the treehouse is torn apart from the back-and-forth swaying of the tree. Homer promises to help Bart restore the destroyed treehouse, but they spend so much time goofing off, Marge decides to call in the Amish to rebuild it. The Simpsons throw a party in the new treehouse, but, because of the Amish's inexperience with electrical wiring, the building catches on fire. Everyone escapes the fire except Homer, who is trapped under a large ice sculpture. Homer sees that Santa's Little Helper is still in the treehouse and entreats the dog to help him, but Santa's Little Helper makes a cowardly exit. It is the Simpsons' cat, Snowball II, who saves Homer. Homer has nothing but kind words for Snowball II, but Santa's Little Helper is, literally, in the doghouse.

The town joins Homer in praising Snowball II as a hero, even changing the old dog park into a cat park, and Homer disowns Santa's Little Helper while being interviewed on television. After Santa's Little Helper further incurs Homer's wrath by eating his unattended burger, the dog is chained to a tree in the backyard. Santa's Little Helper manages to open a can of Duff Beer that Homer has left behind, balancing it on his nose as he drinks its contents. A passing newspaper photographer takes a picture of the dog, and Santa's Little Helper soon captures the attention and marketing imagination of H. K. Duff VII, C.E.O. of the Duff Corporation. The C.E.O decides to fire his longtime spokesman, Duffman, and replace him with Santa's Little Helper. Homer goes along with the idea since it means a lot of money and free beer, and soon Santa's Little Helper, as Suds McDuff, becomes a big success, increasing the sales of Duff Brewery products. Santa's Little Helper's original owner comes back to claim him, using one of Homer's disparaging remarks about Santa's Little Helper to take back the dog. Homer loses his claim on the dog and the riches that come with him, and Bart loses his best friend.

As time goes by, the Simpsons become concerned that Santa's Little Helper's old owner is overworking the poor dog. Plus, Bart misses his dog. They devise

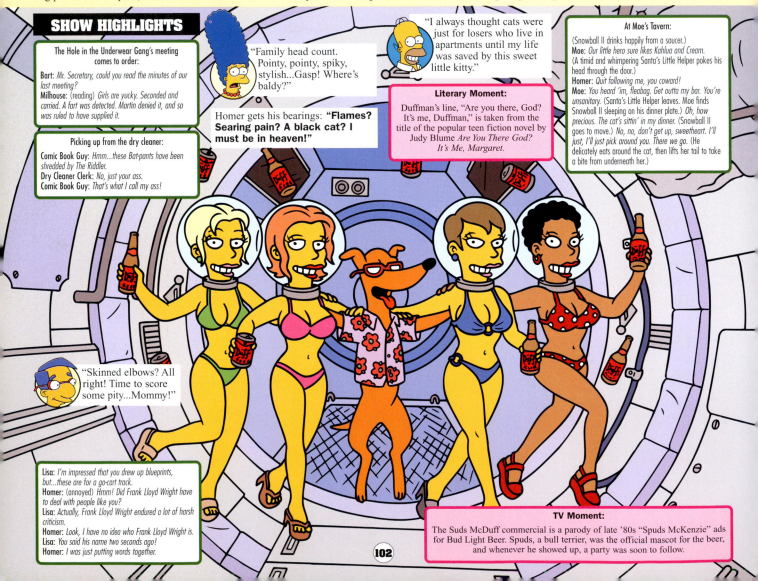

SHOW HIGHLIGHTS

The Hole in the Underwear Gang's meeting comes to order:
Bart: *Mr. Secretary, could you read the minutes of our last meeting?*
Milhouse: *(reading) Girls are yucky. Seconded and carried. A fart was detected. Martin denied it, and so was ruled to have supplied it.*

Picking up from the dry cleaner:
Comic Book Guy: *Hmm...these Bat-pants have been shredded by The Riddler.*
Dry Cleaner Clerk: *No, just your ass.*
Comic Book Guy: *That's what I call my ass!*

"Family head count. Pointy, pointy, spiky, stylish...Gasp! Where's baldy?"

Homer gets his bearings: **"Flames? Searing pain? A black cat? I must be in heaven!"**

"I always thought cats were just for losers who live in apartments until my life was saved by this sweet little kitty."

Literary Moment:
Duffman's line, "Are you there, God? It's me, Duffman," is taken from the title of the popular teen fiction novel by Judy Blume *Are You There God? It's Me, Margaret.*

At Moe's Tavern:
(Snowball II drinks happily from a saucer.)
Moe: *Our little hero sure likes Kahlua and Cream.*
(A timid and whimpering Santa's Little Helper pokes his head through the door.)
Homer: *Quit following me, you coward!*
Moe: *You heard 'im, fleabag. Get outta my bar. You're unsanitary.* (Santa's Little Helper leaves. Moe finds Snowball II sleeping on his dinner plate.) *Oh, how precious. The cat's sittin' in my dinner.* (Snowball II goes to move.) *No, no, don't get up, sweetheart. I'll just, I'll just pick around you. There we go.* (He delicately eats around the cat, then lifts her tail to take a bite from underneath her.)

"Skinned elbows? All right! Time to score some pity...Mommy!"

Lisa: *I'm impressed that you drew up blueprints, but...these are for a go-cart track.*
Homer: *(annoyed) Hmm! Did Frank Lloyd Wright have to deal with people like you?*
Lisa: *Actually, Frank Lloyd Wright endured a lot of harsh criticism.*
Homer: *Look, I have no idea who Frank Lloyd Wright is.*
Lisa: *You said his name two seconds ago!*
Homer: *I was just putting words together.*

TV Moment:
The Suds McDuff commercial is a parody of late '80s "Spuds McKenzie" ads for Bud Light Beer. Spuds, a bull terrier, was the official mascot for the beer, and whenever he showed up, a party was soon to follow.

BELLY

Episode EABF14
ORIGINAL AIRDATE: 05/04/03
WRITTEN BY: John Frink & Don Payne
DIRECTED BY: Bob Anderson
EXECUTIVE PRODUCER: Al Jean
GUEST VOICES: Stacy Keach as H. K. Duff VII

a plan to get Santa's Little Helper back, enlisting the help of Duffman, now living and working in a men's shelter. Homer's plan is to pose as a drowning swimmer at a Duff beach promotion, hoping to reveal the dog's cowardly nature. With Suds McDuff's reputation tarnished, Duffman will earn back his job as spokesman by rescuing Homer. The plan starts to work at first. Santa's Little Helper is too afraid to save Homer, but when a shark arrives on the scene, so is Duffman. Homer is forced to save himself by shoving the keg of Duff Beer he was using as a flotation device into the shark's gaping jaws. The shark becomes drunk on the beer. Seeing that the drunken shark delights the crowd, H. K. Duff VII declares it the new Duff mascot. Santa's Little Helper's old owner gives the dog back to the Simpsons since he is no longer a moneymaker, and Homer vows to never be angry with Santa's Little Helper again, even though the dog's destructive behavior continues.

SUDS MCDUFF SPOKESDOG/MASCOT FOR DUFF BEER

Qualifications:
He's young, slim, and can stand on his hind legs

Benefits of owning him:
Royalties in perpetuity, a bottomless keg of beer, unlimited use of the Duff corporate jet, and wads of cash

Where he can be found:
On international space stations, "Live with Regis and Kelly," game shows, book signings, and beach party coronations

What makes a good mascot:
Guys want to be him, girls think they can change him

Escorts of choice:
Human girlfriends

Title of his autobiography:
I, Suds

His slogan:
"Drink Duff—Man's Other Best Friend"

Movie Moment:

The international space station in the Suds McDuff commercial floats in space to Johann Strauss' "The Blue Danube Waltz," just like the one in Stanley Kubrick's *2001: A Space Odyssey* (1968).

Homer is attacked by a great white shark, as a *Jaws* (1975)-influenced soundtrack plays. He manages to save himself in much the same way Roy Scheider did. Rather than shoving a pressurized oxygen tank into the shark's mouth, he shoves in a huge carbonated keg of Duff beer.

Mayor Quimby endorses Snowball II and more: **"Today I can truly say 'Ich bin eine feline!' And I hereby rename Springfield Dog Park... the Snowball II Municipal Cat Park sponsored by Buzz Cola with lemon.** *(taking a sip from a can of soda)* **Damn, that's a lemony cola."**

Kent Brockman: *Mr. Simpson, how long have you been a cat person?*
Homer: *All my life, Kent. I prefer "catsup" to "ketchup," and to me, "Yusuf Islam" will always be "Cat Stevens."*
Kent: *Heh heh heh. Terrific stuff! You must really love the Broadway musical* Cats.
Homer: *God, no! It sucks!*

Homer: *Why you little...!* (He strangles Santa's Little Helper.)
Marge: *Stop it, Homer! That's inhumane. Use the choke chain.*
Homer: *Fine.* (to dog) *I want you to sit there, look through the window and watch me eat a ham!* Marge? *Prepare the emergency ham!*

THE STUFF YOU MAY HAVE MISSED

The name of Bart's treehouse club, "The Hole in the Underwear Gang," is a play on the late-19th-century Wild West hideout "The Hole-in-the-Wall," a Wyoming refuge for such notorious outlaws as Jesse James and Butch Cassidy, who were dubbed "The Hole-in-the-Wall Gang."

At the dry cleaner, Comic Book Guy picks up his Star Trek, Spider-Man, and Batman costumes.

The Devil, cornered in a barn by an Amish farmer with a pitchfork when Marge calls for help, can later be seen at Bart's treehouse grand opening.

H. K. Duff VIII, the owner of the Springfield Isotopes in "Hungry Hungry Homer" (CABF09), should not be confused with H.K. Duff VII, C.E.O. of the Duff Corporation in this episode. Although they look identical and are both voiced by Stacy Keach, H. K. Duff VII has a distinctive drawl and wears western clothes and a bolo tie. Perhaps that is why Lisa goes to great lengths to refer to him as "Mr. Duff the Seventh."

The "We'll Be Right Back" title card that appears after Krusty has been attacked by the toxic prickle snake pictures an ambulance speeding along, its lights flashing, and a pair of big clown feet sticking out the back door.

Homer's list of his favorites in the family does not include Snowball II, but it does have his Vegas wife at the bottom.

There are several advertisements on the walls of H. K. Duff VII's office featuring Suds McDuff, including: "Share a Cold Duff with Your Best Friend" (with Rainier Wolfcastle), "Drink Duff—Man's Other Best Friend," ¡Me gusto Duff Cerveza tambien! (with Bumblee Man), "Get Your Paws on Some 40s" (with Titania from "Pygmoelian" BABF12), a photo with Krusty, and a "got duff?" ad.

Les, Santa's Little Helper's original owner, was last seen chasing off the dog in "Simpsons Roasting on an Open Fire" (7G08), the first full-length episode of the series.

The sign outside the Springfield Men's Mission reads, "We Add God to Your Misery."

Duffman claims his real name is Barry Duffman. In "Hungry Hungry Homer" (CABF09), he is referred to as Sid, and in "Pygmoelian" (BABF12) his name is Larry. One explanation for the inconsistency is Duffman's line in "Jaws Wired Shut" (DABF05): "Duffman can never die, only the actors who play him!"

Duffman: *Oo...Duffman could use an eye-opener.*
H.K. Duff VII: *Take a hike, Duffman. You're a disgrace to the unitard.*
Duffman: *You're firing me? But, what about my children...Duff-Girl and Duff-Lad?*
H.K. Duff VII: *Oh, those were one-shot characters in a Super Bowl ad!*
Duffman: *(weakly) Oh, yeah.*

Lisa: *Why does a dog have human girlfriends?*
Marge: *People do crazy things in ads...like eat at Arby's.*

Homer: *I'll help you get him back! He may have been a dirty, stinking coward, but show me a Simpson that isn't.*
Lisa: *I'm not a coward.*
(Homer screams and makes scary face at Lisa. She does not react.)
Homer: *All right, you're not a coward. And that's beside the point, because...*
(Homer screams and makes scary face at Lisa again, to no effect.)
Lisa: *Look, to get our dog back, we need a plan!*
Homer: *A plan, eh?* (Homer screams and makes scary faces, then gives up.) *Okay, we'll use a plan.*

Agnes: *That dog is a coward.* (She looks at Principal Skinner.) *And I know cowards.*
Skinner: *Mother! I served in 'Nam.*
Agnes: *And you've been bitching about it for thirty years!*

Bart, upon losing his best friend: **"Who's gonna eat my homework now?"**

MARRIAGE COUNSELOR

His manner:
Quiet and subdued

Believes in:
Making lists and writing on his clipboard

Methods of treatment:
Romantic suggestions and blows to the head with his clipboard

How he sees Homer:
As a big dollar sign

How Homer sees him:
As a big hot dog

How he charges:
By the hour

How effective he is:
Able to reduce a spurned wife's elbow in the face to an elbow in the stomach

YOU'RE AN IDIOT!

BRAKE MY

During a field trip to the Springfield Aquarium, Bart pulls a prank inside a fish tank, but he is soon attacked by the marine life and winds up in the hospital. Marge is unable to find her insurance card and calls all over town looking for Homer, but she is unable to reach him. When Homer does arrive at the hospital, Marge insists he get a cell phone. At Barney's suggestion and for safety's sake, Homer goes to the Try-N-Save to get a hands-free headset for his cell phone. While there, the salesman convinces Homer to purchase all manner of car cigarette lighter plug-in devices—like a DVD player and a snow-cone machine— which makes Homer's car decidedly unsafe. Distracted by all his gadgets, Homer drives off a pier and into the ocean. The Coast Guard rescues Homer and his car, but Homer has his license taken away in court. He is angry about not being able to drive, but it is Marge who suffers, having to drive everybody everywhere and run all the errands. This extra duty, over time, begins to wear on her. Meanwhile, Homer discovers that he is growing healthier and happier from walking, and he no longer envies people in their cars. Homer even sings about his newly discovered mode of transportation, which grows into a big musical production number, until he is unexpectedly hit by a car…driven by Marge.

SHOW HIGHLIGHTS

Tour Guide: *Well, it looks like Mr. Walrus and his family are enjoying their Sunday brunch.* (The crowd laughs good-naturedly.) *Shut up! What am I, some sort of joke to you people? Now, over here is our newest exhibit "The Wonders of the Gulf Coast."*
Kids: *Ooooh!*
Tour Guide: *Shut up! It's not that exciting.*

Homer: *Barney, you ever notice how hard it is to drive with your knees?*
Barney: *Why don't you get one of those hands-free phones? It's the next best thing to paying attention to the road.*
Homer: *Hands-free, eh? Then I could give the brothers the black power salute.* (looking out window he sees Carl, Officer Lou, Dr. Hibbert, and Drederick Tatum driving next to him) *Black power! Black power!*
Carl: *Was that Al Roker?*
Drederick Tatum: *His exuberance is perplexing.*

Homer, after taking a short drive off a long pier: **"I'll never mock the Coast Guard again! You Navy rejects are all right."**

Homer: *I am so screwed! I can't drive to work, I can't drive to the store, and I certainly can't drive to the store at work.*
Marge: *Sigh! I guess I'll have to do all your driving chores. That's what a good wife does, picks up the slack.*
Homer: *That reminds me, we've gotta pick up my slacks at that dry cleaner in Shelbyville.*
Marge: *Why can't you use the local dry cleaner?*
Homer: (ashamed) *I didn't want them to know my size.*

Movie Moment:
One of the videos Homer watches at the video rental store is *Buttercups of Autumn*, a parody of one of the last films of legendary actress Bette Davis, *Whales of August* (1987), which also stars Lillian Gish, Vincent Price, Ann Southern and an actor named Frank Grimes.

While walking to work, Homer runs a stick across a fence and across Mr. Wilson's face—that is, Mr. Wilson, as played by Walter Matthau in *Dennis the Menace* (1993).

Homer: *Thanks for picking my friends up from the strip club, Marge.*
Lenny: *Can we stop for ice cream?*
Carl: *Homer always stops for ice cream.*
Marge: *We'll see.*
Lenny: *That always means no.*

Homer: *Where's your mother? I gotta get to Moe's!*
Lisa: *Dad, Mom's been driving everyone everywhere. Why don't you take public transportation?*
Homer: *Public transportation is for jerks and lesbians.*

(Ralph, sitting in the driver's seat of a police cruiser, passes Homer.)
Ralph: *I let go of the parking brake!*
(Chief Wiggum tries to catch up, riding Ralph's tricycle.)
Chief Wiggum: *Ralphie, if you stop the car, I'll let you play with my gun.*

Homer: (incredulous) *I did it! I walked all the way to Moe's from my house.*
Bart: (calling down the street from the Simpson house) *Way to go, Dad!*
Homer: *You know, I feel pretty good. Maybe I should just keep walking instead of going into a dark, dreary bar.*
Moe: (opening the door and grabbing Homer by the ear) *Hey, get in here, boozy. You're late for your drunkening.*
Homer: *No! From now on, walking is my beer, and feeling good is my hangover.* (He leaves.)

Homer: *Calm down, Stresserella!*
Marge: *I'm stressed because, now that you've lost your license, I'm a full-time family chauffeur.*
Homer: *Now, now, honey. We all appreciate what you do, but real chauffeurs have uniforms and licenses. You could get into a lot of trouble with the Livery Commission.*
Marge: *To hell with the Livery Commission!*
Homer: (worriedly) *Marge, you don't know what you're saying!*

Boys will be boys:
Marge: (to Bart and Milhouse) *How could you both miss the bus to school?!*
Bart: *We touched hands and then we had to wash the cooties off.*
Marge: *Hrrm!*

Homer: *How 'bout we take a family walk around the block?*
Lisa: *Yay! I wanna amble.*
Bart: *I wanna saunter.*
Lisa: *Amble!*
Bart: *Saunter!*
Lisa: *Amble!*
Bart: *Saunter!*
Marge: *Stop saying things!*
Homer: *Honey, you seem frazzled. Why don't you come with us?*
Marge: (perking up) *Hey, I'd like that!* (remembering) *Oh, I can't. I have to go pick up Grampa. He proposed to another hooker at the bus station.*

THE STUFF YOU MAY HAVE MISSED

At the Springfield Aquarium, a sign assures everyone, "Dead Fish Skimmed Daily."

The wall photos of aquarium-related mishaps that Dr. Hibbert shows Marge feature Ralph Wiggum, who has a blowfish in his mouth, a kid with his head stuck in a whale's blowhole, and a giant squid attacking a school bus.

Things Homer buys to plug into his car's cigarette lighter: a DVD player, a snow-cone machine, a lava lamp, a fog machine, a computer, a coffee maker, Lite Brite, a P.A. system, a stereo, a turntable, a portable CD player, a fax machine, a hot plate, a deep fryer with heat lamp station, and a television.

When Bart and Milhouse's Peruvian Fighting Frogs fight, they sound distinctly South American. The Bart and Milhouse fight music plays as their frogs tussle.

As Bart, Lisa, and Homer skip happily past the window several times, they pass the window in one direction with Homer carrying Bart and Lisa on his shoulders, then a final time with Bart carrying Lisa and Homer on his shoulders.

After Homer realizes he is not wearing a fanny pack, he just throws his money away.

At the marriage counselor's office, a sign on the window reads, "The One Who's Wrong Pays."

The note that mysteriously calls Ned Flanders out of town reads, "Dude, Meet Me in Montana. XXOO, Jesus (H. Christ)."

WIFE, PLEASE

Episode EABF15
ORIGINAL AIRDATE: 05/11/03
WRITTEN BY: Tim Long
DIRECTED BY: Pete Michels
EXECUTIVE PRODUCER: Al Jean

GUEST VOICES: Jackson Browne as Himself, Steve Buscemi as Himself, Jane Kaczmarek as Judge Harm

Homer suffers a crushed pelvis and is placed on bed rest, and Marge claims that she accidentally hit the accelerator rather than the brake, causing the accident. She tells Homer that she will take care of him, but while trying to feed him, Marge accidentally scalds him with soup. Homer recovers quickly, and while showing Marge how agile he is becoming again, Marge kicks his cane away, knocking him over. Homer suddenly realizes that Marge is trying to hurt him. When confronted, Marge admits she has come to hate him. They decide to go to a marriage counselor, where Marge declares that Homer does not care about her as much as he cares about himself. With the marriage counselor's guidance, Homer arranges a big banquet in her honor in their backyard to show her how much he cares about her. All of their friends come, and Marge is serenaded by singer Jackson Browne. Marge feels loved, and she and Homer make up. As the party comes to an end, Homer turns on the backyard lawn sprinklers to get rid of the remaining guests.

Lenny: *Morning, Homer. Lookin' good.*
Carl: *Yeah, walking's made a new man out of you.*
Homer: *It sure has.* (pointing to his rear end) *You see this bulge back here? Now it actually is a fanny pack.* (He attempts to stick a dollar bill in it, but cannot.) *No, wait. It's still my ass. But your point is well taken.*

Homer, responding to his crushed pelvis: **"Oh, my feet are inside me!"**

Marge: *I am so sorry, Homie. How is your crushed pelvis?*
Homer: (in bed) *Pretty good! Thanks for asking.*
Marge: *I don't know what happened. I saw you, and I went for the brake, but I hit the accelerator.*
Homer: *It's okay, Marge. It would have been a lot worse if I hadn't been carrying this Bible in my crotch.* (He pulls the Bible out from under the covers.)

Homer: *Marge, you're trying to hurt me!*
Marge: *What? That's crazy!*
Homer: *No, it's true. The car, the soup—it's like you hate me. Your own husband!*
Marge: *That's ridiculous. I don't like you. I mean...hate you. Hate you, hate you, I hate you!*
Homer: (hurt) *I've heard that from coworkers, strangers on the street, even my own children...but I never thought I'd hear it from you.*

At the marriage counselor's:

Marriage Counselor: *All right, before you came in, I asked you each to make a list of the people who are most important to you. Homer, you first.*
Homer: *There's Homer, Homer J. Simpson, and Commander Cool—a.k.a. me.*
Marge: *That's us in a nutshell! I care so much about you, Homer, but I'm not even on your list. Excuse me.* (She leaves.)
Homer: *We gotta help her! If Marge isn't happy, I'm not happy. And if I'm not happy, Moe is very happy. But for once, this isn't about Moe.*

Counselor: *You gotta knock her off her feet with something utterly romantic. Something that says, "I care about you."*
Homer: *I see. Do you have any suggestions?*
Counselor: *I do, but the hour's over.*
Homer: *Here's a dollar.*
Counselor: *Romantic dinner.*
Homer: *Gotta go.*

Musical Moment:

The upbeat melody of Homer's song "I Love to Walk" contains elements of Leslie Bricusse's Oscar-winning song "Talk to the Animals" from *Doctor Doolittle* (1967).

Homer: *I'm gonna treat Marge to a romantic dinner, to make up for all my shortcomings.*
Lenny: *Hey, Homer. If you're havin' a banquet for Marge, I'd like to help.*
Carl: *Hey, me too. I could whip up my famous poulet au vin avec champignons à la Carl.* (He kisses his hand. Homer looks at him blankly.)
Homer: *You can bring a bag of ice.*

 "Lousy Homer. I'll show him. Tonight his beloved mock apple pie will have real apples."

Homer: *Tonight, we're here to serve you. Sit back and enjoy the finest foods Springfield has to offer.*
Captain McCallister: *I brought you me finest catch of the day. We lost a dozen good men, but it's worth it just to see ye smile.*
Marge: (smiling) *Ohh!*
McCallister: (disappointed by her reaction) *That's it, eh? Twelve men...well...I've got some families to inform.* (under his breath) *Unbelievable!* (grumbles)
Marge: *Who–?!*
McCallister: *Nothing!* (under his breath) *Just a curse on your very soul.*

Jackson Browne and Homer sing to Marge:
(to the tune of "Rosie" by Jackson Browne)

Jackson Browne: *You hooked up in high school,*
Now you've come so far,
Then you started to hate him,
And hit him with your car!
Homer: *So I threw you a fancy banquet,*
And now you can't stay mad.
How 'bout a make-up snuggle?
It would be so rad!
Jackson Browne: *But, Margie, you're all right, you wear my ring,*
When you hold me tight, Margie, that's my thing,
When you turn out the light, I've got to hand it to me,
Looks like it's me and you again tonight, Marjorie!

"I'm so full, my control-top panel is in shards."

The party's over:

Homer: *And now, to all my dear friends, I say, "Get the hell out of my yard."*
(He flips a switch and the lawn sprinklers turn on. The remaining guests scatter.)

Bart and Milhouse are enjoying the animated show "South Park," when Marge turns it off due to its violence. The boys go outside and try to find a cure for their boredom. Bart gets the idea to tie a string around a fly, and when the fly goes into the Flanders house, Bart and Milhouse follow it inside. They discover that a cat has eaten the fly, but they set about disturbing the privacy of the home. After causing a mess in the Flanders living areas, they find a secret room filled with Ned's collection of rare Beatles memorabilia. When Ned comes home with his sons and finds the house in disarray, he calls the police. Soon, Chief Wiggum and his men enter the house, and they discover that Bart and Milhouse have damaged much of Ned Flanders' collection.

The parents of the two troublesome boys are called in, and Marge promises to see that Bart gets more adult supervision. After separating Bart from Milhouse, Marge suggests that Bart join the Pre-Teen Braves, a community youth group, and Homer volunteers to lead the tribe. But when Homer's leadership proves less than inspiring, Marge takes charge of the group, which consists of: Bart,

Ralph Wiggum, Nelson Muntz and "Super Friend" Database. Marge arranges for the group to go on a field trip to meet a member of a local Indian tribe and visit the land his forefathers once owned. When they see how littered the land is, the Pre-Teen Braves decide to clean it up. But, when they return to the site ready to work, another youth group called the Cavalry Kids, consisting of Milhouse, Jimbo Jones, Martin Prince and "Super Friend" Cosine, and led by adult supervisor Kirk Van Houten, has already cleaned and restored the land to its original beauty.

A nasty rivalry quickly develops between the Pre-Teen Braves and the Cavalry Kids. Both groups spend more time trying to outdo each other or spoil each other's plans than they do accomplishing good deeds. They become even more competitive when the Springfield Isotopes baseball team announces a candy sale contest, with the winning group given the chance to serve as batboys for a day. Homer takes over as wartime chief, and the Pre-Teen Braves taint the Cavalry Kids' sale candy with laxatives. It looks bad for the Cavalry Kids, but when the old people at the Springfield Retirement Castle purchase the laxative-

SHOW HIGHLIGHTS

TV Announcer: Next on Comedy Central, an all-new "South Park"!
Milhouse: I hear those kids' voices are done by grown-ups.
Bart: Hey, there's nothing wrong with that. I just wonder how they keep it so fresh after 43 episodes.

Milhouse: I'm bored!
Bart: Hey, I've got an idea—let's tie a string around a fly.
Milhouse: Cool! Do you think bugs feel pain?
Bart: If they don't, I've wasted a lot of my life.

Milhouse: I wish I could fly. Then I'd be the most popular kid in school.
Bart: Knowing you, you'd mess it up somehow.

Bart: The fly's stuck in Flanders' house!
Milhouse: I-I'll go contact the nearest adult!
Bart: There's no time. We're going in!
(Bart climbs in the Flanders' kitchen window. Milhouse follows, dropping something on the ground outside.)
Milhouse: My eyeglass repair kit!
Bart: (pulling him back) Let it go.

Bart: These losers are out of peanut butter.
Milhouse: I know how to make some. (filling a blender) Peanuts, butter...now, we just put the top on.
Bart: Hey, I didn't get where I am putting tops on things!

Milhouse, riding a two-man video cart: **"I feel like luge Silver Medalist Barbara Niedernhuber!"**

Music Moment:
The montage of the escalating charitable deeds and destruction of the Pre-Teen Braves and the Cavalry Kids is set to Coven's "One Tin Soldier," made famous in the film *Billy Jack* (1971).

Bart: Wow! Mr. Flanders is really into the Beatles!
Milhouse: What are the Beatles?
Bart: They wrote all the songs on Maggie's baby records.

 "I don't feel so 'fab.'"

Ned Flanders: Well, the folks at the Senior Center sure will love that peach tree we planted.
Rod Flanders: I wish we could see their happy faces!
Ned: Sin of pride, Roddy.
Rod: I'm sorry.
Ned: Sin of regret.

 "The house is slightly askew! To the panic room!"

Todd: Daddy, I'm scared!
Ned: Scared of what? All the funny camp songs we're gonna sing? (singing, to the tune of "She'll Be Comin' 'Round the Mountain")
We'll be safe inside our fortress when they come.
We'll be safe from creeps and killers when they come.
Unless they have a blowtorch
Or a poison gas injector,
Then I don't know what'll happen when they come!

Chief Wiggum: (over bullhorn) Okay, home invaders, we don't want to hurt you! We just want to talk!
Officer Lou: Well, if you just want to talk, why don't we talk about Eddie sleepin' with my ex-wife?
Wiggum: I thought the divorce was final.
Lou: When is a divorce ever final?
Wiggum: Yeah, all right. Let's just move in.

Wiggum: Well, well, well! Looks like a couple of punks are gonna be taking the "Last Train to Clarksville"!
Lou: That's The Monkees, Chief.
Wiggum: Go wait in the car.
Lou: Fine...it was The Monkees.

The laws of grammar:
Bart: Please don't call our parents!
Wiggum: I'm afraid I have to for hijinks like these. Heh. "Hijinks." It's a funny word. Three dotted letters in a row.
Officer Eddie: Is it hyphenated?
Wiggum: It used to be...back in the bad old days, you know? Of course, every generation hyphenates the way it wants to. Then there's "NSYNC. Ha! What the hell is that? Jump in any time there, Eddie. These are good topics.

Homer: I never knew you were such a Beatles fan.
Ned: Of course I am! They were bigger than Jesus. But your boy went Yoko and broke up my collection.

Homer's tom-tom song:
I am Homer, tribal chief.
I am wearing tiny briefs.
Braves teach values boys should know,
Now extended drum solo!

Homer, a chief with a lack of tribal history: **"Let's see. What Native American activities should we do? *(flipping through the handbook)* Making wallets... faking crop circles...respecting nature...Geez, no wonder these guys lost the Civil War."**

White man's burden:
Marge: What are we gonna do to that field?!
Pre-Teen Braves: Clean it!
Bart: And why are we gonna do it?!
Pre-Teen Braves: Liberal guilt!
Marge: Yaaay!

Poor pundit:
Lisa: I'm so proud of what you guys are doing, I've even tipped off the local paper.
Dave Shutton: Yeah, she sure did. And I've already got the perfect headline—"Activity Participated In By Some." Hey, that's great!

WAR

Episode EABF16
ORIGINAL AIRDATE: 05/18/03
WRITTEN BY: Marc Wilmore
DIRECTED BY: Michael Polcino
EXECUTIVE PRODUCER: Al Jean

coated candy, they end up winning the contest. Homer and Bart misdirect the Cavalry Kids on their honorary day, sending them away from the stadium. Then the Pre-Teen Braves, disguised as the Cavalry Kids, attempt to discredit their rivals by offending the stadium crowd with an off-color version of the National Anthem. The Cavalry Kids arrive, but rather than saving the day they begin to fight with the Pre-Teen Braves. The fight soon escalates into a stadium-wide brawl. Marge is very upset by the turn of events, bemoaning the fact that her plan to provide the youths with a life-affirming experience has turned into a free-for-all. Her sobbing image is broadcast on the stadium's Jumbo-tron, and when the combatants see her, they decide to end their conflict. Considering the National Anthem a hymn to war, they join together and sing the nonaggressive and soothing Canadian National Anthem instead.

JIM PROUDFOOT

Indian tribe:
Mohican

Noble tradition:
Encouraging the myth that the Mohican tribe is extinct

Tribal land:
Once stretched from where the Krusty Burger now stands down to Gary's Waterbed Warehouse

The Great Spirit's blessing of beauty and abundance:
The land gave birth to the trees, the animals frolicked in the waters, and the wind was so gentle it would tie your shoes for you

> CHICKS REALLY DIG YOU WHEN YOU'RE THE LAST OF SOMETHING.

THE STUFF YOU MAY HAVE MISSED

Videos seen on Flanders TV cart are *Girls Gone Mild* and *Debbie Does Penance.*

Signs on the door of Ned's Beatles room read, "Beware of God" and "Children Keep Out."

Some of the many, many items that comprise Ned's Beatles memorabilia collection: a book titled *Learn Carpentry with the Beatles* (featuring John on the cover saying, "I'm filling a hole...in my drywall!"); a poster for "Beatles Shampoo"; a set of drums like Ringo played; four mop top wigs; a Beatles Junior Guitar record album; a Beatles metal lunch box; a Beatles mug; a *Yellow Submarine* standee; Mop Top Pop (with flavors "John Lemon," "Orange Harrison," "Paul McIced Tea" and "Mango Starr"); an autographed photo of the Beatles; Beatles figurines; the Beatles' "Ed Sullivan Show" suits; knee-high Beatles figures; a Beatles wastepaper basket; a movie poster from *A Hard Day's Night;* a Blue Meanie doll; a *Help!* movie poster; a *Let It Be* movie poster; a *Help!* advertising display with gloved hands that reads, "Help Is Here"; a turntable; a juke box; a Beatles pinball machine; several framed Beatles LP covers; a gold record; a park bench; an electric guitar; a Peter Max–style poster of John Lennon; and Beatles bobbing head dolls.

Bart takes a drink from a can marked "John Lemon," and the psychedelic transformations he sees Milhouse go through reflect phases of John Lennon's career: from early suit and mop top to the *Sergeant Pepper*–era uniform to a more radical hippie-look with granny glasses to the controversial *Rolling Stone* cover of a naked Lennon balled up next to Yoko Ono.

When Bart says, "Yellow matter custard, dripping from a dead dog's eye," he's quoting from the song "I Am The Walrus" from the Beatles' *Magical Mystery Tour* album.

The spinning handle on Ned's panic room door resembles a cross.

The brochure for "The Future Veterans of Foreign Wars" pictures a one-legged veteran supporting himself on a crutch while handing a rifle with a bayonet to a young boy.

The cover of the Pre-Teen Braves brochure says members will engage in hiking, camping, and listening.

When Homer does his extended drum solo and taps on the boys' heads with drumsticks, Ralph Wiggum's head sounds hollow.

The foreword of *The Pre-Teen Braves Handbook* was written by Larry Storch—actor, comedian, and star of the 1960s TV western comedy "F-Troop."

In Jim Proudfoot's flashback to the time of his forefathers, a flock of birds carry away a moose, snakes are seen jumping around like springs, bunnies are hopping on a reclining bear's belly, and a gorilla is seen chasing a barrel hoop with a stick.

On the *Springfield Shopper* a headline reads "Cavalry Kids Lead Charge in Cleanup," and the sub-header reads "President Shoots Wife."

Marge and the Pre-Teen Braves are seen building a "Domicile for the Destitute." The organization was last seen in action in "Large Marge" (DABF18).

Ralph Wiggum, to his new mommy, the wolf: **"You smell like dead bunnies."**

> Marge: *Those Cavalry Kids are bigger credit hogs than the Red Cross.*
> Apu: *I must disagree, Mrs. Bart. They've painted this town with a fresh coat of "give a hoot."*
> Marge: *Well, you ain't seen nothing till you've seen the Pre-Teen Braves.*
> Apu: *Pre-Teen Braves? Is this another of those youth groups that apes the cultures of those indigenous peoples you invaded and destroyed?*
> Marge: *Exactly! The Pre-Teen Braves.*

> The Pre-Teen Braves' sales pitch:
> Bart: *Get your un-poisoned candy!*
> Homer: *It's laxative-free for today's lifestyle!*
> Nelson: *Melts in your mouth, not in your pants!*

> The Cavalry Kids' (actually the Pre-Teen Braves') version of the National Anthem:
> *Oh say can you see,*
> *Back in row Double-Z,*
> *That the team sucks out loud,*
> *And you fans are all plowed...*

> Marge sobs on the Jumbo-tron:
> Homer: *Oh my God! That's my wife, and she's crying!*
> Groundskeeper Willie: *Oh! Lassie, dry your tears!*
> Otto: *Then show us your boobs!*

> Milhouse: *Well, Bart, we've learned that war is not the answer.*
> Bart: *Except to all of America's problems.*
> Milhouse: *Amen!*

"Let's go, boys. Make sure you use Pine-Sol on those pine trees, for that pine fresh smell."

> Bart: *Hey! Some jerks cleaned our field!*
> Nelson: *It's awful! It looks like Wisconsin.*

TV Moment:
The TV show Marge wants the boys to watch, "Good Heavens," pokes fun at popular angel-themed shows like "Touched by an Angel."

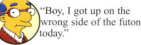

"Boy, I got up on the wrong side of the futon today."

DON CASTELLANETA

Identifying mob boss characteristics:
A raspy voice and an overcoat draped over his shoulders

Falls for:
The old "spill wine on your clothes and excuse yourself to go to the bathroom to get a planted gun" trick

Turns the tables with:
The old "drop a fork on the ground and bend over to reach under the table to get a planted gun" trick

Advice to wine-spilling mobsters:
They should really consider sippy cups

Does not know the difference between:
A bambino and a bambina

I NO SPEAK ANY LANGUAGE SO GOOD.

Lisa leads the Simpsons to the Springfield Botanical Gardens, where the Sumatran Century Flower is about to bloom for the first time in 100 years. Moe, wondering where his regular customers are, discovers that most of the town has turned out for the botanical event. He closes his bar and proceeds to uncomfortably join the throng. Unfortunately, the crowd size for the event has exceeded the garden's capacity by one person, and Chief Wiggum makes Moe leave. When the plant blooms, it releases a ghastly stench that makes the townspeople flee for their lives, destroying the botanical gardens. Moe walks sadly away from the gardens, mistaking the townspeople's screams of horror for screams of delight. While attempting to escape the plant's noxious fumes, the crowd causes a terrible traffic jam that bottlenecks at the Springfield Bridge. Thinking the traffic has finally cleared, Homer floors the accelerator but then must suddenly slam on the brakes, causing Maggie's car seat restraints to snap. Maggie goes flying through the car's sunroof. Moe, having decided to end it all, is just about to jump off the bridge when Maggie lands in his arms. The crowd deems Moe a hero, and when Maggie gives her surprised rescuer a kiss, suddenly life does not seem so bad to the surly bartender.

Moe stops by to see Maggie a few days later, and Marge asks him to watch the baby while she is occupied. Maggie and Moe get along really well, so Marge calls on Moe as a babysitter. Moe is thrilled to have human contact with someone, and Maggie adores the usually crabby bartender. Marge finds that she has plenty of spare time because of Moe's help, but Homer suddenly starts to feel that Moe is replacing him as Maggie's father figure. At

SHOW HIGHLIGHTS

Homer: *How come Lisa always gets to pick the family activities?*
Lisa: *Because I know every time you say, "Pick a number from one to ten," it's always seven.*
Homer: *That's because there were seven apostles.*
Marge: *No, there were twelve.*
Homer: *Boy, that's a big staff. And still, he wasn't that funny.*

Chief Wiggum: *Ah, people? We are officially over-capacity. We've gotta kick one person out. Someone who's alone, already bitter, someone whose feelings have been trampled on so many times, one more won't make any...oh, Moe!*
Moe: *Sigh! Yeah, that's me, all right.*
Wiggum: *Sorry, Moe. You can either walk out with dignity, or I can push you down this muddy hill.*
Moe: *I'd prefer that you push me, seein' how I'm desperate for any human contact.*

Couch pedestrians:
Carl: *Well, at least we're outside, instead of sitting home, watching TV.*
Lenny: *I hear that. Hey! That car has a TV in it.*

Race relations:
Carl: *Can you put on the baseball game?*
Dr. Hibbert: *My kids are watching a movie.*
Carl: *(pressing his face to the window) Come on! Help a brother out.*
Hibbert: *Oh, why don't you call my secretary and make an appointment...brother?*
Carl: *(pounding on the window) A dream deferred is a dream denied!*

Sideshow Mel's faint praise for Moe: **"That hideous man is a hero!"**

Marge: *Moe, I'm glad you're here! I wanted to thank you so much for saving my baby. So I knitted you a nice, warm sweater.*
Moe: *Aw, look at that! That's so soft and thoughtful and—what's the gag? Is it full of chiggers?*
Marge: *No, no! All that's in there is love and gratitude.*
Moe: *Aw geez, there's somethin' in my eye. (plucking out a small object) Oh, it's just some glass.*

(Grampa walks down the street in his bathrobe, banging one of his slippers against a bedpan.)
Grampa: *The Swedish are coming! The Swedish are coming!*
Marge: *Oh Lord. Why do they keep changing his medication?*
Grampa: *(putting the bedpan on his head) Look at me! I'm Speedy Alka-Seltzer! (He runs off.)*

Moe: *So, how's it goin'? Heh. (Maggie stares at him.) Hey! Y-you wanna see me dislocate my arm? Take a look at this! (He pulls his arm out of its socket, and swings it freely as his limb crackles. Maggie laughs delightedly.) It was years before I could do this without faintin'. (grimacing) Uh...heh-heh. Still hurts.*

At the Krusty Burger:
Hot Woman: *(looking at Maggie) Aw, what a face! She looks just like you.*
Moe: *You callin' her repellent? (He cracks his knuckles, ready for a fight.)*
Hot Woman: *Well, n-n-no! I was just...*
Moe: *'Cause you ain't exactly Karen Allen yourself, you know!*
Hot Woman: *You idiot! I was trying to pick you up.*
Moe: *Oh...great! Why don't you play with the baby, while I go rent a room?*
Hot Woman: *Uggh! (She leaves.)*
Moe: *Boy, that's one for the Christmas letter! What a nut.*

Marge: *Well, I have so much free time, now that Moe's our babysitter.*
Homer: *Yeah, it's great that Maggie's got a father figure in her life...Hey, wait! That's supposed to be me!*
Bart: *You could be my father figure!*
Homer: *No way! I'm not getting my fingerprints on that train wreck. But if I lose Maggie, I'm 0 for 3. I've gotta get her back.*
Bart: *I can help you!*
Homer: *I said pipe down, Amtrak!*

THE STUFF YOU MAY HAVE MISSED

The sign made of greenery outside the Springfield Botanical Gardens reads, "Our Stamens Are a Pistil!"

Topiary sculptures seen inside the Springfield Botanical Gardens include: Jebediah Springfield, a rearing horse, Binky—the rabbit from Matt Groening's "Life in Hell" comic strip, and Kang and Kodos from the "Treehouse of Horror" episodes.

A sign promoting the Sumatran Century Flower reads, "The Greatest Show on Dirt."

Maggie's car seat clasp (which breaks easily) is called a "Krap-E-Latch."

The *Springfield Shopper* headline with the story about Moe saving Maggie reads, "Baby Saved By Local Hero, Not Father."

Moe wears the ducky sweater Marge knitted him to Maggie's birthday party.

The character Don Castellaneta is named after and voiced by Dan Castellaneta, the voice of Homer Simpson and many others.

The photo montage of Homer and Moe's play dates with Maggie and Moe's ham at end of the episode includes: Moe carrying Maggie on his shoulders in the park, while Homer carries Moe's ham; Moe, Maggie, Homer, and the ham cycling through the park; Moe, Maggie, Homer, and the ham riding a roller coaster, (Moe sitting with Maggie, Homer with the ham); Homer and the ham getting cotton candy; Homer and the ham getting their picture taken posing as musclemen on the boardwalk; Homer and the ham playing checkers in the park; a drunken Homer carrying the ham out of a tattoo parlor— each with a new tattoo of one another; and Homer and the ham watching the sun set.

BLUES

Episode EABF17
ORIGINAL AIRDATE: 05/18/03
WRITTEN BY: J. Stewart Burns
DIRECTED BY: Lauren MacMullan
EXECUTIVE PRODUCER: Al Jean
GUEST VOICES: Joe Mantegna as Fat Tony

Maggie's birthday party, however, Marge begins to worry that Moe has become too obsessed with Maggie, and then, one night as Maggie cries, Marge and Homer are startled to find Moe in Maggie's room, picking her up to soothe her. They learn that Moe has set up a video camera in Maggie's room and has his very own baby monitor. Shocked by this behavior, Homer orders Moe to leave, and Marge tells him he can no longer see Maggie.

Moe carries on, but he is torn up not being able to see Maggie. A few nights later, Maggie leaves the house when Fat Tony and his gang congregate outside her bedroom window and Fat Tony does an impression of Marlon Brando from *The Godfather*, just like Moe had recently done for her.

Maggie follows the mobsters to Little Italy. When Marge realizes Maggie is gone, she calls the police. Thinking Moe is the most likely suspect in Maggie's disappearance, the police storm into his apartment. Moe is innocent, but he finds clues that quickly lead him, Homer, and Marge to Luigi's Restaurant in Little Italy. They arrive just in time to find Maggie in the middle of a Mexican standoff between Fat Tony's men and a rival gang. Before anyone can shoot, Moe goes in and rescues Maggie. Once Moe points out how adorable she is to the mobsters, they break down crying and the prospect of a gun battle comes to an end. Moe returns Maggie to her happy parents, and Maggie lets everyone know that she wants Moe in her life. Marge tells a grateful Moe that he can continue to spend time with the littlest Simpson.

Moe explains his relationship with Maggie: "It's so nice to be with someone who can't understand the horrible things I say."

(Maggie plays in the sandbox with one of Apu's octuplets.)
Moe: Hey, hey, hey, Osh Kosh B'Gosh. She don't want what you're shovelin'.
Apu: Mr. Moe. My son was only playing next to this girl who is not your daughter.
Moe: Yeah, sure he was, Nahasapasa-l'mraisin'apervert.

Homer's rejection song:
(to the tune "Itsy Bitsy Spider")
The squirmy wormy spider
Squirts out of Daddy's hands.
Daddy feels rejected.
He's gonna eat some cake.

Happy Birthday, Maggie:
Marge: Ooh, a rattle! Thank you, Selma!
Moe: Yeah, great present, Selma. Nice of you to break a five.
Selma: Eh, get a neck, Frankenstein.

Moe: Open my present! It's "Uncle Moe's Play Tavern!" With classic drunk Barney. Look—even the little toilet is broken.
Marge: I don't know if toy drunkards are an appropriate gift for a baby.
Moe: Sure they are! They even talk. Look!
(He flicks a switch on a toy Homer.)
Toy Homer: (drunkenly) I peed my pants!
Homer: (angry) I recorded that for private use!

Music Moment:
Queen's "You're My Best Friend" plays over the Maggie and Moe outing montage, as well as the duo's series of still photos with Homer and the ham.

Homer: Moe? What are you doing here?
Moe: Maggie was cryin'. I heard her on my baby monitor.
Marge: You have your own baby monitor in our child's room?
Moe: I had to. (indicating a pivoting camera in the corner of the room) It's so weird watching the video and not gettin' any sound.

Homer: Get your own family, Moe!
Moe: Hey! You never cared about Maggie 'til I started paying attention to her. Last night at the bar, you called her "Raquel."
Homer: Get out.
Moe: Is that, uh, "get out," like "leave"? Or "get out" as in, "Get out. You banged Bridget Fonda?"
Homer: (pointing to the open window) Get out!

Moe: Boy, I'm like a mess here. I feel so lonely without that kid.
Lenny: You still got us, Moe.
(Moe imagines Barney, Lenny, and Carl as if they were Maggie.)
Moe: You guys mind if I, uh, kiss your tummies?
(The barflies appear receptive.)

Movie Moment:
Moe recounts much of *The Godfather* (1972) and parts of *The Godfather: Part II* (1974) during Maggie's storytime. Later, when Fat Tony and his men spill wine on themselves on purpose and excuse themselves to go to the restroom, we are reminded of the scene where Michael Corleone excuses himself in the restaurant to use the facilities. In both cases, Michael Corleone and Fat Tony are going to the restroom to fetch guns that are planted there.

(Outside Maggie's bedroom window, Fat Tony talks with Louie, Legs, and Johnny Tightlips.)
Fat Tony: Tonight, I want you to take out the Castellaneta family.
Louie: Ah, I dunno, boss. My passion for whacking is waning.
Fat Tony: Perhaps this will cheer you up. (Fat Tony does an impression of Marlon Brando from *The Godfather* with an orange peel in his mouth. The mobsters laugh.)
Louie: Oh, that's better! I could whack my own mother now.
Fat Tony: I'm glad you brought that up.
Louie: Kill my mother? She makes such good pasta sauce!
Johnny Tightlips: It comes from a can.
Louie: She's a corpse!

"Scum, freezebag! A-heh. I mean...freeze, scumbag. You can't write stuff like that. See, that's why sitcoms are dying."

Looking for clues:
Lisa: Well, it looks like Maggie crawled through these bushes, spit up over here, and crashed her tricycle into the wall.
Homer: Ah...no...that was me.

Moe: Marge, do mobsters ever congregate outside your house?
Marge: All the time. Sometimes I bring them lemonade.
Moe: Listen. I think we might have to make a trip to Little Italy.
Homer: I'll get our little passports.

Marge: Gasp! Maggie's right in the middle of that Italian-American Mexican standoff!
Homer: Oh my God! I've got to save her!
Moe: No! You've got a family. I'm the guy with nothin' and no one. (He goes to save her but his sleeve is grabbed.) No, no! Don't try to stop me!
Homer: We're not. Your sleeve got caught on that tree. Here, let me unhook you. Off you go! (He pushes Moe on.)
Moe: Yeah, thanks.

Moe: Here's your baby back.
Marge: Thanks, Moe. I'm sorry we thought you were a baby-napper.
Homer: Or worse! Am I right?

SEASON 14

CHARACTER DESIGNS

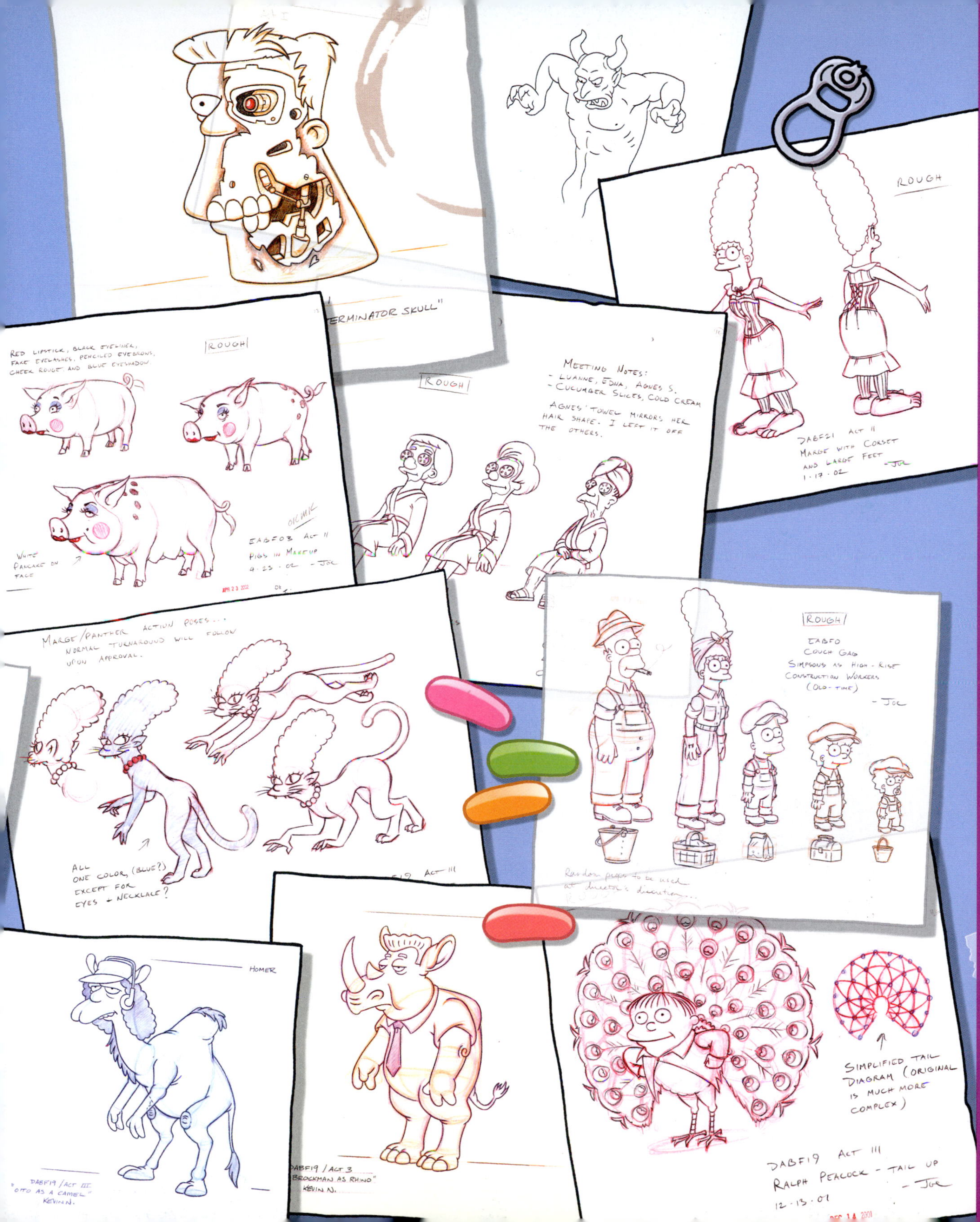
ERMINATOR SKULL"
ROUGH
RED LIPSTICK, BLACK EYELINER, FAKE EYELASHES, PENCILED EYEBROWS, CHEEK ROUGE AND BLUE EYESHADOW
WHITE PANCAKE ON FACE
EABF03 ACT II PIGS IN MAKEUP 4-23-02 - JOE
APR 23 2002
ROUGH
MEETING NOTES: - LUANNE, EDNA, AGNES S. - CUCUMBER SLICES, COLD CREAM
AGNES' TOWEL MIRRORS HER HAIR SHAPE. I LEFT IT OFF THE OTHERS.
ROUGH
DABF21 ACT II MARGE WITH CORSET AND LARGE FEET 1-17-02 - JOE
MARGE/PANTHER ACTION POSES... NORMAL TURNAROUND WILL FOLLOW UPON APPROVAL.
ALL ONE COLOR, (BLUE?) EXCEPT FOR EYES + NECKLACE?
ROUGH
EABF0 COUCH GAG SIMPSONS AS HIGH-RISE CONSTRUCTION WORKERS (OLD-TIME) - JOE
Random props to be used at director's discretion...
HOMER
DABF19 / ACT III "OTTO AS A CAMEL" KEVIN N.
DABF19 / ACT 3 "BROCKMAN AS RHINO" KEVIN N.
SIMPLIFIED TAIL DIAGRAM (ORIGINAL IS MUCH MORE COMPLEX)
DABF19 ACT III RALPH PEACOCK - TAIL UP - JOE 12-13-01
DEC 14 2001

EABF04 / ACT III
" MUSCULAR MARGE AT CONTEST "
KEVIN N / JOE W.

" EABF04 / ACT I
COMIC BOOK GUY IN RUNNING MAN-TYPE OUTFIT "
KEVIN N.

EABF02 / ACT I
EDNA IN CAPRI PANTS
KEVIN N.

ROUGH

SEP 16 2002

FROM SCOTT'S STORYBD.
PUTTING HIM IN A CHAIR
ENABLES US TO SHOW
MORE STRAPS . . .

SHIRT ON'

ROUGH

APR - 3 2002

HE IS WEARING PANTS

EABF01 ACT I
SHACKLED SIDESHOW BOB
4.2.02 . -JOE

DON'T KNOW IF
IS WILL BE ALLOWED,
IT AUGMENTS
STEREOTYPE . . .

ROUGH

IMAGE WILL BE
FLOPPED UPON APPROVAL.

JUL 11 2002

EABF09
ACT II
KRUSTY IN BERET
7.11.02 . -JOE
C.U. 7.25.02

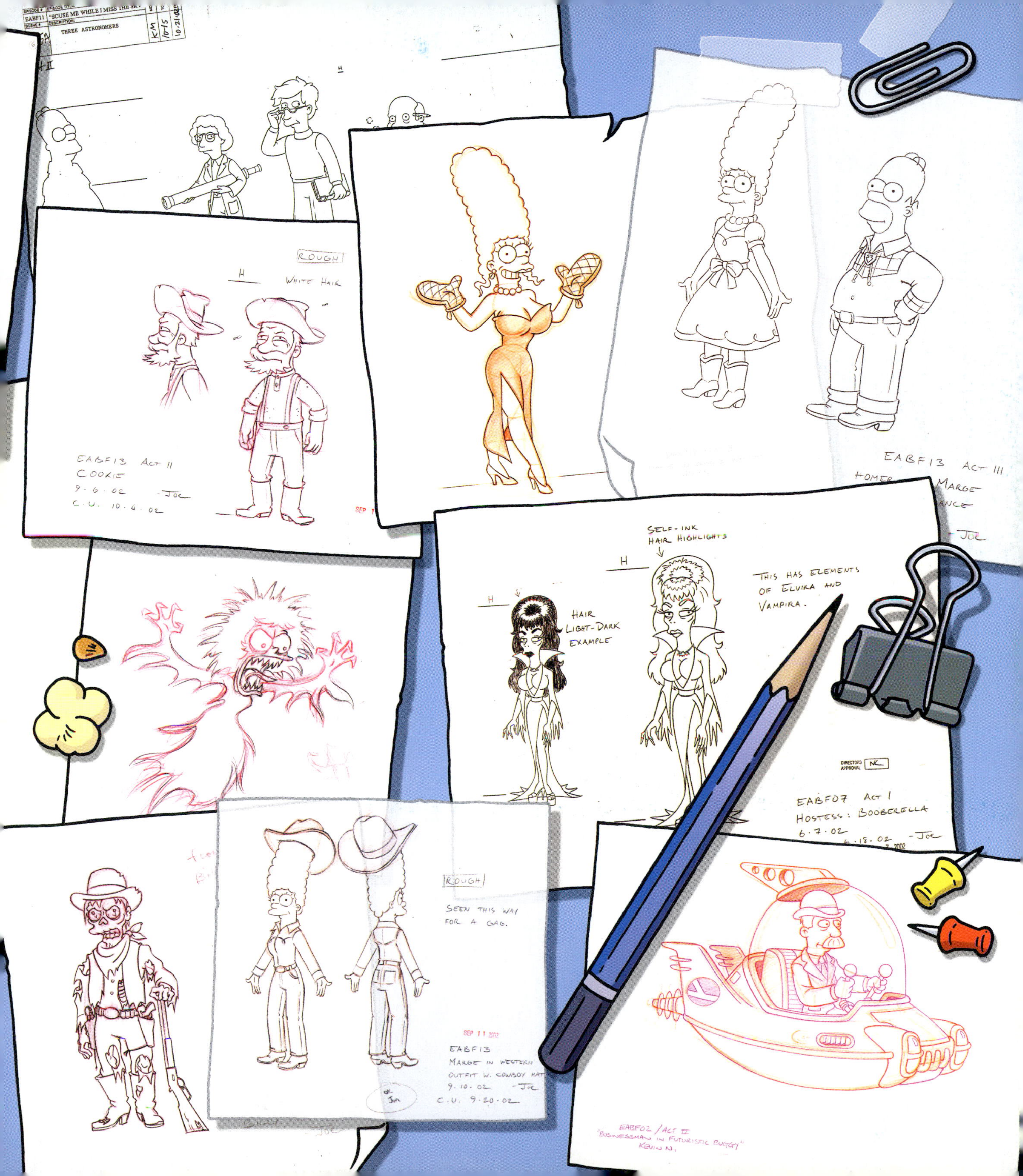

EPISODE # EABF11
EPISODE TITLE "SCUSE ME WHILE I MISS THE SKY"
SCENE # DESCRIPTION: THREE ASTRONOMERS
KM 10-15 10.21.02
ROUGH
WHITE HAIR
EABF13 ACT II
COOKIE
9.6.02 -JOE
C.U. 10.4.02
EABF13 ACT III
HOMER
MARGE
-JOE
SELF-INK HAIR HIGHLIGHTS
HAIR LIGHT-DARK EXAMPLE
THIS HAS ELEMENTS OF ELVIRA AND VAMPIRA.
DIRECTORS APPROVAL NK
EABF07 ACT I
HOSTESS: BOOBERELLA
6.7.02 -JOE
6.18.02
ROUGH
SEEN THIS WAY FOR A GAG.
SEP 11 2002
EABF13
MARGE IN WESTERN OUTFIT W. COWBOY HAT
9.10.02 -JOE
C.U. 9.20.02
EABF02 / ACT II
"BUSINESSMAN IN FUTURISTIC BUGGY"
KEVIN N.

COUCH GAGS

CABF22 The Parent Rap—The Simpsons are standing on the deck of a little sailboat. They jump into the water below, making a splash that covers the screen. The camera pulls back to reveal that they were standing on the sailboat in the picture that hangs above the couch. The family is now sitting on a water-soaked couch, dripping wet, with puddles all around them. The sailboat picture on the wall is askew and water streams out of the frame. Marge throws back her head, flipping her soggy hairdo, as Homer turns on the TV with the remote control. **CABF20 Homer the Moe, CABF06 Skinner's Sense of Snow**—A loose football bounces into the family room. The Simpsons, all dressed in football uniforms, dog-pile on the ball. Maggie emerges from the pile with the football, spikes it, and performs a victory dance. **CABF18 Hunka Hunka Burns in Love, CABF12 New Kids on the Blecch**—The Simpsons' couch and TV are inside the walls of a prison. A siren wails and a searchlight passes over the prison yard as the family attempts to escape by burrowing in separate tunnels underground. But instead of escaping, they all emerge from their tunnels, dressed in black-and-white prisoners garb, and hop onto the couch. Homer clicks on the TV with the remote as the searchlight illuminates them. **CABF21 The Blunder Years, BABF17 Insane Clown Poppy**—The Simpsons run into their family room, but we see

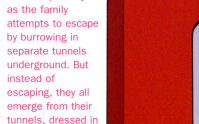

them enter from a different perspective. They are in front of the television with the family room window behind them. As they enter, they leap up with arched backs and freeze in mid-air à la *The Matrix*. In a "bullet time" swivel shot, the camera rotates 180˚ around their airborne bodies so that now we see them in front of the couch. They become unfrozen, land on the ground, jump into place on the couch, and Homer turns on the TV with the remote control. **DABF02 She of Little Faith, DABF12 Gump Roast**—In the Simpson family room, a giant slot machine takes the place of the couch. The slot's spinning images roll to a stop, revealing each member of the Simpson family except Maggie. In her place is a "7." A siren on top of the slot machine lights up and a bell sounds as gold coins spill out of the machine and onto the family room floor. **DABF01 Brawl in the Family, DABF11 Weekend at Burnsie's**—An unpruned shrubbery stands

in place of the couch in the Simpson family room. A gardener enters with a pair of hedge trimmers and quickly cuts a topiary in the shape of the Simpsons. When done, the gardener sighs with relief and wipes his brow. **DABF03 Sweets and Sour Marge, DABF13 I Am Furious (Yellow)**—The Simpsons are sitting on the sofa, watching TV and smiling pleasantly. An arcade game skill crane claw descends, grabs Homer, and starts lifting him upward. Before he disappears, Homer shouts, "Ow, my brain!" **DABF05 Jaws Wired Shut, DABF16 The Frying Game**—The family room is seen as a scratchy black & white film image with the sound of an old projector clattering in the background. Homer enters dressed like Charlie Chaplin's Little Tramp character from the silent film era. He waddles to the couch while twirling his cane, turns and waits, wiggling his mustache. Marge and the kids enter, in period dress, and take their places on the couch. Homer backs up to the couch and sits down. **DABF04 Half-Decent Proposal, DABF14 The Sweetest Apu**—The Simpsons rush in to find that two men from Repo Depot are taking the couch away. Homer starts to sob, Marge looks on, and the kids, noticing the TV is still there, turn around, sit down on the floor, and happily watch TV. **DABF06 The Bart Wants What It Wants, 9F08 Lisa's First Word, 9F13 I Love Lisa, 9F16 The Front, 9F22 Cape Feare, 2F08 Fear of Flying, 3F31 The Simpsons 138th Episode Spectacular, AABF17 Monty Can't Buy Me Love, CABF13 Simpson Safari**—The

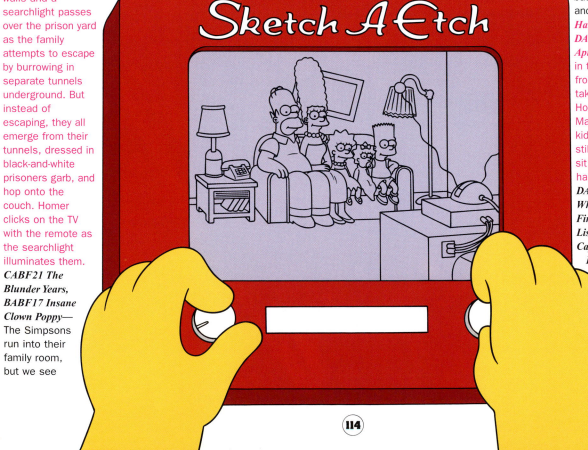

family rushes in. They dance in a chorus line. Soon, they are joined by high-kicking Rockettes, a variety of circus animals (including trained elephants), jugglers, trapeze artists, fire breathers, magicians, and Santa's Little Helper, who jumps through a hoop as circus music plays. *DABF07 The Lastest Gun in the West, DABF15 Little Girl in the Big Ten*—The family runs into the family room, where the lights are off. They stop because there is a couple making out on the couch. Homer turns on the light. It is the pimple-faced, squeaky-voiced teen and a sexy blonde woman. The couple disengages, startled and embarrassed. Marge gasps in shock, and Homer eyes them sternly. *DABF09 The Old Man and the Key, DABF17 Poppa's Got a Brand New Badge* —The Simpsons rush in to find the Blue Man Group playing percussion instruments in front of the couch. When the drummers stop, Homer says, "What the–?!" (In the case of episode DABF17, the "What the–?!" is cut out.) *DABF08 Tales from the Public Domain, EABF10 C.E.D'oh*—The Simpsons are seen running in and sitting down on the couch, as rendered in penciled pages on an animator's flipbook. The camera pulls back to reveal the hands of a live-action person holding the pad of paper and flipping the pages. When the "couch sequence" is completed, the animator gestures to the flipbook in a presentational fashion. *DABF10 Blame It on Lisa, EABF08 A Star Is Born-Again*—The family, as marionette puppets, jerkily enters, only to bump into one another and get their strings entangled. The camera pans up to reveal that the puppetmaster is "The Simpsons" creator Matt Groening. Groening gets annoyed with the tangled puppets and throws the controls down in frustration. *DABF22 How I Spent My Strummer Vacation, EABF11 'Scuse Me While I Miss the Sky*—Two shark fins circle the Simpsons' living room, which is immersed in water. There is also a water ski jump. The family, wearing bathing suits, enters from the right side of the screen on water skis in a stunt formation. The family hits the jump, and the formation comes apart, with everyone flying into the air. The two sharks lunge out of the water and snap at them, but everyone lands in place on the couch (in an extreme close-up). As the camera pulls back, the sharks are each seen gnawing on a leg, and both of

Homer's legs are missing below the knees. Homer picks up the remote and aims it at the television. *DABF20 Bart vs. Lisa vs. the Third Grade*—In a tip of the hat to the title sequence of Mel Brooks and Buck Henry's 1960s spy comedy series "Get Smart," Homer walks down a staircase and through a corridor, with a series of sliding doors that automatically open and then close behind him. At the end of the corridor, Homer enters a phone booth, picks up the receiver, dials a number, hangs up, folds his arms, and waits. The floor of the phone booth suddenly opens, dropping Homer through the floor. He then falls from the top of the frame and into his place on the couch, arms still folded, and joins his family. *DABF18 Large Marge, EABF07 I'm Spelling As Fast As I Can*—We see a "Sketch-A-Etch" toy (a parody of the Etch-A-Sketch from Ohio Art) being manipulated by the hands of an unseen artist (possibly Homer). The artist is using the toy to create a portrait of the family sitting on the couch. When the portrait is completed, we hear Homer exclaim, "Woo-hoo!" *DABF21 Helter Shelter*—The Simpsons run in and take their places on the couch. An arrow-shaped computer cursor picks up Homer and moves him to the other side of the couch, with an accompanying computer sound. The cursor then clicks on the wall, changing it from pink to bright green, again with an accompanying sound. Finally, the arrow changes the sailboat picture over the couch to the *Mona Lisa*, accompanied by an "eep" sound. *EABF01 The Great Louse Detective, EABF09 Mr. Spritz Goes to Washington*—The Simpsons run into the family room and take their places on the couch. Homer aims the remote control at the television and changes the channel. Suddenly, the family appears dressed like cavemen, sitting on a stone couch. They all stare at a blazing campfire. Homer, still holding the remote, changes the channel. And the family now appears dressed in Roman togas. All around them spectators cheer as they watch gladiator battle in the Coliseum. With one final click of the remote, the Simpsons return to the normal setting of their living room. *EABF02 Special Edna, EABF12 Three Gays of the Condo*—The Simpsons are seen frozen and placed inside a deep fry basket. An unseen cook lowers the basket into a deep fryer and quickly cooks them to a golden brown. They

are then lifted out of the hot oil and dumped onto the couch in their family room. As a final touch, the cook seasons them with salt. *EABF03 The Dad Who Knew Too Little, EABF14 Old Yeller-Belly*—The Simpsons are seen in black and white high above a cityscape, circa 1930, being lowered into view while suspended on a steel girder next to a skyscraper construction site. They all wear period workmen's clothing and sit along the girder in their normal order. Opposite them is another girder that holds their television. The family members eat from lunch pails on their laps as they watch television. *EABF04 The Strong Arms of the Ma, EABF15 Brake My Wife, Please*—There is an amusement park cut-out of the Simpsons couch scene set up in the family room, with holes so that people can put their heads through and get their picture taken. The family runs in and the camera pulls back to reveal a photographer in place to take their picture. Each of the family members places his or her head through the hole of a different family member: Lisa is Homer, Homer is Marge, Maggie is Lisa, Bart is Maggie and Marge is Bart. They smile and the photographer takes a flash picture. *EABF06 Barting Over, EABF16 The Bart of War*—The Simpsons run into the family room and take their places on the couch. After a moment, two large hands reach down and grab the family — Homer and Bart in one hand and Lisa, Maggie, and Marge in the other. As the hands lift the family up, knocking over the table with the lamp and phone next to the couch as well as the lamp stand, we realize that the family members are actually figurines in a playset and discover that the hands belong to a big drooling baby. *EABF05 Pray Anything, EABF17 Moe Baby Blues*—The Simpsons enter their family room, but in this version they are gingerbread cookie figures entering a room made of gingerbread and candy. As they take their places on the couch, the gingerbread Homer leans over and takes a bite out of the gingerbread Bart's head and says, "Mmm…" Gingerbread Bart gives him a dirty look. *EABF13 Dude, Where's My Ranch?*—The Simpsons enter the couch-less family room all dressed as mimes. They are "walking against the wind" until they are positioned where the couch should be, and then they sit down, pantomiming the presence of a couch.

HOMER SAYS, "D'OH..."

CABF19–After realizing he has baited his leprechaun trap with Trix instead of Lucky Charms cereal.

CABF18–After being pistol-whipped the first time by Snake, who is holding Homer and Mr. Burns' girlfriend, Gloria, hostage.

CABF21–After jumping into the old quarry and landing in a puddle of mud as a ten-year-old boy.

DABF01–After landing on one of Bart's Monopoly properties (Marvin Gardens), which is loaded with houses and hotels.

DABF03–After trying reverse psychology on a toucan to get his map back while on the island of San Glucose, only to lose it in the process.

DABF05–In writing and pantomimed, after Marge tells him that Ned Flanders rang the doorbell.

DABF04–When he attacks Bart while filming his goodbye video and hits his head on the camera.

DABF08–When Poseidon (Captain McCallister) flicks Odysseus' (Homer's) ship off course, sending him and his crew to the Island of Circe.

DABF08–After the ghost of Hamlet's father (Homer) attempts to choke Hamlet (Bart) but his hands pass right through him.

DABF13–When the voice actor playing Angry Dad, still speaking in Homer's voice, discovers he will not get paid for his work until 2012. (Technically, not a Homer "D'oh!" – but notable because it is Dan Castellaneta performing as Angry Dad in Homer's voice.)

DABF13–When the Piano Lady throws a piano at Homer and it lands on his foot.

DABF15–After getting a Frisbee stuck in a tree while using it in an attempt to dislodge the bubbled Bart, who is wedged in the tree's branches.

DABF16–After being sentenced to 200 hours of community service.

DABF19–Multiple times, as the Homer clones (and as it turns out, Homer himself) fall to their deaths, following large donuts over the edge of the Springfield Gorge.

DABF18–During the Baha Men's song over the closing credits ("Who Let Her Jugs Out?"), several samplings of Homer saying "D'oh!" are heard in the chorus.

EABF04–After packing up the car with his bankruptcy sale purchases and discovering there is not enough room for him.

EABF04–After Bart wakes him up in church by hitting him with a hymnal.

EABF06–After Ned Flanders sinks a half-court basket to win $50,000.

EABF06–Seven times, while swinging on the backyard swing set, looking into Ned Flanders' yard with binoculars and discovering that the grass is, in fact, greener there.

EABF12–After realizing he is late for his date with Marge.

EABF15–While singing happily and walking down the street, he claims he rarely feels the need to utter "D'oh."

EABF15–After being hit by Marge's car, consequently, he utters one.

EABF17–Upon realizing that he has lost his advantage over everyone else to leave the Springfield Botanical Garden parking lot.

HOMER SAYS, "MMM..."

"Mmm...various eggs."
After being served his favorite meal by the Ultrahouse 3000. (CABF19)

"Mmm...unexplained bacon."
Upon awakening to the smell of Ultrahouse 3000's sizzling bacon coming from the automated kitchen. (CABF19)

"Mmm...Pistol Whip."
While being held hostage by Snake, Homer daydreams about repeatedly dipping the barrel of a gun into a tub of dessert topping called Pistol Whip and eating it. (CABF18)

"Mmm...pie pants."
After Bart uses quick thinking and substitutes the words "pie pants" for "science" to control Homer's rage. (DABF02)

"Mmm...that's the next best thing to eating Lenny."
After taking a bite of the swine that looks like (and actually happens to be) Lenny. (DABF08)

"Mmm...caramel baloney."
After hearing Apu bemoan that he "always thought karma was baloney, but not anymore." (DABF14)

"Mmm...donuts."
When the Homer clones (as well as Homer, it seems) see the huge donuts suspended from helicopters. (DABF19)

"Mmm...feed."
After Bart mentions the live NBC news feed. (DABF20)

"Mmm...steamed gentile."
After Krusty frees Homer from the Stagnant Springs steam room and calls out, "Who ordered the steamed gentile?!" (EABF01)

"Mmm...trophy."
After eating a piece of the First Place gummi fish trophy he won by using the gummi worms from his World's Greatest Dad mug as bait. (EABF02)

"Mmm...McNuggets."
After the prospector in Lisa's "Girl Cowboy" video, voiced by Homer, reports that the McNuggets have been stolen by Indians. (EABF03)

"Mmm...garnish."
After Judge Harm garnishes Homer's wages so that he can repay Bart. (EABF05)

"Mmm...far-fetched."
After wondering what it would be like to be with a 7-foot-tall WNBA basketball player, and imagining being lifted over her head and taking a bite out of the moon. (EABF06)

"Mmm...move over eggs, bacon just got a new best friend...fudge!"
After a truck carrying hot fudge collides with a truck carrying bacon and Homer samples the result. (EABF06)

"Mmm...promo."
After noticing, then eating, the "Joe Millionaire" graphic that runs across the bottom of the screen. He then gags and spits it out, saying, "Ew...Fox." (EABF09)

"Mmm...bad eggs."
After hearing Marge comment on marauding vandals by saying, "Looks like some bad eggs are cooking up trouble." (EABF11)

AN ITCHY & SCRATCHY FILMOGRAPHY

To Kill a Talking Bird

(DABF05 "Jaws Wired Shut")

(This episode runs as a public service announcement at the Googolplex.)
Itchy and Scratchy are sitting in a movie theater. They, and the rest of the audience, become annoyed when a duck lets his cell phone ring several times before answering it. When the duck does answer, he chats into it loudly. Itchy replaces the cell phone with a stick of dynamite, and the duck blows up, leaving only his skeleton. The duck says, "Uh-oh," then crumbles into a heap. The audience laughs at the detonated duck, and Scratchy smiles at Itchy. Itchy takes out a knife and slashes Scratchy's belly open, then proceeds to pull out the cat's bloody intestines, flinging them onto the movie screen to spell out "Please No Talking."

Circus of the Scars

(DABF06 "The Bart Wants What It Wants")

Itchy and Scratchy are performing in a circus on the flying trapeze. Scratchy swings towards Itchy, hanging from the trapeze. Itchy hangs upside down, swinging towards Scratchy, as if to catch him. Itchy pulls out a pair of sharp knives and cuts Scratchy's hands off. Scratchy's hands remain holding on to the trapeze bar, but the rest of him falls towards the safety net, spurting blood from his arms. The net dices Scratchy into square chunks, instead of catching him. Scratchy says, "Ow! My body!" as an elephant starts eating him piece by piece to the tune of "Baby Elephant Walk."

DVD Commentary:
(Scratchy appears by himself in a small picture within a picture at the bottom right of the screen.)
Scratchy: We shot this at four in the morning and the crew was getting a little cranky.
(The camera pans right to include Itchy.)
Itchy: You can never get enough takes for Steven Soderbergh.
(Itchy reaches down as Scratchy speaks.)
Scratchy: Always wants more rehears– Aaaah!
(Itchy cuts off Scratchy's head with a pair of garden shears. A splatter of blood fills the screen.)

Itchy & Scratchy's Golden Age Radio Show

(DABF09 "The Old Man and the Key")

Announcer: It's the "Itchy & Scratchy Hour!" Presented by Hansen's Mustache Wax—the mustache wax Hitler doesn't use.
(The "Itchy & Scratchy Theme" is heard. The studio audience applauds.)
Announcer: As we join tonight's adventure, we find Itchy at the counter of his butcher shop.
(We hear the sound of a shop door opening and, a bell jingling as someone enters.)
Itchy: Heya, Scratchy!
(Applause.)
Scratchy: Ga-gaah ga-gaah ga-gaaah! You're grinding my head! (More screams.)

Par for the Corpse

(DABF10 "Blame It on Lisa")

(Itchy and Scratchy are on a golf course. Itchy is golfing and Scratchy serves as his caddy.)
Itchy: Tee one up for me...cat-ty!
Scratchy: Sure thing, mouse-y! Ha ha ha ha ha ha!
(Scratchy stoops and places a ball and tee on the grass. Itchy jumps on Scratchy's back, flattening him out, swings a golf club, and drives Scratchy's head into space.)
Scratchy: Nice follow-throuuuuuuugh!
(Scratchy's head comes to rest, lodging in the Man in the Moon's right eye.)
Man in the Moon: Now that's what I call a "moon shot."
(Back on Earth, Itchy pulls a few dollars out of his pocket and throws them on Scratchy's decapitated body as a tip. He hops off the body and walks away.)

Butter Off Dead

(DABF15 "Little Girl in the Big Ten")

(The college professor cites this short as Episode DABF06)

Itchy is an Amish farmer making toast in his farmhouse kitchen. Unfortunately, he discovers that his butter dish is empty. Just then, an Amish Scratchy passes by Itchy's window.

"Good morrow to thee, neighbor," Scratchy says, tipping his hat.

"Ha-ha!" Itchy gets an idea. A lit candlestick appears over his head.

Itchy grabs Scratchy by the beard and pulls him out to the barn, where he proceeds to feed Scratchy to his cow. Scratchy is digested by the acids in the cow's four stomachs, screaming all the while. Then, Itchy milks the cow. Scratchy's eyes, nose, and whiskers rise to the surface of the milk bucket. Itchy takes the Scratchy milk back into the house and pours it into a butter churn. After a few quick pumps of the churn and amidst Scratchy's still pained protests, out comes a buttery substance. Itchy fills a tub of butter with it and places a lid on top. The lid reads, "I Can't Believe It's Not Scratchy!" Itchy takes the container of butter back to the kitchen table and spreads it on his toast. After a quick prayer, Itchy laughs gleefully then bites into the toast, unconcerned that Scratchy's eyeballs are on the toast, looking at him.

Bleeder of the Pack

(EABF10 "C. E. D'oh")

As Bill Haley & His Comets' "(We're Gonna) Rock Around the Clock" is heard, we see Scratchy as a motorcycle cop in the 1950s, flirting with a roller-skating bunny waitress. Itchy, dressed like a greaser with a leather jacket and DA hairdo, sneaks up from behind and fastens a long chain from Scratchy's tail to a lamppost. Itchy then drives past Scratchy in a souped-up roadster and taunts him.

"Nuts to you, copper," says Itchy.

Scratchy gives chase, and when the slack is taken up in the length of the chain, his skin and fur are torn from his body. When he realizes his skin is gone, he falls off the motorcycle, painfully bouncing and rolling on the pavement. Amidst his screams, he leaves a trail of bloody red asphalt in his wake.

As soon as his body comes to a stop, an ambulance pulls up. Two mice hop out and place Scratchy on a stretcher. They put him into the ambulance and drive a short distance to a small plane preparing to take off.

"You're gonna be just fine!" assures one of the mice, and Scratchy is loaded on the plane. The plane takes off down the runway, and Scratchy slumps in his seat, uttering a big sigh of relief.

"Hello, Scratchy!" comes a deep voice. Scratchy looks up to see three rock 'n' roll stars smiling at him.

"The Big Bopper?" Scratchy says incredulously. "Ritchie Valens? Buddy Holly? Noooooooo!"

Scratchy screams, but it is too late. The rockers turn into vampires, advancing on him, and the plane goes down in a snowstorm, crashing in the distance.

117

WHO DOES WHAT VOICE

DAN CASTELLANETA
Homer Simpson
Abraham "Grampa" Simpson
Arnie Pye
Barney Gumble
Bill
Blue-Haired Lawyer (Burns' Lawyer)
Capital City Goofball
Coach Lugash
Dracula
Frank Nelson-Type (Man with a Mustache)
Gary
Gil
Groundskeeper Willie
Hans Moleman
Itchy
Jimmy the Snitch
Kodos
Krusty the Clown
Louie
Mayor Quimby
Mr. Teeny
Rich Texan
Santa's Little Helper
Sideshow Mel
Snowball II
Squeaky-Voiced Teen (Pimple-Faced Kid)
Fruit Vendor (CABF19)
Leprechaun (CABF19)
Gil Salesbot (CABF19)
Robot Worker #2 (CABF19)
Ultrahouse Standard Voice (CABF19)
Ultrahouse "Dennis Miller" Voice (CABF19)
Milhouse's Prince (CABF19)
Lisa's Prince (CABF19)
Promising Athletes Coach (CABF22)
Chinese Military Official (CABF20)
Professor Huntington (CABF20)
"M" Customer #1 (CABF20)
Woody Allen-Type Fortune Writer (CABF18)
"The Planet from Outer Space" Ensign (DABF02)
Wino (DABF02)
Barking Angel (DABF02)
Strom Thurmond Animatronic (DABF01)
"First Date" Host (DABF01)
Cougar (DABF01)
Overweight Man (Marlon Brando) (DABF03)
Male Marcher (DABF05)
Gay Man (DABF05)
Cell Phone Talking Duck (DABF05)
"Soccer Mummy" Justin (DABF05)
Soccer Mummy (DABF05)
Society Man (DABF05)
Movie Call Announcer (DABF05)
Beer Vendor (DABF05)
Butler (DABF04)
Baron Von Kiss-a-lot (DABF04)
Ant (DABF04)
Ostrich (DABF07)
Helicopter Cop (DABF06)
Butler (DABF06)
Paramountie Studios Tram Driver (DABF06)
"Undercover Nerd" Bully #2 (DABF06)
Canadian Basketball Player (DABF06)
"Itchy & Scratchy" Radio Announcer (DABF06)
Charlie Callas (DABF09)
French Catapult Soldier (DABF08)
English Soldier #1 (DABF08)
Telemarketer (DABF10)
Wounded Man (DABF10)
Man on Fire (DABF10)
Sgt. Scraps (DABF11)
Bill Clinton (DABF11)
Pete (DABF12)
Singer (DABF12)
Monkey (DABF13)
Bin Laden (DABF13)
Voice Actor (DABF13)
Angry Dad (DABF13)
Repo Man (DABF13)
Smooshie Deliveryman (DABF14)
President John F. Kennedy (DABF15)
Student #1 (DABF15)
Screamapillar (DABF16)
Catholic Priest (DABF16)
Man with Braces (DABF16)
Butterfly (DABF17)
T-Shirt Vendor (DABF17)
Otis (DABF17)
Air Force General (DABF19)
Sundance Kid (DABF19)
Kaiser Wilhelm (DABF19)
Kenny Loggins (DABF22)
Rhino (DABF20)
"Touch the Stove" Contestant (DABF20)
Race Track Announcer (DABF20)
NBC News Stagehand (DABF20)
"Who Wants to Marry" Announcer (DABF20)
"Robot Rumble" Robot #1 (DABF20)
Caution Crew Member (DABF20)
Homeless Man (DABF20)
President Jimmy Carter (DABF18)
Television (Humphrey Bogart/ Frankenstein) (DABF18)
Chief O'Hara (DABF18)
Head Veteran (DABF18)
Shoe Buyer #2 (DABF18)
Angelo (DABF21)
Artist (DABF21)
Kozlov (DABF21)
Termites (DABF21)
Bran Producer #2 (DABF21)
Bill Cosby (DABF21)
Elderly Lion (DABF21)
Sad Man (DABF21)
Cameraman #2 (DABF21)
"Law & Order" Cop #1 (DABF21)
"That '30s Show" Dad (EABF01)
Cellmate (EABF01)
Robin Williams-Type Teacher (EABF02)
Teacher of the Year Judge #3 (EABF02)
Bully of the Year Committee Chairman (EABF02)
Reporter (EABF02)
Electric Car (EABF02)
Male ENRON Rider (EABF02)
Cartoon Mouse Voice (EABF02)
Alien Frog Creature (EABF03)
Test Lab Monkey (EABF03)
Mailman (EABF04)
Fox Announcer (EABF06)
Male Skating Announcer (EABF06)
Truck Driver (EABF06)
Bowler #2 (EABF06)
"Perfect Strangers" Announcer (EABF05)
Arthur Miller (EABF05)
Neighbor (EABF05)
Bum (EABF05)
Ray Romano/Referee (EABF07)
Italian Ribhead (EABF07)
Photographer (EABF08)

Diego (Actor) (EABF08)
Larry (EABF09)
John Armstrong (EABF09)
Elderly Congressman (EABF09)
Currency Committee Member #1 (EABF09)
Janitor (EABF09)
Mouse Paramedic (EABF10)
Worker (EABF10)
Lego Land Capitol Dome (EABF10)
Lego Land Tourist (EABF10)
Paleontologist (EABF11)
Astronomer (EABF11)
Streetcar Conductor (EABF11)
Stargazer (EABF11)
Streetcar Man #3 (EABF12)
Large Gay Military Man (EABF12)
Rabbi Krustofski (EABF13)
Wrangler #2 (EABF13)
Brave (EABF13)
Amish Man with Plow (EABF14)
Devil (EABF14)
Duff Commercial American Astronaut (EABF14)
Regis Philbin (EABF14)
Hobo (EABF14)
Parachutist #2 (EABF14)
Editor-in-Chimp (EABF15)
Peruvian Fighting Frog (EABF15)
Turkmenistani (EABF15)
French Busboy (EABF15)
PAX-TV Silver-Haired Man (EABF16)
Junior Dandy Leader (EABF16)
Happy Little Elf (EABF17)
"Godfather" Don Corleone (EABF17)
Don Castellaneta (EABF17)
President of the Italian American Anti-Defamation League (EABF17)

JULIE KAVNER
Marge Simpson
Patty Bouvier
Selma Bouvier

NANCY CARTWRIGHT
Bart Simpson
Maggie Simpson
Database
Kearney
Nelson Muntz
Ralph Wiggum
Todd Flanders
"Soccer Mummy" Tough Kid (DABF05)
Professor Van Doren (DABF05)
"Nookie in New York" Kristen Davis-Type (DABF04)
Bumper Car Rich Boy (DABF06)
Pria (DABF14)
Sandeep (DABF14)
Little Girl Gymnast (DABF15)
Wellesley (EABF07)
Vassar (EABF07)
Happy Little Elf (EABF17)

YEARDLEY SMITH
Lisa Simpson

HANK AZARIA
Apu Nahasapeemapetilon
Bumblebee Man
Captain McCallister (Sea Captain)
Carl
Chef Luigi
Chief Clancy Wiggum
Cletus Spuckler (Delroy)
Comic Book Guy

Disco Stu
Doug
Dr. Nick Riviera
Dr. Velimirovic
Drederick Tatum
Duffman
Frank Grimes
Johnny Tightlips
Kirk Van Houten
Moe Szyslak
Officer Lou
Old Jewish Man
Professor John Frink
Pyro
Snake (Jailbird)
Superintendent Chalmers
Wiseguy
Baby Vendor (CABF19)
Shrunken Head (DABF19)
Hobgoblin (CABF19)
Yoda–Type Minister (CABF19)
Robot Worker #1 (CABF19)
Bart's Prince (CABF19)
Hobo (CABF22)
Wrestling Announcer (CABF22)
Chinese Humongous (CABF20)
Formico (CABF20)
Cecil the Doorman (CABF20)
Homer's Robot (CABF20)
Animal Catcher #1 (CABF18)
Chinese Restaurant Manager (CABF18)
Older Chinese Fortune Writer (CABF18)
Anti-Theft Device (CABF18)
Burly (CABF21)
Mesmerino (CABF21)
Waylon Smithers, Sr. (CABF21)
Astronaut Pitchman Colonel Chet Manners (DABF02)
Money Changer (DABF02)
Ralph Nader (DABF01)
Environmentalist (DABF01)
Las Vegas Minister (DABF01)
Duff World's Records Male Executive (DABF03)
Suicidal Businessman (DABF03)
Deputy (DABF03)
Male Lawyer (DABF03)
Sugar Smuggler (DABF03)
"Soccer Mummy" Announcer (DABF05)
Demolition Derby Announcer #1 (DABF05)
One-Armed Roughneck (DABF04)
"The Krusty the Clown Show" Writer (DABF07)
Headmaster St. John Van Hookstratten (DABF06)
Wolfcastle Lookalike (DABF06)
"Undercover Nerd" Bully #1 (DABF06)
Zack (DABF09)
Whale (DABF09)
"Dude, Where's My Virginity?" Black Best Friend (DABF09)
Hispanic Gentleman (DABF09)
Bronson Man (DABF09)
Bronson Boy (DABF09)
Mr. T. (DABF09/DABF13)
Tennessee Ernie Ford (DABF09)
English Soldier (DABF08)
Viking (DABF08)
Man in the Moon (DABF10)
Mr. Movie Phone (DABF10)
Pilot (DABF10)
Bellboy #2 (DABF10)

Lifeguard (DABF10)
Samba Teacher (DABF10)
Taxi Driver (DABF10)
Brazilian Police Chief (DABF10)
Toucan Man (DABF10)
Seamus (DABF13)
Geoff Jenkins (DABF13)
Danger Dog (DABF13)
Radio Announcer (DABF13)
Stegosaurus (DABF13)
Lou Rawls (DABF13)
Milkman (DABF13)
Divorce Lawyer (DABF14)
Liberace Action Figure (DABF15)
Café Kafka M.C. (DABF15)
Student #2 (DABF15)
Male Student (DABF15)
Glue-Bottle Cow (DABF15)
Student #3 (DABF15)
EPA Scientist (DABF16)
Jury Foreman (DABF16)
Prison Warden (DABF16)
Executioner (DABF16)
Michael Clarke Duncan-Type (DABF16)
Fonzie (DABF17)
Dancing Santa (DABF17)
"Wooly Bully" Beatnik Proprietor (DABF17)
Silent Alarm (DABF17)
Monster (DABF17)
Hammock Peddler (DABF19)
William H. Bonney/Billy the Kid (DABF19)
Salvadoran Rebel (DABF22)
Jeff Probst-Type (DABF20)
"Touch the Stove" Game Show Host (DABF20)
Boob Tubery Cashier (DABF20)
Satellite Monkey (DABF20)
Japanese Chandler (DABF20)
Clock Channel Announcer (DABF20)
"Robot Rumble" Announcer (DABF20)
"Robot Rumble" Robot #2 (DABF20)
Clown (DABF20)
M.C. Safety (DABF20)
Senate Chairman (DABF20)
Grandpappy (DABF20)
Spanish Man (DABF18)
Shoe Buyer #1 (DABF18)
Usher (DABF21)
Hotel Clerk (DABF21)
Mitch Hartwell (DABF21)
"Law & Order" Cop #2 (DABF21)
Dr Mas-Seuss (EABF01)
Attendant (EABF01)
Yoga Master (EABF01)
Decapitating Harry (EABF01)
High-Tech Cell (EABF01)
Frank Grimes, Jr. (Junior) (EABF01)
Jester (EABF01)
Mardis Gras Reveler (EABF01)
Man at Copier (EABF02)
WWI General (EABF02)
Teacher of the Year Judge (EABF02)
Future Sphere Narrator (EABF02)
Maniacal-Looking Teacher (EABF02)
Turbo Diary (EABF03)
Spaceman Rod (EABF03)
Prospector (EABF03)
Dexter Colt (EABF03)
Head Protester (EABF03)
Motel Clerk (EABF03)
The Flying Guiseppe (EABF03)
Mugger (EABF04)
Cooking Show Host (EABF04)
TV Announcer (EABF06)

Ken Burns (EABF06)
Tanker Driver (EABF06)
Larry H. Lawyer, Jr. (EABF06)
Bailiff (EABF06)
Bowler #1 (EABF06)
Buddha (EABF06)
Ornette Coleman (EABF05)
"Perfect Strangers" Balki (EABF05)
Orderly (EABF05)
Bailiff (EABF05)
Skewed Tour Announcer (EABF05)
Frankenstein (EABF07)
Ribwich Commercial Singer (EABF07)
Rib-it (EABF07)
Travel Agent Ribhead (EABF07)
Big Band Singer (EABF08)
Irish Cop (EABF08)
Reporter #3 (EABF08)
Director (EABF08)
"Publicity Tonight" Host (EABF08)
Moe Howard (EABF09)
Airport Official (EABF09)
Jet Pilot (EABF09)
Fox News Anchor (EABF09)
Krusty Campaign Commercial Singer (EABF09)
Southern Congressman (Beauregard) (EABF09)
Currency Committee Member #2 (EABF09)
Congressman (EABF09)
Sgt. at Arms (EABF09)
Stark Richdale (EABF10)
Marrakesh Vendor (EABF10)
Palm Scanner Voice (EABF11)
Alien Life Form (EABF11)
Paramedic (EABF12)
Streetcar Man #1 (EABF12)
Julio (EABF12)
Black Knight (EABF12)
William Shatner (EABF13)
Wrangler #1 (EABF13)
Native American (EABF13)
Square Dance Caller (EABF13)
Amish Man with Sack (EABF14)
Mennonite (EABF14)
Mailman with Hitler Moustache (EABF14)
Duff Commercial Russian Astronaut (EABF14)
Les (EABF14)
Mission Volunteer (EABF14)
Male Aquarium Tour Guide (EABF15)
"Editor-in Chimp" Reporter (EABF15)
Armando (EABF15)
TV Chef (EABF15)
Mr. Wilson (EABF15)
Peruvian Fighting Frog (EABF15)
Turkmenistani (EABF15)
Marriage Counselor (EABF15)
French Busboy (EABF15)
"South Park" O.J. (EABF16)
"The Beverly Hillbillies Down Under" Jethro (EABF17)
"Godfather" Mobster (EABF17)

HARRY SHEARER

Benjamin
C. Montgomery Burns
Dave Shutton
Dr. Julius Hibbert
God
Herman
Jasper
Judge Snyder
Kang
Kent Brockman
Legs
Lenny
Marty
Ned Flanders

Officer Eddie
Otto
Principal Harlan Dondelinger
Principal Seymour Skinner
Rainier Wolfcastle (McBain)
Reverend Timothy Lovejoy
Scratchy
Waylon Smithers
Mailman/Bill Clinton (CABF22)
Baseball Announcer (CABF22)
Dr. "Bob" Kaufman (CABF20)
Male Bargoer (CABF20)
Male Bargoer #2 (CABF20)
Pimento Grove M.C. (CABF21)
Waylon Jr. (CABF21)
"Rain Delay Theater" Announcer (DABF02)
"The Planet from Outer Space" Captain (DABF02)
Executive (DABF02)
Senator Bob Dole (DABF01/DABF09)
Count Fudge-ula (DABF03)
Male Marcher (DABF05)
Feature Presentation Announcer (DABF05)
Teenage Usher (DABF05)
Demolition Derby Announcer #2 (DABF05)
"Nookie in New York" Waiter (DABF04)
BHO Announcer (DABF04)
"McTrigger" Announcer (DABF07)
"The Krusty the Clown Show" Announcer (DABF07)
Dr. Foster (DABF07)
Pilot (DABF06)
CN Tower Security Guard (DABF06)
"Curling for Loonies" Male Host (DABF06)
"Dude, Where's My Virginity?" Jock (DABF09)
Hispanic Sidekick (DABF09)
WOMB Radio Announcer (DABF09)
Yakov Smirnov (DABF09)
Kidnapper (DABF10)
Mr. Blackwell (DABF13)
Mayor of Neuterville (DABF13)
"When Dinosaurs Get Drunk" Announcer (DABF13)
Todd Linux (DABF13)
Tom Brokaw (DABF14/DABF20/EABF01)
Café Kafka Roadie (DABF15)
Student #4 (DABF15)
President George H. W. Bush (DABF16/DABF18)
Army General (DABF19)
Frank James (DABF19)
"MTC" Announcer (DABF22)
"Animal Survivor" Announcer (DABF20)
Mountain Man (DABF20)
TV Announcer (DABF18)
President Bill Clinton (DABF18)
Bran Producer Speaker (DABF21)
Bearded Man (DABF21)
Cameraman #1 (DABF21)
"Law & Order" Announcer (DABF21)
"That '30s Show" Announcer (EABF01)
Wrestling Announcer (EABF02)
Teacher of the Year Judge #2 (EABF02)
Electric Car of the Future Announcer (EABF02)
Awards Announcer (EABF02)
"Turbo Diary" Announcer (EABF03)
Kiosk Productions Announcer (EABF03)
Radio Announcer (EABF03)
Bodybuilding Announcer (EABF04)
WNBA Announcer (EABF06)
David McCullough-Type (EABF06)
Bowler #3 (EABF06)
Walter Cronkite (EABF05)

"Perfect Strangers" Larry (EABF05)
Fresh Breath (EABF05)
Viagrogaine Announcer (EABF05)
Ribhead (EABF07)
Ribwich Commercial Announcer (EABF07)
Hippie Ribhead (EABF07)
Reporter #1 (EABF08)
Assistant Director (EABF08)
"Three Stooges" Announcer (EABF09)
Curly IV (EABF09)
Rep. Horace Wilcox (EABF09)
Channel 6 Announcer (EABF09)
Currency Committee Chairman (EABF09)
Committee Chairman Hayes (EABF09)
Speaker of the House (EABF09)
The Big Bopper (EABF10)
Terrence (EABF10)
Nuclear Inspector (EABF10)
Planetarium Announcer (EABF11)
Streetcar Man #2 (EABF12)
King (EABF12)
Chief (EABF13)
Duff Commercial Announcer (EABF14)
Parachutist #1 (EABF14)
Aquarium Narrator (EABF15)
"Editor-in-Chimp" Announcer (EABF15)
French Busboy (EABF15)
Comedy Central Announcer (EABF16)
PAX-TV Announcer (EABF16)
Nelson's Father (EABF16)
Jim Proudfoot (EABF16)
TV Announcer (EABF17)
Younger Mobster (EABF17)

MARCIA WALLACE

Edna Krabappel

JESS HARNELL

Various Animal Sounds (CABF22)

JOHN KASSIR

Various Animal Sounds (DABF05/EABF14)

PAMELA HAYDEN

Amber
Janey Powell
Jimbo Jones
Milhouse Van Houten
Rod Flanders
Sarah Wiggum
Russian Model #1 (CABF20)
Female Bargoer (CABF20)
Pimento Grove Waitress (CABF21)
"Afternoon Yak" Joy Behar-Type (DABF05)
"Afternoon Yak" Gen X Girl (DABF05)
"Nookie in New York" Kim Cattrall-Type (DABF04)
Snobby Bully #1 (DABF06)
Female Street Merchant (DABF10)
Krusty's Assistant (DABF13)
Poonam (DABF14)
Uma (DABF14)
Nabendu (DABF14)
Carrie (DABF15)
"Taxicab Conversations" Announcer (DABF22)
Third-Grade Girl (DABF20)
Mountain Woman (DABF20)
Stomach Staples Center Receptionist (DABF18)
Gummy Sue (DABF21)
Female Castaway (DABF21)
Asian Masseur (EABF01)
Female Skating Announcer (EABF06)
Baby Stink-Breath's Mother (EABF05)
Uwa (EABF05)
Stenographer (EABF05)
Kathy (Commercial Actress) (EABF05)

Radcliffe (EABF07)
Mount Holyoke (EABF07)
Smith (EABF07)
Hibbert's Son (EABF08)
Reporter #2 (EABF08)
"Buttercups of Autumn" Woman's Daughter (EABF15)

TRESS MACNEILLE

Agnes Skinner
Bernice Hibbert
Brandine Spuckler (Delroy)
Dia-Betty
Cookie Kwan
Dolph
Ginger
Lindsey Naegle
Governor Mary Bailey
Booberella
Wealthy Dowager
Society Matron
Miss Springfield (Quimby's Assistant)
Sickly Woman (CABF19)
Gypsy (CABF19)
Harry Potter (CABF19)
Cora (CABF19)
Karie the Bailiff (CABF22)
Tethering Officer (CABF22)
Russian Model #2 (CABF20)
"M" Customer #2 (CABF20)
Woman with Rolling Pin (CABF18)
Mama Celeste (CABF21)
Moe's Date (DABF01)
Brenda the Negotia-bot (DABF01)
Duff World's Records Female Executive (DABF03)
Woman on Jet-Ski (DABF03)
"Soccer Mummy" Teenage Soccer Player (DABF05)
"Afternoon Yak" Barbara Walters-Type (DABF05)
"Afternoon Yak" Star Jones-Type (DABF05)
"Nookie in New York" Cynthia Nixon-Type (DABF04)
"Nookie in New York" Sarah Jessica Parker-Type (DABF04)
Headmaster's Wife (DABF06)
Snobby Bully #2 (DABF06)
Paramountie Studios Tour Guide (DABF06)
"Curling for Loonies" Female Host (DABF06)
Automated Phone Voice (DABF09)
Old Woman (DABF09)
Bronson Woman (DABF09)
Nurse (DABF09)
Charo (DABF09)
Circe (DABF08)
Female Robot Operator (DABF10)
Ronaldo/Flamenco Flamingo (DABF10)
"Teleboobies" Hostess (DABF10)
Nun (DABF10)
"Three Stooges" Wealthy Dowager (DABF11)
Booking Agent (DABF13)
Paperboy (DABF13)
Piano Lady (DABF13)
Manjula (DABF14)
Annette the Squishee Lady (DABF14)
Sashi (DABF14)
Anoop (DABF14)
Gheet (DABF14)
Brunella Pommelhorst (DABF15)
Tina (DABF15)
Elderly Woman (DABF17)
Newsie (DABF17)
Nurse (DABF22)
Female Cab Driver (DABF22)
Japanese Phoebe (DABF20)

Mrs. McConnell (DABF20)
Teenage Boy (DABF20)
Radio Diz-Nee Announcer (DABF18)
Kiki Highsmith (DABF18)
Termites (DABF21)
Bran Producer #1 (DABF21)
Female Executive (DABF21)
Stagnant Springs Guide (EABF01)
"That '30s Show" Boy (EABF01)
"That '30s Show" Aunt Gladys (EABF01)
Teacher of the Year Judge #1 (EABF02)
Female ENRON Rider (EABF02)
Robot Mother (EABF02)
Waitress (EABF02)
Female MTV V.J. (Sepulveda) (EABF03)
"Turbo Diary" Girl (EABF03)
"Turbo Diary" Bully (EABF03)
Sheriff Lisa (EABF03)
Mugger's Cheap Girlfriend (EABF04)
Bodybuilder (EABF04)
Sonya (EABF04)
Old Lady (EABF05)
Sun Moon (EABF07)
Alex (EABF07)
Barnard (EABF07)
Bryn Mawr (EABF07)
Hibbert's Daughter (EABF08)
Lady Android (EABF10)
Accountant (EABF10)
Lesbian (EABF12)
Clara (EABF13)
Native American Woman (EABF13)
Game Show Contestant (EABF14)
Female Aquarium Tour Guide (EABF15)
"Buttercups of Autumn" Announcer (EABF15)
"Buttercups of Autumn" Southern Woman (EABF15)
Mrs. Wilson (EABF15)
"South Park" Stan (EABF16)
"South Park" Farty the Robot (EABF16)
PAX-TV Silver-Haired Woman (EABF16)
Beautiful Woman (EABF17)
"The Beverly Hillbillies Down Under" Granny (EABF17)
Hot Woman (EABF17)
Tickle-Me Elmo (EABF17)
Happy Little Elf (EABF17)

MARCIA MITZMEN-GAVEN

Helen Lovejoy (DABF18)

MAGGIE ROSWELL

Maude Flanders Ghost/Demon (DABF19)
Helen Lovejoy (DABF04)
Luann Van Houten (EABF08)

RUSSI TAYLOR

Martin Prince
Lewis
Sherri/Terri
Uter
Wendell

KARL WIEDERGOTT

Chinese Delivery Boy (CABF18)
Sad Cowboy (Walter Brennan) (DABF07)
English Soldier #2 (DABF08)
Co-Pilot (DABF10)
Professor (DABF15)
Hair Stylist (EABF12)
Cookie (EABF13)

Songs Sung Simpson!
...continued

Included here are song lyrics and musical number descriptions from Seasons 13 and 14 of "The Simpsons."

"Everybody Hates Ned Flanders"

(Homer at the piano.)

Homer: *Everybody in the USA hates their stupid neighbor.*
He's Flanders, and he's really, really lame.
Flanders tried to wreck my song.
His views on birth control are wrong.
I hate his guts, and Flanders is his name!
(Homer performs with Lenny and Carl at Moe's Tavern.)

Homer, Lenny, Carl: *F-L-A-N-R-D-S!*
Homer: *He's the man that I hate best.*
I'd like to see his house go up in flame!
(Homer, Lenny, and Carl are in the studio with David Byrne.)

Lenny & Carl: *F-L-A!*
Homer: *His name is Ned!*
Lenny & Carl: *D-R-S!*

Homer: *It's a stupid name!*
He's worse than Frankenstein or Dr. No!
David Byrne: *You can't upset him even slightly,*
He just smiles and nods politely,
Then goes home and worships nightly.
His Leftorium...is an emporium...of woe!
(The single starts to be packaged on an assembly line.)

Lenny & Carl: *F-L-A!*
Homer: *Don't yell at Ned.*
(Bill and Marty play it at KBBL.)
Lenny & Carl: *D-E-R!*
Homer: *His wife is dead.*
(Bill pushes a sound effect button on his control panel that elicits a woman's scream and a thud. Bill and Marty laugh.)
Everybody hates that stupid jerk!
(At Styx and Stones Records, David Byrne pipes music directly into Milhouse's, Mr. Burns', Otto's, and Skinner's headphones.)
David Byrne: *Springfield rocks with Homer's joyous loathing.*
Filling clubs (taking a sip of water) *with angry Valentinos.*
(David Byrne is onstage in front of a huge Warhol-esque four portrait psychedelic painting of Flanders. Byrne is wearing his famous long-sleeved white suit.)
You don't have to move your feet.
Just hate Flanders to the disco beat.
(Homer's head pops up next to David Byrne's in the suit.)
David & Homer: *He's your perky, peppy, nightmare neighborino!*
Homer: *If you despise polite left-handers,*
(Flanders sings along in his car. Rod and Todd are in the backseat reading *Billboard for Kids*

magazine. The headline reads "Flan Slam Is #1 Jam.")
Then I doubt you'll like Ned Flanders,
Or his creepy little offspring Rod and Todd!
Todd: *That's us!*
Rod: *Hooray!*
(Apu stands on a stage singing karaoke. The audience joins in.)
Audience: *F-L-A!*
Apu: *His name is Ned!*
Audience: *E-R-S!*
Apu: *He is so white bread!*
(Reverend Lovejoy conducts the church choir.)
Church Choir: *The smiling mustached geek who walks with God!*

(From EABF13, "Dude, Where's My Ranch?")

"The Very Reason That I Live"

Sideshow Bob: *I've grown accustomed to his face*
And dreams of gouging out his eyes.
I've grown accustomed to my hate,
My plans to lacerate...
(Bart burrows under his covers with his mouth taped shut. Bob lifts him out by the collar of his pajamas, then uses a knife to pin his collar to the wall, leaving him dangling. Bart takes a look at his wristwatch and realizes it is taking Bob a long time to do him in.)
...to disembowel, to hear him howl!
The very reason that I live,
Is plotting how to watch him die!
Homer: (pounding on wall from next room) *Bart!* Turn down that original cast recording and go to sleep!

(Homer's pounding knocks Bart free from the wall. He scampers to the door, but Bob catches him, holding him upside down by the ankle.)
Bob: *I know this chubby scalawag,*
Has made my life a living hell.
Surely, if I drank his blood,
I'd be at peace...but, well...
Bart: (taking the tape off his mouth, sings) *You've grown accustomed to my face!*
Bob: (spoken) This isn't a duet.
Bart: (spoken) Sorry. (He puts the tape back on.)
Bob: *I've grown accustomed to your fear,*
Accustomed to revenge,
Accustomed to your face.

(From DABF01, "The Great Louse Detective")

"Jellyfish"
(sung by Hank Azaria)

Jellyfish, along you came,
And right away, I'm stung.
Sweet words I long to whisper,
But you paralyzed my tongue.
Jellyfish, I held you close,
And told you, "I love you,"
But then the ocean took you back,
And now I just hold goo.
Jellyfish, I held you close,
And said that, "I love you,"
But then the ocean took you back,
My jelly, I'll miss you.
For now I just hold goo.

(From EABF08, "A Star is Born-Again")

"They'll Never Stop the Simpsons"
(sung by Dan Castellaneta)

Ullman shorts, Christmas show, Marge's fling, Homer's bro,
Bart in well, Flanders fails, whacking snakes, monorail,
Mr. Plow, Homer space, Sideshow Bob steps on rakes,
Lisa's future, Selma's hubby, Marge not proud, Homer chubby,
Homer worries Bart is gay, Poochie, U2, NRA,

Hippies, Vegas and Japan, octuplets and Bart's boy band,
Marge murmurs, Maude croaks, Lisa Buddhist, Homer tokes,
Maggie blows Burns away...
What else do I have to say?
They'll never stop the Simpsons.
Have no fears, we've got stories for years!
Like, Marge becomes a robot.
Maybe Moe gets a cell phone.

Has Bart ever owned a bear?
Or how 'bout a crazy wedding?
Where something happens,
And doo doo doo doo doo...
Sorry for the clip show.
Have no fears, we've got stories for years!

(From DABF12, "Gump Roast")

The opening number from "That's Familiar!"

(Actors wearing funeral garb enter from both sides of a stage covered in dry ice. A coffin, on end, rises from the center of the stage. The backdrop shows a green mountain with tombstones and a "BRANSON" sign. A death knell sounds, then suddenly the coffin lights up and the actors begin to sing and dance.)

Chorus: *Remember the stars you loved yesterday?*
Where did they go? Did they all pass away?

(The camera pans a variety of people: a man dressed as a syringe, a woman with a steering wheel around her neck and torn clothes, another woman with her face partially wrapped in bandages.)

Was it drugs or a car crash or face-lifts gone wrong?

No, they're right here in Branson and singing this song!
(The actors now wear powder-blue top hats and tails with pink trim and form a chorus line. Moving spotlights highlight the BRANSON sign. Charo enters from out of the coffin.)

Charo: *My name is Charo! I shake my maracas!*
(Mr. T, covered in his typical gold jewelry, enters from the coffin.)

Mr. T: *Remember me, fools? I was B.A. Baracus!*
(Mr. T throws some punches. Bonnie Franklin and Adrian Zmed appear from the coffin together. She wears a star-spangled leotard. He wears a top hat. Both wear sashes with their names on them. They point to each other, then wave to the audience.)

Chorus: *We're the performers you thought were dead,*
Like Bonnie Franklin and Adrian Zmed!
Branson's the place we can always be found!

They took "Nick at Nite" and made it a town!
(Ray Jay Johnson enters from the coffin.)

Ray Jay Johnson: *You can call me Ray, or you can call me Jay,*
Just don't call me washed-up. I do three shows a day!

Charlie Callas: *Charlie Callas doesn't sleep in the ground!*
Yes, I'm still alive, and I'm making my sounds!
(He makes his silly sounds.)

Chorus: *So sit back, relax, and watch our review!*
(Yakov Smirnov is the last to emerge from the coffin for the big finale.)

Yakov Smirnov: *In Soviet Union, review watches you!*

(From DABF09, "The Old Man and the Key")

"You're a Bunch of Stuff"

Homer: *You took a twenty-carat diamond*
And made it gleam,
Like a big spaghetti dinner
Smothered in whip cream!
(Homer picks up a plate of spaghetti and tops it off with whipped cream from a can. Then various male diners sing to and toast Marge.)

Comic Book Guy: *You're like "X-Men #3"*
In a mylar bag.

Snake: *You're a brand-new muscle car*
And all the wheels are mag.
(Mr. Burns is enticed by Marge; however, Smithers, who is with him, just looks annoyed.)

Mr. Burns: *You make me feel as young*
As the blood I get from sheep.

Captain McCallister: *You're like Jacqueline Bisset*

In me favorite film The Deep.

Moe: *You're sexy and exotic*
Like a hooker from Belize.

Dr. Hibbert: *Or a patient with insurance*
Who's crawling with disease.

Men: *You're a sundae underneath two great big cherries.*

Marge: *Keep in mind they're only tempo-ra-ra-rries!*

Men: *Still we'd like to say that we are very, very*
Glad to see you!

Mayor Quimby: *And I decree you!*
(He pulls out a decree and reads it.)
The hottest thing to hit this city since the fire that killed eleven...

Everyone: *Gasp!*

Quimby: *...dangerous criminals!*

Everyone: *Hooray!*

Homer: *And they're all mine!*

(From DABF18, "Large Marge")

"I Love to Walk"

Homer: *I like to walk down the avenue,*
Bust a move with Disco Stu.
(He discos down with Disco Stu.)

Disco Stu: *You shake me from my booty to my 'fro!*

Homer: *Yes, I strut down the boulevard,*
Burning off my excess lard.
(He opens up the waistline of his sweatpants to let steam escape.)
I rarely feel the need to utter "D'oh."
(He walks past Patty and Selma and addresses them.)
Top of the morning, ladies!

Patty: (spoken) *Bite us.*
(Homer walks across a large map of the world to Alaska and greets two eskimos.)

Homer: *I can walk from Springfield to Alaska,*
(Then skips down the coast to California, where he meets Steve Buscemi, who is sitting in a director's chair.)
Then hobnob with the stars in Malibu.

Steve Buscemi: (spoken) *Hi, Homer. I'm actor Steve Buscemi.*

Homer: (spoken) *The guy who got fed into the wood-chipper in Fargo?*
(The actor nods affirmatively.)

(singing) *And when I hear...*
(Two Turkmenistanis point to a crossing signal flashing alternately "WALK" and "DON'T WALK.")

Turkmenistanis: *You can't walk to Turkmenistan.*
(Homer and Steve Buscemi hop across the United States and Atlantic Ocean to the Middle East.)

Homer: *I say, of course I can.*
Screw you!
(The Turkmenistanis brandish sabers. Steve pulls out two tickets.)

Steve Buscemi: (spoken) *Hey, would you guys like tickets to the Independent Film Awards?*

Turks: (spoken) *Would we?!*
(The music builds and Homer and Steve Buscemi pair off with the two Turkmenistanis, dancing in circles. Then we see Homer walk down a street in Springfield, leading a throng of walking citizens.)

Homer: *Oh, I love to perambulate.*
It's standing still I really hate.
So let me please reiterate,
I love to—(Marge runs into him with her car.) *D'oh!*

(From EABF15, "Brake My Wife, Please")

CHURCH MARQUEES

> ## IF YOU WERE A PASTOR, YOU'D BE HOME NOW!

"The Frying Game" (DABF16)

> ## TOMORROW: HOMER SIMPSON FUNERAL

"Poppa's Got a Brand New Badge" (DABF17)

> ## WELCOME PISSED-OFF CATHOLICS

"Special Edna" (EABF02)

> ## NO OUTSIDE EUCHARIST

"The Strong Arms of the Ma" (EABF04)

> ## GOD: THE ORIGINAL TONY SOPRANO

"Pray Anything" (EABF06)

> ## HOUSEWARMING PARTY LET THERE BE LIGHT BEER

"Pray Anything" (EABF06)

INDEX

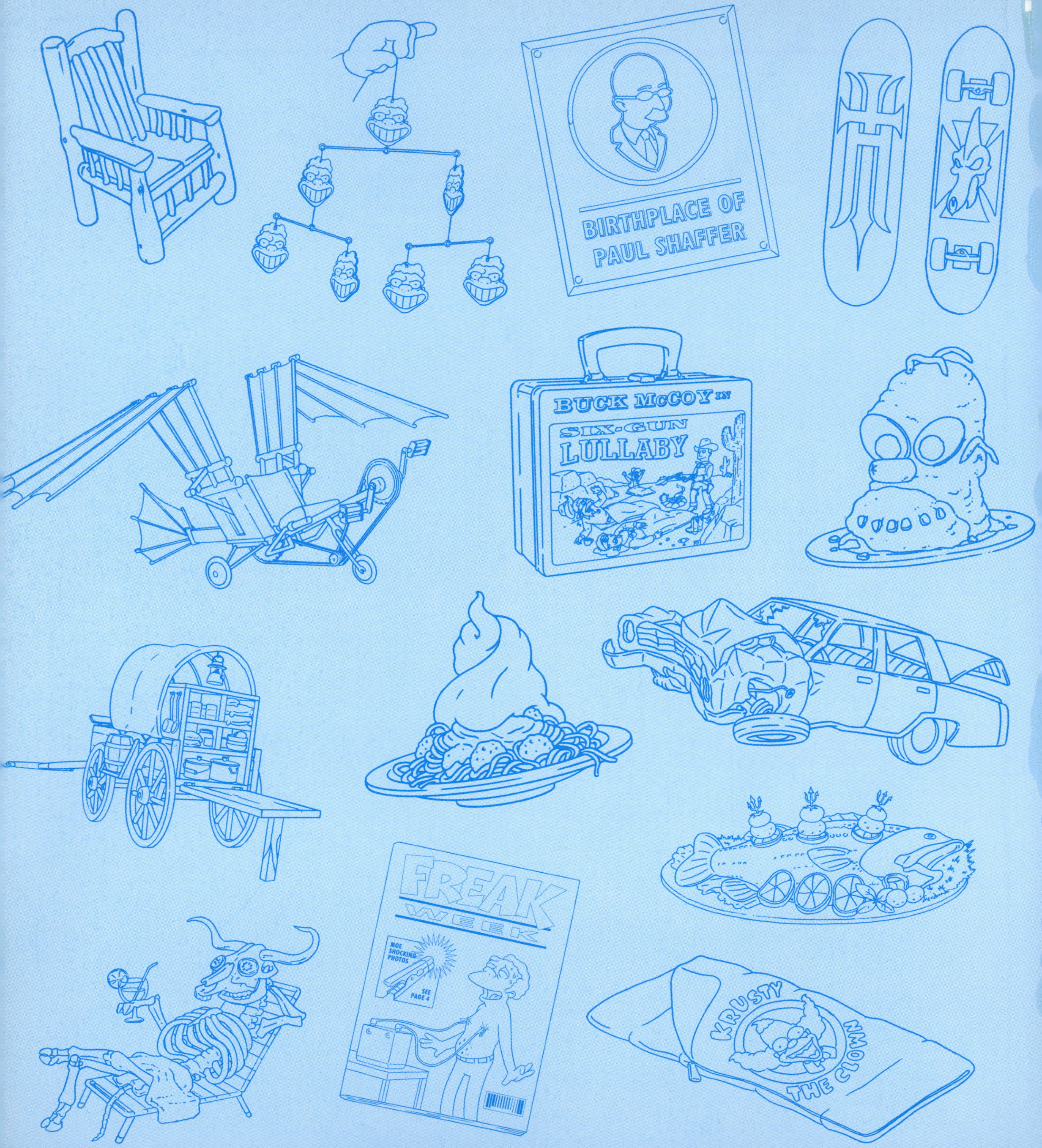
BIRTHPLACE OF
PAUL SHAFFER
BUCK McCOY IN
SIX-GUN
LULLABY
FREAK
WEEK
MOE
SHOCKING
PHOTOS
SEE
PAGE 4
KRUSTY
THE CLOWN